Christmas in Sturcombe Bay

ALSO BY SUSANNE McCARTHY

STURCOMBE BAY ROMANCES
Book 1: A Fresh Start at Bramble Cottage
Book 2: Coming Home to Sturcombe Bay
Book 3: Christmas at Sturcombe Bay

Christmas at Sturcombe Bay

SUSANNE MCCARTHY

Choc Lit
A JOFFE BOOKS COMPANY

Choc Lit, London
A Joffe Books company
www.choc-lit.com

First published in Great Britain in 2025

Cover art by Cover art by Jarmila Takač

ISBN: 978-1781899212

To my lovely cousins, Leigh and Deidre.

CAST LIST

Ellis Family
Jess Bennet
Julia – Jess's twin sister
Luke – Julia's husband
Ben – Luke and Julia's seven-year-old son
Liam – Luke's brother
Robyn – Liam's five-year-old daughter
Natalie – Liam's late wife
Graham and Diane – Luke and Liam's parents

Channing Family
Paul Channing – ex-professional footballer
Cassie Channing – Liam Ellis's fiancée
Lisa Cullen (née Channing) Paul and Cassie's sister, assistant manager of Carleton Hotel
Ollie Cullen – Lisa's husband, the local GP
Richard and Helen Channing – Paul, Lisa and Cassie's parents
Noah and Kyra – Lisa and Ollie's children

Crocombe Family
Alex Crocombe – a Canadian airman
Arthur Crocombe – Alex's elderly grandfather
Marcus – Arthur's carer
Simon Crocombe – Alex's father
Frank Beaumont – Alex's Canadian business partner

Other Key Characters
Shelley – a chambermaid at the Carleton Hotel
Mike Slade – manager of the Carleton Hotel

Kate Rowley – owner of the CupCake Café

Additional Characters
Debbie – Kate's daughter
Amy – Debbie's five-year-old daughter
Bill – Debbie's husband
Tom and Vicky Cullen – friends
Glenn – Jess's ex-boyfriend
Mr Forsyth – Representative of Lytcott Capital Management
Mr Stretton – CEO of Lytcott Capital Management, who have bought the Carleton from Nordicote Asset Management
Alan Cowan and Kelly-Ann (uncredited)

CHAPTER ONE

"I never want to see you again as long as I live!"

"Jess, please, listen to me." Glenn hurried down the stairs behind her as she hefted two large bin bags full of clothes out to her car. "I can explain."

"Explain?" She turned to confront him, fury churning inside her. "Like it was a mistake? You weren't really messaging those women?"

"Well, I . . ."

"And not only messaging." Her voice was a snarl. "Dick pics! Dick pics!"

Glenn glanced nervously up and down the street. "Oh, go on," he protested. "Why not shout it out so all the neighbours can hear?"

"Good." She tossed the bags into the back of the car on top of the boxes of books, shoes and general jumble that were all her worldly possessions. "They should hear. They should know what a dirty, sleazy, low-life scumbag is living in their street." She slammed the boot shut and marched round to the driver's door.

"Where are you going?" Glenn pleaded.

"Anywhere away from here. As far away as I can get."

1

"Jess, we're getting married next month."

"Well, that's not going to happen now, is it? What part of 'I never want to see you again' is so difficult to understand? You can tell everyone it's off. Goodbye and good riddance."

"That car belongs to the business . . ."

"So sue me for it!"

Her hand was shaking as she pressed the ignition button, the wheels spinning as she put her foot down, pulled away from the kerb and headed for the main road. Before she reached it she forced herself to slow down and breathe steadily. She had no intention of giving Glenn the satisfaction of making her have an accident.

Where was she going to go? To her dad? He was happily settled with his new young wife, only a few years older than she was herself, with a toddler in the house and another on the way.

Or to her mum, still bitter more than four years after the divorce, and more than ready to indulge in a diatribe against the whole species of men. Which would be like eating too much chocolate — fine for a while, and then you'd just want to throw up.

So, Julia then — her twin sister. Everyone said it was impossible to tell them apart, but their personalities were complete opposites. Calm, easy-going Julia, never known to lose her temper. Jess had temper enough for both of them, as she'd be the first to acknowledge. A temper that went with her fiery red hair — a living cliché!

Her phone rang, and she ignored it. All calls would go to voicemail anyway, so if they wanted the motorbike shop they would get the office number to ring instead. And if it was Glenn, he could go to hell.

She checked the petrol gauge. She'd need to stop and fill up the tank before she hit the motorway, and she needed to ring Julia and check that it would be okay to land on her.

She knew it would be — they'd always been there for each other, from the time they'd shared a crib. But it would be

2

the considerate thing to do, especially as Julia would probably have sensed, with that crazy twin telepathy they shared, that there was something wrong, and worry.

After making a quick stop on the way out of town to fill up with petrol and buy a large slab of chocolate, she pulled into a layby and took her phone out of her bag.

Julia picked up the phone after just one ring. "Jess? What's up?"

"You knew."

"Of course I knew. Tell me."

"It's a long story." The tears had started — fierce, angry, hurt tears that she'd refused to shed in front of Glenn. Now it felt as if they were never going to stop. "Can I come down to yours for a few days?"

"Of course you can." No hesitation, no questions. "You know that."

"I'll tell you the whole thing when I get there."

"Okay, honey-bun." Julia's voice was gentle, calming. "Drive safely."

"See you in a couple of hours."

Which, apart from a bit of a hold up at roadworks outside Taunton, was a pretty good estimate.

The view as she drove down through the Devon countryside was stunning — gently rolling hills of lush green grass where cows grazed contentedly, ignoring her as she passed, ploughed fields dotted with huge bales of golden hay like giant sausage rolls, and trees just beginning to drop the first leaves of autumn.

And as she approached Sturcombe she caught glimpses of the sea, a vivid shining blue beneath a high blue sky dotted with a few wisps of white cloud.

But it was all wasted on her. All she could think of was getting to Julia's. She ignored the first turn-off for the village and took the second, down past the shops and the quaint old church, and turned right onto the lane behind the Memorial Gardens.

3

The lane led past the white frontage of the old Carleton Hotel. A little further on was a low stone wall surrounding a paved front yard, with a wooden table and chairs and a few half-barrel tubs filled with flowers.

To one side was the house — a rambling, quirky, ivy-clad L-shaped cottage built of the local grey stone. You could see that it had once been three cottages, but they had been knocked together many years ago. The roof-line was a jumble of square chimneys and dormers, every window a different size and a different level.

As she turned in through the gate the front door flew open and Julia raced out, dragging open the car door before Jess had even got her seatbelt off. The hug from her twin was what started the tears pouring down her cheeks again, soaking the shoulder of Julia's sweater.

"Oh, honey. No, don't say a word. Come on inside and sit down, have a cup of coffee, then you can tell me everything. No one else is home right now, so we can be quite private."

Jess hiccupped and scrubbed her hand across her eyes. She let Julia link her arm into hers to draw her inside.

She had always liked the Ellis's family home. Julia's husband, Luke, was a vet, and so were both his parents and his brother. They had horses, dogs, a cat and a couple of rabbits which belonged to Julia's seven-year-old son Ben and Robyn, her five-year-old niece.

"Go on through into the sitting room," Julia urged. "I'll put the coffee on."

The sitting room was comfortable and unpretentious, with rough white-painted walls and dark oak beams across the low ceiling. The big stone fireplace was empty apart from a few withered flowers, and the long sofas facing it were piled with mismatched cushions. An ancient wooden cabin trunk served as a coffee table, but the large television was uncompromisingly modern.

One of the sofas was occupied by an elderly springer spaniel who showed no sign of being willing to move, so Jess

4

sat on the other. Julia brought in two mugs of coffee and a plate of chocolate brownies. She set them down on the cabin trunk, and sat down next to the spaniel, who lifted her head to grumble mildly then went back to sleep.

"Now, tell me what's happened."

Jess huffed out a heavy breath, trying to ease the tension in her jaw. "Okay. Well, you remember last year I found out he was using one of those online sites to hook up with women? And he swore he'd never do it again?"

"But he did?"

Jess nodded. "He'd been acting a bit weird with his phone for the past few weeks, maybe longer, but that's when I really noticed it. At first I thought maybe it was something about the wedding, some kind of secret surprise he was planning."

She took a sip of her coffee, holding it carefully because her hands were shaking so much.

"Then this morning he'd answered a call when he first woke up, and when he went into the bathroom he forgot to turn the phone off. When it pinged . . . I was still half asleep, and I picked it up without thinking."

"And there was a message from a woman on the same site?"

"There were more than a dozen, from several different women. And that's not the worst of it." She took a pause, struggling to force the words past the constriction in her throat. "I checked the messages he'd sent. And there were dick pics."

"*What?*"

"Uh-huh."

Julia's nose wrinkled in disgust. "That's . . . that's . . . ."

"Quite. So, the wedding's off." Oh dammit, she was crying again. "It's all off."

"Oh, love." Julia moved quickly to wrap her arms around her sister. "That's awful."

Jess cuffed away the tears. "Not as awful as being married to that despicable low-life gutter rat."

5

"Too right." Julia's voice was uncharacteristically fierce. "I'm going to have to kill him."

Jess managed a weak laugh. "Oh, I don't think we need to go that far. Castration ought to be enough."

"With a blunt knife."

"That's gone a bit rusty."

"And been dipped in salt."

They were both laughing so much that Bramble the spaniel lifted her head, regarding them with what could only be interpreted as disdain, then lay down again with a huff and continued to ignore them. Which made them laugh more.

"Oh . . ." Julia groaned, holding her side. "I've got a stitch."

Jess brushed the tears from her eyes with her hand. "I knew coming down here was the right thing to do. I feel so much better."

They both leaned back, catching their breath. The laughter hadn't solved everything, but it had helped.

The sound of footsteps at the back door quickly sobered them. Jess sat up sharply, slanting her sister a look of alarm. She hadn't wanted to meet any of the family just yet, didn't want to have to answer any awkward questions. Julia patted her hand, gave her a reassuring smile, and strolled out to the hall.

"Hi, Graham. How's everything?"

"Oh, fine, my luvver. Old Bert Mildon has finally paid his bill from last March. All in used fivers, I'm afraid, but the bank won't mind how grubby they are."

"Lovely." Jess could hear the sardonic humour in her sister's voice. "Is that sheep muck or pig muck on them?"

"Probably pig. Whose is that car in the yard?"

"My sister's. She's come down to stay for a few days, if that's okay."

"Of course it's okay. I'll just get these boots off and get myself a coffee, and I'll come in and say hello."

"Right."

6

Julia slipped back into the sitting room, a question in her eyes. Jess nodded, drawing in a long slow breath to compose herself. By the time he appeared in the doorway she had her smile in place. "Hello, Graham."

"Hello there, my luvver."

Graham Ellis's Devon accent was as rich as Devon cream. In his mid-sixties, with grizzled hair and a weathered face and growing comfortable around the middle, he and Luke ran a farm-animal practice, while his wife Diane ran a small animal clinic, and his younger son Liam's main interest was in horses.

They all lived in this rambling old cottage. Graham and Diane lived in the main section, their two sons and their families each having a separate wing, though they all seemed to spend most of their time jumbled together in this sitting room, the heart of the house.

Graham brought his coffee mug and sat down next to the spaniel. With a small contented grunt she twisted round and laid her head on his lap. "So, you're down for a few days, is it?" he asked.

"That's right."

"Ah." He nodded. He must have noticed the redness of her eyes, but to her relief he didn't ask questions. He was the type to mind his own business unless invited in.

"That new batch of Bangs vaccine has arrived," Julia told him, sitting down next to Jess again and picking up her coffee mug. "It's in the fridge."

"Good, good. Draw up a schedule for me, will you?" He chuckled at the slightly quizzical expression on Jess's face. "Don't worry — no danger of you pouring it on your corn-flakes by mistake. We don't keep it in the kitchen fridge with the milk and cheese — we have a separate one in the mud room for medical supplies."

She laughed. "I thought you must have." She finished her coffee and put down her mug. "I'll just pop out and bring my stuff in from the car."

Julia put down her mug too. "I'll come and help you."

7

"Need a hand?" Graham offered.

"Oh . . . No, thanks all the same. There's not much. We can manage."

"Right then." He tickled the spaniel's ear and picked up the remote to turn on the television.

It took a couple of trips to haul all of Jess's stuff up to Julia's spare room on the first floor. At the far end of the passage, overlooking the stable yard, it was small and cosy, tucked beneath the eaves, with a sloping ceiling and a dormer window. The bed looked comfortable, the wardrobe and dressing table old-fashioned, but more than adequate.

"I'll get some fresh bedding for you." Julia dumped the three bags she had brought up from the car onto the floor. "Will you be all right in here?"

"Absolutely." Jess smiled at her sister. "It's fine."

"It could probably do with a bit of a dust round."

"Don't worry, I'll do that."

"Okay."

The two of them went back downstairs to bring up the last of the stuff from the car, then Julia brought the fresh bedding from the airing cupboard and helped Jess make up the bed. As they were finishing, the sound of hoofs on the cobbled stable yard echoed up to them.

Jess glanced out of the window as a slim, dark-haired young woman slid athletically down from a large chestnut. "Who's that?"

Julia came to peer over her shoulder. "That's Cassie — Cassie Channing. Liam's fiancée. You'll like her. She's loads of fun. They're getting married at Christmas."

Oh. A wedding. Ouch.

Julia was quick to notice the thinning of her lips. "I'm sorry. I shouldn't have mentioned it."

Jess shook her head. "Don't be silly. People get married all the time. I can't pretend it doesn't happen."

The woman was unfastening the horse's girths and lifting off the saddle, all her movements quick and efficient.

8

"She's Lisa's sister. Remember Lisa Cullen from the hotel, the assistant manager?"

"Oh, yes."

"Cassie's been away for ten years, travelling all over the world. But apparently she and Liam had a thing going when they were teenagers, and when she came back they got together again."

"Ah, how romantic." Jess couldn't quite keep the cynicism from her voice. Turning away from the window she began to pull her clothes out of the bags and hang them in the wardrobe. "What does little Robyn think of her?"

"She adores her. It'll be good for her to have a mum again. It was so sad, Natalie dying like that when she was only two. Though Liam's done a great job with her — he's a smashing dad. Anyway, how about some dinner?"

"Sounds good."

"We sometimes have dinner with the family, but I've got a lasagne on for us tonight. There's plenty for the four of us, and . . . I guess you'd prefer to eat with just us anyway?"

Jess smiled crookedly. "Yes, I would, if that's okay?"

"Of course."

"Thanks, Jools." Impulsively she hugged her sister. "Thank you so much. I feel better already."

"That's good. Come down in about twenty minutes. I'll leave you to unpack for now."

Alone in the room, Jess sat down on the edge of the newly made bed. The anger that had sustained her on the drive down here had exhausted her. Now her head was aching. She felt as if she had been hit with a sledgehammer.

Reaching into her handbag she pulled out a small parcel. Glenn's Christmas present. A watch — quite an expensive one, one he had always coveted.

She'd bought it early, looking forward to Christmas with as much excitement as a child. Her first Christmas as Mrs Glenn Howell. Well, it wasn't too late to send it back and get a refund.

9

If only she could get a refund on the past five years of her life so easily.

Oh dammit, it was her own stupid fault. Oh, not Glenn's behaviour — that was entirely on him — but she should never have let it pass the last time he had done it. And the time before.

She hadn't told Julia about that first one — she had been too embarrassed. He had apologised so profusely, promising her so sincerely that he would never do it again. And she had believed him because she had wanted to. Pathetic.

So, the wedding was off. She would never wear the beautiful vintage ivory lace dress she had left hanging up in the spare room of the flat she had shared with Glenn, above his motorbike shop. Her little cousins would be upset that they weren't going to be bridesmaids — she felt bad about that.

There were all the guests to be told, the church and the vicar, the hotel where the reception was to have been held, the photographer, the florist, the caterers . . . Oh lord, the list seemed endless!

In her initial surge of anger she had told Glenn that he would have to deal with it, but that wasn't really fair on all those people. When it came to tasks like that, he couldn't find his backside with both hands. Besides, he'd give his version of the reason — which probably wouldn't be true.

She'd have to do it herself. Dammit. Impatiently, she brushed a tear from her eyes and rose to her feet to continue unpacking her bags. She was *not* going to cry any more. Even though it hurt like hell.

10

CHAPTER TWO

Jess slept badly and woke late. She lay for a long time, staring up at the sloping ceiling, her mind churning with the memory of how she had woken just twenty-four hours ago. If she hadn't picked up the phone and seen those messages . . .

But then she wouldn't have known about Glenn's latest sleazy behaviour, and would have ended up married to him — which was a far worse proposition than not being married to him.

At last she dragged herself out of bed and slipped across to the bathroom, then pulled on some clothes and wandered downstairs.

She found her sister in the small office next to the sitting room in the main part of the house. This was where she managed all the administration for the family's veterinary practices.

Julia looked up and smiled. "Good morning, honey. How did you sleep?"

"Pretty well." Jess's mouth quirked into a wry smile. "No, actually I didn't. But I'll be okay."

Julia came round the desk to hug her. "You can't expect it to be fine all at once. It's been a big shock and upheaval. It'll take time to get over it."

11

"Yes." No tears now — they'd probably all been used up. Anyway, she had things to do, there was no time for wallowing. "Can I link my laptop into your Wi-Fi? I've got a load of messages to send out, cancelling everything."

"Of course. I'll give you the password. Have you had breakfast?"

Jess shook her head. "I don't really want anything. Maybe just a coffee."

"I'll make it. I could do with one myself. And some toast. You really ought to eat something. Don't give Sleazy Glenn the Dick Pic Dick the satisfaction of seeing you waste away."

Jess managed a laugh. "Okay, just one slice. And a couple of Aspirin if you have them."

"Right. If you want to set up your laptop in here, just clear that stuff off the table there. It can go on the bookshelf."

"Fine." She drew in a long, calming breath. "Thanks."

It wasn't a very pleasant way to spend a morning. Messages came pinging back from the guests who had been invited to the wedding — sympathetic, discreetly curious. She had planned a script for responding which gave a brief explanation, but not the whole story.

Her mother, predictably, was the hardest. She couldn't do that one by email — it had to be a phone call. She put it off till last, but it had to be faced. If her mother heard the news from another source, she'd never hear the end of it. She dialled the number, and gritted her teeth through the lengthy diatribe that came down the line to her.

Julia glanced over with a sympathetic smile as she finally put the phone down and rubbed her ear. "What did she say? No, let me guess. *I told you so. They're all the same. Just like your father. You're better off without him*?"

"Something like that."

"How about the rest?"

"Not good." Jess smiled crookedly. "Cancelling so late means that we're going to lose our deposits. That's a few thousand quid down the drain."

12

"Better that than being married to that scumbag, though."

"Too right."

"Has he been in touch?"

Jess rolled her eyes. "There's a string of emails from him. I haven't opened any of them."

Julia laid a hand on her shoulder. "Do you want me to look at them?"

"No . . . Yes. Tell him not to contact me." She huffed out an angry breath. "Tell him I've notified everyone and cancelled everything. I've pulled my half of the savings out of the joint account we had for wedding expenses, and taken my name off it — though I'll pay my share of the bills, of course."

"Okay."

Jess moved out of the chair so that her sister could sit down at the laptop.

"I've cancelled the business insurance on the car, too, and taken out my own. The only thing I want from him is to transfer my car into my name from the business."

"Right. I'm on it."

Jess stood behind Julia, watching as she scrolled through the dozen or more emails Glenn had sent.

"I'm sorry . . . *blah blah blah* . . . Please come home so we can talk about it . . . *blah blah blah* . . . Everyone's ringing me to find out what's going on . . . Oh, you poor thing." Julia's voice dripped with sarcasm. "Are you getting hassle over it? All the rest are pretty much in the same vein. Ah, here's an interesting one." She laughed as she read it. "He's forgotten the password for the office computer!"

"Tell him he can have it when he's signed the car over."

"Right."

Julia tapped out a reply with swift fingers. *This is Jessica's sister Julia* . . . When she had finished, she clicked on 'send'. "There, that's it. All done."

"Thank you." Jess managed a smile. The headache that had lingered since yesterday was slowly easing at last. "Do you want a coffee?"

"I'll tell you what, let's get out of here for a while. Why don't we pop over to the hotel and have one? It's lovely sitting out on the terrace over there."

"Okay. Sounds like a plan."

It was a bright sunny day, but the slight chill in the air warned that it was already well into October, and Jess was glad of her thick sweater. She'd been to the hotel several times — Julia's wedding reception had been held there, and sometimes they'd dined in the restaurant when she'd come down to visit.

The place had probably seen better days. The wooden floor in reception was a bit scuffed and the carpet in the lounge was showing signs of wear. But the view from the terrace made up for everything.

The bay spread out to the far horizon, a pure sapphire blue, sparkling beneath the clear blue sky. The red-gold beach curved in a long arc from the rocks beneath the hotel, past the village of Sturcombe nestled in its dip of green hills, to the russet cliffs on the far side.

Although the main season was over there were still quite a few holidaymakers strolling along the Esplanade, past the amusement arcade, the fish and chip shop, the beach shop and the CupCake Café — mostly older people or families with children not yet in school.

Jess sat down at one of the tables with her coffee, leaning back, closing her eyes and breathing in the cool, fresh sea air. "Ah, this is good."

"Isn't it? I love it here."

"I'm not surprised. It must get packed with tourists in the summer, though."

"Well, yes, quite a few. Then in the winter it's almost dead. But that's how it is with seaside towns."

"I suppose so. What do people do for jobs in the winter?"

Julia laughed. "Not much, once the tourist season's over. There's a bit of farming, but that doesn't employ many people. There's Tom Cullen's organic animal-feed business, and a couple of small factories still going on the industrial estate

14

on the edge of the village. Some people commute into town, or even Exeter or Plymouth. But a lot have to move away."

"That's a shame."

"It's the same with housing. A lot of places have been sold off as second homes that are only lived in for a few weeks of the year, or they're Airbnbs or guest houses. So local people get priced out." She shrugged. "Ah. Well. It is what it is."

Jess nodded, sipping her coffee. She hadn't given much thought to her own future plans yet, but she was going to need a job, and somewhere to live. She couldn't freeload from her sister for ever. But any thought of staying here in this pretty village looked like it would be a non-starter.

"Hi, mind if I join you?"

Julia glanced up as a smiling dark-haired young woman strolled out onto the terrace. "Oh, hi, Lisa. Of course. Come and sit down. Do you remember my sister, Jess?"

"Of course." The other woman laughed merrily. "It would be hard to forget you, seeing your living image around the place most days. I bet you had fun when you were kids, swapping places."

"We did." Jess's eyes danced. "We used to drive the teachers crazy. They tried to insist that Mum put us in different colour jumpers, but we used to just swap them over."

Lisa shook her head. "You must have been a nightmare, the pair of you."

"We were."

"Where's the baby?" Julia asked.

"With my mum. I just popped down to help out for a while. With Vicky still on her honeymoon and the student temps back at university we're a bit short. Fortunately it's quiet at the moment. A lot of our custom at this time of year comes from the golfers," she explained to Jess. "But there's a big tournament this weekend up at Wentworth. Even the ones who aren't playing will have gone to watch."

"Do you get many guests apart from the golfers?" Jess asked.

15

"Not many." Lisa smiled wryly. "Not enough. We're struggling a bit, like a lot of seaside hotels. Those sort of holidays have pretty much had their day."

"I suppose so." Jess glanced around at the terrace and the white-painted building behind it, a rambling jumble of buildings and extensions, with a white-framed conservatory wrapped around two sides, and a lush garden full of semi-tropical palm trees and flowering shrubs. "It's a shame, though. It's a nice hotel."

"It is, or it would be if the owners would put a bit of money and effort into it."

"Who owns it?"

"Some investment trust — bean counters. They don't seem to care about it at all."

"It looks pretty old."

"It is. This main part was built in 1860 something, a bit before my parents' house was built." She pointed to the row of tall Victorian townhouses which climbed the hill on the far side of the bay, from the Esplanade up to the caravan site on the cliffs.

"Wasn't it taken over by the army during the war?" Julia remarked.

"That's right; some kind of recuperation centre for injured pilots. Then after the war they just abandoned it, and it was pretty much left to fall apart before it was bought up by a big hotel chain. It's changed hands a few times since then. Unfortunately, most of the owners haven't been too bothered about the place, so it's been a bit neglected over the years."

"Yes, I can see that. But mostly it only needs some paint and polish. It's not like it's crumbling or anything."

"The structure's sound enough, but it needs more than a bit of paint and polish." Lisa sighed. "Some of the window frames on the side facing the sea need replacing, and those are our best rooms. It's about due for rewiring throughout, the central heating boiler's on the blink, and the guest lift has broken down twice in the past three months."

"Not good," Jess conceded.

"Ah, well. We keep plodding on. Quite a lot of our guests have been coming down here for years, celebrating anniversaries and such. Sadly, a lot of them are growing older now, and each year there are fewer of them. But the golfing enthusiasts keep us going, just about."

Jess gazed around. "You know, it's got a lot of potential. With that view, it could be really popular."

"It could. There's been a rumour that there's going to be another takeover. I just hope the new owners are a bit better than the current ones. Anyway . . ." She sipped her coffee. "How long are you staying?"

"Oh, I don't know. A few days . . ." She drew in a long breath, struggling to suppress the tears that were welling up again. "I really don't know. I was supposed to be getting married next month, but I found out the scumbag was cheating on me."

Lisa's eyes widened, appalled. "The rat! So you dumped him? Good for you."

"Yes, I suppose." Impatiently she scrubbed her eyes. "It's difficult, even though it wasn't the first time. But we'd been together for five years, and I really thought that he was my future. I feel . . . cheated of so many years of my life. And stupid, for not bailing out sooner."

"Oh, honey, not at all." Lisa leaned over and took her hand, squeezing it. "It can happen to anyone. You ought to speak to Vicky — she was in more or less the same boat. Her fiancé was screwing her step-sister, of all people. Now she's just got married to Tom Cullen, who's a really nice bloke as well as being absolutely gorgeous, and they're off in Spain on their honeymoon."

Jess laughed without humour. "I can't see that happening to me. I'm seriously off men."

"Well, I suppose I don't blame you. So, what are you going to do now?"

Jess shook her head. "I've no idea. Glenn's got a motorbike shop — that's how I met him. I used to ride out with his

17

group, then I got a job there. I worked on sales, did the admin and stuff. Now . . . Well . . . No job, no home, no boyfriend."

"You're welcome to stay with us for as long as you like," Julia assured her quickly.

"Well, if you want something for a stopgap, we need a receptionist," Lisa suggested. "And you could live in, if you want to."

Jess's eyes widened. "Really? That would be perfect."

"It would be perfect for us, too. With Christmas coming up, it can get a bit crazy."

"Oh, yes." Julia's eyes danced. "The Turkey-and-Tinsel invasion."

"Turkey and tinsel?" Jess queried, bemused.

Lisa grinned. "Coach parties. They come from all over, for three or four days, starting in late November. There can be anything upwards of fifty guests at a time, and it's full on. Christmas on steroids: entertainment, decorations, excursions."

"Sounds like fun," Jess remarked uncertainly.

"It is. But it's hard work. An extra pair of hands would be more than welcome."

"And it would be great if you were working here, at least for a while," Julia pointed out. "It would give you a chance to sort out what you want to do long-term, without having to bother about Glenn."

Jess laughed. Yes, it was the perfect solution. "Okay. When do I start?"

"No time like the present!"

* * *

The quiz show they'd been watching had ended, and Luke glanced at the programme page in the newspaper. "There's not much on now, unless you want to watch the news," he remarked. "Fancy popping down to the Smugglers for a drink?"

"That sounds like a good idea." Julia glanced across at Jess. "Fancy it?"

"Okay." Better than sitting here pretending to watch television, trying to still the thoughts churning through her brain like a washing machine on an endless wash cycle.

"Come on then. I'll just let Mum know we're going out. She'll keep an ear open for Ben. Liam and Cassie will probably be coming down later. Better put your jacket on — it's a bit windy out there."

Jess swung to her feet. In the hall she hooked her black leather motorbike jacket down from the rack and shrugged into it, tucking her hands into the pockets.

She was glad of its warmth as they strolled along the Esplanade. The sea, which earlier in the day had been a peaceful blue-green, lapping quietly against the sandy beach, had run in on a high tide and was now thumping against the sea wall, throwing up showers of white spray.

"Phew!" She had pulled her hair into a loose bun with a scrunchy, but the wind was tugging it loose and blowing long, curling strands across her face. "This is some weather!"

Julia laughed. "This is nothing. It's only October yet. Wait till we get really into winter. It can blow up some fabulous storms, straight in off the North Atlantic."

At least the pub looked welcoming, warm amber lights glowing through its windows. As Luke pushed open the door, that warmth greeted them — the rich dark oak of the slightly uneven floor and the beams across the low ceiling, a bar of the same gleaming wood, and rows of bottles and glasses and brass beer pumps. People were chatting and laughing, the jukebox playing some classic rock-'n'-roll hit from the sixties.

With the main season for holidaymakers over, the place wasn't crowded. Most of the customers looked like locals, and Jess realised as she looked around that they were probably the youngest people there.

"Ah, there's Lisa and Ollie." They were sitting at a table in the corner. Julia raised her hand to acknowledge them. "Let's join them."

"I'll get the drinks in," Luke said. "What are you having?"

19

"Oh, a white-wine spritzer please."

"Right."

Lisa greeted them with a smile. "Hi, I thought you might be down. Jess, I don't expect you remember my husband, Ollie."

A tall man with floppy brown hair and glasses rose to his feet and held out his hand. "I think we've met, probably at Julia's wedding. Come and sit down."

There was plenty of room on the banquette seat for Jess and Julia to squeeze in. "How did you get on in Exeter?" Julia asked Lisa.

Lisa rolled her eyes. "It was packed, and the shops are all putting out their Christmas stuff already. Honestly, they seem to start earlier every year."

Julia laughed. "How many shopping days to go?"

"It must be about ten weeks, I should think. Noah's already started making his wish-list for Santa."

"So have Ben and Robyn. Santa's going to need an extra-large sleigh if they get half of what they're asking for. Still, I expect we were the same — Tracy Island, My Little Pony . . ."

"Ah, those were the days! Anyway, I managed to get a couple of things I wanted. A new coat for Noah for school — that boy's just shooting up! And a cute little winter onesie for Kyra. It's yellow teddy-bear fur, with teddy-bear ears and a teddy-bear face on the tummy!"

"I'll turf out those school trousers for Noah if you like. Ben hardly wore them — he grew out of them so quickly. Ah, thanks, my luvver," Julia added as Luke brought their drinks over and sat down beside her.

Jess thanked Luke and sipped her drink, letting herself absorb the atmosphere of the pub. It was very different to the pub she and Glenn had usually drunk in — that was at least three times the size of this place. The wood had all been an ugly yellowish veneer, and the floor was covered in a lurid red-and-green carpet that was sticky when you walked on it.

It had always been busy, noisy, with a young crowd and music that was too loud to hear yourself think. And she had usually been with Glenn and his mates from the motorbike club, talking about the relative merits of mechanical slide or CV carburettors, struggles with changing out oil filters and great runs to Pendine Sands.

It felt . . . odd not to be with Glenn. He had always been the loudest, the centre of the group, sometimes a little overpowering. Good-looking too. She had always been aware that other women were attracted to him, were envious of her for being with him.

But . . . she had often felt uncomfortable. Especially after having twice found out about him messaging women online, quite possibly meeting up with them. Quite possibly for sex. Quite possibly with any of the women in the pub.

Here . . . She had a feeling she could be much happier.

* * *

Paul Channing parked his car on the gravel hard standing in front of his house at the top of Cliff Road. He leaned back in the comfortable leather seat, closing his eyes to relax for a moment. It had been a long drive from Manchester, though the Aston Martin ate up the miles as if it was riding on silk.

But it had been a productive trip. The start of each football season brought in a new crop of eager young players earning more than they could ever have dreamed of, with no idea what to do with it. Having been there himself he knew what that was like, and they trusted him.

When he'd signed his first professional contract, at seventeen, he'd felt invincible, as if his career would go on for ever. But wiser heads had warned him that the bubble could burst at any time, and he'd been sensible enough to listen. And he'd found that he had as much flair for picking good investments as he had for scoring goals.

By the time he'd retired from the game, fourteen years later, forced out by an aggravating knee injury, he'd had a very successful portfolio and a growing group of fellow players

21

asking for his advice. So he'd gained legal authorisation and set himself up as an investment consultant.

Now he had a client list of several dozen footballers, plus a few tennis players and athletes. All of them had come to him through recommendations from his old teammates.

And his second string — commentating on matches, writing a newspaper column or occasionally sitting as a pundit on the regional match-day sports programme — was going pretty well too.

Yes, life was good.

He climbed out of the car, tucking his hands deep into the pockets of his cashmere overcoat, and strolled across the road to the rough stone wall to stand gazing out across the bay.

Some of his mates in the game had thought he was slightly mad to tuck himself away down here, in a mid-Victorian townhouse overlooking a pretty seaside village in South Devon, instead of buying a swanky apartment in Chelsea Harbour or a mansion in Hertfordshire.

Well, this was much of the reason — the sea. Summer was ending — it would be winter soon. The wind was blowing in cold from the North Atlantic, whipping up the waves into a fury.

He loved it when it was in this mood — wild and powerful, the waves really meaning business as they thumped against the cliffs below, sending up showers of spray.

Actually, he loved the sea in all its moods. Having been brought up right beside it, he got a weird kind of claustrophobia if he was away from it for too long. He wouldn't want to live anywhere else.

Drawing in a long, deep breath of the refreshing, salt-tanged air he turned and sauntered down the hill to the Esplanade.

* * *

Jess sipped her spritzer, listening to the conversation around the table.

"Liam got called out to look at one of the ponies up on the moor. Some bloody idiots wild camping up there had left

22

one of those disposable barbeque trays behind, and the poor thing tried to lick it."

"Oh no! Was it badly hurt?"

"Fortunately it wasn't too bad, but it could have been very nasty."

"I thought they were going to ban those things. They could start fires too."

"They are banned, if the Rangers can catch them."

"Shame they didn't wander onto the firing range," Luke remarked fiercely. "Or fall into one of the bogs."

"It'd be a real shame if a few idiots end up getting wild camping on the moor banned altogether. It's the best. Remember that time we all went camping up on Shelstone Tor?"

"Oh lord, yes!" Lisa hooted with laughter. "And it poured with rain all night and the tents got flooded. And we had to walk all the way home in the morning, dripping wet, with everything water-logged and weighing a ton."

"And Alan Cowan offered Liam a fiver to carry his stuff for him, and Liam told him to shove it where the sun don't shine!"

"Then he just dumped it. He told his dad it had got stolen, but the Rangers found it and he'd dropped his school library card with it."

"And they got in touch with Dad, and he had them come into school to give a talk about caring for the environment."

"And Cowan's dad heard about it and grounded him for a week."

They all laughed at the memory.

Jess glanced across at Lisa. "Your dad?"

"He's the headmaster of the Community College. Well, it was St Urith's back then."

Jess laughed dryly. "I bet you got some ribbing over that!"

"A bit. But Dad was always dead fair. He never favoured us, and he was never harder on us. Mum was Deputy Head at Fowey Road Primary as well, until she took early retirement a few years ago to look after our nanna."

23

"Oh, I remember your grandmother. Sometimes when we came down we'd go and watch the cricket up at that place behind the church, and she'd be there. Waving her walking stick at the players and telling them what to do."

"That'll be Nanna." Lisa chuckled. "She could be a real old curmudgeon, but we all adored her."

"Is she still . . . ?"

Lisa shook her head, her eyes darkening. "She died a couple of months ago."

"Oh . . . I'm sorry."

"She was ninety-three."

"That's a good age. But you must miss her."

"We do." Lisa smiled fondly. "Anyway, anyone for another drink?"

"I'll get these," Jess offered, rising to her feet. "What are you all having?"

* * *

Paul pushed open the door of the Smugglers. This was another reason why he wouldn't want to live anywhere but Sturcombe. A friendly pub, unpretentious, where he was just Richard and Helen Channing's son, Lisa and Cassie's brother. He greeted a few friends as he moved over to the bar, catching Wes's eye to order his beer.

He smiled as he spotted who was at the bar ahead of him, being served with a tray of drinks. Long and slender in slim-fitting jeans, curling red hair cascading halfway down her back. Julia Ellis. They were old friends, and soon she'd be his sister-in-law when his sister Cassie married her brother-in-law Liam.

He crept up behind her and slipped his arms around her waist. "Hey there, kiddo. What have you . . . Ooof! Ow!"

He gasped, dragging in a painful breath — she had back-elbowed him sharply in the ribs. No defender on the football field could have dealt out a fiercer tackle.

24

It wasn't Julia — though she looked remarkably like her. From the back of his brain a memory surfaced. "You're . . . Oh lord, I'm sorry! I thought you were Julia. You're her sister."

Julia herself appeared at his side, shaking with laughter. "That's right. My twin, Jess. Meet Paul Channing — village idiot."

Jess didn't look amused. Though they were very much alike, he could now see the small differences between them. Julia's face was softer, her eyes a warm grey, where her sister's eyes were a beguiling amethyst above sharply-defined cheekbones.

Those eyes were glaring at him now, and he turned on his most charming smile. "I really am sorry. I'm not usually so crass. And we have met before — certainly at Julia's wedding, and I'm sure a couple of times since."

He held out his hand, but she didn't take it, her eyes remaining ice cold. "I don't recall."

"Oh, well. That puts me in my place." Ah — a flicker, just the slightest flicker, of amusement, swiftly quenched. "Can I buy you a drink, to apologise?"

"That won't be necessary. I accept your apology."

She didn't look as though she did. That flicker of amusement was probably as much as he was going to get. For now. But he wasn't one to give up easily — not when pursuing goals on the football field, nor when pursuing an attractive woman.

And she was attractive. Not beautiful, perhaps, and certainly not his usual type, but intriguing. A challenge. This could be interesting.

"I see you've met my brother," Lisa remarked as Jess returned to their table with the tray of drinks.

"Oh . . . ." Her brother. That could be awkward, with Lisa being more or less her new boss. "I'm sorry. I had no idea he was your brother."

"Don't mind him. He's an idiot."

"I'm sorry." Jess smiled crookedly. "He startled me, and I probably overreacted. It's just . . . Like I said, I'm a bit off men at the moment."

25

"I get it. But don't let your sleazebag ex put you off for good. That would be a terrible waste. And Paul's really nice when you get to know him."

"You have to say that," her husband teased. "He's your brother."

The door opened again with a rush of wind that brought Liam inside, with the young woman Jess had seen in the stable yard. They stopped by their table for a brief chat, then went to the bar for their drinks, taking them over to the pool table at the back of the room.

To Jess's relief, Paul Channing went to join them instead of coming over to their table — although unfortunately that meant that he was right in her eyeline.

Okay, she'd prefer not to admit it, even to herself, but he *was* attractive. And she did remember him from the previous times she had met him — he was an old friend of Luke and Liam.

Lisa had mentioned that he had been a professional footballer, and he certainly kept himself in shape: tall and lean, with wide shoulders, and an easy, athletic way of moving.

His hair was dark, curling thickly around a face that was hard-boned and handsome. His nose had possibly been broken at some point, but the slight kink did nothing to detract from his good looks. If anything, it enhanced them.

And his eyes . . . deep brown and glinting with amusement beneath long, dark lashes that any woman would envy. She could hear his laughter — a nice laugh, low-pitched and slightly husky.

She could see that he wasn't trying to dominate the conversation, as Glenn often did when he was with his biker friends. He listened to other people's comments and didn't try to top them with his own anecdotes or talk about himself.

But she wasn't going to let herself fall for his charm, she reminded herself briskly. She was off men, especially men like Paul Channing. Good-looking, charming, sure of himself. There may be some differences, but he was still a bit too much like Glenn.

26

CHAPTER THREE

"Are you ready for your nap, Grandpa?" Alex Crocombe leaned forward and gently took the teacup from Arthur's thin hand before he spilled the contents in his lap.

Arthur opened his pale eyes and smiled. "Well, maybe I'll have a bit of a snooze," he conceded. "Nothing like a nice snooze in the afternoon."

Marcus, his carer, came in from the kitchen. "Yes, it's time for his nap. You settle down comfortable now, Arthur." He picked up the control and pressed it to recline the old man's armchair and raise the footrest, then gently laid a blanket over him. "Alex will come back this evening."

"Yes, yes . . ."

"Goodbye, Grandpa. I'll see you later." Alex rose to his feet, and patted his grandfather's shoulder. Marcus walked him to the front door.

"How's he doing?" he asked quietly.

"He's fine, all things considered. He's determined to score his century." Marcus's dark face broadened into a grin. "Doctor Cullen reckons he could actually do it."

Alex glanced back at the old man. "It's a shame he's lost his two old friends, Molly and Edie."

27

Marcus nodded. "Ah, well. That generation is passing away now. Not too many of them left."

"No, I suppose not." Alex smiled. "Anyway, I'll be back in a couple of hours, if that's okay."

"Of course." Marcus had a gentle warmth of manner, but he could be firm when necessary — perfect for managing the intractable old man. "He's really enjoying your company. How long will you be staying?"

"I don't know yet — maybe until Christmas. It's really nice here — so peaceful, after . . ."

Marcus nodded his understanding. He was an ex-army medic, so he knew. "I guess it would be. Anyway, I'll see you later?"

"Yes. I'll come back after he's had his dinner."

"Right. Cheerio then."

"Cheers."

Though it was the second week in October it was still a pleasant walk in the afternoon sunshine, down the hill and past the old church. Ahead of him the bay spread far out to the horizon, silver-blue beneath the pale-blue sky.

A few white gulls were soaring and swooping over the waves. Down on the beach a couple of dogs were chasing each other over the sand, and a cluster of small children were building a sandcastle.

He smiled to himself, childhood memories drifting into his mind. His family had lived in Bristol, where his dad had worked for a local television station, but they had come down to Sturcombe regularly to visit his grandparents.

Then when he was nine years old, his dad had devised a new quiz show. None of the British channels had wanted it, but a channel in Canada had snatched it up, so they had moved across the Atlantic to Toronto. It was still running, nearly twenty-five years later, with his dad as producer.

Visits to his grandparents had become fewer until he was in his late teens. Then he had joined the Royal Canadian Air Force and gone to Military College to train to fly fighters

— his dream since he'd been a kid. He hadn't been back to Sturcombe since then, almost fourteen years ago.

Now he could see the small signs of decline: the empty shops on Church Road, the slightly shabby paintwork on the large Victorian houses opposite, mostly now guesthouses instead of private homes.

He read the quaint names on the boards in their front gardens, smiling again — Sunny Dene, Bella Vista, Bay View. How very English!

The hotel, the Carleton, had seen better days, too. Or maybe memories had painted it grander than when he and his brother had chased each other around the terrace or played hide-and-seek in the gardens. It was a shame that the owners didn't seem bothered about spending a little money on it. It could be a lovely place.

The attractive redhead was behind the reception desk. "Good afternoon, Mr Crocombe," she greeted him with a professional smile. "Your key."

"Thank you."

"Are you enjoying your stay?" she asked pleasantly.

"Very much, thank you." He picked up the key card. "It's a very pretty place. Have you lived here long?"

She shook her head. "No, just a few days, as a matter of fact. I came down to visit my sister."

"And you decided to stay?"

"For a while."

He smiled. "I can understand why."

For a moment he considered whether to ask her out for a drink, if she wasn't working late. But though she was friendly enough, in a professional way, he sensed a kind of 'keep off' force field around her. Probably best not to go there.

Another cool smile as she turned back to the computer screen. "Well, anything you need, just let me know."

He could take a hint. "Thank you. I'll see you later then."

"Of course."

His room was on the second floor, and he took the stairs. The corridor was quiet at this time of the afternoon. In fact, the place was always quiet. It seemed to be barely half full. But his room was comfortable and clean, with another stunning view over the bay.

He stood for a long moment at the window, gazing out. Peace, tranquillity, stillness.

He had loved flying jets. But after ten years of the noise, the smells, having to think faster than the speed of sound and the constant awareness of the price of making a mistake, he had felt the need to slow down.

Visiting his grandfather had been his initial reason for coming to Sturcombe, but even though he'd only been here for a couple of days, he already knew that he could easily fall in love with the place. He could live here . . .

"*No! Stop!*" A woman's voice, shrill, cut through the quiet. "Leave me alone."

"Ah, come on. You know you . . . OW!"

Lightning reflexes. Alex darted across the room and snatched open his door. The door opposite him was wrenched open and a young woman flew out into the corridor, cannoning into his arms.

Small and fragile as a bird, she gasped and pulled away from him, retreating a couple of steps down the corridor. Behind her, the man in the doorway of the other room was dripping blood from his nose and was hunched over in the cramped posture of a man who had been soundly kneed in the nuts.

Uh — maybe she wasn't quite as fragile as she looked.

"The bitch. She attacked me!" The man's bellow of indignant rage wasn't quite convincing. Sweaty face, balding, puffy around the middle — not a very prepossessing figure. "I'm calling the manager. Careful — she's crazy, I tell you. She might go for you too."

Alex took in the situation in an instant. "Yes, call the manager," he ground out harshly. "Right now. Or I will."

"Oh no . . . please." The girl — her uniform indicated that she was one of the domestic staff — backed further down the corridor. "I can't lose my job."

"You won't." He could see now that some of the buttons on her shirt had been torn off. "In fact, we should call the police."

"No!" Her voice spiked in panic. "Just . . . leave it. I'm fine."

Alex hesitated, all his instincts telling him not to let it go. But it was her decision to make — she was the one who'd been assaulted. He held up his hands in a gesture of conciliation. "Okay, okay, it's up to you."

"See?" The man was cocky now, in spite of the blood still seeping from his nose. "She won't call the police because she knows what she did. I caught her trying to steal my wallet out of my jacket, and when I tried to stop her, she went for me."

"That's not true! I never did." The girl's eyes were wide, wild. "You grabbed me. You were slobbering all over me."

The man laughed — a fake laugh. "You're in big trouble, girlie. You'll go to prison for this."

"No! You're lying!"

"If that's what happened," Alex asserted, fixing the man with a hard glare, "you really should call the police."

The girl stared at him in horror, shaking her head. "No . . . please . . ."

"I will. Right now." But the guy hesitated, looking nervous.

"Go on then," Alex prompted, deliberately needling him. "Call them."

The man took a step back, looking hunted. "Look, I . . . I'm willing to let it go," he stammered. "She didn't manage to get my money."

"I wasn't trying to steal your stupid money!"

"What's happening up here?"

They all turned as Lisa, the hotel's assistant manager, appeared at the top of the stairs.

31

"Ah!" Alex laughed dryly. "Well, that settles that debate."
She arched one questioning eyebrow.

"This . . . um . . . *gentleman* is claiming that one of your staff tried to steal his wallet, but he seems oddly reluctant to call the police."

Lisa's eyes widened. "*Shelley* tried to steal your wallet?"

"I didn't, Lisa," the girl protested, distressed. "I'd never do a thing like that."

"So why are you scared of us calling the police?" the man challenged.

"Why are you, eh?" Alex countered. "She seems to have assaulted you as well. That seems to me to be quite serious."

"Ah, well, she's just . . . I mean, I wouldn't want to get the poor girl into trouble."

Alex snorted with derision. "You were very quick to make accusations, but now you don't want to call the police?"

"Shelley, what happened?" Lisa's voice was quiet and calm.

The girl drew in a ragged breath, but Lisa's manner seemed to have reassured her. "I'd just been dropping off fresh towels in the empty rooms when he came out of his room and asked me to go and clean his bath. So I got the cleaning things out of the cupboard here. Then once I was in the bathroom, he . . . he grabbed me. He tried to kiss me, and he tore my shirt." She was trying to tidy it, holding it closed with one hand.

Alex brushed past the man and went into his room. "The cleaning things are there in the bathroom," he pointed out.

"Well, she . . . that was her excuse for coming into the room."

"She wouldn't be cleaning the bathrooms at this time of the afternoon unless specifically asked by a guest," Lisa asserted.

"You claim she tried to steal your wallet." Alex glanced around the room. "Where was it?"

"In my jacket pocket."

32

"And where is your jacket?" His voice dripped sarcasm. "It's not on the bed, nor on the chair, nor on the hanger on the back of the door."

The man hesitated, his face reddening. "In the wardrobe."

"And where were you?"

"I . . . I . . ."

"I think it's fairly clear who's telling the truth here," Alex remarked, skewering the man with a cold glare.

Lisa nodded her agreement. "Shelley, do you want to call the police?"

"No, please." She still looked agitated. "I'd rather not."

"Okay, that's your decision to make." She turned on the man. "But you'd better leave. Pack and go now. I want you out of this hotel in half an hour."

The man puffed himself up with indignation. "You can't just evict me like that. Do you know who I am?"

"I know exactly who you are," she responded coldly. "And I'm going to inform the president of your golf league that you won't be welcome here ever again."

"You can't do that!"

"I can and I will."

"Hmph!" With a final glare he turned back into his room and slammed the door.

Lisa laughed without humour. "Well, that seems to have sorted him out."

"Thank you." The young woman's voice was shaking. "Will you really tell the golf league?"

"I most certainly will. Look, let's go down to my office and get a coffee. It's okay, there's no one around, it's a very quiet afternoon."

As the young woman — Shelley — hesitated, Alex smiled at her. "Come on. You look as if you could do with a coffee, eh?"

"Okay."

She smiled up at him, a dimple appearing in her cheek, and he felt his gut tightening. She really was very pretty, with

33

an elfin face and large blue eyes, and silky blonde hair in feathery curls around her head.

Suddenly the temptation to shove through the door opposite and knock that sleazy git's teeth down his throat was almost overwhelming. The thought shocked him — he usually had his emotions well under control. You couldn't react erratically when you were at the controls of a fifty-million-dollar fighter jet, armed to the teeth.

Relaxing his fingers to uncurl his fist, he followed the two women down the stairs.

* * *

Shelley's heartbeat was slowly returning to normal. That vile man! She hadn't been afraid of him — she'd met plenty of men like that, and she knew exactly how to deal with them. What she'd been afraid of was losing her job.

This job, this safe place where she had lived for the past three years, had been the most settled time of her life. Her whole life. Growing up in one foster home after another, some of them lasting no more than a few weeks, she had never known that stability.

Thank goodness Lisa was here today. She knew her, and trusted her. Actually she was supposed to be on maternity leave, but Vicky, her temporary replacement, was on her honeymoon, so Lisa was helping out for a few hours most afternoons. There was Mike, of course — the manager. He was a sweetheart, but she doubted he'd have stood up to the scumbag the way Lisa had.

And the other man, the American . . . He'd been brilliant.

She slanted a cautious glance at him from beneath her lashes as he sat opposite her in Lisa's small office. He could have been a film star. Were all Americans that tall, that handsome? He must be a good couple of inches over six feet, with wide, powerful-looking shoulders.

His hair was dark and neatly clipped. She suspected that if it was any longer it would curl. And his face, with those hard cheekbones, that sculpted jaw, and that finely drawn mouth . . .

But it was his eyes that drew her in — eyes the colour of espresso coffee, with long silky lashes. And so kind. When he had smiled at her . . . And he had believed her, and tied that horrid scumbag up in knots when he'd questioned him.

He was smiling at her now as Lisa poured them all coffee. "Are you okay?"

"Yes, thank you." She managed a smile. "I'm fine."

He looked as if he doubted that but he didn't argue, instead taking his coffee from Lisa with a word of thanks.

She sat down behind her desk. "Now, I can understand you not wanting to speak to the police," she said, "but will you speak to the people at the golf league?"

"Yes." Shelley drew in a long, deep breath to steady her nerves. "In fact . . . I will speak to the police."

"You will?" Lisa's approval was warm in her voice. "That's very brave of you. Are you sure?"

"Yes." Tension was coiling in the pit of her stomach, but she had never been a coward. "I just don't want to see him get away with it, and maybe try it on with someone else."

"Right." Lisa picked up the phone. "I'll ring them now." The words *before you change your mind* lingered, unspoken.

Across the room the American smiled at her again, and mouthed a silent, "Good for you."

She managed to return the smile. Was it his presence that had given her the courage to agree to speak to the police? There was something very reassuring about him, a warmth in his eyes . . .

Lisa had been talking on the phone, but now she ended the call and put it down. "I've arranged for you to go to the police station to make a statement." She frowned. "Look, I really should go with you, but I can't make it this afternoon. I have to get home for the baby, and I can't ask Jess to leave reception. Tomorrow would be better."

"No!" Shelley insisted quickly. "I'll be fine on my own. I'd rather get it over with as soon as possible."

35

"Don't worry," the American intervened. "I can take you."

Lisa looked uncertain. "Well . . ."

"It's okay," Shelley assured her. "I don't mind."

"Well, if you're sure." She glanced up at the American. "I'm sorry, I don't mean to imply . . ."

He shook his head. "No. I quite understand.

"Well, all right then," Lisa conceded. She turned to the American with a smile. "Thank you. It's very kind of you."

"No trouble. I can give them a supporting statement at the same time."

"Of course. Well, goodbye then."

* * *

The police station had been built in the nineteen seventies, and was showing its age. The waiting room was lit by a fluorescent tube that was flickering as if it was about to go out. The floor tiles were cracked and crumbling in a few places, and the blue plastic chairs had clearly been designed to discourage sleep.

Alex yawned and stretched his back. There was nothing to read but a few peeling posters, and he had been required to leave his phone in reception. He had closed his eyes, beginning to doze in spite of the uncomfortable seat, when the door of the interview room opened and Shelley came out.

She was looking pale and nervous, as if she had been the accused. "All done?" he asked.

She nodded, managing some kind of smile. "Yes." She glanced up at the police officer who had followed her from the room. "Can I go now?"

"Of course. We'll be in touch."

"Thank you."

"Come on then," Alex urged. "Let's go home, eh?"

They didn't speak as they walked across the car park. He opened the car door for her, then walked round and slid in

36

behind the wheel. As he pulled out of the car park and turned towards Sturcombe, he glanced across at her.

"How did it go?"

She hesitated. "Not too bad."

Her hands were in her lap — small, neat hands with well-trimmed, unvarnished fingernails. In spite of her casual words, he could sense her tension. "You're not too keen on the police, are you?"

She laughed without humour. "Who is?"

He arched a questioning eyebrow.

"Just . . . I haven't always been the type of public they're supposed to protect and serve." She turned her attention out of the window for a moment, then turned back. "We don't get many Americans in the hotel."

He accepted her change of subject without argument. "I'm not American, I'm Canadian. Well, Canadian-British — I have dual citizenship."

"How come?"

"I was born here, and my father's British, but my mother's Canadian. We moved to Canada when I was nine, when my dad got a job there."

She was looking up at him, those pretty blue eyes bright with interest. "Whereabouts in Canada do you live?"

"Toronto." At her puzzled frown he realised he had pronounced it the Canadian way, and repeated it more clearly.

"Oh. Is it nice there?"

"Very nice. It's on the shore of Lake Ontario. It's got loads of parks and loads of skyscrapers. And the CN Tower is amazing. It's got an observation deck fifteen hundred feet up. You can actually feel the tower swaying in the wind from up there."

He was talking trivia to try to help her relax a bit. There was something in her manner that intrigued him. It wasn't shyness — it was more a wariness, as if she was constantly alert for any sign of trouble.

She reminded him of a fox that had often come into their garden when he was a kid. It would creep in under a

37

hole in the fence, and peer out cautiously from among the bushes. At the slightest sound, the slightest movement, it would vanish.

He had put out food for it regularly every night, and had often sat on the back deck, very still, watching for it. It had taken almost a year for it to creep closer to the house. It had been curious, but there had always been a suspicious glint in its eyes, constantly alert to the slightest hint of danger.

The girl was a little older than he had first thought — when she had given her date of birth at the police station he had realised that she was in her middle twenties.

She appeared so delicate, but he guessed that she was tougher than she looked. She'd certainly given that guy who'd attacked her a very sharp lesson.

She smiled up at him. "So why did you choose to come here for a holiday?"

"To England?"

"Yes. Well, to Sturcombe. It's a bit out of the way, especially now the holiday season's over. You haven't come to play golf."

He laughed. "How did you know that?"

"I clean your room," she reminded him with a touch of dry humour. "No golf clubs."

"You're right. I've never played golf in my life. Yes, I came for a holiday, and to visit my grandfather — Arthur Crocombe."

"Arthur? The old guy who lives up the road from the hotel?"

"That's the one."

She smiled, a warmth in her blue eyes. "How is he?"

"He's doing fine, considering he's nearly ninety-four."

"He's really nice. He spoke at the funeral when old Mrs Channing died. It was a nice funeral, not one of those gloomy things with everyone in black. She'd wanted everyone to wear bright clothes, so we did, and lots of people stood up to talk about her, stuff no one else knew about. I went because she

38

was Lisa's grandmother. I didn't really know her myself, though I'd seen her sometimes at the village cricket matches. Your grandfather said he'd promised to outlive her, and everyone clapped."

Alex laughed. "That sounds just like Gramps."

"How long are you going to stay?"

"I don't know yet. A month or so, maybe."

"Don't you have a job?"

"Not at the moment. I was in the air force — the Canadian Air Force. I completed my ten years' service last month and decided I didn't want to sign up for another ten."

"Why not?"

His mouth quirked into a wry smile. "Ten years was enough. So I decided to come and see Gramps, and have a look around the country I was born in."

She seemed a little more relaxed, the hint of tension around her mouth smoothed away.

"Why did your family decide to move to Canada?"

"My dad got a job in television there."

"Wow! That's exciting. What does he do?"

"He produces a quiz show. It's very popular."

"Oh."

He sensed her beginning to withdraw again, the fox stepping delicately backwards across the lawn to the screen of the bushes. What had he said to make her uneasy?

Was it because she'd figured out very quickly that if his father was a successful television producer, his family was quite well-to-do? Why would that bother her?

Most of the women he had dated would have been delighted. He had never been quite sure if they were attracted to him because of his bank balance, or maybe the hope of wheedling a way into television themselves.

But it seemed to have the opposite effect on Shelley. He smiled to himself. If she knew about the very successful side hustle in real estate he had run while he was in the air force, she'd probably freak.

They had reached the turning from the main road, down Church Road to the hotel. As he drew into the car park, Alex glanced across at his passenger. He'd like to ask her out for a drink, but he had a feeling she'd run a mile.

He drew the car to a halt, and she swiftly unfastened her seat belt. "Well, um . . . Goodbye then. Thank you for the lift."

"No trouble. Goodbye."

She flicked him a quick smile and clambered out of the car, scurrying across the car park to the staff entrance at the side of the hotel. Escaping? The thought was unavoidable.

He shook his head wryly and glanced at his watch.

There was time to get a coffee before visiting his grandfather again. Then after dinner he could choose between dropping into the pub down on the sea front for a pint of warm British beer, or a night alone in his hotel room reading or watching British television.

CHAPTER FOUR

Mike Slade sat at his desk, staring at his computer screen. The news was unwelcome, but not unexpected. Nordicote Asset Management, of which the Carleton Hotel was a very minor element, had been taken over by a larger investment fund, Lytcott Capital Management.

Another takeover, another owner who knew little about the hotel industry and probably cared even less. In the thirty years he had worked at the Carleton Hotel, the past twenty-two as manager, the chain that owned it had changed hands more than half a dozen times.

At least the first couple of times it happened it had been taken over by hotel groups, who'd at least had some knowledge about the business. There'd been some strategic planning and money spent on it.

But since then there had been a series of investment funds, and now this latest one. As soon as he'd heard the rumours that this company might be planning a takeover, he'd looked them up and read every online report he could find.

It didn't look good. They seemed to have little tolerance for any element which wasn't making what they considered to be a significant profit. Those elements would be sold off or closed down in short order to raise the bottom line for the rest of the group.

And Mike had to admit that the Carleton hadn't made a significant profit for years.

It had just about kept going, mostly on the Stay'n'Play golfers who came to play on the course on the rising ground behind the hotel, or the occasional amateur tournament, and return visitors who had been coming for many years, often to celebrate birthdays and anniversaries.

The local people were fond of the old place — it had stood here above the bay for more than a hundred and fifty years, through many different incarnations. And it was a traditional treat to come up for a Devon cream tea on the terrace with home-baked scones, or for a meal in the restaurant.

As for him, it had been a major part of his life for all those years. And since his wife had died, almost two years ago, it had been his whole life. If it was sold off, would anyone actually want to buy it? Or would they just close it down, leave it derelict, or even demolish it to build a hideous concrete block of holiday apartments?

He rose to his feet and walked out of his office to reception. The new girl was on the desk, and he forced a friendly smile to greet her.

"Hello, Jessica. How's it going?"

"Fine thanks, Mike. Mr and Mrs Wright have booked in. They've got their dog with them — a little spaniel with the cutest face. I upgraded them to suite ten, like you suggested. They were delighted."

"Good, good."

"They're a really sweet old couple. They were showing me pictures of their great-grandchildren. They said they've been coming here for nearly sixty years."

"That's right. They came on their honeymoon, and they've been coming back on their anniversary every year since then."

"So they said. Isn't that lovely?"

42

He nodded, and strolled over to the ballroom. Memories — the place was full of them.

The ceiling in here had been blue at one time, now it was white. Well, it could do with being painted again. There had been wallpaper on the walls back then, with tiny blue flowers, but it hadn't worn well; now they were painted a rather dull beige. And the brown carpet that covered the parquet dance floor was wearing thin — he remembered when it had been laid.

Soon they'd be dressing it up for Christmas. For the Turkey-and-Tinsel groups, the mainstay of their winter bookings. Hard work, but a lot of fun, everyone fizzing with Christmas spirit and determined to enjoy themselves.

If Lytcott were going to close the hotel down, he could only hope that they would wait until after Christmas.

He wandered out into the conservatory, a large airy space around two sides of the building that caught the sun. On hot days in the summer it was almost tropical, a lush green jungle of kentias and arecas, strelitzia and aechmea and natal lily, with cane trellises smothered in hibiscus and bougainvillea which, in season, were bright with vivid red and purple flowers.

His wife, Sarah, had loved gardening, had loved to spend time in here, plucking off any dead flowers, tugging up the odd weed that had dared to show its head. She had loved to watch things grow, from tiny shoots to thriving pageants of colours and greenery.

And then there was the terrace, paved in old York stone with a stone balustrade around it, and a spectacular view over the wide sweep of the bay. The sky was pale blue, streaked with drifts of white cloud like the sweepings of a lazy broom, and a cool breeze was blowing in from the sea.

He loved to stand out here and just gaze at the ever-changing panorama. It was wonderful first thing in the morning, when the beach was empty and the horizon was veiled in a lilac mist, the sea shimmering like mother-of-pearl, ruffled with lazy, lace-edged waves that whispered halfway up the sand.

It was still beautiful in the heat of the afternoon, when the laughter of children building sandcastles rivalled the squealing of the white seagulls dipping into the waves. Or even late in the evening, when the sea lay tranquil beneath a dark velvet sky spangled with stars.

It was fascinating to watch when a winter storm was blowing up the English Channel from the wild North Atlantic, whipping the waves into a fury as if there were dragons dancing just beneath the surface, throwing up fountains of white spray as they thumped against the sea wall.

"Ah, Mr Slade. How nice to see you again."

He turned as an elderly couple came out onto the terrace, a small King Charles Spaniel trotting happily at their side on a red leather lead. "Hello there." He recognised them at once — Mr and Mrs Wright — and greeted them with a welcoming smile. "It's Beryl and George, isn't it?"

"That's right. And this is Tansy."

"Well, you're cute, aren't you?" He bent and tickled the little dog's ear. "Did you have a good journey down?"

"Not too bad. The roads get busier every year, of course."

"Of course. Are you having coffee?"

"Yes. Your girl's bringing it out to us."

He nodded, smiling. "I'll join you, if I may."

"Of course."

They settled at one of the white-painted bistro tables. George sighed contentedly as he glanced around. "It's good to see the old place still going. I was just saying to Beryl, I bet it's seen some things in its time."

"Ah, yes indeed. It has quite a history. This main part was built in 1862, you know."

"Oh yes?"

"It was built by a man called Edmund Bould, from Staffordshire. He owned an iron smelting works, and was pretty well-to-do. He built it as a summer retreat for his family, away from all the smog of the Midlands."

44

When he'd first come to work here, all those years ago, he'd been fascinated by the hotel and had spent time tracing its history, but he hadn't really thought about it much until the prospect of seeing it demolished had brought it to mind.

"He was from the Midlands, eh? I don't blame him," George remarked. "Who wouldn't want a summer retreat down here?"

Jess brought out their coffees, and Mike thanked her with a smile. "You've met our Jessica, haven't you?" he said to the guests.

"Oh yes, of course." They both smiled up at her. "She booked us in."

"She's quite new. Her sister lives just round the corner, and she's come down to visit for a while. Which was lucky for us. We have a few university students come down over the summer to work here, but of course they've gone now. She's fitted in very nicely."

Beryl was stirring a generous swirl of cream and two of the paper sachets of sugar into her coffee. "Why did this Edmund choose Sturcombe for his house?" she asked. "Wasn't it an awfully long journey from Staffordshire in those days?"

"Ah, well, the railways made a big difference, you see. By the 1850s there was a regular train service coming down to Plymouth. It would only take a few hours, instead of days by the old stage coaches. We even had our own train station then. Sadly, it's been closed for many years now."

He stirred his own coffee before continuing.

"I believe his wife chose the location. She was from Plymouth. He met her when he was trading with the dockyard at Devonport, supplying iron for the new iron-hulled ships. Ah . . . I hope I'm not boring you?"

"Not at all," Beryl insisted. "It's really interesting. Did Edmund and his wife have any children?"

"They had three girls and two boys, but the boys both died in infancy."

"Oh . . . That's sad."

"The daughters all married, and rarely came down here." Encouraged by their interest, he plunged on with the story. "The old house began to fall into disrepair. Then in the First World War it was requisitioned by the War Office as a recuperation centre for soldiers who'd been gassed in the trenches. That was when they built the extra wings — they needed more accommodation."

"Didn't I hear that at one time it was a sanatorium for tuberculosis patients?" George asked.

"That's right. They didn't have any antibiotics then for treatment, so it was all about sunshine and fresh air and exercise. That was when they added the conservatory and the indoor swimming pool."

"Oh, yes. I remember the swimming pool. We haven't used it for years. Is it still there?"

Mike smiled sadly. "I'm afraid it's closed. It's rather too expensive to heat."

"Oh, that's a shame."

"Anyway, by the 1930s the tuberculosis cases were beginning to decline, with better general health and hygiene standards. The sanatorium was closed in 1934. That was when the place was first opened as a hotel . . ."

"Mike? I'm sorry to bother you." Jessica had reappeared in the doorway. "The council are on the phone. Something about the potholes on Church Road?"

"Oh . . . Yes, thank you, my dear. If you'll excuse me," he added to the Wrights, "I need to take this call."

"Of course. It's been really interesting talking to you."

"I'll see you later."

He hurried through to his office to take the call. The council were supposed to have repaired those potholes months ago, but it had been put off and put off until there was more pothole than road. Not a good impression for visitors coming to the town.

Not that he was going to have to worry about that for much longer. As he ended the call he swung his chair round

46

to gaze out of the window at the blank whitewashed brick wall opposite.

Chatting to Mr and Mrs Wright had reminded him that this place was more than just a hotel. It was history. Part of the fabric of this small town, part of people's lives.

What would people like the Wrights and their other loyal repeat visitors do if the place was closed down? In just another couple of years it would be the Wrights' diamond anniversary, and they had already expressed their wish to spend it here. It would break their hearts to learn it wouldn't be possible.

And then there were the staff. They weren't a large group, but several of them had worked here for as long as he had himself. Tracey, the housekeeping supervisor, was almost sixty — it would be difficult for her to find another job. And Pete, the night manager, would be in the same situation.

It would be nothing short of criminal to let the place fall into ruin, but if that was what the new owners chose to do there was nothing he could do to prevent it. Shaking his head with a sad sigh he turned back to his desk to finish checking through the pile of invoices, his least favourite task.

47

CHAPTER FIVE

Memories. Alex strolled along the Esplanade, his mind drifting back . . . what, twenty-five years and more to when he was six, seven, eight years old, visiting his grandfather with his mom and dad and his older brother David.

The sand here was perfect for sandcastles. They'd built the most amazing constructions, with moats and drawbridges and battlements. And they'd swum in the sea. He'd like to do that now, but it was probably a bit too cold at this time of year.

There was something so very English about this small town, with its fish and chip shop, its noisy amusement arcade, and a shop defiantly displaying colourful baskets of plastic buckets and spades, beachballs and frisbees in spite of the dwindling number of tourists.

Next to it was a shop selling all sorts of kitsch knick-knacks: glass paperweights with tiny mermaids or pirate ships inside them, mugs with garishly painted seaside scenes, colourful tea cloths with images of the sea front and 'A Present from Sturcombe' printed on them.

Maybe he'd buy his brother one of those china trinket trays decorated with sea shells. It would be perfect for holding paperclips, but look suitably embarrassing on his desk in his high-powered law office.

Did people really buy this sort of thing these days? There must be a market for them he supposed. Perhaps, like him, people bought them as tongue-in-cheek gifts for family and friends.

Ah, that was more like it. There were some framed water-colours of the bay and the village which were quite good. His dad would love one of those.

Inside, the shop was like an Aladdin's cave: postcards, a rack of plastic wallets and purses, and another of fridge magnets. And a shelf of Christmas knick-knacks — cheery red-cheeked Santas and elves in green pointy hats, popping up out of colourful cardboard tubs like jack-in-the-boxes, and plush reindeer with bright button eyes and long curling lashes, lined up as if ready to be harnessed to a sleigh.

The elderly woman behind the counter looked a little surprised to have a customer. "Hello, my luvver. What can I do for you?"

Alex smiled. "I see you have your Christmas stock in early."

"Oh ah — people are buying them already. Did you want one of them?"

"No. I was looking for something for my mom and dad. Something like this."

There was a display of pretty jewellery made of sea glass. He chose a pair of earrings for his mother — blue pebbles set in coils of silver. And the trinket tray for David, of course.

"Those paintings," he asked as he took his selection to the counter. "Are they by a local artist?"

"Oh, ah." She chuckled with delight. "They're by my husband. He always dabbled, but after he retired he took it up a bit more." Another chuckle. "He's never going to get hung in the National Gallery, but they do well enough down here for folks as want a souvenir. Which one would you like?"

"That one, I think." He pointed to one of the bay. "Where's that view from?"

"Ah, that's from up the top of Cliff Road there." She gestured to the left, where the Esplanade ended and the road climbed to the higher ground to the east of the bay. "It's one of his favourite places."

"Well, it's very nice. Tell him I said so." He passed his phone over the scanner. "Actually, it's for my dad. He was born here in Sturcombe."

"Oh?"

"Simon Crocombe."

"Simon?" Her eyes widened. "You mean old Arthur's boy?"

"That's right."

"Well I never!" She was deftly wrapping his purchases as she spoke. "I was at school with him! How's he doing now?"

"Very well. He moved to Canada, you may know?"

"Really? Oh yes, I remember hearing that. Years ago, weren't it?"

"That's right. He's a television producer — a quiz show. It's very popular."

"Goodness, he has done well for himself. Give him my best. Tell him Annie Bickle, as I was in those days. Though I don't suppose he'll remember."

"I'll tell him." He took the paper carrier she handed over to him. "Goodbye."

"'Bye, my luvver. Don't forget now — Annie Bickle."

"I won't forget." He smiled back over his shoulder as he stepped out into the sunshine . . . and almost collided with Shelley.

"Oh!" She gasped in shock, quickly stepping back. "I'm sorry . . ."

"No, it was my fault. I wasn't looking where I was going."

"Uh . . . Ah . . . ." She was blushing, embarrassed.

He smiled, trying to convey reassurance. "Actually, I was just thinking of getting a coffee. Will you join me?"

50

She hesitated, that wary look in her eyes.

"Please?" He laughed. "It can be a bit lonely sitting on your own."

Another hesitation, then she conceded with a small smile. "Well . . . okay. I was just going to get one too."

"Good. Where . . . ?"

"Not the hotel," she insisted quickly. "Debbie's café's right here. It's really nice."

She indicated the small café next door. It was a charming place, the window frame painted ice-cream pink, with the words CupCake Café on the board above, alongside three dancing cupcakes.

"Excellent."

Shelley's heart was thumping so hard she was afraid he would hear it. Why had she agreed to have a coffee with him? Of course, it wasn't so bad going into Debbie's place. She really couldn't have a coffee with him in the hotel.

She liked the little café — it was clean and bright, but had an old-fashioned charm, with its cool black-and-white tiled floor, Formica-topped tables and white-painted chairs. The pale-blue walls were hung with colourful framed 1950s-style posters: '*Welcome to Sturcombe*'.

The glass-fronted cabinet at the back displayed a very tempting selection of cakes and scones, all sorts of savouries, and the famous cupcakes.

"This looks nice." Alex smiled as he glanced around. "Especially those scones."

"They're all homemade."

"Great!"

Debbie's mum Kate was serving a table, and she glanced over, smiling. "Hi, Shelley. Sit down. I'll be with you in half a tick."

There was an empty table by the window. Shelley sat down before Alex could hold her chair out for her and picked up a paper sachet of sugar, twisting it in her fingers, feeling it crunch as she sought for something easy to talk about.

"What have you bought?" she asked.

"A couple of presents for my folks. Earrings for my mom, and a picture of Sturcombe for my dad. The lady in the shop said it was painted by her husband."

"Oh, yes, George Foale. He does nice pictures. But have you heard about our famous artist?"

"No?" He looked interested.

"His name was Juan-Jorge Conejelo. He was Spanish, but he lived here with Vicky's Aunt Molly in her cottage up at the top of Church Road. He painted a really weird portrait of her — it looked as if she was made of wood, but it sold for a fortune. He did sketches of quite a few other people in the village too. All women — I don't think he drew men at all."

Alex laughed. "A bit of a Don Juan, was he?"

"Who?" Oh, lord. Should she know that? Would he think she was stupid?

He just smiled. "Another Spaniard — a renowned seducer of women. At least according to Lord Byron."

"Oh. Well, I don't think our Juan seduced women. But the sketches were sold as well. They were bought by an art gallery in Spain." Phew. If he had noticed her ignorance, he had let it pass. "One of them was of Kate's mum," she added as Kate came to their table to take their order. "Wasn't it, Kate? I was just telling Alex about Juan-Jorge."

"Oh, yes." The older woman's eyes danced. "Our gorgeous Spanish artist."

Alex arched one dark eyebrow in amused question. "Gorgeous?"

Kate chuckled. "We found him on the internet. He really was very handsome. Lucky Molly! Anyway, what can I get you?"

"You have to have the scones," Shelley insisted. "You can't come to Devon and not have a proper cream tea. Oh, Kate, this is Alex Crocombe. He's old Arthur's grandson."

"Really? Oh, it's lovely to meet you. Arthur's a real old rogue, but everybody loves him."

52

"Thank you." He rose to his feet to shake her hand.

"So how long are you staying?" she asked.

"I don't know yet. My plans are quite flexible."

"Well, I hope you'll enjoy your stay."

"I'm sure I will."

Shelley was aware of the slight blush of pink that had risen to her cheeks as Alex slid back into the seat opposite her. She really would like him to stay.

Which was stupid. He'd said before that he might be staying a month or so, but she doubted that he'd stay much longer. He'd surely want to be at home with his family for Christmas.

But at least for this moment she could enjoy just sitting here chatting with him.

Mustn't stare. Even though his face was so beautifully designed, with slanting cheekbones and a hard jaw, and those dark, dark eyes . . . Look at his hands instead. Beautiful hands, with strong wrists and long, sensitive fingers . . .

No, better to look out of the window.

The summer had been glorious, and though it was colder now the blue skies had lingered into October. The sun was sparkling on the sea, and far out beyond the bay a few white-sailed yachts were tacking down the English Channel.

"It's certainly beautiful here," Alex remarked.

"It is."

Kate had brought a tray to their table, with a pretty teapot, milk jug and teacups, four scones, a ramekin of thick golden Devon cream and a small pot of jam. "Enjoy."

"Thank you." Alex surveyed the spread. "This looks good. Is it supposed to be cream first or jam first?"

Shelley laughed. "Cream first when you're in Devon; it's the other way round in Cornwall."

"Ah! And they're wrong, of course?"

"Of course! If you put the jam on first, the cream could slide off into your lap." She picked up her knife, sliced her scone in half, and scooped a generous spoonful of cream onto it, then dabbed on a little jam. "See?"

They both laughed, and Shelley could feel herself relaxing, beginning to enjoy herself.

"Do you miss your job, flying aeroplanes?" she asked.

"Some elements of it." He took a bite of his scone. "Flying jets is the most amazing feeling. I flew Hornets, beautiful machines. They can reach a speed of almost Mach two, and climb to fifty thousand feet."

"What's Mach two?" She felt safe asking that — it sounded like something technical which an ordinary person wouldn't be expected to know.

"Twice the speed of sound. That would be fifteen hundred miles an hour. The Hornet can do around twelve hundred."

"Phew, that's fast!" She laughed. "Does it have guns and missiles and things?"

"Of course — it's a fighter. It can take Sidewinders, Sparrows and Mavericks — those are missiles. And it's got a Vulcan rotary canon with a firing rate of up to six thousand rounds per minute."

Her eyes widened. "Did you . . . did you ever have to fire them?"

A shadow crossed his face, and she saw memories there of a darkness he wanted to forget. "A couple of times. But mostly we flew defence — securing Canada's airspace."

"It sounds really exciting. Why did you leave?"

He laughed dryly. "Flying those things is a young man's game. If I'd signed on for another tour, I'd have likely been shunted into a desk job, and that's not my thing. But enough about me." He spread the second half of his scone. "What about you? Tell me about your life."

A flicker of an edgy smile. "Oh, there's not much to tell. I've never done anything exciting."

"Were you born here? In Sturcombe? Or in Devon, eh?"

"No."

54

"Where then?" He smiled encouragingly. "I assume you didn't just spring up out of the ground like a daffodil."

That dragged a laugh from her, though she could feel the familiar knots twisting in her stomach. "No . . . I was born in London."

"But you didn't want to stay there?"

"No. I like it here. The sea and the beach and the countryside." She paused to pour the tea, taking the moment to find a new topic of conversation. "Is England very different to Canada?"

To her relief he accepted the change of subject without question. "Well, Canada's a lot bigger, obviously. And there's some fantastic scenery — a lot of it's really wild. And there's a *lot* of lakes — some figures put it at nearly two million."

Her eyes widened. "That many?"

"Uh-huh. But England has some very pretty scenery, too, though obviously on a much smaller scale. And some things are similar — most places feel safe, the cops are friendly. Though it took me a while to get used to driving on the wrong side of the road."

"The wrong side?" she protested, laughingly indignant.

"Well, the other side, I guess." He picked up his teacup. "And like you Brits, we're fond of our tea."

"And you play ice-hockey instead of football."

"That's right. Well, we do play football — we call it soccer. We're not in the top rank, though we have been in the World Cup a couple of times. And it's not nearly so popular as it is here."

They chatted easily as they ate their scones. So long as they kept well away from any questions about her past, Shelley felt comfortable. She liked listening to him talk — he had a deep, soft voice, with that fascinating Canadian accent. And when he laughed . . .

"Well, that was good." At last Alex set down his teacup and smiled at her across the table. "Thank you for keeping a lonely Canadian company."

"Oh . . ." She returned the smile. "That's okay."

"I was just wondering . . . If you have a day off, maybe we could take a drive up to the moors? It's a long time since I've been up there. I used to love going up to see the ponies."

"Uh . . ."

It was tempting — she really liked him. And he was a real gentleman — she hadn't met many of those. But it wouldn't be wise to let her guard down, she reminded herself sharply. It would be all too easy to let herself like him too much. Hadn't she learned, her whole life, that getting too close to someone only ended in disappointment?

She had to get away before she started to imagine that this could be something more than just a casual encounter, a friendly chat over a cup of tea.

"No. I'm sorry, I can't." She flashed him a quick smile. "Hotel policy." She glanced at her watch. "Oh, excuse me. I have to get back — I'll be late." She scrambled to her feet. "I . . . Um . . . It's been nice talking to you. Goodbye."

Outside, she turned towards the hotel and almost collided with Mike, the manager. Mumbling some sort of apology, she stepped past him and hurried away along the Esplanade.

Dammit, how stupid was she? One smile from those deep brown eyes and she had been ready to throw caution to the wind, step over the line that she had so carefully drawn for herself. Let herself dream.

Impatiently she brushed a wayward tear from the corner of her eye. From now on she would be very careful to avoid him — she was far too attracted to him, and that could be dangerous.

CHAPTER SIX

"Oh, sorry." Mike stepped back sharply to avoid colliding with Shelley as she hurried out of the café, looking flustered. "Is everything okay?"

"Ah . . . Yes, Mike. Fine. Thank you. I just . . ." She paused to catch her breath. "I didn't realise the time."

"Well, there's no need to rush." He smiled down at her in gentle concern. "It's your afternoon off, isn't it?"

"Yes, but . . . I need to get back." She shuffled aside, not meeting his eyes. "See you later."

Bemused, he watched her hurry away. Whatever had upset her, she clearly didn't want to talk about it.

He pushed open the door of the café. The big Canadian guy who was staying at the hotel was sitting at a table by the window, looking equally bemused, two empty plates and tea-cups in front of him.

It seemed reasonable to assume that he was the reason why Shelley had been looking so distressed. But wasn't he the one who had rescued her from that unpleasant chap who'd tried to attack her?

So what was going on? Maybe he shouldn't jump to conclusions. He'd mention it to Lisa — she'd be the best person

57

to deal with it. Anyway, a moment later the guy got to his feet and left the café. He didn't follow Shelley — he crossed the road and went down the steps to the beach.

Well, that was a relief. He hadn't wanted to be forced to confront the guy — he wasn't very good at that sort of thing.

Kate came through from the back room with a plate of her delicious home-baked scones. "Mike, hello." She smiled warmly. "Your usual?"

"Yes, please. Especially if I can have a couple of those straight from the oven. They smell delicious."

She laughed. Nothing pleased her as much as a compliment on her cooking. "Of course. Sit down and I'll bring them over."

The café was quiet, only a couple of tables being occupied. Mike sat down in a corner by the window, and Kate brought his coffee and scones.

"Is everything okay?" she asked gently. "You look a bit worried."

"Mmm." He smiled wryly. "You could say that."

"Wait, I can take a moment to sit down. I'll get myself a coffee." She was back a moment later and sat down opposite him. "So, what's wrong?"

"We've been taken over again." He sighed heavily. "Another capital management group. I don't know what's going to happen."

"But surely it won't affect the hotel directly?" Her eyes were warm with sympathy. The afternoon sun was shining on her soft brown curls, bringing out highlights of red, and just catching a few threads of silver.

His mouth thinned. "It depends. If they decide its worth investing to spruce the place up a bit, attract a new clientele . . ."

"That would be good."

He sighed, shaking his head. "More likely they'll consider that to be throwing good money after bad, and just close us down."

58

She looked shocked. "But why would they do that? They've just bought the place — why close it down? That doesn't make sense."

"They bought it as part of the package, with the rest of the Nordicote Group. But they'll be wanting to get a good return for their money. And we're down pretty badly on room occupancy year on year. We're barely turning a profit."

"That's because it's been neglected for so long," she asserted indignantly. "It's got real potential — surely they'll be able to see that?"

He shook his head sadly. "They're just bean counters. All they see is the bottom line, and that isn't good."

She reached across the table and laid her hand on his. "It'll be okay, Mike. You'll see."

He felt the warmth of that simple touch spread through him. Maybe it would be okay — maybe he was worrying for nothing. His wife would have told him not to anticipate trouble — there'd be time enough to worry if it happened.

Oh, how he missed Sarah. Though the sharp edges had worn off, he still felt the aching loneliness. He knew Kate missed her too — they'd been best friends since they were at primary school.

"It was a lovely wedding you put on for my Debbie," Kate urged. "You could be doing more of that. People would love to come down to a beautiful place like this. And the guests would be able to stay in the hotel, make a whole weekend of it."

Mike smiled. "It was good, wasn't it? And lovely to see her so happy with Bill, after . . . everything."

"Pfttt!" She snapped her fingers. "That Alan Cowan is nothing but a wasp at a picnic."

"I enjoyed dancing with you." He smiled a little uncertainly. "I was just wondering . . . I haven't been to our old ballroom dancing sessions very often since Sarah's been gone. It feels . . . uncomfortable."

Kate laughed. "You mean you don't like being a babe magnet?"

He felt himself blush. "Well, I wouldn't say that. But, well, any man on his own is going to have the ladies wanting him to be their partner. So I was wondering . . ." He took off his glasses, polished them with his handkerchief and put them back on again. "I was wondering if maybe you might like to come with me? I'll understand if you'd rather not," he added quickly, feeling awkward. "I mean, if you're too busy with the café and that."

He watched anxiously as she hesitated. It had taken him a while to work up the courage to mention this, and he just hoped it wouldn't risk damaging their friendship — he really valued that.

"No, I'm not too busy. As you can see, with the season winding down it's quite slow." She really did have a very pretty smile. "And now that Debbie and little Amy have moved in with Bill up at the farm it can get a wee bit lonely of an evening. So . . . yes, I'd love to come dancing."

"You would? Ah . . . that's . . . good." Suddenly he could breathe again. "It's Thursday evenings. I could pick you up at seven."

"Thursday, seven o'clock. That's fine . . . Oh, excuse me." An elderly couple had come into the café. She rose quickly to her feet, and smiled back at him. "I'll see you then."

"Yes. I'll . . . look forward to it."

Kate smiled as she watched him go. She could just imagine how he must feel at his dancing sessions, with all the single women flocking around him.

She'd known him for . . . what, more than thirty years, since he'd first come down to Sturcombe to work at the Carleton. He'd met his beloved Sarah at a ballroom dancing competition, and came down to be with her.

Thirty years. Where had the time gone? She'd been a young bride herself then, with her Terry. She'd been so glad that her friend had found the same happiness.

60

But life hadn't turned out quite how each of them had been hoping. Sarah and Mike had tried for years to have a baby, but it hadn't happened.

And a few years after she herself had had her Debbie, just when they had been thinking of trying for another, Terry had started to get that nasty pain in his leg.

He thought he must have knocked it at work, but it didn't get any better. Typical man, he had refused to go to the doctor until it had got so bad that he could barely walk.

The cancer diagnosis had been a terrible shock. And even worse, it had already spread, so amputating the affected leg wouldn't help. They had given him six months — he had lasted seven.

With a small sigh Kate tucked the memories away in the safe place in her heart, where she had kept them for so long. There were tables to be cleared, and Debbie would be back soon, having been up to collect little Amy from school.

She had made a life for herself — she'd had no choice. Terry's life insurance had enabled her to put down a substantial deposit on the café, which had given her a job and a place to live in the flat upstairs. She had never asked for more.

61

CHAPTER SEVEN

Jess woke with a mild headache again. She hadn't slept well, but she didn't want to think about what had disturbed her dreams. A glance at the small clock on her bedside table told her that it was almost nine thirty. But that was okay — she wasn't due to start her shift on the reception desk until two, so she had the whole morning to kill.

Wearily she rolled out of bed, shrugged into her dressing gown, and padded over to the bathroom. Maybe a shower would make her feel better. The staff corridor was deserted, only four of the rooms being occupied at the moment anyway. No one to talk to.

After scrubbing herself dry on the rough towel, she wandered back to her room to get dressed. The headache was fading and she was feeling restless.

The strange thing was that it was nothing to do with Glenn or thoughts of her abandoned wedding that kept dancing an irritating tap-dance through her brain, but images of another man — a man with wide shoulders and curling black hair.

But she didn't want to acknowledge that.

Sitting down at the small dressing table she dragged a comb through her long wet hair. Maybe she'd get it cut — it would be easier to manage. Wasn't that what women did when they left a long-term relationship? Reinvent themselves? What a cliché!

She didn't need to reinvent herself to leave Glenn behind. It was her future she needed to figure out. But there was no rush for that. If the hotel closed, which the rumours suggested it might, that would be time enough. For now, drying her hair and getting some breakfast was as far ahead as she wanted to plan.

Forty minutes later saw her strolling over to the Ellis's house. She found Julia in her office. She glanced up from her desk with a smile.

"Hi, honey. How are you?"

"Oh . . . fine."

She wandered listlessly round the small room, reading the labels on the files stacked on the bookshelves, admiring the child's drawing — Ben's, of his mum and dad. Hobo, the three-legged grey Lurcher, was reclining on an old pink blanket in the corner. Jess hunkered down and scritched the magic spot behind his ear.

"You're a handsome chap, aren't you?" she murmured to him. "Are you a good boy?" The dog stretched out his long pink tongue and licked her wrist. "How did he lose his leg?"

Julia smiled grimly. "Remember that Alan Cowan we told you about the other night?"

"The one they went camping with, when they all got soaked?"

"That's the one. He got him as a puppy, but he never took proper care of him. Poor Hobo hurt his leg on some barbed wire, and instead of taking him straight to the vets, he just wrapped a bit of old cloth round it and left it. By the time he did take him in to Diane's surgery it was really bad — the infection had got into the bone, and the only thing she could do was amputate."

"Oh, that's awful. Poor Hobo."

The dog seemed to appreciate her sympathy, resting his head heavily on her hand.

63

"Cowan got really stroppy about it, refused to pay for the treatment — told her to put him down. Diane just about blew his head off." She laughed dryly. "I'd have loved to have seen it. She doesn't look it, but she can be quite a force to be reckoned with when it comes to any kind of animal cruelty."

"I can imagine."

"Anyway, she threatened him with the RSPCA, and made him sign Hobo over to her."

"Ah, bless." She fondled the dog's whiskery grey head. "So now you have a nice cosy home and a blanket to sleep on, and lots of treats. He does seem to manage pretty well with only three legs."

"Oh, it doesn't bother him at all. Would you like to take him for a walk?"

Jess glanced up in surprise. "Would that be okay?"

"Of course. Take him down to the beach — he loves the sea."

"Oh, right. But if I let him off the lead, will he run off? What if he won't come back to me?"

Julia laughed, taking a packet of dog treats out of her desk drawer. Hobo heard the rustle and was instantly alert. "Take these and he'll be your best friend forever."

A walk on the beach was exactly what she needed to blow the cobwebs away. Jess felt her steps lightening as she strolled through the Memorial Gardens.

The trees were beginning to shed their leaves, but the grass was neatly mowed, the flowerbeds all weeded. Some of the rose bushes were still in bloom, and so were the pansies, chrysanthemums and pretty mauve asters, asserting their bright colours against the slow creep of autumn.

She paused by the War Memorial to read the names engraved on the weathered brass plaques, of the men killed in the Boer War, both World Wars and even the Korean War. Some of the surnames told that they were from families who still lived here in Sturcombe: a couple of Channings, three Cullens, three Crocombes.

64

The dates showed they had almost all been young men — nineteen, twenty, twenty-one. Now they would have been great-grandfathers, great-great-grandfathers, but they had never had that chance.

But Hobo was quickly bored, so she let him tug her out to the concrete ramp down to the beach.

The sky was a pale misty blue above a silvery sea, but the October sun gave just enough warmth to take the edge off the cool breeze blowing in across the bay. She paused for a moment to breathe in the fresh, salt-tanged air, feeling it chase away the last of that lingering restlessness.

The beach was almost empty, just a few elderly couples in deckchairs, a young mum with a toddler looking for shells to collect, a few dog walkers throwing balls for their pooches to chase.

The moment she let Hobo off the lead he raced away joyfully, hirpling down the beach to splash in the shallows, where the waves rolled in gently, lazily unfurling their long ribbons of white lace over the wet sand.

She stood and watched him for a moment, smiling at his sheer *joie de vivre*. Put him down? No wonder Diane had blown her top at that horrible man. He should have been put down himself.

A little further out she spotted a dark head moving through the water. Incredibly, someone was swimming out there. It must be freezing! But he seemed to be wearing a wetsuit and was carving through the waves with a powerful overarm stroke.

She watched as he swam across the width of the bay, then back. As he finally stood up and started to wade in towards the beach, Hobo barked ecstatically and bounced over to him, cannoning into him and licking at his face.

"Hobo!" As she had feared, he ignored her. "Hobo, here! I'm sorry, he . . . Oh!" She stopped dead. Paul Channing. "It's you!"

A slow, lazy smile curved his well-made mouth. "Ah, what a wonderful warm greeting. It does so much to revive my poor bruised ego."

65

"I doubt your ego needs much reviving," she retorted tartly. "It seems to be in perfectly good health."

He laughed, not at all troubled by her barb. "I really did get off on the wrong foot with you, didn't I?"

"I'm not sure there'd be a right foot."

Hobo was still splashing around him with boundless enthusiasm. Weren't dogs supposed to have a sixth sense about people? The stupid Lurcher seemed to lack a brain along with his leg.

Though her own brain really couldn't lay claim to much sense either. She couldn't help but be aware of how good he looked in that wetsuit, all wide shoulders and tapered torso and taut butt. It was a very unforgiving garment, showing up any lumps and bumps, but when the package inside was that good it could be spectacular.

"Isn't it a bit cold for swimming?" she remarked, to distract herself from the way her heart was thumping.

He shook his head. "Not if you swim every day — you get acclimatised to it."

"Every day?" Her eyes widened in surprise. "Even during the winter?"

"Pretty much, whenever I'm home. It's the best exercise in the world. Do you swim?"

"Yes. But only when the water's warm."

"Chicken."

"Huh!" But she couldn't quite suppress a bubble of laughter. He really did have more charm than was recommended under health and safety guidelines.

He laughed too, and picked up the towel he had left lying on the beach, indulging Hobo in a brief game of tug-of-war with it before scrubbing it over his hair and tossing it round his shoulders.

"Well, now that I've got a laugh out of you, perhaps I'd better quit while I'm ahead. See you around." And he strolled away to the steps that led up to Cliff Road and the tall, elegant Victorian townhouses there. Was that where he lived?

66

It seemed a rather incongruous choice for an ex-professional footballer.

But then she had to admit that Paul Channing didn't entirely conform to the stereotype. Calling to Hobo, who was looking distinctly disappointed at losing his friend, she turned and walked back along the beach.

CHAPTER EIGHT

Shelley had been doing her best to keep out of Alex's way since that awkward moment in Debbie's café. She was familiar with his routine by now. He would usually go down to visit his grandfather at around ten o'clock, and sometimes stay for lunch with him, or sometimes he would go into town to eat, to Debbie's or the pub.

Which left her plenty of time to clean his room extra thoroughly. Sometimes she when she was changing his pillowcase or tidying away one of his sweaters, she would let herself pause and breathe the unique male scent of his skin.

Stupid. But it was too tempting to resist. For that short time she could safely let herself indulge in foolish fantasies . . .

"Shelley?"

"Hi." She turned quickly. "I'm in here."

Tracey, the housekeeping supervisor, appeared in the doorway. "Ah, there you are. Lisa wants you to pop down to the office."

"Oh, but . . ." She glanced back at the room.

"Go on. You can come back and finish off in here later."

"What does she want?"

"I've no idea. Hurry up. Don't keep her waiting."

68

Shelley hurried down the stairs, anxiety coiling in her stomach. Maybe she was a pessimist to always think there was going to be trouble, but life had taught her that there usually was.

Jess was at the reception desk. "Hi. They're in the lounge." Her smile was bright — that was reassuring, anyway. "I'm bringing coffee. Do you want one?"

"No . . . um . . . yes, please." Coffee? Surely that had to be reassuring too?

Lisa was seated in a corner of the lounge with two smartly dressed women that Shelley recognised. One of them was the Chair of the Ladies' Golf League. As she hesitated, Lisa glanced up and beckoned her over.

"Ah, here she is. Sit down, Shelley. I asked you down to meet Mrs Lewis and Mrs Booth."

"Ah, yes. We've met before, haven't we, dear?" The two women were smiling at her. "We just wanted a moment to thank you in person."

She stared at them, startled. "Thank me?"

"Roland Gibbons. He's been a thorn in our side for some time, with his inappropriate behaviour, but it was difficult to do anything about him as the other women were all reluctant to make a formal complaint. You going to the police about him has given them the courage to speak out."

"Oh!"

"He's been suspended from the committee," the second woman went on. "And the police are charging him with several counts of assault. It'll be some time before the case comes to court, of course, but at least it's being taken seriously at last."

Jess had brought the coffees over and set them down on the low table between them. As she turned away, she gave Shelley an encouraging wink. Shelley smiled back. She had never really had a female friend, but she really liked Jess.

One of the ladies — Mrs Booth? — picked up her coffee cup and took a delicate sip. "It must have been a most unpleasant experience."

69

Shelley was tempted to tell her that dealing with their sleazy Mr Gibbons hadn't been the most unpleasant thing. Dealing with the police had been the difficult part. But these two genteel ladies wouldn't understand that.

So she just smiled and sipped her coffee, wondering how soon it would be okay to make an excuse to get away. They were probably very nice women. It wasn't their fault that they made her feel uncomfortable. It was just that they reminded her of the magistrates she had encountered as a child — well-meaning but completely unable to understand the reality of her life.

At last they finished their coffee, and one of them glanced at her watch. "Well, we've time to get in a practice round before lunch," she declared. "Come on, Iris."

The two of them rose to their feet, smiling graciously at Shelley. "Well, goodbye, my dear. It was so nice to meet you. And thank you again."

"Yes. Um . . . thank you." She put on a smile which she hoped looked genuine. "It was nice to meet you too."

She moved to pick up the empty coffee cups, but Lisa shook her head. "No, leave that. I'll do it. I haven't had a chance to speak to you since Wednesday. How are you?"

"I'm fine. Really. It was nice of them to say thank you like that."

"It was probably the least they could do. As for suspending him, I'd like to suspend him. By his ankles. With cheese wire."

Shelley laughed. For all she was the assistant manager, Lisa had no side to her. "That would be good. Anyway, I've got rooms to clean. See you later."

She hurried back up the stairs to the second floor, and along the corridor. Tracey had locked the door to Alex's room, so she opened it with her pass-key . . . and stopped dead on the threshold.

Alex was in there. There was a suitcase on the bed, and he was packing it.

Something cold swept through her, like being caught by a rogue wave on the beach. "You're leaving."

He turned and smiled. "I'm leaving the hotel. As I'm staying in Sturcombe longer than I'd initially intended, I thought I might rent a flat for a while instead."

"Oh . . ."

"I've found quite a nice one, on Pear Tree Road. It's got a sea view."

"Oh . . . That's nice."

"It'll be good to have my own space, to be able to spread out a bit. Make a cup of tea in a kitchen instead of the bedroom."

"Yes."

Such a simple conversation, but it felt so stiff, so awkward. She took a step back, ready to escape, reluctant to leave. If he moved out of the hotel, she probably wouldn't see him again. Which would be good. Wouldn't it?

"Well, I . . . I'll leave your room for now then, till you've finished. I have a couple more on this floor to do."

"Right."

Oh, that smile. Did he feel the same sizzle of attraction? Sometimes the gleam in his eyes when he looked at her made her begin to hope that he might. *Dammit. Be sensible.* He just wanted a friend, company while he was here on holiday.

And probably convenient sex.

Oh, yes. She could be tempted into that, easily. But sooner or later he'd be gone, back to Canada, leaving her feeling more rejected and lonelier than ever.

With an effort of will she returned him a cool smile as she turned away. "See you around then."

* * *

"There. That ought to do it. I'll just reboot it." Paul turned the computer off and waited a few seconds before turning it on again. The screen opened instantly.

71

Mike beamed. "Oh, that's much better. Thanks, Paul."

"No problem. You just need to clear your cache every now and then to stop it clogging up."

The older man shook his head. "I'm afraid I'm pretty useless when it comes to computers."

"Don't worry. I'm always happy to help if I can." And all the more so as it gave him an excuse to drop into the hotel. Jess was on reception. He'd breezed past her on his way in, ignoring the dirty look she'd shot at him.

He checked again that the computer was loading properly, then rose to his feet and invited Mike to take back his chair. "There you go. All done. Any more problems, just give me a call."

"Yes, yes." Mike was already intent on the screen. "I'll see you later."

Paul laughed softly to himself as he strolled from the office and out to reception. Jess was chatting to a couple of guests, so he wandered over to the lounge and poured himself a coffee at the small bar.

He waited until she was free then sauntered over and leaned casually on the counter. "Good morning."

Those amethyst eyes were ice cold. "What are you doing here?"

He smiled blandly, knowing it would annoy her. "Just helping Mike with a little computer glitch."

"That's nice. Have you finished? Good. Goodbye."

"Now that's not very friendly," he protested, putting on a hurt face.

She glared at him down her nose. "Why would I want to be friendly?"

"Because secretly you like me."

"No, I don't."

"You should." He rested his chin on his hand, turning on his most charming smile. "I'm a really nice person once you get to know me."

"I have no wish to get to know you," she returned dismissively, turning her attention back to the computer screen.

"You don't know what you're missing."

"Actually, I do. Your sister told me about you. Warned me, to be more precise."

"Oh?" He grinned. "What did she say?"

"That you change your girlfriends more often than you change your socks."

"Ah, now that's not fair. I change my socks every day. My mother taught me that."

She snorted. He suspected that she was trying not to laugh.

"I'll tell you what," he coaxed. "Why don't you have dinner with me tonight? It'll give you a chance to get to know me properly."

"I told you, I don't want to get to know you."

"Scared?" he teased, grinning.

"Scared?" She arched one finely drawn eyebrow. "Why would I be scared?"

"Maybe of finding out that the shark-infested moat you're hiding behind isn't quite wide enough after all?"

She sighed with impatience. "For the last time, I do not want to get to know you, I don't want to go out to dinner with you, and if you don't go away, I'll ask Mike to throw you out."

"He wouldn't do it. He's too nice." That won him a flicker of a smile.

"Lisa then."

"Oh, yes. She'd throw me out," he acknowledged, laughing. "Even though she's my sister."

She conceded another reluctant smile. "Are you always this arrogant?"

"I like to think of it as persistent."

"You're certainly that."

"Ah, now you've hurt my feelings." His desolate expression was entirely bogus — he knew she wouldn't be fooled for a moment.

"I doubt you have any feelings," she snapped.

"I have lots of them. Like I feel all fuzzy when I look at you. Like I just want to run my fingers through that gorgeous flaming hair."

"Try that and I might have to break your arm."

"That wouldn't hurt as much as if you broke my heart." He laid a hand over the threatened organ. "And you've already bruised it by refusing to have dinner with me."

She laughed, shaking her head. "Is this how you do it?"

"Do what?"

"Wear a girl down until she agrees to go out with you just to shut you up."

"Are you going to go out with me?"

Her mouth thinned. "Will it shut you up?"

"Of course. How about tonight? I know a nice little place on the edge of Dartmoor. Very classy, very romantic. Great food."

"Not tonight. I'm working late."

"Tomorrow then?"

"I'm washing my hair."

"That takes a whole evening?"

"It takes as long as I want it to take."

"Well, it's very nice hair, so I guess it can take as long as it takes. Okay then, Wednesday?"

She rolled her eyes. "You don't give up, do you?"

"I told you, I'm known for my persistence."

She sighed. "Okay, if it'll shut you up. Make it Thursday."

"Good decision. I'll pick you up at seven." He winked, and sauntered away.

Jess shook her head in exasperation as she watched him stroll out of the front door, the set of his wide shoulders conveying pure arrogance. Dammit, why had she agreed to have dinner with him? He was exactly the type she didn't want anything to do with, but it seemed that she had some kind of stupid addiction to good-looking, arrogant men.

Somehow she was going to have to find a way to wean herself off them. Though letting Paul Channing wheedle her into agreeing to a date probably wasn't the best way to go about it.

For a few moments she turned her attention back to the computer, noting that an elderly couple were due to arrive tomorrow. A note attached to the booking told her that they were another couple like Mr and Mrs Wright, regulars who had been coming for years to celebrate their anniversary, having spent their honeymoon here.

She loved that about this place, that little personal touch. Housekeeping would put fresh roses in their room, and there would be a complementary bottle of champagne with their dinner.

She glanced up as a man came through the front doors, then frowned slightly — he wasn't their usual type of guest. Apparently on his own, he was wearing a smart charcoal-grey business suit, highly polished shoes and a pristine white shirt with a dark-blue striped tie.

It was hard to guess his age; she'd peg him at maybe around his middle forties. His hair was closely trimmed with not a hint of curl. Everything about him — including the slim leather briefcase he carried — proclaimed him to be a high-powered businessman. But what business could bring him here to sleepy Sturcombe?

He paused halfway across the hall and looked around as if wondering how he had found himself in a place which was probably not up to his usual standards.

Jess pinned a professional smile in place. "Good morning, sir. How can I help you?"

"I'd like a room." His voice was crisp, no-nonsense.

"Certainly, sir. How long will you be staying?"

"Just one night."

"That's fine." She clicked on the computer. "May I have your name?"

"Forsythe."

"Thank you, Mr Forsythe. Room 11 is on the first floor, just at the top of the stairs, opposite the lift. Do you have any luggage?"

75

"Just one bag."

"Would you like to have the porter take it up for you?"

"Yes, please."

Ah, the first 'please' she'd got from him. She rang the bell for Eric the porter, and handed over his key card. "Have a pleasant stay."

"What time is dinner served?"

"From six o'clock."

He nodded briskly and took the key card. Jess watched him as he crossed the hall and climbed the stairs. For some reason she felt an uncomfortable sinking sensation in the pit of her stomach.

She didn't think his arrival was going to bring good news.

CHAPTER NINE

Mike put down the phone and propped his elbows on his desk, dropping his head into his hands. He had been expecting this news since Forsythe's visit, but that didn't make it any easier to take.

Two days. Why had he even bothered to visit? The speed of the decision suggested that it had been a foregone conclusion. At least they'd had the decency to ring him instead of just sending an email.

> *Regrettably, Lytcott Capital Management don't see a future for the Carleton in their portfolio . . . blah blah blah . . . Thank you for your loyalty and hard work over the past thirty years . . . blah blah blah . . . Hoping to find a buyer . . . blah blah blah . . . If there's no interest, it will go to auction in a month.*

So that was it. He had little hope that a buyer would be found. The old place would be closed down and demolished to make way for a block of holiday apartments or another caravan park.

77

With a small sigh, he picked up the phone again and clicked on Lisa's number. She was the first one to tell, then he'd have to call a staff meeting. He'd speak to Chef as soon as he came on.

* * *

Shelley stared at Jess. "A staff meeting? Now?"

"In half an hour, in the ballroom."

"What's it about?"

"I don't know." Jess shook her head. "It could be something to do with that bloke who came the other day — Mr Forsythe."

Shelley furrowed her brow. "Who was he? Someone from the golf league?"

"I've no idea." Jess shrugged. "He only spoke to Mike. I suppose we'll find out soon enough."

"Yes . . ."

She was horribly afraid that she could guess. Though that sleazy guy had been suspended from the golf league's committee, maybe they had decided that after the trouble it had caused, they didn't want to have anything to do with the Carleton anymore.

If they'd cancelled the contracts for their tournaments and their Stay'n'Play packages, that would be a massive blow. And would people blame her for it? She knew Lisa didn't, but some of the other staff might.

Dammit, she'd just stay up here, finish the rooms on this corridor. This whole floor was empty, and would likely stay empty until the Turkey-and-Tinsel groups began to arrive in another couple of weeks.

They were coach parties of mostly pensioners, many of whom came every year to kick off their Christmas. They spent their time gossiping in the lounge, going on shopping trips to Exeter or excursions to Newquay Zoo or the Eden Project.

She'd find out soon enough what was going on.

78

Room 306 had probably never been so clean. She'd scrubbed the bathroom to within an inch of its life, cleaned the windows, even got down on her hands and knees to sweep out every awkward corner of the floor.

She was polishing the dressing table, bringing it up to a gleaming shine, when Tracey put her head round the door.

"Are you coming down to the staff meeting? It's nearly time."

"Oh . . . I . . . Do I really need to be there?" There was a small smudge on the dressing table mirror. She rubbed at it fiercely. "I'm trying to crack on with the rooms on this corridor."

"The rooms can wait," Tracey insisted. "Come on. Mike wants everyone there."

"Okay." Reluctantly she put down the polishing cloth. "What's it about?"

"Mike will tell you."

Shelley could tell from Tracey's expression that it wasn't going to be good news. Her heart was heavy as she followed her supervisor along the corridor and down the stairs.

The staff were gathered in the ballroom, apart from a few who were off duty this afternoon. Chairs had been set out in a semi-circle. Mike was sitting in front of them, looking nervous.

Shelley took a seat at the end of the row, folding her hands in her lap to stop herself fidgeting with them.

"Hello, everyone," Mike began, a slight quaver in his voice. "Thank you for coming. I have some news which I need to share with all of you. And I'm afraid it isn't very good news."

He took off his glasses, polished them on his handkerchief, and put them back on again.

"As most of you know, we — that is, the hotel group which we're part of — has been taken over several times over the years by various investment funds. Well, it's been taken over again, by another investment fund."

79

There was a murmuring around the room, some people enquiring what an investment fund was.

"A couple of days ago we had a visit from a representative of the fund. A Mr Forsythe. Some of you may have seen him around the place."

Nods, more murmurs.

"This morning I had a . . . long telephone conversation with him. He told me that the fund has assessed the hotel and decided that it isn't making sufficient profit to warrant the cost of much-needed repairs and renovations. So, after *careful* consideration . . ." There was an uncharacteristic note of sarcasm in his voice. ". . . he has decided to recommend that the hotel be sold off."

The ripple of murmurs spread again.

"It's to be sold at auction next month. And if it isn't sold as a going concern . . ." He paused, evidently struggling to speak. "It will be closed down."

"What?"

"No! They can't do that!"

The protests rose, angry, distressed.

Mike shook his head. "I'm afraid they can. They're only interested in whether we're making enough profit, and we've been on the edge for years. I wish I could be more optimistic, but . . ."

Shelley felt her heart bounce to her throat and then sink like lead to her feet. The Carleton had been her home for three years — the best home she'd ever had. If it closed . . .

Several people were already in tears, and not just the women. They were a small staff group, and very close, like family. And everyone loved this place. It had stood here above Sturcombe Bay for so long, had seen families grow up here, couples come back year after year for sentimental reasons.

And now it was probably going to close.

Why had she let her guard down? Why had she let herself begin to trust that she had finally found a safe haven? Hadn't

80

life taught her the hard way for as long as she could remember that nowhere was safe, nowhere was forever?

So, in maybe no more than a few weeks, she'd be packing up her rucksack again and moving on. Maybe she'd go sooner, just pack up and slip away, avoid all the goodbyes. She hated goodbyes.

CHAPTER TEN

"Goodnight, Grandpa. I'll see you tomorrow."

"Goodnight, son. Mind how you go."

Alex laughed. "I'm only going about two hundred yards up the road, Grandpa."

"Ah, you can never be too careful. You never know who's about these days."

Alex laughed again, shaking his head. "Okay, Grandpa, I'll be careful."

It was a pleasant evening for a stroll. The sun was sinking slowly beneath the horizon, the sky tinted with watercolour shades of gold and magenta, darkening to indigo in the east as a few stars began to glimmer.

But it was still quite warm. Instead of going straight back to his empty flat and cooking himself some dinner (something straight from the freezer to the microwave), he was tempted to take a walk on the beach.

The waves were rolling in lazily and uncurling with ribbons of white foam sliding in over the red-gold sand. Alex paused at the bottom of the ramp down to the beach and drew in a long, deep breath of the salt-tanged air.

He'd only been here for a couple of weeks, but already he was falling in love with the place . . .

Someone was sitting on the rocks beneath the hotel — someone he recognised instantly. Her shoulders were hunched, and her whole posture signalled dejection. He hesitated, then walked over.

"Hi."

She glanced up, startled, and he knew at once that she'd been crying. She brushed a hand across her eyes and turned her head away from him.

"Mind if I join you?"

She didn't answer, so he climbed up and sat on a rock just below hers, careful not to startle her.

"What's wrong?" he asked gently.

"Nothing."

"There clearly is. Is it something to do with that sleazebag who attacked you?"

"No." Her voice was ragged. How long had she been crying? There was a long pause, then she said, "They're closing the hotel."

Astonished, he glanced up at the building above them. "Closing it? But why?"

"It's been taken over by some greedy investment fund who just want to make money, and we're not making enough, apparently." Now it was bitterness in her voice. "So, they're putting it up for auction next month, and if it doesn't sell . . . Which it probably won't. I mean, who wants a great big white elephant like that these days? Nobody wants to come to the seaside for their holidays any more when they can go to Greece or Spain and be sure of getting the sun. So they'll just close it, and leave it derelict until it falls down."

"That's ridiculous! It's a great place. All it needs is a little bit of polishing up, a bit of advertising in the right places . . ."

"Who's going to pay to polish it up?" She turned to him, her eyes red-rimmed. "It doesn't make enough profit for it to be worth putting money into it."

"You have to invest to make money."

"Yeah, well, all we need is a millionaire with more money than sense."

He paused for a moment, the figures his accountant had sent him a few days ago flickering through his mind. "Most millionaires have more money than sense."

"They'd have more sense than to throw money at this place."

The tears were streaming down her cheeks. Carefully, Alex eased up closer to her. "How long have you worked here?"

"Three years. But it's not just a job. It's my home. I've never had a proper home before."

The ache in her voice tore into his heart. "Never?"

"Oh, I've had a lot of homes, but they weren't really mine. Just foster homes. I was even adopted once, but they gave me back."

"They what?"

She laughed bitterly. "I wasn't the good little girl they wanted."

Her words shocked right through him as he remembered his own close, loving family. "That's appalling."

"So I got moved on." She shrugged her slender shoulders in a gesture of casual dismissal which he recognised as just a front for a world of hurt. "To another foster home, and then another. I can't even remember most of them. By the time I was fifteen, I couldn't be bothered with them anymore, so I ran away from the last one."

"What did you do?"

"Survived." The acid in her voice could have etched steel.

He took a moment to choose his words — it would be very easy to say the wrong thing. "That must have been tough."

"Oh, it was a laugh a minute. A bit of begging, a bit of shoplifting. Living in squats which were filthy and had no water or electricity. I lived with a couple of prostitutes for a while, kept house for them. I never sold sex myself." Her eyes were sharp. "Except for a couple of hand jobs."

84

He knew she was expecting him to recoil, but all he felt was a profound compassion that she had been forced to such extremes. But he sensed that she would reject sympathy, at least at the moment.

"So how did you end up down here?"

Another casual shrug. "I'd been sleeping rough round behind Oxford Street for a couple of weeks, and this charity that looks out for homeless young people offered me a room in their hostel. I stayed there for a while, then they found me this job." At last a smile. "It was the best thing that's ever happened to me."

The tears started again, and he reached out tentatively to take her hand. She didn't withdraw it. They just sat in silence for a while as the waves rolled in, splashing against the rocks beneath them.

"Are you hungry?"

A wary look.

"Fish and chips?"

She smiled, that tiny dimple popping into her cheek. "That would be nice."

"Come on then." He drew her to her feet and they walked along the beach, the cool evening breeze from the sea stirring their hair, the stars appearing one by one as if lit by an invisible hand.

CHAPTER ELEVEN

Kate studied her reflection in the mirror. It wasn't something she did very often, except for a quick check that she looked tidy, her soft brown hair brushed, her shirt buttoned straight.

But this evening she was going out. It wasn't a date — it was just an evening with an old friend, enjoying a favourite hobby. She had always loved dancing. They all used to go together when her Terry was alive, the two of them with Mike and Sarah.

After Terry died she hadn't had the heart for it any more. But she hadn't forgotten the steps. Debbie had always laughed at her when she had waltzed or tangoed around the sitting room when *Strictly* was on the television.

And now she was going dancing again, after all these years. It had been difficult to decide what to wear. She didn't really have a 'going out' wardrobe any more.

Would the dress she had bought for Debbie's wedding be suitable? It was pale blue, quite a simple style without the embroidered jacket that went with it. Maybe she could pair it with a dark-blue cardigan and give it a twist with her purple paisley-patterned silk scarf, and a nice pair of earrings.

86

At least shoes wouldn't be a problem. She had several pairs of plain black court shoes with low kitten heels which she wore when she was working in the café, so she knew they were comfortable as well as smart.

A glance at her watch told her that it was almost seven o'clock, so she picked up her bag and her jacket and went downstairs to watch for Mike's car. She didn't want to keep him waiting.

At exactly two minutes past seven the car pulled up to the kerb. Kate smiled to herself as she went to open the door. Mike had always been punctual. But as soon as he stepped out of the car she knew that there was something wrong.

"Mike? What is it? What's happened?"

His shoulders were slumped and he looked utterly defeated. "They're closing the hotel."

"They . . . what?" She stared at him, startled. "Who is?"

"This new investment fund that's bought it. They sent a representative down to have a look around, and he decided that we're not making enough profit for them, so they're putting it up for auction next month. And if it doesn't sell, they're just going to close it."

"Oh no! Look, come on inside and tell me all about it." Without thinking, she took his hand and drew him into the café, urging him to sit at one of the tables. "I'll get us some coffee."

The barista machine was turned off, but she had some instant for emergencies. In a few moments, she brought two mugs over to the table and sat down opposite him.

"I don't get it." She shook her head, frowning. "Why did they buy the place if they don't want to keep it open?"

"They didn't particularly want to buy it. It just came as part of the package when they took over the Nordicote Group. Nordicote had bought it as part of another group four years ago, and there was another group that owned it before that. None of them have taken much interest in it, they haven't wanted to invest in it. They've just let it get more and more run down, until we're where we are now." His voice was laced

87

with a bitterness she had never heard from him before. "Not worth keeping open."

"But it's not that run down," Kate protested, indignant on his behalf. "Yes, it needs a bit of work — the paintwork could be freshened up, a few new carpets — but people come back year after year because they love it."

He sighed heavily. "Our old faithfuls. The trouble is that there's not enough of them, and they're all elderly. In a few more years there won't be many of them left. We have the golfers through the summer, and the Turkey-and-Tinsel people around Christmas, but . . . Do you know, the swimming pool's been empty for five years? It was hardly used, and we couldn't afford to heat it."

"Oh, Mike . . ." She reached across the table and took both his hands in hers. "But if they're putting it up for auction, someone might buy it."

"But not to keep it open. They'll demolish it for . . . I don't know, another caravan site or something. At least that would be better than just leaving it derelict."

"And what about you?" she asked gently. "What will you do?"

"I don't know." He shook his head. "I'm fifty-seven years old — too young to get my pension, too old for anyone to employ me. Except for stacking shelves in a supermarket, maybe. Collecting trolleys."

She felt her heart crease. "Don't fret about it, Mike. Something will turn up."

"Maybe." He managed a smile, squaring his shoulders. "But worrying about it won't butter the parsnips, as my mother used to say. Come on, let's go dancing."

* * *

The dance school was on the upper floor above a row of shops. Kate was a little hesitant as they climbed the stairs, not sure what to expect. It was so long since she'd been dancing.

88

There was a small lobby where patrons could leave their coats, and a hatch into a kitchenette where teas and coffees could be prepared.

The ballroom was a good size, with a gleaming hardwood floor and wooden chairs round the walls, and soft lighting from amber LED bulbs set in the ceiling.

There were about two dozen people there, the women outnumbering the men by almost two to one. Kate could see why a man on his own, especially a good dancer like Mike, would be very much in demand.

And not only for his dancing. In his mid-fifties, he was still a good-looking man. His hair and his beard were both neatly trimmed, though touched with grey. His eyes were grey and gentle, with a faint tracery of smile lines around them.

He was tall — close to six feet — and lean without being skinny. And very smart in a navy-blue suit, with a crisp white shirt and maroon tie. Her presence was going to cause a lot of disappointment.

She slanted a quick glance up at him, and he smiled reassuringly. "Come over and say hello to Theresa, our teacher."

The teacher was an elegant woman with neat auburn hair, wearing a pale-blue skirt with a white blouse, her make-up immaculate. She extended a perfectly manicured hand when Mike introduced her to Kate.

"Ah, yes. Welcome. Have you danced before?"

"Well, a long time ago."

"We've danced at a couple of weddings recently," Mike put in. "She's really good."

"Oh . . . well, I wouldn't say that," Kate protested.

Theresa smiled. "Don't worry, you'll be fine with Mike. Let's just see how you get along." She turned towards the hall and clapped her hands. "Okay, people. Are we ready to begin?"

Kate felt a flutter of nerves in the pit of her stomach as the music started and Mike put his hand on her back, turning her towards the dance floor.

It was one thing dancing with him at Debbie's and Vicky's weddings, but here, with all these experienced dancers watching her, probably wondering who she was and what she was doing with Mike, she was desperately aware of being an absolute beginner.

For the first time she understood what they meant by that expression 'two left feet'. She felt as if hers were three times their normal size, and they were refusing to do what her brain was telling them.

"I'm sorry," she muttered as her knee knocked against his, forcing him to stop and restart.

"Don't worry." He smiled down at her. "Just relax and listen to the music — it'll tell you what to do."

She nodded and closed her eyes, letting the simple melody with its underlying three-beat rhythm seep into her brain. And somehow the old memories came back to her, as if her body knew what to do without her having to think about it. It seemed to lift her inches above the polished floor as Mike led her into a swirling turn around the room.

For a fleeting moment she was dancing with her Terry, but then, with one of his cocky grins, he faded away and she was dancing with Mike. And it felt . . . right.

* * *

They danced a waltz and a slow foxtrot, but the Viennese Waltz was Mike's favourite. He loved the swoop and flow of it, the simplicity of the steps, the music. Whether they were dancing to Strauss or Shostakovich, or something modern, it had a grace and elegance unmatched, in his opinion, by any other dance.

And Kate was a delight to dance with — light on her feet and following his lead as if they had been dancing together for years. Why hadn't he thought of asking her before?

Because . . . it had felt a little awkward. She'd been his wife's best friend. He had so many memories of them together:

coming home from a shopping trip laden with bags, laughing in the kitchen as they cooked up a lasagne or a Thai curry.

Kate sitting with Sarah as she had slowly slipped away from them.

He had valued the comfort of her friendship since then as someone who had known and loved Sarah as he had. They had often spoken of her: 'Sarah would have laughed at that'. And he knew the flowers that often appeared on Sarah's grave were from Kate.

Then he had danced with her at Vicky and Tom's wedding . . . and something seemed to have slipped a little sideways. He wasn't just thinking of her as Sarah's friend any more. He was thinking of her as a woman. An attractive woman.

Oh lord, she'd be so embarrassed if she ever guessed.

CHAPTER TWELVE

Paul bowed in mocking amusement as he held open the passenger door of the dark-green Aston Martin. "Your carriage awaits, Madame."

He had half-expected that Jess wouldn't show up, or that she'd be wearing jeans and trainers when he had promised to take her somewhere classy. But she had emerged from the hotel's staff entrance at seven on the dot, and she'd gone for the classic little black dress. Simple, elegant, skimming over her slender figure — and short enough to start a riot.

And her legs. Long, long legs in sheer black tights. And strappy black sandals with killer heels. And a provocative sway of her hips as she strolled across the car park.

She slanted a sardonic glance along the sleek lines of the car. "Am I supposed to be impressed?"

Paul laughed. "No, you're supposed to relax in supreme comfort as you're whisked to our destination."

She rolled her eyes. "Are you ever lost for words?"

"Rarely."

She shook her head, conceding a reluctant laugh as she slid into the comfortable leather seat. "Okay, where are we going?" she challenged. "I warn you, I'm expecting something special."

92

"It will be." He walked round the long bonnet and climbed behind the wheel. He fired the ignition and the engine purred into life like a sleeping lion. "Music?"

"What have you got?"

"What do you like?"

"Springsteen?"

He shouldn't have been surprised at her choice — she wasn't a soupy ballad type of woman. "Certainly. Classic or recent?"

"Oh, classic, of course."

He clicked through his listing and chose the *Darkness* album, and as 'Badlands' blasted through the speakers, she sang along, beating out the rhythm on her knees.

He smiled across at her. "Ah, I finally got something right."

"It had to happen eventually."

Oh, he liked her. He liked her a lot. She was fun, challenging — he'd never known a woman quite like her. She'd be great in bed — hot, wild, exciting. It wasn't going to be easy to get her there, but it would be worth it.

* * *

It was a beautiful car. Glenn would have been green with envy, Jess mused with a touch of dark humour. Aston Martins were one of the few cars he would choose over a motorbike.

Paul turned out of the hotel's car park, drove past the Memorial Gardens, and accelerated smoothly up Church Road. "So, what brought you to Sturcombe?" he asked conversationally.

She gave him a flickering glance. "A slightly rusty hatchback."

"Not an Aston Martin then?" His eyes glinted with amusement. "There aren't too many of these babies on the road." There was a distinct note of pride in his voice. Men and their modes of transport!

93

"It's a nice car," she acknowledged.

"Something else I got right?"

She conceded a smile.

"You didn't answer the question," he prompted. "What brought you to Sturcombe?"

She took a pause to consider what, if anything, she was going to tell him. "I just dumped my boyfriend of five years, six weeks before we were due to get married."

"Drastic. What did he do?"

"I found out that he was sexting women on one of those hook-up sites."

"Unacceptable."

"And he was clearly meeting up with them for sex."

"Definitely unacceptable."

"And he was sending them dick pics."

"Where did you bury him?"

She laughed. "Tempting, but he wasn't worth going to prison for." She arched one questioning eyebrow. "I assume you'd never do anything like that?"

"I've never needed hook-up sites." His voice was bluntly matter-of-fact. "Sexting — fun, but only if you're in a relationship. Sleeping with random women — not since I was about sixteen. I may have had a lot of girlfriends, but only ever one at a time. As for dick pics — that's just sleazy."

"So you're Mr Clean?" she taunted.

His smile was one of pure wickedness. "Oh, I can be very dirty, given the right circumstances."

Jess forced herself to breathe slowly. She wasn't going to follow that topic of conversation any further. He had turned onto the dual carriageway, and the car was eating up the miles, as smooth as silk.

"So what about you?" she asked. "Lisa said you used to be a professional footballer."

"That's right."

"Used to be?"

94

"I picked up a knee injury, tore my cruciate ligament. It put me out for most of a season, but even once I was fit again, I rarely made it off the subs bench."

"So you retired?"

"Football careers rarely last much past the middle thirties, especially for strikers. Some go into coaching or management, but that wasn't my thing. I'd already accepted that none of the top clubs were going to come bidding for me. I could have dragged out my time in one of the lower leagues, but that didn't appeal either. So . . ." He shrugged those wide shoulders. "I retired."

She sensed that he wasn't quite as unconcerned about it as he was pretending to be. "A torn cruciate ligament can be pretty painful," she remarked with sympathy. "Glenn tore his falling off his bike."

He arched one dark eyebrow. "Your ex? I didn't have him pegged for a cyclist."

"Motorbike."

"Ah."

"He's got a bike shop in Bristol. I helped him run it." She smiled dryly. "He's going to struggle with it now, until he can get someone else in to help. He never was any good with paperwork."

"Which bothers you not at all?"

"Not at all. Bloody well serves him right. I hope he goes bankrupt."

He laughed. "Did you ride yourself?"

"Pillion." She pulled a face. "I used to ride a Moto Guzzi. I loved that bike. That was how I met Glenn, riding out with his group. But I came off it and broke my wrist quite badly. It never really healed properly, so I struggled to control the rear brake."

"That's a shame. Do you miss it?"

"Well, yes. I suppose like you miss playing football. There's something about being in the zone, you know?"

He nodded, his eyes dark. "I know."

"You can never quite get that feeling any other way."

95

There was that wicked smile again. "Oh, I know of one other way."

She turned her head away sharply, watching the twin beams of the car's headlights stab through the gathering twilight. It had started to rain, just a drizzle, and the slow rhythmic swish of the windscreen wipers was almost hypnotic.

Maybe this had been a mistake. She'd been ready twenty minutes early, then she'd paced around her small room, her mind bouncing between the two poles — stay or go.

Then she'd seen the car pull into the car park in front of the hotel, and she'd told herself firmly not to be a coward. She could cope with a man like Paul Channing.

But now, in the quiet confines of the car, she wasn't sure that she could.

She'd seen him in casual jeans and sweater, and in — *oh boy!* — that clinging wetsuit. Tonight he was wearing a dark-blue suit, stylishly cut and immaculately tailored over those wide shoulders.

But even the best of tailoring couldn't disguise that aura of lithe male power, like a panther prowling the fringes of the jungle. She'd seen it in action — an internet search had shown her a clip of him scoring a Championship League Goal of the Season, several years ago.

He'd slid past three defenders with an effortless, almost laconic grace, and arced the ball from over thirty yards out to curl it round the goalkeeper and into the back of the net.

She'd probably watched that clip at least a dozen times.

* * *

Springsteen was singing mournfully about his '69 Chevvy as Paul turned the car into the gravelled car park in front of a beautiful seventeenth-century manor house — two storeys, with square chimneys and a slate-tiled roof, ivy clinging to the grey stone walls. The latticed windows glowed a warm amber, and the front door was standing open in welcome.

96

"Very nice," she approved.

"Three for three?"

She laughed, nodding.

He came round to open her door, and they scampered through the rain to the shelter of the stone porch. The entrance hall was as beautiful as the exterior. The gleaming dark wood of the floor contrasted beautifully with the rich walnut wainscoting on the walls which were hung with gilt-framed portraits of fine ladies and gentlemen.

A large well-polished table stood in the centre of the room, holding a fabulous display of lilies and roses beneath a chandelier worthy of Versailles hanging from the high coffered ceiling.

The imposing head waiter came forward with a smile. "Ah, Mr Channing. We have your usual table."

"Thank you."

Jess shot him a narrowed look. "You bring all your girlfriends here? You just lost a point."

He returned her one of those bland smiles. "Not all my girlfriends. And not always girlfriends."

She shook her head. "No, you don't get the point back."

The head waiter glanced from one to the other, slightly puzzled by the exchange. "Um . . . this way, please."

They followed him into the dining room. This was the last word in elegance. Softly lit by antique-style sconces, the walls were panelled to the ceiling in that rich dark walnut and the floor was covered with a carpet in subtle shades of olive-green and gold.

The circular tables were covered in pristine white cloths over olive-green table skirts which matched the velvet curtains and the cushioned chairs. Gleaming crystal glasses and white tableware graced the tables, each holding a centrepiece of white roses.

The head waiter led them to a corner table and produced two menus in olive-green leather binders.

"Ah, a point awarded for a proper menu," Jess accorded. "Not some stupid edgy thing in chalk on a garden spade."

Paul laughed at that. "Certainly not."

Jess forced herself to focus on the menu, not the man sitting opposite her, but that was far from easy. He was wearing a pale-blue shirt, the collar open, and she could just glimpse a smattering of dark curling hair at the base of his throat.

And his hands were strong and sensitive. They looked like hands that would know how to caress a woman's body . . .

But it was more than just a physical attraction that tugged at her. She liked his sense of humour, and she liked that he got hers. Glenn could sometimes get annoyed when she teased him.

She was going to have to be careful, she reminded herself firmly. She could be standing on a very slippery slope.

Pushing those troublesome thoughts from her mind, she glanced through the menu. The selection was small, but it looked delicious. Jess chose pulled crab with crème fraîche and chives for a starter, followed by Suffolk lamb with mint and white asparagus. Paul opted for fillet of veal with fingerling potatoes and rapini.

"And I'll have mineral water with that, as usual," he added. "Would you prefer wine, Jess?"

"Ah . . . not a whole bottle. Do you have a house wine?"

"Of course."

"Then I'll have a glass of that, please."

The waiter smiled and withdrew.

Jess picked up a breadstick and nibbled on it. "Has Lisa told you what's happening with the hotel?"

"Yes."

"It would be a real shame if it gets closed down. There's this lovely old couple — the Wrights — who had their honeymoon there nearly sixty years ago, and they've come back for a long weekend every year since, on their anniversary. They brought their little dog with them. They want to celebrate their sixtieth wedding anniversary there. It'll break their hearts if they can't. And there are quite a few people like them — regulars who come back every year. I've been looking back over the old guest lists."

Paul's eyes were dark. "I know. They pretty much keep the place going through the off-season. Unfortunately there aren't enough of them, and they're gradually getting older and dying off."

"What about the golfers?"

"They bring in a lot of business over the summer, but not so many want to play in the winter when it's windy and the ground's wet. There are only two tournaments for the whole six months."

"But if the hotel closes, what will happen in the summer when they do want to play?"

He shrugged his wide shoulders. "They'd just go somewhere else."

She shook her head sadly. "It's a lovely old place. It could be really nice if only someone would invest a bit of money in it. If no one buys it, it could just get demolished."

"It won't be as easy as that — it's actually a listed building. They'd need to get it delisted and then apply to the council to knock it down."

"Can they do that?"

"Yes, though it can be a long and expensive process. But if the owners are unscrupulous enough they'd just leave it empty and derelict until it's beyond recovery — unsafe. Maybe a convenient fire that can be blamed on squatters. Then the council doesn't have much choice."

She stared at him, aghast. "Oh no, that would be even worse. You could do so much with the place, with a bit of input."

"Such as?"

"Well, weddings, for a start. Lisa told me they had two there this summer. It's a wonderful venue, especially with those views. When we were looking for somewhere for ours, we'd have jumped at it, if it had been closer."

"Yes, closer. That's one disadvantage. Sturcombe's pretty tucked away, off the beaten track."

"So you play that up as a plus," she argued, her enthusiasm rising. "You could offer the whole package, with the bridal party and even the guests staying for the weekend as well."

"That could be expensive."

She waved the breadstick in a dismissive gesture. "There'd be people willing to pay. Destination weddings are a big thing. Some people go to Ibiza or even the Caribbean for their wedding. Why not South Devon?"

"Hmmm."

"It would be cheaper and certainly less hassle for the guests to get there, particularly older guests. Of course, if you were going to go for that you'd need to smarten the place up quite a bit," she added judiciously. "Go more upmarket. Maybe think about a spa, a hairdressing salon. And you could upsell by offering it as a package for hen and stag weekends."

"What? Hordes of screaming women running around in feather boas and pink cowboy hats, blokes getting pissed up and hiring strippergrams, and tying the groom butt-naked to a lamppost? No, thank you."

She laughed, shaking her head. "Not that sort of thing. You market it as something classy. Five star. Not the sort of thing that would attract the cowboy hat and strippergram brigade."

He nodded slowly. "Okay . . ."

The waiter had brought their starter. Jess thanked him with a smile, and took a forkful of her pulled crab. "Mmm . . ." She closed her eyes, savouring the delicate blend of flavours. "This is delicious."

He grinned. "Do I get a point?"

"Two points," she conceded.

"So, go on," he prompted. "Weddings wouldn't be enough to sustain the place. You'd still be likely to have a drop off of bookings in the off-season. What else?"

"Okay . . ." She thought about it. "You could push the dog-friendly angle, especially as dogs are allowed on the beach. A lot of places ban them during the summer or even all year round. Dog owners are always looking for places to go. A lot

100

of them don't want to have to deal with all the paperwork to take their pooch abroad. And there are already websites and magazines — there's your promotion right there."

He nodded thoughtfully. "Good one."

"And I'm sure there are lots of other things they could do. Business conferences, and maybe . . . corporate team-building events. You know the kind of thing — paintballing, trekking. Being so close to Dartmoor, that could be really popular."

"It could."

She sighed. "All we need is someone with a few million to toss around."

"Yes . . ."

* * *

The waiter had taken away their empty starter plates and brought their main course. Paul was particularly fond of fingerlings, with their slightly nutty, earthy tang. He ate in silence for a while, thinking over Jess's suggestions.

He was fond of the old Carleton. When they were kids, he and Tom Cullen and the Ellis brothers used to run wild about the place, exploring all the hidden nooks and crannies that had been disused for years. That could maybe be turned to something productive.

He knew from Lisa how little had been put into it over the past . . . well, probably twenty years or so. Just barely enough to keep it up to the basic health and safety codes.

The structure was basically sound, but it would take an awful lot of money just to buy the place, never mind to renovate it to the kind of standard that would be needed. And he couldn't bring any of his clients' money in — not yet anyway. That would be unethical.

But if he could find a way to turn it into an attractive venue, where people would be willing to pay good prices, with a range of facilities which would free them from relying on the unpredictable English weather, it would be worth thinking about.

101

"You're very quiet," Jess remarked, a question in her eyes.

"I'm enjoying my dinner." He wasn't ready to share his thoughts about the hotel yet. "How's yours?"

"Excellent."

"More points?"

"Don't get greedy."

He laughed. She was fun to be with, that sharp sense of humour keeping him on his toes. He was enjoying the evening more than he had enjoyed a date with a woman for . . . a long time.

Maybe Lisa was right, he acknowledged with a quirk of wry humour. Choosing his girlfriends on the basis of having great legs might not be the best way to achieve a lasting relationship. Not that Jess didn't have great legs, starting in a pair of sharp high heels and going all the way up to heaven.

But then he wasn't looking for a lasting relationship. No way. Tom and Liam might have bitten the bullet, but he enjoyed the single life. Domestic bliss wasn't his thing.

CHAPTER THIRTEEN

"Mmm." Alex bundled up his fish and chip paper ready to throw it in the bin. "Those were about the best fish and chips I've ever tasted."

Shelley smiled up at him. "Do you have fish and chips in Canada?"

"We sure do. In many ways Canada is a lot like Britain. We even have red mailboxes, though they aren't round like they are here."

"What about Christmas? Do you do it the same as here?"

"Oh yes." His eyes twinkled. "Christmas trees, turkey with all the trimmings. The main difference is the snow."

"You get a white Christmas?"

"Of course. Well, not quite so often now as when I was a kid, but still about half the time. And we have a Santa Claus Parade, and ice skating in Nathan Phillips Square."

"It sounds like fun."

"It is. Maybe you should come visit one day?"

"Oh no . . . I . . . That isn't going to happen. I'm happy just to stay here in Sturcombe." She glanced up at the hotel above them. "If I can."

"What will you do if the hotel closes?" he asked gently.

103

"I don't know." Her voice was bleak. "I don't have anywhere else to go."

He reached out and took her hand. His impulse was to tell her that it would be fine, but he couldn't be sure of that. And besides, he suspected that she'd rarely had cause to trust anyone, so why should she trust him?

Shelley felt a slow, melting warmth spreading up her arm. Alex was holding her hand. It was nice, but she probably shouldn't be letting it happen. Hadn't she learned, her whole life, that anything nice invariably came to a sticky end?

But oh, it was so nice.

She'd never really understood when people had talked about attraction. She'd had a few relationships. Well, more 'friends with benefits' arrangements, to be honest.

Maybe it was just because he had been so nice to her. And he'd been great at dealing with that sleazebag from the golf league, too.

But no, it was more than that. Every time she saw him she felt a little fizz, like static electricity running over her skin. And when he smiled, those dark eyes warm . . .

The romantic atmosphere wasn't helping: the stars were as bright as diamonds in the dark velvet sky, and the sea was quiet, whispering softly over the sand.

Drawing in a deep breath she forced those foolish thoughts from her mind. But she left her hand in his as they walked slowly along the beach and up the ramp, and past the Memorial Gardens to the hotel.

As they reached the car park she turned to him with what she hoped was a confident smile. "Thank you for the fish and chips. Um . . . goodnight."

He arched one dark eyebrow in question. "I thought maybe we could have a nightcap in the lounge?"

She shook her head. "Staff aren't allowed."

"Oh . . . right. Well, now that we've kinda broken the ice over eating together, maybe we could have dinner somewhere

104

tomorrow night? Just to keep a poor lonely Canadian airman company?" he added with a quirk of humour.

She laughed, but shook her head again. "Staff aren't allowed . . ."

"To date guests. But I'm not a guest anymore."

"No, but you were. I could get the sack." That wasn't strictly true. There might be some sort of policy about it, but she'd never known it to be enforced. He wouldn't know that, though, and it was a good excuse.

"Right." His mouth quirked into a crooked smile. "Well . . . goodnight then."

He held out his hand, and she put hers in it. "Goodnight . . ."

For one wild moment she thought he was going to kiss her, and the smile in his eyes almost unravelled all her defences. But she managed to draw her hand away, and fumbling for her key she hurried across the car park.

She opened the door and hurried up the three flights of stairs to the staff accommodation on the top floor. To her relief there was no one around.

The little room below the eaves was her haven, somewhere she could be at peace. The smallest room in the hotel, but that meant she didn't have to share it.

She sat down on the bed and kicked off her shoes, still feeling that odd little fizz. Alex had actually asked her out — to dinner, no less. There was no way she could accept, of course. He'd take her somewhere posh, and she had nothing to wear that wouldn't make her look as though she should be out the back washing the pots.

And it would be dangerous to let herself be tempted. He wasn't for her. Apart from the fact that he'd been a guest of the hotel, he must be worth a few bob, to be able to stay here in England for several weeks, at least, when he had no job. And that posh Jaguar he was driving — it was a rental, but even so.

She was going to have to find a way to brush him off. It should be easy. She'd done it loads of times before. Except . . .

105

she hadn't been that attracted to those guys. She'd always tried to let them down gently, but if they wouldn't take a hint, she hadn't hesitated to be blunt.

But with Alex Crocombe . . .

She had been almost sure that he had been going to kiss her. She'd wanted it so much, she could almost feel how his lips would have touched hers. Why hadn't he?

Because he knew, as she did, that it wasn't going to go anywhere.

With a small sigh, she pulled her jumper over her head, dragged off her jeans, and shrugged into her dressing gown to go down the corridor to the bathroom to get ready for bed.

It wasn't eleven o'clock yet, and she was pretty sure that she wouldn't be able to sleep. And when she did, there would be dreams.

CHAPTER FOURTEEN

"That was a pleasant evening." Jess gave Paul a cool smile as he turned into the car park in front of the hotel. He drew up by the steps and smiled back.

"Pleasant?"

"Very pleasant. The food was delicious, the restaurant elegant and charming."

"And the company?"

"Entertaining."

"So how many points have I scored?"

"Oh . . ." She let a provocative smile play over her lips. "I think . . . eight out of ten."

"Is that all?"

"I'm a hard marker."

The glint in his dark eyes told her very clearly that he wasn't abashed. She hadn't expected him to be. Climbing out of the car, he strolled round to open her door for her. She smiled to herself at the gentlemanly gesture as he held out his hand to help her to her feet.

"Thank you."

"Thank *you* for a very . . . *pleasant* evening." His eyes glinted with lazy mockery as he drew her closer.

She put her hand up against his hard chest. "You haven't earned enough points for that yet."

"How many do I need?"

"I'll let you know."

He laughed in wicked amusement. "So how do I earn more?" He slid his arm around her waist and curled one finger beneath her chin, tilting her face up to his. "Like this?"

She forced herself to hold his gaze, refusing to give him the satisfaction of seeing the effect he had on her.

But as his head bent slowly over hers and she felt his breath warm on her cheek, the ground beneath her feet begin to shift. She closed her eyes as her lips parted softly . . .

And then abruptly he let her go. "I'm going up to London for a couple of days next week. I'll see you when I get back."

She opened her eyes and glared at him as he leaned past her to close the car door, then sauntered round to climb in behind the wheel again.

"Goodnight."

She was still standing there struggling to get her head straight as he executed an efficient three-point turn and drove out of the car park and back down the lane.

* * *

Jess lay awake, staring at the ceiling. She really ought to get up. Sounds around the hotel told her that everyone else was way ahead of her, but she didn't feel able to move just yet. Fortunately, she didn't have to as she was on a late shift today.

Last night . . . Paul. She had really enjoyed the evening, far more than she was willing to admit. But then when she had thought he was going to kiss her . . . he hadn't. The bastard.

How contrary was that? She hadn't wanted him to kiss her, so why was she so annoyed that he had just walked away?

Dammit, maybe she should just use him as a rebound fling to get over Glenn. Although she really didn't need to get over Glenn. She was over him already, apart from a lingering

108

annoyance with herself that she hadn't dumped him the first time she'd caught him cheating. Or at least the second. At least then she'd have been spared the cost and complications of cancelling the wedding.

A clatter of horses' hoofs on the lane below her window drew her out of bed. She crossed to the window and drew the curtain aside. Liam and Cassie were riding up from the beach, side by side, Cassie laughing at something he'd said.

Love. It seemed to work out for some people, but not for her.

She stood watching for a few moments as the couple turned in through their front gate and rode across the yard. Then, giving herself a mental shake, she shrugged into her dressing gown, picked up her towel and washbag, and hurried over to the bathroom.

Half an hour later, refreshed from her shower and having scoffed a bowl of cornflakes in the kitchen, she was strolling down the lane to the Ellis's pretty cottage.

The gate into the stable yard was latched, and she remembered the importance of latching it again behind her. Cassie was walking a horse in a wide circle round the yard. She wasn't holding the bridle, the horse was just following her, peering over her shoulder as if curious about what she was doing.

Jess waited quietly and as Cassie turned, she smiled a greeting.

"Hi, Jools . . ." A quick frown, then she laughed. "Oops, sorry. Hello, Jess."

"Hi." Jess laughed, dismissing the mistake. "I hope I'm not in the way. I saw you through the window, coming up from the beach. I've got the morning off, and I thought I'd just come down to say hello to the horses."

Cassie's smile widened. "You're more than welcome. They all like saying hello to people. Well, maybe not Sykes at the end there. He can be a bit grumpy."

Jess glanced around the yard. There were a dozen sturdy brick-built stables in one block, and three more in a separate wing, with a corrugated iron roof and wooden split doors. Only a couple of them appeared to be occupied, the horses peering out like nosy neighbours looking for gossip.

Beyond the yard she could see a long grassy paddock, shaded by trees, where horses, ponies and a few donkeys were contentedly grazing.

"Julia said you're taking on the care of the horses from the rescue society," she remarked.

"That's right. It'll take some of the weight off everyone else. I worked with horses in Montana, on a dude ranch. Great fun." She laughed. "The guests all loved my English accent. They thought it was 'real cute'. And they did some rehabilitation work with horses that had been traumatised by bad treatment or accidents."

"Is that what you're doing now?"

"Uh-huh." She was still walking slowly around the yard, the horse following her closely. Even to Jess's inexperienced eye the animal looked thin and badly out of condition. "This is Cody. He came to us a month ago. He'd been really badly neglected, but he's coming along nicely now, learning to trust me. Aren't you, my luvver?"

The horse nodded his head as if agreeing with her.

"How many horses do you have here?"

"We've got fifteen rescues in at the moment, as well as our own. Plus the ponies and donkeys. The society has another couple of dozen living out in foster homes. We usually keep them here for a while to begin with, so Liam can assess them and we can build up their health if they need it. Then some of them can be loaned to people we know are reliable. But some are retired and will be with us long-term."

"It must cost a fortune."

"Not really. They're mostly out to grass. And Tom Cullen supplies us with organic feed. Plus we have a group of regular donors and some support from a couple of charities, and a regular GoFundMe page attached to our website. Do you ride?"

"Horses? No."

"Would you like to?"

"Could I?"

"Of course. Jools said you ride motorbikes."

"I used to."

"Well, you should get the hang of horses dead easy then." She patted the nose of the horse that was following her. "Good boy, Cody. Want to go back to your field?" She glanced back at Jess. "Come on, let's choose a ride for you."

Jess followed Cassie over to the five-barred gate which led into the paddock where the horses were grazing. As she climbed nimbly onto the gate, several of the horses lifted their heads and ambled over to greet her.

"You could try Bella," Cassie suggested. "She used to be with a riding school, so she's used to novices and she's very sweet natured." She singled out a russet-coloured mare with a white streak down her nose. "Come on then, Bella. Do you fancy a little outing?"

The horse nuzzled against her shoulder as she stroked her neck. Cassie skipped down from the gate and opened it, and the horse walked through. She put her hand in her pocket, produced a Polo mint, and gave it to Jess.

"Here, give her this and she'll be your friend for life."

Jess smiled. "Thanks." She laid the mint on the palm of her hand and held it out to the horse. With a lap of a soft pink tongue and lips, it disappeared. She stroked her hand down the long muscular neck. "She's a beauty."

"She's a three-quarter bred Irish Draught. She's twenty-four years old so she's come here to retire, but she still likes a nice steady walk now and then. I'll saddle her up for you while you find yourself a helmet that fits. There's plenty to choose from in the tack room."

"Thank you."

She followed Cassie to the room at the end of the row of stables, the horse ambling along behind them. A rich smell of wood, leather and liniment hit her nostrils. It was like an equestrian Aladdin's cave with every kind of horse-riding equipment stored neatly on hooks and shelves.

"I'll saddle up Missie and come out with you," Cassie said. "She likes a steady walk too."

"Can I help?" Jess asked, eager to learn.

Cassie smiled. "Of course. I'll show you what to do. You can be my first pupil."

"Oh?"

"I'm going to set up my own training school." Cassie's voice lilted with enthusiasm. "Working with horses and owners, teaching the natural horsemanship methods I learned in Montana."

"That sounds great!"

"My nanna left me some money and I've found the ideal place for it, just up by the main road. There was an old farmer called Harry Ellicot, and when he died Tom Cullen bought his land. But there's a good-sized paddock and a big barn which will be ideal for what I want."

She selected a bit and bridle from the hooks along the wall, and walked back out to where Bella was waiting patiently. "Okay now, you always approach them from the left."

"Why's that?"

"It's standard practice, so they expect it. It's supposed to date back to when soldiers wore their swords on the left, so mounting from the left kept the swords out of the way. Speak softly to them, to let them know you're there."

Jess nodded as Cassie murmured sweet nothings to Bella, stroking gently down her sleek neck.

"You need to be smooth and easy with them. They're big, but they evolved as a prey animal so they startle easily, and they have a helluva kick."

Jess smiled. "Thanks for the warning."

"Okay, to fit the bit, coax the horse to open her mouth with your left thumb," Cassie went on. "Guide the bit in gently and be careful not to let it knock against her teeth. Then you lift the bridle with your right hand. See how it moves the bit up into the corners of her mouth?"

"Oh, yes. I always thought it looked a bit cruel, putting that piece of metal in their mouths."

"They don't mind it," Cassie assured her, "so long as you're gentle with them." She went on fitting the tack, explaining as she went. "Now, check that it's all straight, then tuck the reins up while you put on the saddle, so she doesn't tangle her foot in them."

She went back into the tack room to fetch a saddle.

"Pad first, then take the saddle and hike it onto your hip like this. Then swing it up and lay it gently over the pad. Never, ever, just dump it on her back." She huffed out a sharp breath as she hoisted the saddle over the horse and lowered it carefully.

"It looks heavy," Jess remarked.

"This one weighs about twenty pounds. English saddles are a lot lighter than American ones." As she spoke, she continued demonstrating how to adjust the saddle and tighten the girth. "Right, all done. Take her over to the mounting block. She only needs a light hand on her bridle — she knows what to do. One foot in the stirrup, a hand on the pommel, then up and over. And lower yourself gently . . . perfect."

Jess laughed. "It's pretty much like getting on a motorbike."

"Feel okay?"

"Yes." Jess couldn't help smiling. "Fine."

"Good." Cassie adjusted the stirrups to the right length. "Now, let yourself relax. Don't squeeze her with your knees, just give her a gentle nudge with your heels to coax her forward. Walk her slowly round the yard to get used to it while I saddle up Missie, then we can get going."

Jess found that Cassie had been right. She felt comfortable on the back of the big horse, accustomed as she was to using her sense of balance and her core muscles to maintain her position. After walking Bella round the yard a couple of times she followed Cassie out onto the lane.

There were several walkers strolling along the bridleway, some in sensible walking shoes and carrying rucksacks and

113

Nordic walking poles, others in shorts with small children and dogs in tow. They shared greetings as they passed.

"We'll just go out for half an hour today, or you won't be able to move tomorrow." Cassie laughed. "You're using muscles you never knew you had."

"It is a bit like riding a bike, though a lot wider. And nicer." She glanced around, over the hedges that lined the path. To her right the golf course spread up the gentle slope towards the main road, giving way a little further on to ploughed fields.

The trees were showing gold, the leaves beginning to fall and drift along the path. To her left the sea glittered in the cool October sunshine, silver-blue far out to the horizon. "You can see so much more, going slower and being higher up."

"Yes. I've ridden motorbikes too, but I do prefer horses."

"Jools said you worked at a water-sports resort in Australia."

"That's right. I started out in Florida, then I worked on the dude ranch for a year. But my work visa for the US was due to run out so I went to Africa — I worked in a water-sports resort and safari park in Tanzania for a year."

"Wow, that sounds exciting!"

"It was. The Serengeti is just amazing — miles and miles of open grassland, and huge herds of wildebeests and antelopes. And the skies are just incredible, especially in the rainy season."

"Did you see many elephants and giraffes?"

"Of course, loads. And zebras, hippos, and lions and cheetahs. And I visited Victoria Falls, and climbed Kilimanjaro to help raise money for a wildlife reservation. But now I'm home." She smiled, and there was no mistaking the happiness in her eyes. "And that's the best."

"You're getting married soon, aren't you?"

"Yes, at Christmas."

"Oh, that'll be lovely." If she felt a fleeting regret for her own abandoned wedding, she dismissed it impatiently. Better

114

no wedding than being married to a sleazebag like Glenn. Dick pics — the memory still grated.

"And we'll be kind of in-laws," Cassie pointed out. "Your sister will be my sister-in-law. She's really nice. It must be fun, being twins."

"It is. We used to have a great time when we were kids, winding everybody up by swapping clothes. Mum and Dad could tell us apart, but most other people couldn't — not even our aunts and uncles."

"I think I can when you're together, but when you're apart it's quite difficult. As my dear brother discovered, to his cost."

"Yes . . ." Jess paused to decide whether to continue down that line of conversation, though if she was completely honest with herself that was why she had come down to the stables. "I went out with him last night."

Cassie's eyes glinted with amusement. "So I heard."

"I didn't intend to say yes," Jess admitted. "I'm actually rather off men at the moment. But he's very . . . persistent."

Cassie laughed. "He's certainly that. When we were kids he could talk you out of your last red jelly baby."

Jess laughed too. "I can just imagine! Lisa said he's had a lot of girlfriends."

"He has, but don't let that put you off. Oh, I know I'm a bit biased because he's my brother, but I love him to bits."

Jess smiled. "It shows."

"Will you go out with him again?" Cassie asked.

"I don't know. I don't intend to, but I said that before."

"Well, all I'm saying is, if you want someone to help you get over your ex . . . Well, Paul's the perfect guy to have fun with."

"Nothing serious, no strings?"

"That's right."

Jess's mouth quirked into a wry smile. "I'll think about it."

They turned and began to amble back.

115

"You've done well today," Cassie remarked. "Would you like to ride out again?"

"Yes, I would. Would it be okay?"

"Of course. Mornings are the best time, if you're on a late shift. I'd be able to ride out with you then."

"That's great." She patted Bella's sleek neck. She was already growing fond of the big, placid horse. "Thank you."

But her mind was still drifting back to the conversation about Paul Channing. Someone to have fun with — no strings. Maybe. But . . . she was already far too attracted to him.

She needed to be very careful. Not let him talk her out of her last red jelly baby.

* * *

"Hi." Paul strolled into the stable yard and greeted his sister with a cheerful grin.

Cassie glanced over her shoulder. "Good afternoon, brother dearest. Have you just come to pester me, or are you planning to go out for a ride?"

"That's the general idea."

"Good." Cassie held out a shovel. "You can help me muck out first."

Paul rolled his eyes, but took the shovel. "Okay. Which one do you want me to do?"

"You do that one, I'll do this one."

"Right."

He pulled off his jacket and hung it over one of the half-doors. He really didn't mind helping his sister with the chores. He liked the horses, and he knew that caring for them required a lot of hard work.

And oddly, he quite liked the rich organic smell as he heaved shovel loads of old straw into a wheelbarrow and trundled it to the compost heap where Tom Cullen would come to collect it to use as fertiliser for his organic crops.

116

By the time the job was finished he was breathing hard. "Phew! That's warmed me up. Are you coming out?"

"Yes." Cassie took the two shovels and scraped them clean with a piece of wood. "I want to give Cody an outing."

"How's he doing?"

"Pretty well. He's putting on weight and he likes a good canter. Do you want to take Smudge?"

"Okay."

The two horses were very happy to come out of the paddock and have their saddles put on. Hobo came hirpling out from the back door of the house, eager to join them.

They let themselves out through the gate and set off along the bridleway at an easy trot, Hobo snuffling happily along the hedgerows beside them.

The sky was a pale, cool blue, drifted with white cotton-wool clouds, and a cool breeze was blowing in from the sea. Paul was glad he'd put his jacket on again after saddling Smudge.

The big bay gelding was inclined to be wayward. A string of owners had found him too difficult to manage, which was why he had ended up with the Horse Rescue Society. But he seemed to like Paul and the feeling was mutual.

"So, did you have a nice time last night?" Cassie enquired, eyeing him sideways with a look of sardonic amusement.

Paul laughed dryly. "I'm not sure if 'nice' applies. She's got a very sharp tongue, that lass. I suppose I should have been forewarned."

His sister raised a questioning eyebrow.

"The red hair."

"That's a terrible cliché," she dismissed scornfully.

"It's easier than thinking that it's just me she doesn't like."

Cassie thought for a moment. "I don't think she doesn't like you."

"You think she does like me?"

She laughed. "Who wouldn't?"

117

He grinned mischievously. "Ah, but you're my sister. You have to like me."

"It's not compulsory," she countered with a touch of dry humour. "You like her, don't you?"

"Yes." He gave the question some consideration. "She's . . . interesting. She's got a sharp sense of humour, gives as good as she gets."

"And great legs?"

"That goes without saying."

Cassie chuckled, her eyes teasing him. "You know, you could have met your match . . . at last."

He returned her a look of sardonic humour. "We'll see."

She held up crossed fingers. "We will. Fancy a gallop?"

He grinned. "Race you to Spiney Point."

"You're on."

CHAPTER FIFTEEN

"Well, here we are, Grandad." Alex smiled as he parked the Jaguar beside the front steps of the hotel.

"Hmph! Weren't worth getting in the car for just that little distance," Arthur grumbled. "We could have walked."

"You could have come down on your skateboard."

The old man chuckled. "I could at that."

Marcus grinned as he climbed out of the back seat. "Don't encourage him. We'll have him doing backflips and kick-turns down the Esplanade."

Arthur's pale eyes were twinkling with amusement as he let Marcus take his arm and help him to slowly climb the three shallow steps that led up to the front entrance. The glass doors whispered open and they walked into the reception hall.

Lisa and Vicky were there to greet them. "Arthur! Lovely to see you. You're looking well."

"So are you, my luvvers, so are you. Are you coming to my birthday party?"

"Of course. Everybody's coming."

He beamed in delight. "Well, there's a thing."

"It's not every day you get to be ninety-four years old."

119

"That's right. Molly Marston only got to be ninety-two. Edie Channing only got to be ninety-three. I told 'em both I'd outlive 'em, and I did!"

Lisa laughed. "You certainly did."

"We're going out onto the terrace," Alex said. "But you let us know if you get cold."

"Don't fuss. You're like an old woman."

Alex shook his head in amused exasperation. "Okay, okay. I just want to make sure you get to ninety-five."

"I'll get to a hundred," Arthur asserted with a grin. "You'll see."

"I'm sure you will. God and the Devil will be arguing about who's going to have to put up with you for eternity."

That made Arthur chuckle with glee.

Although it was late October, the sun was still bright in the high blue sky. Out on the terrace a long table had been set up with a traditional-style buffet — mini sausage rolls, cheese straws, salmon and cucumber sandwiches.

And in the middle, a large square cake, iced in pale green, with a cricket bat, a ball and a wicket made of icing. And piped around the edge, the words *94 not out*.

Arthur gazed at it in delight, laughing. "Well, I never! That's wonderful. Who did that?"

"Our chef, of course," Lisa told him. "Now, here's your throne, your majesty, all ready for you."

They had brought a comfortable armchair out for him, covering it with a red throw, and tied on two gold foil balloons, a 9 and a 4, which bobbed merrily above it.

"Ah, now — this will do me." He sat down, head erect like a king surveying his subjects. "Welcome, everyone."

Quite a few people had come. Alex recognised several of them, having seen them around the hotel or down in the town. There was the red-haired receptionist, Jess, and another woman who looked so much like her that they had to be sisters, if not twins.

They were with a good-looking couple he'd seen riding horses on the beach in the early morning, and an older couple whom he took to be their parents.

The manager of the hotel was there, chatting to Kate from the little café on the seafront, and the woman who ran the convenience store just round the corner from Arthur's house.

Marcus had plated up a few items from the buffet for Arthur, and brought him a cup of tea. Alex thanked him with a nod and moved over to the table to load up a plate for himself.

He found himself standing next to a tall, dark-haired man of around his own age. The man turned, greeting him with a genial smile.

"Hi. You're Arthur's grandson, aren't you?"

"That's right. Alex Crocombe."

"I'm Paul Channing. My sister's the assistant manager here." He held out his hand. "Pleased to meet you."

"Ah, yes." Alex shook his hand. "Lisa. She mentioned you. You're the soccer player?"

"I was. And you're the fighter pilot?"

"I was." They both laughed, acknowledging the shared experience. "How are you enjoying retirement?"

"I'm working on it. You?"

Alex smiled wryly. "I haven't entirely figured it out yet."

By unspoken agreement, they moved away from the table to allow other people to get to it.

"Are you staying in England long?" Paul asked.

"I don't really have any plans at the moment," Alex acknowledged. "I'm just enjoying a holiday, and spending time with my grandfather."

Paul nodded. "Oh, yes. Everyone's very fond of old Arthur."

"So I see." Alex glanced around at the crowd on the terrace. "We were very grateful for the way everyone looked after him when he had his fall. My dad couldn't get over — he'd had a hip replacement. And I was . . . abroad."

He saw a flicker of interest in the other man's eyes, but he didn't pry.

"Well, if you're staying a while, why don't you come down to the pub one evening?" Paul invited genially. "The Smugglers, down on the Esplanade."

"That would be good. I was thinking of looking in there."

"Do you play darts or pool?"

"Of course. Not much else to do between shouts, apart from sleeping."

Paul's grin spread. "Just don't let my sister Cassie hustle you into playing pool against her." He nodded his head towards the dark-haired young woman he'd seen with the horses. "She's a killer."

"Really?"

Paul shook his head in mock regret. "Many have tried, many have fallen."

"Thanks, I'll remember that."

As Paul Channing strolled away, Alex glanced around again. There was no sign of Shelley. Of course, since he had moved out of the hotel he'd had much less chance of bumping into her, but he had taken to dropping in here for an afternoon coffee instead of going down to the café on the Esplanade, in the hope of seeing her.

Was she deliberately avoiding him? He didn't want her to feel as if he was stalking her, but he really wanted to see her again. There was something about her, that intriguing mix of feistiness and vulnerability.

There had been women in his life — plenty of them, over the years. Easy relationships, no complications, no strings. He had expected little of them, and they had expected little of him — just fun.

But with Shelley, it couldn't be like that. Was he up for something more serious? That was something he needed to think about . . .

"Okay, everyone. Gather round." Lisa clapped her hands for attention. "We're ready to cut the birthday cake. First, blowing out the candle."

There was a round of applause as she set a cupcake with a single candle on the buffet table in front of Arthur.

"What's this?" he demanded, indignant. "There's supposed to be ninety-four."

"That many would have set the fire alarms off."

"Huh!" He chuckled with laughter. "You thought I wouldn't have enough puff to blow out ninety-four candles."

"I would never even dream that!"

She held up a hand to start a rousing chorus of 'Happy Birthday', then with a huff, Arthur blew out the single candle, and with a swift movement that belied his great age he snatched up the fondant cricket ball from the cake and popped it into his mouth, grinning in triumph.

Then it was time to open his presents and read the pile of cards. Most of the presents were bottles of brandy or whiskey, much to his delight. "Well, well. This'll keep me going for a week or two!"

"He's loving this," Marcus murmured to Alex.

"He certainly is. Better try to ration the booze a bit, though."

"It's okay, I can hide most of the bottles and just bring them out one at a time."

Lisa had cut the cake, and Alex took a slice to his grandfather, drawing up a chair to sit beside him. "I guess you have a lot of memories of this place, Grandpa," he suggested.

"Oh, ah. Backalong we was always up here, me and my pals. During the war, that was."

"To chat with the soldiers?"

The old man shook his head. "Not soldiers — pilots. Pilots as had got shot down. Mostly they'd got burned — hands, faces. Some of them was blinded, noses and ears gone, fingers gone."

"Oh . . ." Alex was startled. "I never knew that."

"They'd been in the hospital up at East Grinstead, then they'd come down here for a bit of convalescence. We used to

123

chat to them, Freddie Mogford and Stanley Lerwell and me. Keep their spirits up, read to them, help them with their dinner when they couldn't hold their knife and fork. Take them for walks along the coast path there if they could manage it, or down on the beach."

Alex stared at his grandfather, impressed. "That's amazing. You've never talked about that before."

"Ah, well, it was just one of those things. After the war no one talked about it much. Well, what was the point? But families round here used to have them in for tea, make them feel at home. And sometimes there'd be parties, with showgirls coming down from London in a charabanc. Then when it was all over, they just closed the place down, just like that. One day there, next day gone! The men all went off home, and we settled down to our old lives again."

He sighed in sad reminiscence.

"But she did her bit, the old Carleton. Stood here more'n a hundred and fifty, hundred and sixty years now. But come the war, she did her bit."

Alex glanced around the terrace and up at the white facade of the hotel, his mind conjuring up images of those long-ago airmen with their bandaged hands and faces.

Airmen like him. He felt the connection tug at his spirit.

And now it was at risk of being left to fall into disrepair, dereliction, until in the end it was demolished. No, for the memory of those airmen, he wasn't going to let that happen.

* * *

The conservatory windows had probably never been this clean. At least not this pane. Shelley had managed to remain concealed behind a large Chinese fan palm while discreetly watching Alex at his grandfather's birthday party.

He was really good with the old man, chatting easily to him and making him laugh. Everyone loved Arthur Crocombe — he was a proper character.

And Alex . . . The memory of walking on the beach with him, of eating fish and chips from the paper, would stay with her for a long time . . .

As if the thought had conjured him up, she heard his voice behind her.

"Ah, so this is where you're hiding."

She stiffened. "I'm not hiding. I'm . . . just cleaning the windows."

"So I see." His voice was warm with gentle amusement. "Aren't you going to join the party?"

She shook her head. "That . . . wouldn't be allowed. I'm staff."

"So? So are Lisa and Jess."

"They're management, office staff," she protested desperately, wishing he'd go away before she made a fool of herself by blushing. "I'm just a chambermaid."

He arched one dark eyebrow. "That sounds like inverted snobbery."

"Yeah, only someone who's never had to worry about losing their job would say a thing like that."

"Fair enough." He smiled, a smile that did funny things to her insides. "Can I at least get you a slice of birthday cake? No one can object to that. I paid for it, so I can give it to whoever I like."

She hesitated, then conceded reluctantly. "Okay, thank you."

He grinned, satisfied. Shelley watched as he strolled back to the buffet table and collected two plates of cake and two glasses of wine. But as he turned to bring them back out to the conservatory, Lisa spotted him.

"Hi. Where are you off to with . . . Oh, hi, Shelley. What are you doing hiding out there? Come on in and join the party."

"I already invited her." Alex slanted her look of teasing amusement. "She said it wasn't allowed."

"What? Oh, don't be silly. Come and wish Arthur a happy birthday."

125

Shelley hesitated, but reluctantly joined them. Arthur spotted her at once and beamed broadly. "Ah, here's another pretty girl come to wish me a happy birthday. Come and get some cake, my luvver."

She smiled warmly. "I've got some, thank you. Happy birthday, Mr Crocombe."

"Arthur. Call me Arthur, my luvver," he insisted, reaching for her hand.

"Arthur." On an impulse she bent and kissed his papery cheek. "Happy birthday."

He chuckled richly. "And I'm going to have a whole lot more of 'em. You just wait and see!"

"I'm sure you will."

She drew back discreetly, taking a careful sip of her wine — she didn't want to risk it going to her head. She was very aware of Alex beside her. Were the little shivers running through her bones because of his closeness, or because she was worried that someone would notice and comment that she shouldn't be here?

Arthur was holding court again with his stories of times long past.

"Then there was Bill Bamfield — Squadron Leader William Frederick Bamfield, DFC and Bar, to be correct. He were an Ace, flew Hurricanes. Shot down eleven till he got shot down hisself over Normandy in forty-four. Blinded, he was."

Shelley was fascinated. "He's got a very good memory," she murmured to Alex.

"He has, though this is the first I've heard about the Second World War. Mostly he loves telling stories about doing his National Service and the Korean war. He remembers every detail of that."

"And there was Chalkie White and Clive Darrow." Arthur was pausing only to pick up crumbs of his birthday cake. "Crew mates, they was. Their Lancaster got shot up badly on a bombing raid over Berlin. The pilot managed to

126

limp it home, but the undercarriage was stuck and it crashed on landing."

Alex turned to Lisa. "I was just wondering . . . Are there any old papers from those days?"

Lisa frowned and shook her head. "Not that I know of. They've probably all been sent back to the Ministry of Defence."

"I'm not talking about official records or anything like that. But photos, diaries . . . ?"

"I don't know."

"There's some old boxes down in one of the storerooms, full of papers and things," Shelley suggested. "There might be something in there." She dug deep to find her confidence. "I can show you where it is."

Alex turned to Lisa. "Is there a key?"

"I'll get it."

The basement was reached by an old door behind the kitchen, and a steep flight of stairs. At the bottom was a long, narrow corridor with a stone floor, lit by stark fluorescent strips in the ceiling, one of which was flickering as if ready to go out.

There were several wooden doors down each side, all in need of a coat of paint. Shelley stopped at one of them. "It's this one."

Alex fitted the key into the lock and opened the door.

"It's a bit dusty in here," Shelley warned. "And there are spiders."

"Never mind."

She switched on the light — more fluorescent strips. An old copper boiler lay on its side in the corner, there were a couple of deckchairs with torn canvas seats, the floor was covered with a litter of old rubbish, and the place smelled of ancient dust.

"Here's the boxes."

At the back of the room a haphazard pile of cardboard boxes was stacked against the wall. They certainly looked old enough to date from the war years, being rubbed ragged at the edges, and some of them showing from the faded printing on their sides that they had once held bars of carbolic soap or tins of Spam.

He eased his fingers into one of the torn cartons. Inside, he could see the edge of what looked like a photo album. "Ah, this could be interesting."

He opened the top. The carton was jammed with a random selection of papers, notebooks and photo albums, as if someone had just cleared out some drawers or filing cabinets and stuffed everything into the box.

He tugged at one of the albums until it came out.

There were pages of black-and-white photos of young men, some with bandages on their hands and faces, some with the puckered scars of healing injuries.

Some were sitting on beds in pyjamas, but most wore their service uniforms. There were snaps of them standing round a piano for a sing-song, with nurses in their uniforms too.

And some of them were recognisably taken on the terrace of the hotel, with the bay in the background. The Carleton had done its bit.

He pulled out another album, filled with similar photos. "I'd like to show these to my grandpa."

Shelley smiled warmly. "He'll love them."

She leaned over to see the pictures, her hair brushing against his cheek. A soft scent — her shampoo or her skin — drifted to him. The impulse to kiss her almost knocked him off his feet, but he forced himself to pull back . . .

"Argh!"

She jerked back suddenly, bouncing off the stack of cartons and into his arms. He caught a breath — had she sensed . . . ? But it wasn't what he had feared. A black spider bigger than his thumbnail was crawling on her shoulder.

"Wait . . ." Carefully he cupped his hand, flicked the spider into it, and set it down on a broken stepladder leaning against the wall.

She laughed, her eyes dancing. "Oh, lord! I'm not really scared of spiders. It just made me jump!"

Her face was inches from his, her lips parted, those pretty blue eyes gazing up into his . . . It would have taken more will power than he possessed to resist. And as his mouth met hers, she wasn't resisting either.

* * *

Shelley felt as if her bones were dissolving into warm honey. She reached up to wrap her arms around his neck, curving her body against his as his fingers tangled in her hair.

This had to be a dream . . . Except it wasn't. Those strong arms around her were real, and that warm, tender mouth on hers was real. The subtle scent of his skin — sandalwood and something uniquely male — was real.

His tongue swept sensuously over the sensitive inner membranes of her lips, then sought the sweet depths within, stirring the heat in her blood. How could she never have known that kisses could be like this? It felt like magic . . .

But then, abruptly, he lifted his head and stepped back. "I'm sorry. I didn't intend . . ."

Opening her eyes, she glared up at him, the melting honey boiling to hot lava. "You're *sorry?* Oh dear. You kissed the chambermaid by mistake? Well, pardon me for breathing the same air as you . . ."

She had to escape. But as she moved to shove past him, he caught her arm.

"No. I didn't mean it like that. I'm sorry because I didn't intend for the first time I kissed you to be in a dusty old store-room full of litter and spiders." He laughed in wry self-mockery. "I imagined it would be on the beach, in the moonlight, with the sound of the waves whispering over the sand."

She stared up at him. Could she believe a word of it? As she hesitated, he smiled, tipping his head down and laying his forehead against hers.

129

"What I'd really like to do is take you out to dinner, then stroll along the beach and see what happens. Would you like that? Please say yes."

"I . . . ah . . ." She let go of the breath she had forgotten she was holding. "Yes . . . Yes, okay then."

"Good." The smile in his eyes could melt any defences she had. "Look, let's take a couple of these albums up to show my grandpa. He'll be ready to go home soon, then I'll pick you up at seven . . ."

"No, not tonight." Panic surged briefly. "I . . . um . . ."

"Tomorrow?"

"Yes, okay. Tomorrow."

"Good." He tucked the albums under his arm, and took her hand. "Come on, let's take these up to Grandpa."

CHAPTER SIXTEEN

"What a nice old man." Jess leaned back against the stone balustrade around the terrace and sipped her wine. "Everyone seems to love him."

"They do." Paul smiled, glancing back to where Arthur sat enthroned amid his entourage. "He and my grandmother were a right lively pair, along with Vicky's Aunt Molly."

"The two he was boasting that he'd outlived?"

"That's right. My grandmother died a couple of months ago."

"Oh, I'm sorry."

"She was ninety-three, and a real grand old dame. We were all terrified of her, but we adored her." He moved over to lean against the balustrade beside her. "That was her house — you can see it from here. See that row of houses that runs up the hill over on the far side of the bay? It's the one second from the top."

She followed to where he pointed. A road sloped up from the end of the Esplanade, lined with a row of tall, double-fronted Victorian townhouses, three storeys of ruddy-brown brick with dormer windows in the rooves.

"Ah, yes. It looks nice."

131

"It's very nice. I live there now."

"Oh?"

"She moved down to live with my mum and dad a few years ago, when she needed to be looked after full time. That's their house, three doors down. So rather than leave it empty, I moved in and rented it from her. I wanted my own space anyway, so it was ideal."

"You actually paid her rent?"

"Of course."

There was no 'of course' about it, Jess mused, taking a sip of her wine. A lot of people would have taken advantage of a grandmother's affection to live rent free. She silently awarded him an extra point for that. "So what will happen to it now? Will you stay there?"

He nodded. "She left it between the three of us — me, Lisa and Cassie. So I bought them out."

She gave him a questioning look. "You're planning to stay here in Sturcombe long-term?"

"It's my home." With a sweep of his hand, he gestured to the wide crescent of the bay spread below them, the sea blue-grey beneath the cool blue sky, the village clustered like children's toys in the cradle of the green slopes around it. "Why would I want to live anywhere else?"

"It is a beautiful place," she acknowledged, turning to look out over the view. "But don't you ever hanker for the bright lights of London?"

He shrugged his wide shoulders in a gesture of careless dismissal. "I can go up there when I need to. I did look at a couple of serviced apartments, but it didn't seem worth it when I can stay in a hotel for a couple of nights and get everything I need."

"The Dorchester?"

He laughed. "No thank you! There's a nice little hotel near Russell Square. I prefer it there. Quiet, but close enough to the centre of town."

"Sounds good."

132

"What about you?"

"I don't know." She had been trying not to think ahead. "I really like this place. But if the hotel closes . . . I don't suppose it would be easy to find another job here."

"Probably not," he conceded. "Would you go back to Bristol?"

She shook her head. "No . . . Exeter, maybe. It depends where there's work. Anyway, I'm supposed to be at work now." She pulled herself up briskly. "I'd better get back to the desk." She spared him a cool smile. "See you around."

* * *

Paul watched Jess as she disappeared into the reception hall, all long-legged elegance. He hoped she wouldn't leave Sturcombe, but as she had said, if the hotel closed, she may not have a choice.

If it closed.

He glanced around the terrace and up at the rambling white facade of the building. It had stood here, overlooking the bay, all his life. He had always assumed that it would stand here forever.

He saw his sister chatting to Arthur's carer, Marcus. He went over, winking an apology to the man for butting in, and dropped a casual arm around her shoulders. "Ah, Lisa. My favourite sister."

She gave him a glance of sardonic amusement. "Don't let Cassie hear you say that."

"That's okay." He grinned. "I'll always be her favourite brother."

"You're her only brother," she retorted dryly. "Anyway, what do you want?"

"Why would you think I want anything?" He knew she wouldn't be fooled by his bland smile. "Can't I just enjoy the pleasure of your company for a while?"

She rolled her eyes. "What do you want?"

133

"Can I borrow the keys to the annexe?"

Her eyes widened in surprise. "What on earth do you want them for?"

"I'm having a fit of nostalgia." He wasn't ready yet to explain what was on his mind. "I was just remembering how we used to run wild in there, me and Liam and Tom, playing hide-and-seek and cricket."

"Collecting spiders to bring home and put in my bed."

"I never did that!" he protested.

"Did too. Ask Cassie."

"Keys? Pretty please?"

"Oh, all right," she conceded. "Excuse me, Marcus."

He followed her as she led the way over to her office behind the reception desk. The keys were on a long chain hanging on the wall, and she hooked them down and handed them to him.

"Just tell me one thing. You're not planning to lure Jess down there and have your wicked way with her, are you?"

"Of course not! You have a very dirty mind."

"No, I've been your sister for a long time."

"Well, for your information, I absolutely wouldn't dream of it. Down there with all the dust and spiders? Give me a break."

"And don't fall in the swimming pool."

"I thought it didn't have any water in it?"

"It doesn't. That's why I don't want you falling in it. Drowning's clean, but smashing yourself on the bottom at the deep end would make an awful mess."

He dropped a kiss on her forehead. "Ah, you're so considerate."

"It's not you I'm thinking about. It's my cleaning staff who'd have to mop up all the blood."

He laughed as he strolled away, jangling the keys.

The annexe was part of the extension which was built onto the side of the hotel in the First World War to provide a couple of extra wards for the soldiers. Later on, the lower floor had been excavated to build an indoor swimming pool for the tuberculosis patients.

There were two locks and it took him a while to find the right keys, but at last he got the door open and switched on the lights. Only three of the bare bulbs swinging from the ceiling were working, lighting a bleak, echoing space lined with cold white tiles, a lot of them cracked and dulled with age.

The pool itself was twenty-five metres long — a good size. Two of the walls were glass which would give great views of the gardens and the bay, but they'd long ago been boarded up.

He took out his phone and began taking photos as he strolled round the perimeter, visualising how it could look with those windows opened up again, softer lighting, aqua-blue tiles lining the pool with maybe darker blue around the edge.

The changing rooms were in a pretty poor state, and he didn't care to breath the air in the toilets for too long. They could all be knocked down to provide a wider lounging area beside the pool, a small bar for drinks.

Another door to one side opened into a long empty room, thick with the cobwebs and dust of decades. A couple of dismembered bits of hospital-style iron bedsteads lay around on the floor, and a broken table leaned drunkenly against the wall.

But it was a big enough space to provide new changing rooms. There could be creamy marbled floor tiles in here, with lilac walls in the women's and teal blue in the men's, and a couple of single cubicles for those who would prefer them.

There would be showers and lockers, and a baby changing area. And a sauna and jacuzzi.

He took more photographs, estimating the size and dictating his thoughts into his phone. Then he left, locking the door and climbing the stairs to the upper floor.

He could see a well-equipped gym in here, a luxury massage room and spa, maybe a hair salon. Pale wooden floors, more soft lighting, lots of lush green plants in copper pots.

He wasn't ready to share his thoughts with anyone else yet — not even Lisa. He didn't want to raise hopes which might all too likely be dashed. There was a lot to look into, and a lot would depend on what price the owners would be asking for the place. Then he'd need to cost out the renovations, and set that against the possible income.

But he had so many good memories of this place, and it didn't sit easy with him to just let it be knocked down and replaced by heaven only knew what.

* * *

The staff sitting room was at the end of the accommodation corridor. Like the rest of the hotel, it had seen better days. There were half a dozen mismatched armchairs, an ugly mustard sofa with sagging cushions, and a patch of thin rug over the lino floor.

At one side was a tiny kitchen unit with a kettle, a toaster that had to be closely watched or it would stick and burn the bread, a fairly new microwave, and a sink.

Shelley had been watching television when Jess walked in. She glanced up, greeting her with a smile. "Hi."

"Hi." She strolled over to the kitchen unit. "Want a coffee?"

"No, thanks. I've got one." Shelley held up her mug. "Not going out tonight?"

"No."

"I thought you might be seeing Paul again."

Jess rolled her eyes. "No, thank you. He's the sort of guy who should have a Government Health Warning tattooed on his forehead."

Shelley laughed. "He's very good-looking. And he does seem to be keen on you."

Jess's mouth quirked into a wry smile. "Oh, he's good-looking, I'll grant you that, but Lisa warned me about him — he changes his girlfriends more often than he changes his socks. Besides . . ."

136

"You're off men."

"I am. I don't know how I let him persuade me to go out to dinner with him in the first place. Cassie said when they were kids he could talk her out of her last red jelly baby!" The kettle had finally boiled, and she poured a mug of coffee. "Anyway, how about you and Alex?"

Shelley felt an awkward blush rise to her cheeks. "Oh . . . well . . ."

"He seems like a really nice bloke."

"Yes."

"There aren't many nice blokes like that around. When you find one, you should hang on to him."

The blush deepened and Shelley looked away. "I don't know . . . I'm not . . . It's not . . ."

"He likes you." Jess brought her coffee over and slumped into one of the armchairs. "And you like him, don't you?"

Shelley laughed awkwardly.

"Well then . . . ?"

"Well . . ." She drew out the syllable. "Actually . . . I'm going out with him tomorrow night."

"Yay!" Jess smiled in delight. "Good for you!"

"But nothing's going to come of it," Shelley insisted. "I mean, he's just looking for a bit of company while he's here. He won't be staying long. He'll be going back to Canada soon."

"Did he say so?"

"No, but . . ."

"Well, don't worry about it. Just enjoy yourself. Where's he taking you?"

"I don't know. Dinner, he said. He didn't say where."

"What are you wearing?"

"Ah, there's the problem. I don't really have anything decent to wear."

"Hmm." Jess frowned, thinking. "Tricky, if you don't know where you're going."

"I just hope he doesn't take me anywhere posh. I wouldn't know which knife and fork to use, or what to choose off the

137

menu. All the waiters would look at me as if I should be out the back on the pot-wash. And they'd be right."

"Don't be daft. If they're that snobby, that's on them. And if Alex takes you somewhere like that, he isn't as nice as I think he is. Look, don't worry — he's not going to take you anywhere you'd feel uncomfortable. Now, let me think . . . What about your navy-blue trousers? They're really smart."

"I bought them in a charity shop!"

"So?"

"Anyway, I don't have anything to wear with them."

"What about that cream sweater of mine? The one with the big cowl neck."

"Oh, I couldn't borrow that!" Shelley protested. "What if I spilt something on it?"

"It'll wash. What shoes have you got?"

"A couple of pairs of trainers. And my boots."

"Oh, yes. Those nice ankle boots. They'd look great, give it an edge."

Shelley looked doubtful. "How will I know what to pick from the menu?"

"Let him choose for you. And watch which cutlery he uses then just copy him. And if you don't want wine, just ask for mineral water. He probably will anyway, as he'll be driving."

Shelley laughed. "Maybe I ought to be taking notes. Okay, one more thing. What should I talk about?"

"That's simple." Jess snapped her fingers. "Get him talking about himself. There's not a man on the planet who doesn't like that."

CHAPTER SEVENTEEN

"Hi, Dad. How's things?"

"All good, son. How's your grandad?" Alex smiled at the sound of his father's voice echoing from his phone's speaker from three and a half thousand miles away across the Atlantic. "Did he enjoy his birthday party?"

Alex laughed. "He was in his element — King of the World. He got loads of presents, mostly brandy! The hotel put on a great do for him, and the cake was something else. I'll send you the photos."

"Thanks, son. I'd have liked to have been there."

"You were here just a couple of months ago," Alex reassured him. "And you'll be over in the new year."

"That's right. And what about you? Have you got any plans yet?"

"I do." He took a brief pause. "I'm thinking of buying the hotel."

"What, the Carleton?" His dad was startled. "Why?"

"It's being sold off to some investment fund — Lytcott Capital Management. The hotel has already been warned that they're likely to be offloaded, as they're not making enough profit. And if they can't find a buyer, the place will just be closed down."

139

"Ah, now that'd be a crying shame, eh," his dad protested. "It's a grand old building. The trouble is that no one's spent any money on it for years. I was sad to see how run down it was when I was over in July."

"Exactly. Did you know what it was used for during the war?"

"Well, Dad told me it was something to do with the military — a convalescence home for injured soldiers."

"Airmen. With burns injuries."

"Ah . . ."

Alex had known that his father would understand at once the connection he felt — that almost mystical bond between anyone who had served in the military.

It made no difference whether they were airmen, army or navy, what flag they had served under, even if they were generations apart. It was there.

"It's not only a sentimental thing," he explained. "The place has a lot of potential. I was talking to some of the people here and they have some really good suggestions."

"Well, it's certainly in a very attractive location."

"It is." He had wandered over to the window to gaze out at the bay, looking tranquil in the moonlight. The coloured lights strung from the streetlamps along the Esplanade reflected like shimmering jewels in the sea, which at high tide had come right up to the sea wall.

The amusement arcade was a neon-lit circus of reds, blues and greens, the fish and chip shop was a bright white glow, the windows of the pub on the corner were a warm amber.

Behind the seafront, the town was a star-scape of street-lights and house lights. On the far side of the bay, Cliff Road climbed to the roundabout where it met Haytor Avenue and the entrance to the caravan site.

It was a small town, caught in the paradox between catering for tourists and second-home owners which were virtually its only source of income, and the lack of affordable housing for the local people along with the lack of jobs during the winter months.

140

If the hotel closed, the place would be reduced to a shell.

"The trouble with Sturcombe is that it's a bit off the beaten track," his father pointed out. "That's always been against it."

"So we give people a reason to want to come here. I'm thinking wedding packages, an upmarket spa, corporate events . . ."

"Sounds good. How will you finance it?"

"Frank's been talking about retiring, so it seems like a timely moment to sell. The real-estate market's pretty buoyant, and he's had a couple of offers he's considering. If I sell my share of the company with his, as one unit, we could probably get an even better offer."

"Well, good luck with it, son. I hope it works out."

"Thanks, Dad. How's Mom?"

"She's fine. She's out at her book club this evening, but she sends her love."

"Tell her the same. Speak to you soon."

"Sure will. 'Bye, son."

"'Bye, Dad."

He closed the call and put the phone down on the coffee table. Buying the hotel, renovating it, taking it upmarket, was going to be a huge undertaking, but it was a very interesting challenge.

And a challenge was just what he needed. Not the challenge of flying fighter jets in war zones — he was done with that — but he was never going to settle for a quiet life, fishing or tending his garden.

Money wasn't an issue. He'd been investing in real estate almost since the beginning of his air-force career. Initially, he'd just bought a plot of land, intending to build a house for himself at some point.

Then the area had been re-zoned, and the larger adjacent plot had been bought up for housing development. Frank Beaumont, the developer, had offered him a good price for his land, or the alternative of a share in the new project.

141

Due for deployment overseas, he'd opted for the gamble, and it had paid off handsomely. The partnership had been so successful that they'd agreed to continue it with Frank's next project, and every one since. And over the years they'd become good friends.

Once he knew how things stood with the hotel, he'd ring Frank and discuss it with him. In the meantime, he had dinner with Shelley to look forward to.

* * *

Alex had guessed that Shelley wouldn't want to dine in the sort of restaurant she'd call 'posh', but he wasn't going to let her think he thought so little of her that he'd take her to a greasy spoon.

An internet search had given him several options. He'd chosen a place on the edge of the moor. On the website it had looked cosy and unpretentious, with cream painted walls, a plain wooden floor, and lots of leafy green plants in terracotta pots.

He made sure he arrived at the hotel a few minutes early as he didn't want her to feel uncomfortable having to wait for him. He had a feeling that she'd never been on what she'd call a 'proper' date before.

It was ten minutes past seven when she appeared, and he smiled to himself, guessing that the timing had been deliberate. A test. Just long enough to keep him waiting, but not so long as to justify him being impatient.

She'd always be one to test the limits, always prepared for something to blow up in her face.

She'd pushed the line just a little with her outfit too. Navy-blue trousers and a chunky cream sweater with brown ankle boots. Smart, but a bit too casual for anywhere 'posh' — a message, if he'd needed one.

He climbed out of the car and went round to open the passenger door for her. She smiled up at him, but hesitated before getting in.

142

"Where are we going?"

"A place called the Old Mill. It's not far."

"Oh, yes." The slight tension in her shoulders visibly relaxed. "Some of the hotel guests have been there for lunch or dinner. They've said it's nice."

"It looks it on the website. I hope you like it."

She slid into the passenger seat and smiled at him as he slipped in behind the wheel. "This is a nice car."

"It is."

"I've never ridden in a Jaguar before," she confessed.

"There's a first time for everything."

"Lisa's brother's got an Aston Martin — like James Bond."

He laughed. "I saw it. Now that *is* a nice car."

"Better than this one?"

"Hmm. Probably. I've never driven one."

They turned onto Church Road and drove up the hill. The car was smooth and quiet, a pleasure to drive. If he was going to stay in England, he'd need to buy a car instead of hiring one. Should he buy a Jaguar or an Aston Martin, or something else?

He glanced across at his passenger. Maybe he wouldn't mention the car purchase to her. Some women might be drawn like magnets to a man who could afford to buy one of the most expensive cars on the road, but he suspected that it would have the opposite effect on Shelley.

For the same reason, he wouldn't tell her about his plans to buy the hotel. At least, not yet. He didn't intend to tell anyone until the deal went through.

* * *

In spite of her wariness, Shelley was enjoying herself. The car was beautiful; sleek and comfortable, and smelling of new leather. She'd already guessed that Alex was quite well off. Cleaning his room, she'd seen his clothes — mostly casual but of very good quality. His shoes and his luggage were too — always a good tell.

Which meant that the gulf between them was very wide indeed. She'd known that from the start. So, as Jess had said, she should just enjoy this while it lasted. He'd said he might be staying in Sturcombe for a month or so, and then he'd be gone.

Okay, that was fine. Nothing in her life had lasted much longer than that, except for her time at the Carleton. And now that was coming to an end too. Oh well . . .

She hadn't meant to sigh, but it had slipped out, and Alex glanced across at her, one dark eyebrow raised in question.

"What's wrong?"

"Nothing." She managed a smile. "Just admiring the sky. It's so pretty, with all the stars coming out."

"Ah, yes. It is pretty."

"Do you think there really are people on other planets up there?" she mused, hoping to distract him from questioning whether she was all right or not.

"I don't know about people, but there are so many billions of stars out there that it's quite likely there's some form of life. But I doubt if they'll be landing on Earth any time soon, unless they've got some weird sort of propulsion system that we don't know about. The distances are just too great."

She laughed. "Well, that's good to know, anyway!"

They had turned onto the main road. Alex accelerated smoothly, overtaking a caravan and tucking back into the left-hand lane.

"Music?" he suggested.

"That would be nice."

"What would you like?"

"You choose."

He smiled and tapped the screen, and a soft female voice filled the car.

"Who's this?" she asked, curious. "It isn't Adele."

"K.D. Lang — a fellow Canadian."

"She's got a lovely voice."

"She has."

Shelley leaned back in her seat and closed her eyes, listening to the soft, melancholy music, relieved at not having to try to keep up a conversation.

It was all very well telling herself that she could just enjoy this while it lasted, but she had an uncomfortable feeling that she was already getting in too deep. Sitting beside him in the car she was all too aware of the hard muscles in his shoulder, close to hers, and the way his dark hair was just starting to curl over his ear.

And the memory of how he had kissed her . . .

They drove for about fifteen minutes, then turned off the main road onto a narrower one beneath overhanging trees. A few minutes later they turned into a car park in front of a low building of local grey stone, not much larger than a bungalow. As Alex opened the car door for her, she heard the soft babble of water running over rocks.

A neatly trimmed box shrub in a wooden half-barrel stood beside the front door. Inside, there were only about fifteen tables, half of them occupied. A cheerful waitress in a pink tabard greeted them with a friendly smile.

"Ah, hello. Come on in. A table for two?"

"Yes please. I phoned earlier — Alex Crocombe."

"Oh yes, of course. Would you like to sit by the window?"

"That would be nice."

She led them over to an empty table with a view over the stream Shelley had heard. The banks were overhung with lush green shrubs, lit up in places by amber lanterns slung from the branches of the trees. A little further upstream was an old stone bridge, spanning the water in a single curved arch.

"Oh, it's so pretty!" Shelley exclaimed as she sat down. "You could just imagine there were elves or fairies living there." She felt her cheeks flush with heat. *Oh, lord. What a stupid thing to say!* Alex was going to think she was completely crazy!

145

But he was smiling, his eyes warm. "You could."

Taking one of the laminated menus on the table, she studied it, then laid it down on the table, remembering Jess's advice.

"I really can't decide. It all looks good. You choose."

A flicker of surprise, but he smiled. "Okay, how about . . . salmon ceviche with mango, followed by pan-seared lamb cutlets in rosemary sauce?"

"That sounds good."

"And I'll have the same," he told the waitress. "And I'll have mineral water, please. Would you like wine with yours, Shelley?"

"Oh . . . No, mineral water will be fine for me too. Thank you."

Relief — she'd got through that part without too much trouble. Now the conversation bit.

"Why did you decide to join the air force?" she asked.

He laughed. "It's every boy's dream, isn't it? To fly, faster than the speed of sound. I must have watched *Top Gun* a hundred times — I wore out the DVD, not to mention Mom's patience. And the *Battle of Britain*, *The Dambusters*, *Flight of the Intruder* . . . When I was a kid I dragged the family to the Spitfire Museum at Biggin Hill at least half a dozen times. They actually restore Spitfires there, and they fly them most days. You can even fly in them. Unfortunately I was too young for that."

She smiled at his boyish enthusiasm. "Did you have to train for a long time to fly your plane?"

He nodded. "You do a basic officer training course at the Royal Military College, then go on to the Flight Training School in Manitoba. You have to do academic studies too. Once you've got your Wings you move on to Moose Jaw, then Cold Lake to complete your Fighter Lead-in Training."

Her eyes widened. "What a weird place name — Moose Jaw. Is it really called that?"

146

"Oh, Canada's full of names like that. A lot of them are even weirder. There's a place called Sober Island, and Punkeydoodles, and Head-Smashed-In."

She laughed. "You're joking!"

"Not at all. I bet you have some weird place names in England too."

"Well, yes, we do." She thought for a moment. "There's a river in Dorset called the Piddle. One of the hotel guests told me about it. They said it's very good for salmon fishing."

They were both laughing as the waitress brought their starter. She smiled as she set down their plates. "There. Hope you enjoy your meal."

"Thank you. It looks delicious."

"She seems very nice," Shelley murmured as the waitress left. "I was afraid they'd be snooty."

"If they were, we'd leave."

"Really?"

"Really."

A warm glow spread through her. She had been afraid he would dismiss her anxieties as foolish, but he had taken her seriously. She took a forkful of her salmon and mango — the mingle of flavours melted on her tongue.

"Mmm!"

"Good?"

"Very good."

Why had she been so anxious? She was really enjoying the evening. The food was simple but delicious, and Alex was such easy company that she forgot to worry about keeping up the conversation. It just seemed to flow.

He was smiling at her across the table. The warm amber glow from the garden sculpted his features in shadow and darkened his eyes. She would dream of this tonight — she would dream of it for a very long time.

* * *

147

Alex watched Shelley as she ate. She seemed to have relaxed in his company at last, and was chatting happily, telling him funny stories about some of the hotel guests and the odd things they left behind.

"False teeth! Wouldn't you think they'd notice they'd forgotten their false teeth?"

He laughed. "I suppose you get all sorts."

"Oh, yes. Most of them are really nice, especially the elderly ones. They like to chat. They tell me about their grandchildren, show me photographs."

"What about the golfers? Are they nice too?"

"Most of them are okay. They really just want to get out on the course. Some of them bring their wives. Well, some of the wives play too, of course. The ones that don't, they can get a bit bored, and they don't all want to spend their time on the beach. Sometimes they go into Exeter, shopping. It would be nice if the hotel could lay on excursions for them. Down to the Eden Project or something."

He nodded slowly. "That's a good idea." Something to think about if his plans for the hotel worked out.

They finished their meal and the waitress came to take their plates. "Would you like a dessert?"

Alex glanced across the table at Shelley, one eyebrow arched in question.

She shook her head. "Ah . . . um . . . Do you?"

"No, I'll just have coffee. But you have a dessert if you want one."

"Oh . . . no, I don't think so. Just coffee for me, too. Thank you."

The waitress nodded. "Be right with you."

Alex watched Shelley gazing out of the window, maybe looking for those elves and fairies? She would fit right in with them. She was such a dainty little thing; she looked as if a puff of wind would blow her away.

But that was misleading. He hadn't forgotten the injuries she had inflicted on that sleazy guy who had attacked her. And he had seen how hard she worked around the hotel — shifting tables, carting boxes around. On one occasion he had even caught a glimpse of her in one of the rooms, turning a double mattress by herself. When he had offered to help, she had laughed him off. "It's done," she'd told him.

Even so, he had to be careful with her. Physically, she might be stronger than she looked, but emotionally she was very vulnerable. The memory of her sitting on the rocks beneath the hotel, crying her heart out because the hotel might be closing down, had hit him hard.

That had been when he'd first thought of buying the place himself, an idea reinforced by his grandfather's stories about the airmen during the war. The day after tomorrow he had an appointment with a Mr Stretton at Lytcott Capital Management. Then he would see if it was a realistic proposition or not.

The waitress had returned with a carafe of coffee and two cups, plus a jug of cream. Shelley smiled up at her.

"This is a lovely place." She gestured towards the window. "We were just saying there could be fairies living out there."

She laughed. "Oh, yes, there could be. We call them piskies here. My husband's quite a folklore buff."

"Really?"

"Uh-huh. Bernard." She called to a tall, lanky man with a thick brown beard who was wiping down one of the other tables. "These people were asking about the piskies."

"Oh, yes?" He came over, beaming. "Dartmoor's a favourite haunt for piskies. They're supposed to look like bundles of rags, and they live in caves and holes, and under oak trees."

Alex was amused. This man clearly loved to talk about his pet subject.

"Are they friendly?" Shelley asked.

"Oh, yes. They can be very friendly and helpful, if you're friendly to them. There's a legend about a woman who got lost on the moor with her children. The youngest disappeared,

149

and she searched for hours but couldn't find him. Then, as she sat down to cry, two little piskies appeared, holding little lanterns, and guided her to where he was lying. Then they disappeared into thin air."

"Oh, that's lovely!"

"Mind, if you treat them badly, they can be very mischievous. Sometimes they'll force you to dance with them for hours and hours until you collapse with exhaustion."

Shelley laughed. "I'll make very sure that if I meet them, I'll be nice to them, then!"

They had finished their coffee. "Another cup?" Alex asked.

She shook her head. "Oh . . . No, thank you. Unless you're having another one."

"No. Shall we go then?"

"Yes, okay." She rose to her feet and swung her bag onto her shoulder.

"Goodnight, then." The waitress beamed. "Do come again."

"We certainly will. The food was excellent."

"Thank you."

As Alex held the door open for Shelley, she glanced back over her shoulder. "What a nice place." She smiled up at him. "I'm glad you didn't take me somewhere posh."

He laughed. "Maybe next time?"

"Oh . . ." She froze, like that fox in the garden when he was a kid, darting back behind the hedge. "No . . . I . . ."

"Never mind." He tried a reassuring smile. "I was joking. I'm more than happy with fish 'n' chips on the beach."

The smile wobbled and faded, and her eyes flickered away again. "Maybe . . ."

She intrigued him. Just when he thought he was beginning to earn her trust, something would cause her to dart back behind her defences. As he had back then with the fox, he was going to have to exercise a lot of patience to win her over.

CHAPTER EIGHTEEN

Kate glanced at Mike as he drew the car to a halt at the kerb beside the café. "Thank you. That was a lot of fun."

He smiled. "I enjoyed it too. Next week again?"

"I'd like that." Should she invite him in for coffee? It was so many years since she had been in the dating game — not that this was a date, of course. "I never knew you could waltz to the music of *Pirates of the Caribbean*. That's little Amy's favourite film. Well, second to *Frozen*, of course."

"There's a very good waltz in *Frozen* too. We could ask for it next week."

"That would be good. I'm afraid I was a bit clumsy with the Foxtrot. I couldn't seem to get the rhythm."

"Don't worry, it'll come to you. Just relax and follow my lead. You're very good in the Viennese Waltz."

"Thank you. Well . . ." Impulsively, she leaned over to kiss him on the cheek, but he turned towards her, and it landed on the corner of his mouth instead. "Oh . . . uh . . ." Mortified, her cheeks hot, she fumbled to free her seatbelt and open the door. "Goodnight. I'll . . . um . . . see you next week then."

"Yes. Though . . . I might pop into the café over the weekend, as usual. If that's okay?"

"Of course." She was out of the car and digging in her bag for her keys. Dammit, why did they always have to fall into the deepest, most awkward corner? She managed to grasp them, thrust them into the lock and push the door open. Mike waited until she was inside before he drove away.

Of course, he had always been a real gentleman.

She locked the door behind her and hurried up the stairs to her flat above the café. She hadn't quite got used to Debbie and Amy not being there.

She was more than happy that Debbie was settled at last with Bill, the stockman up at the Cullen's farm. They had moved into a cottage up there which was really cosy. And Amy was ecstatic that they had adopted two young cats — sisters — from the animal shelter.

But she missed them.

Was that why she was thinking more and more about Mike? That was a very bad reason to start a relationship. Not that she was really thinking about starting a relationship. It was just . . . a pleasant dream to indulge in when she was feeling a bit lonely.

On the sideboard were several framed photographs of Debbie growing up, and of Amy. And her own wedding photo. She picked it up and gazed at it.

Her Terry. Oh, how she had loved him, from the first moment she had met him — running up out of the sea, laughing, shaking his head like a seal and spattering her with wet drops.

He had dropped to his heels beside her, apologising with a cheerful teasing, and insisting he had to buy her an ice cream to make up for it.

Right then she had known that he was The One. And to her joy and amazement, he had felt the same. They had been so happy, so in love, and she had thought it would last forever.

She used to watch the elderly couples who came down to Sturcombe for their holidays, walking slowly hand in hand along the Esplanade or eating fish and chips on the beach, and imagine her and Terry like that in forty, fifty years' time.

152

Instead, they had barely had five.

Brushing a tear from her eye, she put the photo down. In those five years she'd had more love and happiness than most people had in a lifetime.

* * *

Mike drove carefully down the Esplanade and into the hotel car park. He let himself in through the staff entrance and slowly climbed the stairs to his flat on the second floor.

He had lived here for thirty years, and it fitted him as comfortably as the old pair of tartan slippers waiting for him by the front door. Taking off his jacket, he hung it carefully in the hall cupboard then strolled into the kitchen to make himself a cup of tea.

Sarah had always been very proud of her kitchen, and he had always tried to keep it as spotless as she had herself. Same with the rest of the flat, though there was only himself now to appreciate it.

Sometimes they had thought of moving out, buying a little house. *When the children come along*, they'd promised themselves. But the children hadn't come along.

That had been their biggest regret. They'd considered adoption, but somehow it hadn't felt right for them. So it had been just the two of them, and they'd stayed here. And they had been happy for all those years.

Taking his tea, he strolled through to the sitting room and over to the glass-fronted cabinet beside the fireplace, its shelves filled with the cups and medals he and Sarah had won.

And photographs, he in his smart dinner jacket, she in a dozen different spectacular dresses, all swirling skirts and sequins. She had made those dresses herself.

Maybe one day he could reach that standard again with Kate.

He had really enjoyed tonight. Kate was a natural — she had picked up the steps quickly, and she was so light on her feet. She seemed to really feel the music.

153

He had wondered, driving home, if she would invite him in for a last drink. Had she been worried that he might take it the wrong way?

He laughed, shaking his head. Hardly, at their age. But that kiss . . . Well, it hadn't really been a kiss. She had really only intended a friendly peck on the cheek, but then, like an idiot, he'd turned his head at the wrong moment, and embarrassed them both.

At least she had agreed to come dancing again next week.

CHAPTER NINETEEN

"Well now, you two seem to be very busy." Mike smiled at the two small girls sitting at a corner table, the drawing paper and coloured pencils strewn across it giving the clue to what was engaging their attention.

It was Saturday afternoon, but by this time of the year there were few customers — mostly locals, who greeted him cheerfully.

"What are you doing?" he asked.

Kate's granddaughter Amy beamed up at him. "Writing to Santa."

"Really? Isn't it a little bit early for that?"

Robyn, Amy's best friend, shook her blonde head. "You have to write them early," she explained earnestly. "Because Santa lives a long way away at the North Pole, so letters take a long time to get there."

"Ah — I see. And what are you asking Santa for?"

"First you have to tell him your name and where you live, or he won't know where to go," Amy insisted. "And that you've been good."

He chuckled softly. "And have you been good?"

155

"Well . . . Mostly." Her soft brown eyes, so like her grand-mother's, were slightly evasive. "I didn't mean to let the kittens play with the toilet roll and unwrap it all. But they wanted to play with it and it ended up all over the sitting room floor."

He had to stifle the bubble of laughter that sprang to his lips. "Oh dear."

He glanced round as Kate came over, her pretty mouth curved into a shy smile.

"Hello Mike."

"Hello." He'd been worrying since Thursday evening how it would be, seeing her again. After that awkward sort-of-kiss would she be embarrassed? Would it make things uncom-fortable between them?

But that smile told him that everything was going to be alright.

* * *

Kate suppressed a sigh of relief — at least she hadn't scared him off with that clumsy kiss. Her little granddaughter beamed up at her. "Are you going to sit with us, Nanna? I need you to help me with my letter."

"Of course, sweetie," Kate responded, smiling. "Mike, I've brought your coffee, and I thought you might like to try one of these mince pies I've made."

"I'd love to — thank you. Is it okay if I join you, girls?" he added solemnly to the children.

They giggled at the grown-up request. "Of course it is!"

"Thank you."

He took the seat next to Robyn, and Kate the one next to Amy. She smiled across the table at him. "I've tried a new recipe for these — I hope you like them."

"Can I have one, Nanna?" Amy asked politely.

"Of course. Do you want one, Robyn?"

"Yes please."

"Help yourselves then. How are you getting on with your letters?"

156

"Do you think I should tell Santa that my Daddy's getting married, and we're coming to visit him on our honeymoon?" Robyn asked, a lilt of excitement in her voice.

Kate nodded. "That would be nice."

Her small blonde head bent over her paper, deep in concentration. "How do you spell married?"

Kate watched as Mike patiently spelled out the letters for her, his eyes twinkling with amusement. "And what are you going to ask Santa to give you for Christmas?"

"I want a Skip Ball," Amy said.

"What's that?"

"It's got a ball and a hoop and you put the hoop round your ankle and jump over the ball as it goes round."

"Oh . . . right."

"It's not as complicated as it sounds," Kate assured him.

"Ah. And what about you, Robyn?"

"I want a Singing Sammy and a jungle animals set. But that isn't what I want most of all."

"Oh? What do you want most of all?"

She cupped her hands to her mouth and leaned up to whisper in his ear — though loud enough for Kate to hear. "A baby sister."

He was struggling to contain his laughter. "Well, um . . . I expect your Daddy and Auntie Cassie will have a good think about that."

The little girl frowned. "Is that how you make babies?" she asked, wide-eyed. "With a good think?"

"Well, you certainly need to have a good think about it," Kate chipped in, rescuing him. "Do you like your mince pie?"

"Yes! They're scrummy!"

"Good."

Across the table Mike's smile was filled with warmth and humour, and she felt her heart skip. It was so nice sitting here with him, with the children. He was so easy and natural with them — he would have made a lovely grandpa.

157

CHAPTER TWENTY

Alex had been to London before, several times, but never to the financial district east of St Paul's Cathedral. He had expected it to be similar to downtown Toronto, all high-rise glass towers, and indeed there were plenty of those.

But there were also many dignified old buildings still preserved — the imposing Royal Exchange, with its frontage that looked more like a Greek temple, the neo-classical facades along Cornhill and Leadenhall Street.

His taxi dropped him outside the offices of Lytcott Capital Management, a discreet building in the shadow of the weirdly shaped glass edifice appropriately nicknamed the Gherkin.

He pressed the buzzer beside the anonymous black door and gave his name. A disembodied voice invited him to step inside and take the lift to the fourth floor.

The lift doors opened onto a reception area, subtly lit and decorated in muted shades of grey, with several modish arm-chairs arranged around a low glass table that held an enormous arrangement of silk flowers.

A very elegant blonde woman was sitting behind a long, curved desk. She smiled up at him as he approached. "Mr

Crocombe? Please take a seat. Mr Stretton will be with you in just a few moments."

"Thank you."

The armchairs had clearly been designed to be looked at rather than sat on. The few moments stretched to five, then ten, until at last one of the office doors opened.

Mr Stretton was a tall man, with neatly trimmed dark hair and a perfect shadow of designer stubble. His charcoal-grey business suit was immaculately tailored, his tie almost certainly identifying the public school he had attended.

Alex was greeted with a genial smile which he instinctively mistrusted.

"Ah, Mr Crocombe. Won't you come in." *To my parlour, said the spider to the fly.* "Olivia, we'll have coffee, if you please."

It was a corner office, in more shades of grey, with a huge beechwood desk and an acre of carpet so thick he could feel his feet sinking into it. Invited to take a seat, he was amused to note the subtle power play in the layout — the executive chair with its back to the bright window so that Stretton's face was not quite clear, the lower visitors' chairs intended to put supplicants in their place.

"Did you have a pleasant journey?" Stretton enquired, all polite solicitation.

"Reasonable. I wouldn't say that your train service is the most comfortable I've ever experienced, but your London taxis are excellent."

"Ah, yes. And how do you like England?"

"Very much. I was actually born here and lived here as a child, and I've been back several times over the years. And over it several times," he added with a dry smile. "But rather too high and too fast to get more than a fleeting impression."

"Of course. Should I be calling you Flight Lieutenant Crocombe?"

Alex shook his head. "It's Captain. And no, we don't retain our rank after leaving the Service."

159

"I see, I see." The door opened and the receptionist entered with a tray carrying two cups of coffee. "Ah, Olivia, thank you. Just put them here on the desk. Cream and sugar, Mr Crocombe?"

"Just cream, thank you."

Stretton pushed the cream jug towards him.

"So, I believe you're interested in one of the hotels we've recently acquired in Devon. The . . . ah . . . Carleton. Is that right?"

Alex was mildly amused by the portrayal of smooth charm. Through his partnership with Frank Beaumont he had met many characters like this — and had learned how to handle them.

He took his time, stirring a swirl of cream into his coffee, taking a sip, and putting the cup down on the desk. "Yes, the Carleton Hotel. I understand that your Mr Forsythe's report didn't favour retaining it in your portfolio."

"That's correct. And you have some interest in it?"

"That's correct." He matched the smooth smile, the relaxed posture.

"Well now." Stretton turned to the computer on his desk and clicked a few keys. "The hotel itself — no, we're not interested in it. The site, on the other hand . . . That could be of some interest to us."

"The site would have the same disadvantage of location as the hotel has suffered from."

"And which you would continue to suffer from if you purchased the hotel."

Alex reached over and picked up his coffee cup again, taking another slow sip. "I have plans. I'm prepared to invest for the longer term."

"I see. Well, Mr Crocombe, let's see if we can find some common ground here."

* * *

160

"Well, Mr Channing, let's see if we can find some common ground here."

Paul wasn't misled by Stretton's charming manner — he was a shark. That was how he had made Lytcott Capital Management one of the most successful investment funds in the business.

This vast office, with its subtle shades of grey and its luxurious pale-grey carpet, was designed to display discreet wealth. You could get a good game of five-a-side football going in here.

"However." Stretton's voice carried a heavy emphasis in spite of the smile. "I have to tell you that we've already received a very good offer for the property."

"Oh?" That was unexpected, and unwelcome, but Paul was careful to keep all trace of his reaction from his face and his voice.

"I need hardly explain that I'm duty-bound to get the best return I can for our partners. If you can see your way to improving your offer . . . ?"

"May I ask who the other party is?"

That shark's smile again. "Ah, well, I'm afraid I can't tell you that. Commercial confidentiality, you understand. But they already have some plans for re-development of the site."

Paul nodded slowly. Damn. He could increase his offer, of course — it was still well within the sum he could afford — but was this a bluff? Did Stretton really have another offer in the bag? It seemed unlikely, but not impossible.

Across the wide desk he studied his . . . It was hard not to think of him as his opponent — the goalie looking to block his penalty shot. Stretton was watching him, too, those sharp eyes cold, no doubt calculating how far could he push without losing the deal.

Half an hour later Paul was standing on the Millenium Bridge watching the silver-grey waters of the Thames drift slowly down towards the sea. He'd agreed a price with Stretton — more than he wanted to pay, but less than he was willing to pay.

161

Now it remained to be seen what would happen next. Stretton would contact the other party, of course — if they existed — and try to persuade them to increase their offer. Then he'd hear from him again, probably spinning another line about a higher bid and trying to get him to top it.

Well, he'd deal with that when it happened. Meanwhile, he had an appointment with a couple of new young players at their training ground out in the suburbs, then dinner with some old mates now playing for one of the top London clubs.

CHAPTER TWENTY-ONE

November, and summer was fading. A cool sun still shone in the pale-blue sky, but the air was beginning to chill. Alex was strolling on the beach when his phone rang.

The call was from Stretton. He perched himself on a convenient flat rock below the hotel to take it.

"Ah, Mr Crocombe. Good to speak to you again."

"And you." Alex smiled to himself. "How's the weather at your end?"

"I'm afraid we've got rain."

"Too bad. The sun's shining here. Matter of fact I'm on the beach right now. Anyway, what can I do for you, Mr Stretton?" That was a trick of Frank's, to put the ball back immediately into his opponent's court.

"Ah, well now, regarding the bid for the hotel."

"Yes?"

"I have to tell you that someone else is showing an interest."

Alex's jaw clenched. He hadn't expected that. Maybe he should have. But was it genuine? Would the place really attract that much attention?

"As you came in first, I felt it only right to give you the opportunity to revise your original offer." Oh, so smooth.

163

"I see. Well, that's very considerate of you, Mr Stretton. I'm sure you'll understand that I can't respond immediately. I'll need to consult the figures again."

"Of course. Perhaps you could get back to me . . . tomorrow?"

"Of course."

Alex cut the call and swore fluently. Fortunately only a couple of seagulls were around to hear him, and they used far worse language themselves.

For a long moment he gazed out at the distant horizon. It wasn't the money that was the issue here — well, only partially as he did have deeper reserves to call on. But it stuck in his gullet to play that game, when the future of the hotel was at stake.

Swinging round, he looked up at the building, sitting like a grand old lady in white on the top of the low sandstone cliff. She deserved so much better than to be left derelict, then demolished to make way for a caravan site.

He glanced at his watch. Almost two o'clock. Nine o'clock in Toronto. He tapped on Frank's number. It was answered promptly.

"Hey there, Flyboy. What's with you, eh?"

Alex smiled at Frank's booming jollity, a very effective disguise for one of the shrewdest business brains he'd ever come across. "The game's in play, but I'm not sure if it's chess or checkers."

"Oh? Hit me with it."

"I agreed a price for the hotel with Stretton. Now he's come back to me claiming there's another bidder in the game."

"Genuine?"

"Possibly not. I've no way of knowing."

"Uh-huh. What you gonna do?"

"I can up my offer, but how many times is he going to walk me round the mulberry bush?"

Frank took a pause. Alex could just see the way his white eyebrows would be moving together as he furrowed his brow. "How much do you want the place?"

164

Alex sighed. "I want it."

"You're being sentimental. Sentiment has no place in business."

"If it wasn't for sentiment, I wouldn't be bidding."

"Okay." Frank spared a laugh. He understood — he'd been in the navy, and Alex knew that he made a point of giving jobs on his construction sites to veterans. "Remember the frog?"

"What?"

"You drop a frog in cold water and boil it up slow, frog don't move. Chuck the critter in a pan of boiling water and it leaps right out."

"That sounds cruel," Alex responded with a note of dry humour.

Frank chuckled. "I don't think it's real. But it's the principle. You drop this Stretton guy in the boiling water."

"I'd like to, but I don't think it's legal."

Another dry chuckle. "Okay, here's the thing. You let the guy play you off against this other bidder, real or not, and up creeps the price. Or you slap him with your best offer, take it or leave it, but sign the contract now."

Alex drew a breath in between his teeth. "Bit of a gamble."

"Sure is. But whoever this other guy is, I'd be willing to bet he ain't gonna want it like you do. No sentiment, so he'll be sensible about it. Besides, if he's just wanting it for the site, he's only going to offer what the land's worth — probably less the cost of demolition. So, if you're offering him better than that, he's gonna deal."

Alex laughed. "Okay, I'll think about it."

He ended the call, stuck the phone back in his pocket, and strolled off up the hill to his grandfather's house.

Frank's advice was sound. After all, he had made himself one of the most successful real-estate developers in the Toronto Metro area. And had made Alex himself a comfortable eight-figure bank balance in the process.

But as he had said, it was a gamble. He'd take a little while to think about it.

165

* * *

The lad Alex had hired to tidy up his grandfather's garden was hard at work digging up weeds from round the rose bushes. He greeted him with a casual salute and let himself into the house.

Arthur was watching a quiz programme on the television, but he looked up with a toothless grin when Alex walked in. "Ah, there you are. I was hoping you'd come. My new scooter's come, and it should be all charged up by now. I'm going to take it out for a ride."

Alex rolled his eyes. He hadn't been sure that the mobility scooter was a good idea, but Arthur had found an advertisement for them in the local paper, and insisted Alex take him along to the shop to try one out. Well, that was it — he was going to have one.

"Okay, Grandpa. Where are we going?"

"All round the town. You'll have to walk fast to keep up with me."

"You're only allowed to do four miles an hour on the pavement," Alex reminded him.

"Pah! Come on. Just give me a minute to put my teeth in." He accepted a hand to get out of his chair, and let Alex help him on with his coat.

Marcus was in the kitchen. "You drive safely now," he warned. "It's not a Ferrari, you know."

The old man chuckled. "I'm getting one of those next week."

Alex shared an amused glance with the carer, and gave Arthur his arm out of the back door and down the garden to the shed. Inside stood a gleaming brand-new bright-red mobility scooter.

"There she is. Ain't she a beauty?" he declared proudly. "Come on then, my luvver, let's show you off to the town."

Alex unplugged the charger, and Arthur settled himself on the seat and started her up. "Brrm brrm! Off we go!"

166

Alex hurried to open the gate, watching with some anxiety as his grandfather steered the scooter out onto the back lane. By the time he had shut the shed and the gate he had to hurry to catch up with him as he turned down Church Road, heading for the Esplanade.

"Grandpa, slow down!" he pleaded. "You'll get arrested."

"Whoo hoo! I'm enjoying this. What are they going to do? Throw me in jail? I'm ninety-four, you know."

"I know that. But if the police catch you speeding they might stop you riding it."

"Pah!" But the warning was enough to persuade him to slow to a walking pace.

Fortunately, the pavement wasn't as crowded as it would have been in the high season, and nobody seemed to mind stepping aside for the grinning old man waving and whooping as he bowled along.

At the far end of the Esplanade he crossed the road and turned back along the pavement beside the sea wall, then into the Memorial Gardens with its neatly trimmed lawn and well-tended flowerbeds, all weeded and mulched down for the winter.

In the middle of the gardens the old clock tower stood like a sentinel in the cool November sunshine. To Alex's surprise, Arthur drew the mobility scooter to an abrupt halt beside it. He levered himself to his feet and stepped carefully up to it, peering closely to study the names of the fallen etched onto the weathered brass plaques.

"Mogford, Ernest: Corporal — Freddie's dad," he murmured. "Pym, Albert: Sargeant. Waycott, Dennis: Private."

"You knew them?"

"Oh, ah." He nodded. "Dennis Waycott were apprentice to old George Stanbury as had the garage over on Haytor Avenue. That's gone now. And Albert, he were the postman's son."

He drew himself up proudly erect and lifted his hand in a smart parade-ground salute. He stood like that for a long moment, his eyes gazing back into some long-ago time, a single tear tracking down his cheek.

167

Alex watched him in silence. His grandfather was prone to these sudden mood swings, from happy and rumbunctious to sentimental and full of memories.

It really wasn't a surprise that the Memorial should have triggered him, carrying the weight of the years and all the sacrifices that had been made. All those men who hadn't come home, and those who had, but with changes that would last their lifetimes.

He glanced across at the rambling white facade of the Carleton. Eighty-something years ago other airmen would have stood here, looking up at that building.

Of course, the white walls would have been streaked with smoky-grey camouflage paint then, and the gardens would have been given over to growing vegetables: 'Dig For Britain'.

The Carleton had done her bit.

Arthur stepped back and grinned, rubbing his hands together. "Right. Let's be getting up to the hotel. I could do with a nice cup of tea." Back on his scooter, he swooped out of the gardens and round to the hotel car park, jerking to a halt again beside the front entrance.

Alex offered his arm to walk him up the steps. Jess was on duty in reception and she greeted them with a warm smile. "Hi there, Arthur. Have you come down for afternoon tea?"

"Of course, my luvver. Out on the terrace, if you please."

She glanced at Alex and he guessed she was thinking the same thing that he was. "Don't you think it might be a bit chilly out there?"

"Pah! I've got my coat on. I'll be warm as a bug in a rug."

Alex smiled wryly, and helped him out to the terrace, settling him comfortably at one of the tables.

"I've got a blanket if he'd like it over his knees," Jess murmured to Alex.

"Wait till he's distracted by the scones, then bring it over."

She laughed quietly and went off to get their scones.

168

CHAPTER TWENTY-TWO

The tyres of the sleek green car crunched on the gravel hard standing of his front garden, and Paul leaned back with a sigh. After three days in London, with all the noise and grey pavements and tall buildings crowding in, it was good to be back where he belonged.

He sat there for several minutes, just slowly winding down.

Stretton. Fortunately, he didn't have to deal with scurvy like that too often. When you were the one doing the investing, if you didn't care for them you could just walk away.

Did he really have another potential buyer for the hotel? Possibly. Or it could be just an invention, to push him to increase his bid.

How much would he be willing to pay? Probably considerably more than it was worth. His business head told him he was an idiot to let sentiment intrude on a deal, but this was more than just another business deal. This was important.

Trying to shake off the mood, he climbed out of the car, but he didn't immediately go into the house. Instead, he crossed the road and stood for a moment by the cliff wall, breathing in deeply, savouring the cool, salt-tanged air.

169

There was a stiff breeze blowing in from the sea, and the waves were dancing, crested with frills of white foam as they chased each other over the sand.

At the far end of the beach, the Carleton gleamed white in the cool autumn sunshine. Sentiment . . . Well, so what? Smiling to himself, he turned and strolled down the hill.

With each week there were fewer holidaymakers. Soon the town would sink into its winter torpor, with just the locals dropping in for a coffee at the CupCake Café or walking their dogs on the beach.

He had reached the far end of the Esplanade and was crossing the road to the Memorial Gardens when he heard someone call his name.

"Paul! Hi!"

He glanced over his shoulder to see his sister, Lisa, walking down Church Road with little Kyra in her baby buggy.

"Hello, there. And hello you." He bent to tickle his little niece's toes. "Ah, she smiled at me."

"Wind."

"Huh! Anyway, where are you off to?" he asked Lisa.

"I thought I'd just pop over to the hotel to see if Vicky needs any help with the preparations for Christmas. It can be a bit full on with the Turkey-and-Tinsel crowds."

He laughed. "You really can't just relax and enjoy your maternity leave, can you? I bet you're over here every day."

"Well, not *every* day. And I do try not to interfere. But I love the old place. It's kinda special."

"It is." No, he wouldn't tell her his plans just yet. If there was going to be a bidding war, it could get . . . difficult.

"Anyway, how about you?" she asked.

He shrugged in casual unconcern. "Oh, nowhere in particular."

She wasn't fooled. "No? Just in the general direction of the hotel, then?"

"Well . . ."

Lisa's eyes danced. "Hoping a certain redhead may be on reception?"

170

"Has anyone ever told you that you're a nosy little madam, Annelise Cullen?"

"You did — frequently — when we were kids," she returned smartly.

"And you still are."

They both laughed.

"Well, let's get a coffee anyway, and I promise not to pry if Jess should happen to be there."

As they strolled through the front doors Vicky was coming out of the dining room with a clipboard on her arm. She greeted them with a warm smile. "Hi."

"Hi. Just popped in to see how you're getting on with the prep for Christmas."

Vicky laughed. "It's fun. We've brought up the boxes of decorations — they're in the ballroom. And the trees are on order."

"Great. How about the arrangements for the T'n'T groups?"

"Oh, boy — I'm glad you warned me about that! It'll be great to have the place so lively, but all the comings and goings are hard to keep track of. Three days, four days, mid-week, weekends, which days they want early calls, which evenings they want dinner. Nightmare!"

"I hope my spreadsheet helps."

"It does. Without that it'd be impossible. Anyway, come and have a coffee, then if you've got time maybe you could go through it with me and let me know any little quirks we need to take account of."

"That's why I came over, to see if I could help."

"And you brought the little one over for a visit." Vicky bent over the buggy. "And just look at you, little Kyra. Aren't you growing?" The baby waved her chubby little arms as Vicky tickled her tummy. "Ah, she smiled at me."

"Wind," Paul asserted. "What?" Lisa had rolled her eyes at him. "That's what you always say when she smiles at me."

171

"Ignore him," Lisa advised. "So, you next?" She nodded towards the baby.

"It's on the agenda, but listed for next year."

Lisa laughed. "Babies don't do lists."

Paul was glad that they didn't notice him roll his eyes. Babies, already! Vicky and Tom Cullen, one of his oldest friends, had only been married a few weeks, and were just back from their honeymoon.

He had to admit that she was looking well on it. She positively radiated newlywed happiness, her hair streaked light blonde by the Spanish sun, her skin tinted pale gold.

Shaking his head, he strolled out to the terrace and was mildly surprised to see old Arthur sitting out there with his grandson. Though it was sunny it was November, and there was a distinct chill in the air. But the old man was well wrapped up against the cold in a warm overcoat, with a blanket over his knees.

"Hello there, Arthur. I thought you'd be here — I saw your Batmobile outside."

The old man chuckled. "Smart, ain't it? Goes like the wind, too. Come and join us. Want a scone?"

Lisa lifted the baby out of her buggy, and Paul held out his arms for her. "Here, I'll take her." He only had a partial ulterior motive. He enjoyed bouncing the tot on his lap, but it didn't hurt that women were supposed to melt over a man holding a baby. If Jess happened to be around . . .

He settled the tot comfortably in the crook of his arm, and she gazed up at him with huge blue-grey eyes, her chubby cheeks dimpling as she smiled.

"There! She really did smile at me."

"Wind."

"Of course it wasn't. You recognised your Uncle Paul, didn't you, Toots?"

"Go on believing that," Lisa advised dryly. "She's probably filling her nappy."

He glanced at her in alarm, but Lisa laughed.

172

"You're okay. She had a fresh one on before we came out."

Arthur was chuckling again. "Ah, she got you there!" He leaned over and gave the baby his finger to clutch, her tiny pink hand wrapping around his thin, wrinkled one as she stared up at him — and smiled again. "There, now, that was a smile," he insisted with glee. "A proper one."

Paul had been watching for Jess, but she didn't seem to be around. She hadn't said if she was planning to stay, but if he let the hotel be closed down she would certainly be leaving.

That was another reason to keep it open. Maybe more of a reason than he was willing to acknowledge.

Vicky came out with a tray of cups and a fresh cafetiere of coffee, and sat down at the end of the table. "I just need to keep half an eye on the desk," she explained.

"Paul, you haven't seen Vicky's photos from the Pradera yet, have you?" Lisa asked.

"Oh, no. Show me."

Vicky pulled out her phone, called up the images, and passed it over. "They had a whole wall of Juan-Jorge's paintings in one of the rooms, along with the sketches he did of Tom's grandmother and the others. That's the one of my Aunt Molly, in the centre."

"I heard about that," Alex remarked. Paul passed the phone across the table to him. "It must have been amazing to see them hanging in a prestigious art gallery like that."

"It was." Vicky glanced at Lisa. "Why didn't he do one of your Nanna Edie?"

Arthur snorted. "Pah! Too ugly!"

"Grandpa!"

"What? I'm just telling the truth. If I can't tell the truth at my age . . ."

"Yes, I know." The big Canadian rolled his eyes. "You're ninety-four. You outlived them all. I wonder why you never mention it?"

"Pah!"

173

"What did you think about those old photo albums, Arthur?" Lisa asked, trying to distract him.

"Ah, very good, my luvver, very good. Lots of those guys I remember. Johnny Leadbetter — now, he was a proper 'un. Lungs had been damaged when his plane caught fire, but he was always laughing and joking. Then he died."

A shadow crossed his face.

"He always used to sit out here, over there in the corner." He looked across as if he could still see his old friend in his usual place. "We came up one day, me and my pals, and his chair was empty. They just told us he'd gone, but we heard later he'd died in his sleep. Just like that. Still, it was a good way to go, I suppose, even though he weren't no older than twenty-one."

"Oh, that's so sad," Lisa murmured.

"It's awful that the place could be closed," Vicky sighed. "It ought to be kept as a memorial to all those brave men."

Paul smiled down at the baby on his lap, and put his finger to his lips. "Shhh," he whispered softly. "Secret."

Arthur was chuckling with laughter. "Oh, don't you worry," he declared, beaming broadly. "My grandson's going to see it right. Ain't you, lad?"

There was a moment's startled silence.

"My Alex is going to buy it," the old man crowed. "What do you think of that, eh?"

174

CHAPTER TWENTY-THREE

Alex shook his head, laughing. "How did you know about that, Grandpa? I never told you."

"Your father told me, of course! Why, was it supposed to be a secret?"

Paul Channing was staring at him, then he started laughing too. "*You're* bidding for it?"

"I am. I wasn't going to say anything yet, until the deal's done."

"And Stretton's giving you the runaround, telling you there's another bidder, trying to push the price up?"

"That's right . . ." The cogs in Alex's brain whirred and clicked into place. "*You?* You're his other bidder?"

"I am." Paul was laughing. "It looks like our scheming Mr Stretton has been playing us off against each other. But he overlooked one small but very significant detail."

Alex nodded slowly. "That we both live here in Sturcombe. And if we decided that instead of competing against each other, we combined our efforts . . ."

"We could beat him at his own game!"

Alex leaned back in his chair, his mind working at Mach speed. Years ago, his instincts had told him to trust Frank

175

Beaumont, and that had worked out extremely well. Now his instincts were telling him to trust Paul Channing.

"Partners." He reached out his hand across the table. "Yes?"

Paul's handshake was firm. "Yes."

"Wow, that's amazing!" Lisa was beaming as she glanced from one to the other. "I had no idea that either of you were planning to buy the place."

Paul smiled wryly. "I was keeping quiet about it too. I didn't want to get people's hopes up."

"So what happens now?" she asked.

Alex raised a questioning eyebrow at his new business partner. "First we agree on a figure for our offer to Stretton. Lower, I think, than either of us offered in the first place."

Paul nodded grimly. "And it's a one-time offer — no more games. I very much doubt he's going to get any more interest in it."

Alex smiled in grim satisfaction. "It's going to give me a great deal of pleasure to tell him."

"Well!" Vicky rose to her feet. "I think we should celebrate with a bottle of bubbly!"

* * *

"Is it right, what Vicky just told me?" Jess came out to the terrace and began clearing the tables. "You're actually buying the hotel?"

"That's right." Paul was sitting with his feet propped on a second chair, bouncing little Kyra on his lap, pulling faces at her and making her giggle. "Me and Alex Crocombe. We're going into partnership."

She shook her head, laughing. "I know we talked about what a shame it would be if it closed down, but I didn't realise you were actually planning to buy it yourself."

"I didn't really know myself at that point — it was just a vague idea." He blew a soft raspberry at the baby. "But the

176

more I thought about it, the more I knew I was going to do it. This place has stood here since my great-great-grandparents' time. I'd like to think it might still be here in this little one's great-great-grandchildren's time. Isn't that right, Kyra? It should be, shouldn't it?"

The tot splatted one tiny pink hand across his nose and cheek.

"Was that a yes?" he asked her solemnly. "I think it was, wasn't it? When you're a little old lady of Arthur's age, you'll still be able to come up here for tea and scones on the terrace. What do you think about that?"

Oh damn, what was it about men and babies? All her hormones were racing around her bloodstream, making her feel all squishy and broody. *Get a grip.*

"So what are you planning to do with it?" Jess worked briskly around the table, sweeping the debris of several empty plates onto one and stacking them up, in an effort to take her mind off the way he was playing with the baby.

Paul shrugged his wide shoulders. "Where to start? I've got no illusions — it's going to need a major overhaul."

"It's going to cost a lot."

"We've factored that in."

Yes, he would have. For all his playboy, ex-footballer image, she guessed that he was very shrewd with money. Lisa had mentioned that he had been running a very successful investment consultancy since he'd retired from the game. And he drove an Aston Martin.

If she dated him — *if* — she would look like a gold digger. Well, so what? Let people think what they liked. It was between her and Paul. He was the only one whose opinion mattered.

And if he thought she was a gold digger, he really didn't know her at all.

"So, are you going to run the place?" she asked.

He shook his head. "Not me, I'll be more of a sleeping partner. Mike will still be the manager, of course, but

177

Alex will be taking the leading role in developing our new plans."

"He seems nice." She really shouldn't be finding ways to continue hanging around out here. "Wasn't he a fighter pilot?"

"He was. That's why he feels such a strong connection with this place."

"Ah, of course. Old Arthur's stories of the war. They were fascinating. He has a wonderful memory."

"We'd like to set up some kind of memorial to record the whole history."

"That's a great idea. Maybe a website? Shelley said there are loads more photo albums and diaries and stuff down in the basement. We could scan them and load them up. People are often dead keen on that sort of thing. It could be quite a feature. Anyway . . ." She'd stayed long enough — any longer and her brain would turn completely to jelly. "I'd better take these things into the kitchen and get them washed up."

CHAPTER TWENTY-FOUR

Shelley brushed another tear from her eyes with an impatient hand as she stuffed her second-best cotton sweater into her backpack. Why was she crying anyway? She had known all along that the fairy tale would come crashing down round her ears sooner or later. She just hadn't expected it to end quite like this.

Why hadn't he told her the truth? She had known he was quite well off, but to be able to buy the hotel, outright, just like that! Like someone might decide to buy a packet of crisps. That was a whole different league.

After struggling to fasten up the backpack, she sat down on the bed and looked around the room.

It wasn't much — just a narrow single bed, an ancient wardrobe, a dressing table with a wonky drawer, a slightly threadbare carpet — but it had been her home, her haven, for the past three years. The closest thing to a home she had ever known.

The tears were flooding down her cheeks now. She had to go. She couldn't stay, knowing she'd see Alex every day. It had been bad enough when he was a guest, but now . . . The owner of the hotel didn't have a relationship with a chambermaid — it was as simple as that.

179

Or not a proper relationship anyway. She smiled bitterly. He might sleep with her, keep her on the side while he dated women on his own level. Married a woman on his own level.

She couldn't live like that. And if she was crying now, it was her own stupid fault for letting herself fall in love with him. She should have known better.

The only things left to pack were those on her bedside table — a box of tissues, a packet of mints, and her small alarm clock, a gift from the charity who had got her this job three years ago.

The tissues could go in the bin, the mints into her pocket, and she tucked the clock into the side pocket of her backpack. If she left now she could catch the bus into town before anyone realised she had gone.

Slipping across to the tiny bathroom the staff shared she splashed her face with cold water to try to cool the redness of her eyes. But as she stepped back across the hall she almost collided with Jess.

"Oh, sorry . . ." She ducked her head and tried to dodge past into her own room.

"My fault," Jess responded, her voice buoyant. "I wasn't looking where I was going. Isn't it great news about Alex and Paul buying the hotel? I didn't know a thing about it, did you?"

"No, I . . . never heard anything."

"It's brilliant. They've got so many ideas. They're really going to make something of the place . . ." She stopped suddenly, her hand on Shelley's arm. "What's wrong? Have you been crying?"

"No."

"Yes, you have. What's the matter?"

"Nothing. Leave me alone." The tears were welling up again, and she dived into her room before they started to fall, trying to shut the door.

"What's going on?" Jess stood in the doorway, her gaze taking in the empty wardrobe, the stuffed backpack. "Where are you going?"

180

"I don't know. I don't care." Her heart felt like a lump of cold lead. "I'm just leaving."

"But why?" Jess stared at her. "Everything's going to be okay now. The hotel isn't going to close."

Shelley shook her head fiercely. "That's got nothing to do with it," she insisted. "I've been here long enough. I hate to stay in one place too long."

Jess's expression told her that she didn't believe her, but she stood aside as Shelley shoved past her and hurried for the stairs.

It had started to rain. It wasn't heavy, but it was cold. Shelley pulled the hood of her parka up over her head as she walked briskly past the front of the hotel and up to the bus stop on Church Road. She only had a few minutes to wait for the bus, so hopefully no one would see her.

No such luck.

"Shelley! Shelley, wait!" It was Lisa running after her.

Shelley scowled angrily as she turned. "What?"

"What are you doing? Where are you going?"

"It's none of your business." She felt as if the pressure inside her was going to burst. "Just . . . Just go away. Leave me alone."

Lisa's eyes widened in shock — Shelley had never spoken like that since she had come to Sturcombe. "Why? What's the matter? Has someone done something? Said something? Tell me."

Shelley turned away, hunching her shoulders, squeezing her eyes shut to try to hold back the tears. "Just leave me alone."

"Whatever's wrong we can sort it out," Lisa coaxed.

Shelley shook her head fiercely. "I said leave me alone."

Lisa sighed. "Okay," she conceded after a moment. "But you can't walk out just like that. You have to give a week's notice."

"Why?"

"It's in your contract."

181

"What contract?"

"You were given a copy when you started." Lisa's voice was beginning to sound strained. "Didn't you read it?"

"No."

"Why not?"

Ah, there it was. The crunch. Her stomach roiled — dammit, was she going to be sick?

Lisa laid a gentle hand on her shoulder. "Why didn't you read it, Shelley?"

Shelley looked away. There was no point trying to come up with an excuse. Lisa knew. She was too astute not to have guessed.

"You can't read, can you?"

Where the hell was that bus? It never came along when you needed it. As the tears spilled over, Lisa folded her in a warm hug.

"It'll be okay. Look, let's not stand here in the rain. Come on over to my house and we'll get a cup of tea and talk about it."

"What about the baby?"

"She's fine. She has her Uncle Paul and a whole squad of honorary aunties and uncles making a big fuss of her. Come on."

There was no point trying to resist Lisa when she was determined. They crossed the road and walked a little way up the hill, turning right past Lisa's husband's surgery.

Her house was a short distance further on — a large white detached house with bay windows and orange roof tiles, and a pretty front garden behind a low brick wall, with a neat lawn and well-tended flowerbeds where roses were still blooming bravely.

Shelley had been here a couple of times before and it always seemed like paradise to her. She hesitated on the door-step as Lisa opened the front door.

"I'm wet. I'll drip all over your floor."

"Don't worry," Lisa insisted. "It won't hurt the tiles. Come on in. Give me your coat."

She hung their coats in a closet beside the front door and led the way through to the kitchen.

182

The whole house was light and bright, with white walls and pale wooden floors, and at the back there were huge windows looking out over a lovely garden and beyond to a view of the rain-drenched bay.

"Sit down while I put the kettle on."

Shelley perched on a stool at the granite-topped centre island, wiping her eyes on her cuff. Lisa put a box of tissues beside her, and Shelley took several, scrubbing her eyes and blowing her nose. She had never felt more miserable or ashamed of herself in her life.

"Now." Lisa brought over two cups of tea and sat down opposite her. "Tell me."

Shelley shrugged, still feeling sick. "There's nothing to tell. I can't read, that's all."

"Are you dyslexic?"

"No. Just thick."

"No, you're not," Lisa retorted sharply. "I've known you for three years, and I know darned well you're not thick. So, tell me."

Shelley drew in a deep breath. "It was just that I changed schools so often, every time I moved to a different foster home. Sometimes I'd be at one only for a few weeks before I got moved again. It was all so confusing."

She could feel the tears welling up again as the bitter memories surfaced.

"I couldn't understand what was going on and the teachers never had time to help me catch up. And sometimes the other kids could be really nasty, called me dumbo and that. In the end I just gave up."

"I'm not surprised. It sounds like a right mess." Lisa reached across and took her hand. "But you're bright, Shelley. I know that. You could learn, if you want to."

Shelley shook her head. "I tried, when I was at the hostel in London. I went to classes, but it was just like being at school all over again."

183

"It doesn't have to be like that. Listen, my mum was a primary school teacher. She's taught hundreds of kids to read. She'd be really happy to teach you."

"Oh, I couldn't." Shelley drew back. "No. I wouldn't want to bother her."

"Rubbish, it wouldn't be a bother. She's retired now, and since my nanna died she's been complaining that she hasn't got enough to do. She'd really enjoy being able to use her skills again. One-to-one tuition. What do you say?"

Shelley hesitated. "I'd pay her."

She saw Lisa ready to refuse, but then she smiled wryly. "Okay, if you insist. I'll call her now and arrange for you to meet with her and talk about it."

Before Shelley could change her mind, Lisa had picked up her phone and clicked on her mum's number. It rang a couple of times, then Shelley heard Helen Channing's voice.

"Hello, dear."

"Hi, Mum. What are you doing?"

"Not much. Tidying the kitchen drawers, as a matter of fact. Just sandpapering the anchor, as your grandfather used to say. Why?"

"Can you spare half an hour or so?"

"Happily. What do you want?"

"How would you like to take on a pupil for literacy lessons?"

"You mean Shelley?"

Shelley felt that roiling in her stomach again.

Lisa laughed. "How did you know?"

"Sweetheart, I taught primary school for thirty years, give or take. I know how to recognise when someone's trying to cover up."

"Brilliant. Look, she's here at my house. Could you pop down and have a chat with her about it?"

"Right now?"

"If you can."

"Of course — no time like the present. Give me ten minutes."

As they ended the call, Shelley gazed bleakly across the table. "Does everyone know?"

Lisa shook her head. "No, only Mum, and you heard why. And she won't have said a word."

"*You* knew."

"It was just a guess." Lisa smiled. "Like I said, I've known you for three years. I had a feeling that might be why you didn't want to try the reception job. Shelley, not being able to read isn't something to be ashamed of. The system let you down when you were a kid."

"Yeah . . . ." She'd always tried to tell herself that, but it was hard to believe when your teachers, your foster parents and your classmates were telling you that you were stupid, lazy, wicked.

"Anyway, what about Alex?" Lisa asked gently.

Shelley stiffened, instantly wary. "What about him?"

"Were you really going to leave without telling him, without saying goodbye?"

No words would come. Shelley turned her head away, staring with unseeing eyes at the garden and the cloud-smudged sky.

"Shelley, he likes you — a lot. And I thought you liked him."

Shelley laughed bitterly. "I did. Until I found out about him."

Lisa's brow furrowed. "What? What did you find out?"

"Only that he's a millionaire — a multi-millionaire. He never told me that. I only found out when I heard he was going to buy the hotel."

"So he's rich? What's the problem?" Lisa sounded genuinely puzzled.

"You can't see it? He's going to be the owner of the hotel. I'm just a chambermaid."

Lisa shook her head. "If that's all, well . . . I think you're doing both him and yourself a great disservice. He's a good man. Look at how kind he is with his grandfather."

185

"I know, but . . . It's just a fairy tale, isn't it — Prince Charming and Cinderella. That sort of thing doesn't happen in real life. Although it probably didn't in the fairy tales either," she added cynically, "before they got all prettied up with pink and glitter. The prince probably married some princess from the neighbouring kingdom and kept Cinderella in a nice little cottage in the village, visiting her twice a week and every other Sunday. Well, I'm not going to be that Cinderella." The tears were welling up again, and she blinked them back, struggling to maintain what was left of her fragile pride. "I won't live like that. I can't. So, that's why I have to leave."

"You've just agreed to have literacy lessons with my mum," Lisa pointed out gently.

"Well, yes, but . . ."

"Look, I don't want you to leave, especially knowing you've nowhere to go and no job. I'll just be worrying about you all the time. Stay. Just give it a month. You can keep out of Alex's way now that he's moved out of the hotel. It's probably best that you back off anyway if it's making you feel uncomfortable."

"I don't know. I . . ." She could feel herself wavering. Running away had been an impulse, something she had always done when things had seemed too much for her. But this time, was it really what she wanted?

"Hello-o?" Helen Channing's voice called from the front door.

"Hi, Mum," Lisa called back. "We're in the kitchen."

The older woman appeared in the doorway. "Hi. I left my coat in the closet. Is there a cup of tea going?"

"Of course. Sit down, Mum. You know Shelley, don't you?"

"Of course I do. How are you, dear?"

"I'm . . ." Shelley had to swallow the catch in her throat. "Fine."

"That's good."

186

Shelley had always liked Lisa's mother. Warm and friendly, her dark hair laced with threads of silver, her eyes full of smiles. If any of the teachers at the schools she had attended had been like her, she was sure things could have been different.

Helen came over and sat down at the centre island. "So, you want to catch up with your reading." Her voice was very calm and matter-of-fact. "Were you ever tested to see if you were dyslexic?"

"Yes, twice. They said I wasn't."

Helen nodded. "Okay. So tell me, what parts of reading do you have trouble with?"

"All of it, really. No . . ." She shook her head. If she was going to do this, she had to start in the right place. "I can read some things. Like a notice or something, where there's just a few words. But if it's a whole sheet of paper . . ."

"Well, that's a good start. Maybe it's your confidence as much as anything — that's not unusual. And, of course, you have a very good vocabulary — I've heard you speak. In fact, haven't I heard you speak a little French, and even German?"

"Well, yes," Shelley confessed awkwardly. "Just how to say hello and things like that. I've picked it up when we've had people over for the golf tournaments."

"See." Lisa grinned. "I said you were bright."

Shelley managed a smile. They both seemed to have so much faith in her. Maybe she could do this.

187

CHAPTER TWENTY-FIVE

Kate looked up with a smile as Mike opened the door of the café. "Hi, Mike."

He hesitated in the doorway. "Um . . . It's nearly your closing time. Am I too late for a coffee?"

"Of course not. Have a seat and I'll fetch it over."

"Thank you."

She poured his coffee, and one for herself, and took both over to his table.

"Isn't it great news about the hotel?"

"Yes. Yes, it is." He smiled, but it looked a little forced. "Very good news. You found out very quickly?"

"Debbie met Julia when she went to fetch Amy from school." She stirred a swirl of cream into her coffee. "It's really exciting. Fancy old Arthur's grandson being so wealthy he can afford to buy it just like that."

"Apparently he made his money in real estate in Canada." Mike hadn't touched his coffee. "He and Paul Channing are going into partnership."

Kate frowned. "You don't seem very happy about it."

He sighed heavily. "I don't really think I'd fit into their new plans."

"Whyever not?"

"It's just . . . I'm not very dynamic." He had picked up one of the small packs of sugar — which he didn't take in his coffee — and was twiddling it in his fingers. "It's probably my fault that the owners have invested so little in the place. I haven't been assertive enough."

"You can't blame yourself," she protested, indignant on his behalf.

"I should have insisted on what we needed to do to keep the place looking smart. Used a bit of imagination to come up with new ideas."

She leaned across the table and took his hand. "Mike, don't even think it. You've kept the place running smoothly all these years, in spite of everything. You always turned up a regular profit, even if it wasn't the sort of profit those greedy bean counters want. It isn't your fault that the owners were so short-sighted. Paul and Alex will be much better."

"They've got so many plans. I'm just afraid I'll hold them back."

"Oh, Mike. You mustn't think like that. You've got so much knowledge, so much experience. They'd be lucky to have you. But whatever happens, you must do what's right for you. Whether you stay or leave, it will all work out in the end. You'll see."

He smiled and lifted her hand to his lips, brushing a kiss across the back of her fingers. Just a fleeting touch, but it send a flood of warmth through her veins.

"You're a good friend, Kate."

Yes, a good friend. That had to be enough.

* * *

Mike strolled back along the Esplanade, past the beach shop and the chip shop and the noisy amusement arcade. Some of the shop windows were already dressed up for Christmas, with snow scenes and fairy lights and garlands of holly.

189

Thirty Christmases he'd spent here in Sturcombe Bay — but this could be his last. Maybe . . .

The sky was darkening from the east, but enough light lingered to show the dim line of the horizon. It was cold, but he didn't feel like going back to his empty apartment just yet.

Crossing the road, he turned back down the ramp to the beach. The tide was half out, and the sand crunched beneath his feet. It was a while since he had walked on the beach — ten years, fifteen? He stooped and picked up a pebble. He used to be good at this. With a flick of his wrist he sent it skimming across the lazy waves — once, twice, three times.

He smiled in satisfaction and strolled on to the middle steps. The café was up there, just across the road, and Kate would be finishing clearing up, loading the dishwasher, wiping the tables, sweeping the floor.

Do what's right for you. He hadn't thought for a long time about what was right for him, what he wanted. He hadn't needed to — his life had been settled, content. But since he'd lost Sarah, he'd felt as if he was drifting in a kind of limbo.

But now . . . Maybe the changes to the hotel were his wake-up call. Did he really want to cling on as manager? Or after thirty years, did he want to seize the chance for something else, while there was still time?

In his heart he knew what he wanted. But would Kate feel the same? Or would she think it was too soon, after Sarah? It had only been two years next January. Would she even be interested in being more than his friend, his dance partner?

And if he pushed it, would he risk losing her friendship? That was the last thing he wanted to happen. The music of his favourite waltz drifted through his head. *Don't rush your steps — let it flow naturally.*

He nodded, and turned back towards the hotel.

190

CHAPTER TWENTY-SIX

"Mmm. I think all my Christmases must have come at once."

Jess was perched on the top of a stepladder, hanging baubles on the magnificent Christmas tree at the front of the ballroom. It was twelve feet tall — the angel on top almost touched the ceiling — draped with gold tinsel, hung with large gold and purple baubles, and sparkling with twinkling golden fairy lights.

Glancing down over her shoulder, her mouth twisted into a crooked smile. "Huh! I might have known it would be you."

"Ah, don't come down yet. I'm enjoying the view."

As it was her backside in her slim-fitting black slacks that Paul Channing was admiring, she wasn't going to thank him for the compliment — it would only encourage him.

After making sure the bauble was secure, she started to climb carefully back down. Paul took hold of the stepladder and held it until she reached the bottom.

"Thank you," she rapped sharply. "But there was really no need. I've been up and down this ladder half a dozen times with no problem."

191

"I didn't want you to fall," he explained blandly. "Health and safety. I'm your employer, so I'd be liable for any accidents."

She glared at him, and shifted the stepladder around to the other side of the tree.

"The place is looking good," he remarked, glancing around the room. "Very festive. You've all been working hard."

"Of course, boss. The new owners are slave drivers."

"Make you work from dawn to midnight for tuppence a week?"

"Uh-uh. We start at two in the morning, work our fingers to the bone for thirty-six hours a day knitting Christmas trees, all for a stale sausage roll and half a cup of weak tea."

"A whole sausage roll, eh?" His eyes glinted with amusement. "We'll have to take a look at our wages bill. We're obviously paying you far too much."

Jess was forced to laugh as she climbed the ladder again to hang more baubles.

She had to agree with him that the ballroom was looking good. The walls were all draped with curtain falls of twinkling golden fairy lights. There were half a dozen smaller Christmas trees down each side of the room, their sharp, piney scent already drifting through the air.

In the lounge there was another large tree, and several pots of tall twisted willow branches, sprayed gold and hung with more baubles. A third large tree stood at the foot of the stairs in the reception hall, the walls were festooned with tinsel and pine garlands.

There were fairy lights and a couple of bunches of mistletoe in the conservatory, and the dining room sparkled with gold and silver and pretty table centre-pieces of holly and tall slim scarlet candles.

And outside beside the steps was the biggest tree of all, sixteen feet tall and glowing with multi-coloured lights.

"Phew!" Jess sighed as she climbed down the stepladder for the last time. "That's it. All done."

"You deserve dinner for that."

"Oh?" She eyed him warily.

"At mine. I'll cook for you."

"You can cook?"

"Of course. I live alone. If I want to eat, I have to cook. Or pop down to my mum's," he added with a mischievous grin.

She rolled her eyes. "Which is just three doors down. Convenient."

"You were paying attention."

"Of course. I was taught to have good manners."

"So what do you say? Are you going to let me show off my culinary skills?"

She hesitated. She really ought to say no. Wasn't she supposed to be off men? Especially men like Paul Channing. But somehow the message from the sensible part of her brain hadn't reached the part that formed speech, and she heard herself say, "Okay."

"Great. See you at seven. Number twenty-two, Cliff Road."

And before the sensible part of her brain could catch up he had strolled away to chat to Alex Crocombe.

* * *

Dammit, she must have been mad to agree to this. Had she learned nothing from experience? Another good-looking, arrogant man — just like Glenn.

Although . . . maybe not really like Glenn. It wasn't quite fair to call him arrogant. He was certainly confident, self-assured, but then he had good cause to be. He had reached very close to the top as a professional footballer, and had gone on to forge a second successful career in the equally competitive world of finance.

Whereas Glenn . . . His arrogance had been that of a big fish in a small pond. Why had she put up with him for so

193

long? Five years . . . She'd been pretty down at the time when they had first got together, having been in a nasty accident on her motorbike and fracturing her wrist.

He'd been fun and charming and very, very sexy, and he'd given her a real boost when she'd needed it most. It had been easy to fall in love with him in those early days — and much harder to fall out of it as she had gradually come to see the other side of him.

She shook her head. Tomorrow was the eighteenth of November. The day she had been supposed to marry him. She couldn't even imagine that now — it seemed like another lifetime.

But like an idiot, here she was again. Fun, charming and very, very sexy — far too easy to fall in love with.

Lisa had warned her, Cassie had warned her, Julia had warned her. None of his . . . liaisons — you couldn't really call them relationships — had lasted more than a couple of months. Then it was 'goodbye and thank you, don't leave your toothbrush on the shelf when you go'.

When everyone was pointing and shouting 'shark', it was probably a good idea to stay out of the water.

Instead, she was walking up Cliff Road, past the row of elegant Victorian townhouses. Each had stone steps leading up to their front doors, with bay windows on each side. They were the sort of houses that would have been converted into holiday flats, but she knew that number nineteen was where Lisa's parents lived.

And three doors up was Paul's, with his gleaming Aston Martin on the hard standing at the front.

The front door was painted a traditional glossy dark blue, with a smart brass knocker, but tradition gave way to twenty-first-century technology with the neat security camera on the wall.

She rapped on the knocker, struggling to keep her heartbeat steady as footsteps approached. The door opened. And breathe . . .

He was wearing a charcoal-grey cashmere sweater, smooth across his wide shoulders, the V-neck revealing a smattering of dark hair at the base of his throat, the sleeves pushed up over strong forearms.

"Good evening." Oh, that smile . . . "Come on in."

She wasn't sure what she had expected, but as she stepped into the hall her first reaction was surprise. And disappointment. The walls were covered in a flowery wallpaper, slightly faded and scuffed in places. The paintwork would have once been white but was now yellowed, and the wooden floor was covered with a dull red-and-green runner.

"Ah." She glanced around, a hint of sardonic humour curving her mouth. "Nice place you've got here."

He laughed, untroubled by the barb. "My grandmother's taste. I haven't got round to decorating all of it yet."

"I thought you said you'd lived here for a while?"

"Five years, since Nanna moved down to live with my mum and dad. But as I was only renting it from her, it didn't seem right somehow to make any big changes."

Ah, that was a sensitivity she hadn't quite expected from him. "And now?"

"I've made a start on doing it up how I want it. Come and see the sitting room."

He opened a door on one side of the hall and flicked on the lights. It was a huge room running from the front to the back of the house. Above the ivory-cream marble fireplace the wall was painted a soft pale grey and was hung with a large abstract painting — wild swirls of blue and grey, with a pop of vivid yellow.

On each side of the fireplace the alcoves were a darker grey with gleaming ebony sideboards. There was a television the size of a small cinema screen, two long sofas upholstered in pale-grey leather with grey and yellow scatter cushions, and a large cream wool rug on the pale wooden floor.

The effect was cool and modern, but comfortable. It was a bold thing to do in a Victorian house, but it worked.

195

"I like it," she approved. A large Christmas tree stood in the bay at the front, its white fairy lights winking and making the silver baubles and stars sparkle. She moved over to look out of the window. "You must have a fabulous view from here."

"I do." He moved over to stand beside her. "It's the view I grew up with from my bedroom window."

The moon hadn't yet risen. It was too dark to see the sea, and the high ground on the far side of the bay was invisible against the dark sky. The village, by contrast, was sparkling with lights, along the Esplanade and rising against the surrounding hills.

"You never wanted to move away from Sturcombe?"

"I moved away while I was playing, but I always intended to come back. Why wouldn't I?"

"Why indeed."

"Would you like to see the rest of the house?"

She turned to smile up at him. "Yes, I would."

He was clearly very proud of it. He opened the door on the other side of the hall. "This is the dining room. I haven't touched it yet. I haven't decided what to do with it."

A large walnut dining table dominated the room, gleaming with polish. Clearly Paul wasn't neglecting it, even if he didn't use it. Matching walnut sideboards flanked the marble fireplace, but the faded floral wallpaper and heavy old-fashioned crystal-drop chandelier dated the room badly.

"The furniture looks like it's antique."

"It is. It was bought by my great-grandfather. If I decide to keep it, I'll do the room in a traditional style, like my mum and dad's. When Nanna lived with them she had the dining room, but after she died they put the furniture back and painted the walls dark green. It really works."

"Sounds nice."

"The alternative is to sell all this stuff and go modern. But . . . I don't know. I'm still thinking about it."

"I can see why you don't want to rush. Once it's gone, it's gone."

196

"Right. And there are memories tied up in this room, more so than in the sitting room. Birthday parties, Christmas dinners. My nanna was a great cook." He glanced around the room, smiling. "She lived here all her life — she was born in one of the upstairs rooms. Her grandfather had bought the place when it was first built."

"What about your parents? Did they buy their house to be close to her?"

He shook his head. "My mother's family had owned it for the same amount of time. My mum and dad grew up together."

She smiled with sardonic humour. "Childhood sweethearts?"

"More just friends when they were kids. Then they both went away to different universities and it was when they came back that they got together. They've been married for over thirty-five years now."

"I'm impressed. Mine managed twenty-five, less one day. They were due to celebrate their silver wedding when my dad announced that he was leaving."

"Cold."

"I don't entirely blame him. For my mother, nothing's ever right. She could complain that the sky's the wrong shade of blue. But he didn't exactly go about things in the right way. He'd been seeing someone else, someone a lot younger, for more than a year, and they had a baby on the way."

Paul nodded. "It would have been better if he'd been honest about it."

"It would."

"Anyway, come and have a look upstairs."

* * *

Paul smiled to himself as he climbed the stairs. If you were talking about fabulous views . . . Long, long legs, a very neat backside in tight jeans. Hair the colour of autumn leaves tumbling

197

halfway down her back — hair he could imagine spread across his pillow . . . That was what he called a fabulous view.

He was going to show her his bedroom, though he doubted if he'd be able to persuade her to share it with him tonight. But that was okay — he was enjoying the game.

"That's Nanna's room." He gestured towards the door on the right, but didn't open it. "I haven't started on it yet. It . . . feels kinda weird to go in there."

Jess nodded. "Vicky said the same thing about when she inherited her cottage from her Aunt Molly. She felt really awkward going into her room at first, going through her things. She could still smell her perfume."

"We went in there when Nanna first moved down to live with Mum and Dad, to pick up some clothes and things for her." He laughed, shaking his head at the memory. "We were all afraid she'd suddenly burst in and demand to know what we were doing, messing with her stuff! And the fuss she made . . . Anyone would have thought she was moving to Australia. It took months to persuade her to move — she'd had a couple of falls, and they were really worried about her. Even when she finally agreed to go, she wouldn't let them put in a stairlift for her so she could use one of the upstairs bedrooms. She said it looked like a toilet!"

Jess hooted with laughter. "She sounds like a wonderful old woman."

"She was. We all adored her, though she could be as cantankerous as they come."

"And you still miss her."

"Yes, I do. Anyway, this is my office." He opened the next door.

"Ah." Her eyes danced with amusement. "The hub of your financial empire!" She glanced around, taking in the long desk, the two large computer screens. And the weight bench and rower. "Not just for exercising your brain, then?"

"Unfortunately, when you give up professional sports it's all too easy to let yourself go to seed."

"Hmm." She flickered a speculative glance over him, lightly mocking, and he arched one eyebrow in unspoken question. She returned him a cool smile, and turned away.

It amused him that she'd tease him. None of his past girlfriends would have challenged him like that. Oh boy, he really liked this woman, on a level way beyond the thought of getting her into bed.

"That's the bathroom." He ignored that door. "I haven't bothered with that yet, but I've had an en-suite installed in my bedroom. Which is here." He opened the door and stood aside for her to step through.

He was pleased with how this room had turned out. He'd been inspired by the hotel he'd stayed in when his team had gone on a trip to Jakarta to play a few friendlies during the off-season.

Rich plum-coloured walls and gleaming dark mahogany furniture, and a long built-in wardrobe with frosted glass doors. Three paintings of swirling Indonesian dancers lined up on one wall.

And the bed — big and wide and covered with a plum satin spread. Would she be tempted?

She glanced into the room, then stepped back, but the slight wobble in her smile told him that she had felt the tug. "It's . . . um . . . a big place just for you on your own," she remarked as she preceded him down the stairs.

"I like a lot of space. Besides, as neither Cassie nor Lisa wanted it, if I hadn't taken it on it would have gone out of the family. That didn't seem right."

"No, I can see that."

"Okay, dinner?"

"Sounds like a plan."

* * *

Jess's heart was fluttering alarmingly. That bedroom . . . The image of Paul Channing sleeping in that bed, probably naked, had burned itself into her brain as vividly as if she had seen it for real.

199

As she reached the bottom of the stairs she wondered for one wild moment if she should just run straight out of the front door and keep running until she was a safe distance away from him.

John O'Groats might just be far enough.

"We could eat in the kitchen, if that's okay? The dining room's a bit grand for just the two of us."

"Oh . . . Yes, fine."

That would probably be better. The dining room could well involve candles and a romantic atmosphere.

The kitchen was at the back of the house. It faced north, but she guessed that the wide French doors overlooking the garden would let in plenty of light during the day.

As in the sitting room, he had gone for simple lines and monochrome shades. Inset lights in the ceiling cast a bright glow. The cupboards were all a dark granite-grey with gleaming black granite worktops, and the backsplashes matched the pale-grey marble-tiled floor.

She leaned against the granite-topped central island, watching — fascinated — as he moved efficiently around the kitchen, collecting ingredients — rice noodles, tofu, garlic chives, tamarind puree — and began chopping and boiling and mixing up a sauce.

"What are we having?" she asked.

"Pad Thai. Is that okay?"

"Mmm. One of my favourites."

"Do I get points?"

She laughed. "Oh, I think so."

"Good." Before she realised what he intended, he had put down his chopping knife and whirled her round, and she found herself backed up against a cupboard. His dark eyes glinted with mocking amusement — and something else that she wasn't ready to analyse.

And then his mouth came down on hers, tempting, tantalising, igniting her response.

200

Oh boy, this was kissing. She had closed her eyes and lifted her hands to tangle them in his hair, and all the world seemed to have shrunk into this single point in time and space. His sensuous tongue was swirling deep into the sweetest corners of her mouth, stirring a fever in her blood.

She shouldn't be allowing this to happen — or was it exactly what she had wanted when she had agreed to come here? Her head was all over the place . . . But before she could gather her thoughts, he stepped back, those dark eyes glinting wickedly.

"I thought maybe I'd spend a few points. Seems silly to save them all up. Why don't you take the wine out of the fridge and pour us a couple of glasses."

She stared up at him, not sure if she could even stand, let alone breathe.

He grinned. "Wine. Fridge." He pointed behind her, and she realised that she was leaning against it.

"Fridge. Yes. Wine. Okay."

She turned and dragged open the fridge door, staring blankly at the contents, trying to remember what she was supposed to be doing. Her head cleared slowly and she saw the wine — a Sauvignon Blanc. She grabbed the bottle and closed the door.

"Um . . . Where's your corkscrew?"

"No corkscrew, it's a screw top."

"A screw top? You just lost a point."

"Don't be so hasty. It's a good wine, and the screw top eliminates the risk of spoiling it with a cork taste."

She regarded him through narrowed eyes. "That sounds like an excuse for being a cheapskate."

He put on an expression of affronted dignity. "Would I?"

"I don't know." She was forced to laugh. "Would you?"

"Not with you." For a moment his eyes reflected warm sincerity, then they flashed with wicked humour. "I wouldn't dare."

She snatched a tea towel from the worktop and flicked it at his shoulder. He caught it and pulled her towards him, dropping a kiss on the tip of her nose.

201

"Pour the wine."

She retreated behind the island and perched on one of the stools as her heartbeat slowly returned to normal. He had moved over to the glassy hob and was deftly stirring the noodles, prawns and scrambled egg in a large wok.

This was crazy. She had decided weeks ago that she wasn't going to let herself fall in love with him . . .

Whoa! She wasn't in love with him. Of course she wasn't. Paul Channing was the last man any sensible woman would fall in love with. He was an unashamed player — all his relationships were easy come, easy go. In fact, according to Lisa, he chose his girlfriends on the basis that they had great legs. That was hardly a recommendation.

To distract herself from that unsettling train of thought she picked up the wine bottle, unscrewed the top and filled the two glasses, taking a deep swig of hers.

It was better than she had anticipated, light and slightly sweet, with a faintly fruity, smoky flavour.

"Hey!" Paul chided her, laughing. "Careful, I don't want you to get drunk."

"Don't you?"

"Of course not." Those dark eyes glinted with wicked intent. "When I take you to bed, I want you wide awake and sober. I don't want you claiming I took advantage of you the next morning."

"You think you're going to take me to bed?" she challenged, aware that the slight tremor in her voice betrayed her.

"Or you can take me — I don't mind which. But for now . . . dinner."

His abrupt change of subject caught her still struggling for breath. She was sure he did that deliberately, to keep her off-balance, unable to think straight.

But the plate that he placed before her was a powerful distraction — a fiesta of colours and textures and rich aromas, tantalising her taste buds.

202

"Looks good," she approved, picking up her fork. "Oh, wow!" The subtle blend of flavours on her tongue more than lived up to the promise. "This is fabulous! How did you learn to cook like this?"

"I had a teammate from Thailand — Tommy Thongchai. He loved to cook, and he taught me this and a few other Thai dishes."

"Well, it's really excellent. And before you ask, you get five points."

He laughed, that low, husky laugh that did crazy things to her heartbeat. How did you disentangle sexual attraction from love? Or liking from both? Was it even possible to fall in love with someone you'd only known for a little more than a month?

Or was she just on the rebound? That was a sobering thought. Just because she was sure she was over Glenn didn't mean she wasn't susceptible to a rebound reaction.

* * *

They ate in silence for a while. Paul watched Jess, fascinated by the changing expressions flickering behind her eyes. What was she thinking? Was she remembering that kiss? He hadn't planned it — it had been pure impulse. But if it had taken her by surprise, she hadn't objected. And she had stayed.

He had kissed a lot of women — a *lot*. But none had been as fiery and as sweet as Jessica Bennett. He'd wanted a lot of women, but he'd never wanted one quite as much as he wanted her.

Which was moving into dangerous territory.

"How's the wine?" he asked.

She took another sip. "Actually, it's quite good."

"Told you so."

She laughed. "I was going to award you a point for it, but you just lost it again. Nobody likes a smart-arse."

Oh, he liked that provocative sense of humour. Most of the women he had dated over the years tended to just sweetly agree with everything he said. Which could get rather boring.

"What do you think of the work on the hotel so far?" he asked.

"I had a peek in at the annexe. I like the new tiles for the swimming pool."

"We have to get new covers for the drains. The flat ones can be dangerous. Too much suction apparently. The new ones are dome-shaped."

"Are they starting on the windows and rewiring straight after Christmas?"

"Uh-huh. Then we'll start on upgrading the décor throughout. The main public areas will be first — reception and dining room, and the ballroom. Dan Tuckett's a local guy. He was at school with me and Liam and Tom. We aim to use local labour as much as possible."

"That's good. But if you're going to upgrade, you'll be putting up the prices." Her brow furrowed. "Then what about people like the Wrights? They probably wouldn't be able to afford it."

"Ah, we have a plan." He took a long sip of his wine. "We're going to award our long-term regulars Gold Star Status, with special discount prices which would bring them down to the same price bracket as they're paying now."

"That's a great idea!" Her eyes were bright. He had guessed that she would like that scheme. "What about the Turkey-and-Tinsel groups?"

"We've discussed that with the agents. They also do premium groups, so we'll be looking to upgrade with the new contract."

They carried on chatting as they ate. Talking about the hotel felt like a safe distraction from thinking about where this might be heading. He wasn't ready to look that far ahead yet.

He brought out a tiramisu for dessert. His culinary skills didn't extend to sweet stuff, so he usually kept one in the fridge for when he had a date round for dinner.

They finished the bottle of wine as the conversation moved on to talking about his football career, the places he'd been, and Jess told him about a motorbike trip she'd done through France and Spain.

"We were planning to go on to Morrocco, but the heat was a bit too much. And after fifteen hundred miles on a motorbike, your bum begins to ache!"

He'd intended to suggest a move into the sitting room to settle on the sofa and watch a film, but by the time he glanced up at the clock on the wall it was almost eleven o'clock.

"Oh . . ." Jess's eyes widened in surprise. "I . . . I ought to be going. We have the first of the T'n'T groups arriving this weekend, and it's likely to be a bit full on, getting everything ready."

Instinct told him not to try to persuade her to stay — this had to go at her pace. She gulped down the last of her wine and rose to her feet. He followed her out to the hall, lifted her jacket down from the hook, and helped her to shrug into it. Then he reached for his own overcoat.

"Oh . . . Uh . . . You don't need to . . . It isn't far."

He smiled, shaking his head. "A gentleman always walks a lady home."

She rolled her eyes, but didn't argue.

* * *

Instead of turning down Cliff Road, Jess crossed over to rest her hands for a moment on the rough stone wall. A cold wind was blowing in from the Channel, nipping at her nose and ears, whipping up the waves to thump against the cliffs below.

Over there on the far side of the bay stood the Carleton, spotlit in white, still proud and elegant as she reigned over the small town. It was good that Paul and Alex Crocombe were buying it, saving it from being demolished.

She had seen how important it was to the local community, how it was the focus of the town, sitting up there on its cliff, surrounded by its gardens, watching out over the sea.

And that story old Arthur had told, about its role during the war — she could understand how that had fired people up to defend the place. She had felt it herself, and she'd only been here for a few weeks.

Paul came to stand beside her. "So, are you going to tell me that was a pleasant evening?" he teased, smiling down at her.

"It was."

"Very pleasant? Extremely pleasant?" His face held a doleful expression that she had no trouble in recognising as entirely bogus. "Mildly pleasant?"

Her eyes narrowed. "Your sister told me you used to talk her out of her last red jelly baby when you were kids."

"She did? The traitor! Family aren't supposed to grass up family."

"I'm glad she warned me."

He picked up her hand and lifted it to his lips, brushing a light kiss across her knuckles. "For me, I would say it was an exceptionally pleasant evening. I've rarely enjoyed an evening so much."

She laughed, shaking her head. "Ah, smooth operator."

"Uh-huh." He slid his hand around her waist and drew her closer. She felt his breath warm against her cheek, and then his mouth met hers, warm and firm, his tongue swirling deep inside, exploring all the secret corners within.

A whimpering moan escaped her throat, and she felt the ground beneath her feet slipping away . . .

A shower of spray from a crashing wave startled her out of the moment, and she drew back, her eyes misted. As they cleared, she shook her head, laughing.

"It's much too cold to stand around here," she declared, aiming for a note of casual unconcern but not sure that she'd hit it right. "Come on. If you're going to be a gentleman, let's go."

He laughed. "I could warm you up."

"I think I'll stick with my hot water bottle, thanks."

They strolled on down the hill. Maybe it was the wine, maybe it was the spirit of Christmas already infusing the atmosphere, but she was beginning to feel more relaxed in his company.

Maybe she could take the chance of taking this a little further. It could be fun . . .

CHAPTER TWENTY-SEVEN

They crossed the Memorial Gardens, the fallen leaves crunching beneath their feet, and turned into the hotel's car park. And she stopped dead. There was a large motorbike parked beside the front steps.

Paul slanted her a questioning look. "That's Glenn's bike?"

"It is." Her mouth was a grim line. "What the hell's he doing here?"

"Just go in through the staff entrance," he suggested. "You don't have to see him."

She shook her head, gritting her teeth. "No. I might as well get it over with. Let him know once and for all that I want nothing to do with him."

His eyes were dark as they searched her face. "Is that true?"

"Yes, it is." She could hear the jagged edge in her own voice. "You don't think I'd forgive him after what he did, do you? Not in this phase of the universe."

He nodded. "Look, I know you wouldn't want me to interfere . . ."

"I don't. I can deal with him. Though there might be a few broken bones," she added on a note of acid humour.

"Okay. But I'll be right behind you if you need me."

She smiled grimly and marched up the steps.

Neil, the relief night manager, looked up a little nervously at her entrance. "Ah, Jess. There's someone here to see you."

"I know. Where?"

He pointed to the lounge.

Glenn was sitting in an armchair reading the paper. He tossed it aside and rose to his feet as Jess stalked across the reception hall. "Where have you been?" That old familiar whine when things didn't quite go his way. "I've been waiting hours."

She felt her anger spike like hot lava. "How *dare* you ask where I've been? What I do is absolutely none of your business."

She watched as he struggled to rein himself in. "No. I'm sorry." He held out a hand to her. "Jess . . ."

"That's my name," she snarled. "I'm surprised that you can remember it, among all those other women you've been texting."

"That's all over now. I don't do that anymore." Oh, that little throb of sincerity in his voice — she could almost believe he meant it. "I made a huge mistake and I hurt you. I'm sorry."

"Sorry doesn't cut it. I don't want to hear it."

"Jess . . ." He took a step towards her. "You were in love with me. We were getting married this weekend."

"And am I glad that's not happening!"

"Are you saying you don't love me anymore? Can you really say that?"

"Watch my lips." She could sense Paul standing a few paces behind her.

Glenn shook his head in disbelief, reaching out to grasp her shoulders. "Jess, please, don't say it's over . . ."

"Let me go." Her voice would have etched steel. "Don't touch me."

"Jess, I still love you. And I can't believe you don't love me, not after everything we've been to each other."

208

"Let. Me. Go."

"Jess . . ."

There was a note of anger creeping into his voice, and she felt Paul move up beside her. "I believe you heard the lady." He spoke slowly and clearly. "She would like you to let her go."

Glenn blinked at him as though he hadn't even noticed him before. "Who the fuck are you?" he demanded belligerently.

"I'm a friend of Jess's."

"Oh, yeah? Well, she's my fiancée, so butt out."

"I am *not* your fiancée." Jess could feel the tears of anger stinging her eyes, and blinked them back fiercely. "I haven't been since the moment I saw those dick pics on your phone."

"She's not your fiancée."

Paul's voice was quiet and calm, and for a moment that seemed to work. Glenn stepped back, but then abruptly swung his fist. If Paul's reactions hadn't been lightning quick it might have connected, but he missed by inches.

"Hey, stop!" Jess pushed herself between them. "Glenn, stop it this minute. If you think hitting Paul . . ."

"It's okay, Jess." Paul drew her safely back out of the way. "He isn't going to try that again. Are you?"

Glenn was still glaring at Paul and for a moment it looked as though he would. Neil was hovering behind them anxiously, though he couldn't do much if it came to a proper fight — he was nearer sixty than fifty.

The stand-off lasted for several long seconds, but then Glenn broke the stare, shaking his head and uncurling his fist.

"Look, Jess, can we just talk?" The force had drained from his voice. "Five minutes? Please."

She hesitated, then sighed. "Okay. Five minutes, and that's it." She turned to Paul. "Thank you, Paul. Goodnight."

"I can wait?" he offered.

"That isn't necessary. I'll be fine. Goodnight."

209

He didn't argue with her, but she suspected that he would wait anyway. She watched as he nodded to Neil, and walked out of the front door.

* * *

The night air was sharp with frost. Paul thrust his hands deep into his pockets and strolled over to the low wall along the front of the car park. He sat down, well in the shadow of a large horse chestnut that grew in the corner.

It would be better if the guy didn't see him when he came out — he didn't want to provoke another fight.

He was a good-looking dude, and the black leather motorbike trousers and heavy leather jacket made him look like something out of a Marvel comic.

From what Jess had told him he knew that their relationship had ended badly, but if he was here to plead with her to go back to him what would she do? They'd been together for five years . . .

He waited. Five minutes stretched to ten, then fifteen. He was tossing up between going back inside or giving up and going away when the doors opened and the guy came striding out. He paused to pull on his crash helmet, then swung onto his bike, revved it up, and turned out of the car park.

Paul waited until the noise of the bike's engine had faded, then climbed the steps and walked back in through the front doors. Neil pointed to the terrace. "She's outside," he murmured.

Nodding his thanks, he crossed to the terrace. Jess was standing by the stone balustrade, gazing out over the bay. He moved over to stand close to her, but didn't speak.

After a long time she turned. "He tried to hit you."

"He missed."

"Thank you for not hitting him back. Oh, not because he didn't deserve it." She shook her head, unsmiling. "But that would have been just what he wanted — a good ruck."

210

"I thought as much." He laughed with a touch of dry humour. "When I was playing, I'd often have defenders try to rile me up, try to get me sent off. I learned pretty early how to handle those situations."

Her brow furrowed. "What is it with some men? Thinking they can just say sorry, and carry on as if nothing has happened?"

He shrugged his shoulders. "I guess some of us are just idiots."

"He brought me this." She had a small box in her hand, a jeweller's box. "Earrings." She flipped open the lid to show him.

Diamonds winked in the light spilling from the reception hall. Diamonds in a pretty flower-shaped setting. He knew enough about diamonds to know that they were almost certainly real.

"Bloody diamonds." She snapped the box shut. "They're probably fake. He thought he could give me diamonds and I'd go running back to him. Well, this is what I think of his bloody diamonds." She swung her arm back to throw the box into the sea.

In a swift movement he caught her wrist, folding his other hand over her fist to close it over the box. "Don't do that. If you really don't care about him anymore, it doesn't matter what you do with them. Wear them, sell them, give them to charity."

She laughed — bitterly, angrily, then shading into a wry amusement. "You're right. Why should I throw them away? They're very pretty. I'm surprised he had such good taste. I bet someone else chose them for him. Probably his sister." She dragged in a deep breath, and held out her hand. "Anyway, thanks for . . . Thanks. Goodnight."

He took her hand and held it. "There's a comedy night at the Corn Exchange in Exeter on Wednesday. It's usually a pretty good evening."

She shook her head. "No, thank you." She looked away, then back again. "I'm sorry, but as a . . . relationship, this isn't going to go anywhere. I hope we can still be friends, but . . ."

She drew her hand from his, and with a brisk nod, she turned and walked back across the reception hall to the staff door.

He watched her go. Well, that had been pretty clear. He'd been given the brush-off before, a couple of times, but they really hadn't bothered him much. They'd mostly been just a case of who would say it first.

This time . . . He felt like one of those cartoon characters who'd been hit over the head with a giant hammer.

But it was no surprise. Her ex showing up like that had thrown her for a loop. She was going to need a bit of space. He drew in a long, deep breath, and sighed wryly. He'd give her space, but he wasn't going to give up.

Cassie had warned him that he could have met his match. Maybe she wasn't far wrong.

CHAPTER TWENTY-EIGHT

"That was fun." Kate smiled at Mike as they drove back towards Sturcombe. "I love the Viennese Waltz — or I will when I get the hang of that turn. What did you call it? The flicker?"

"The fleckerl. It is a bit tricky to do, but I'm sure you'll get the hang of it with practice."

"I hope so. I wouldn't want to be holding you back."

"You're not." His eyes were warm. "I really enjoy dancing with you."

"Really?" She felt a glow around her heart. "I'm glad about that."

He turned down Church Road. "How's Debbie?"

"Oh, she's so happy in the cottage!" She sensed that he was deliberately changing the subject. Thank goodness. It was a struggle to keep her feelings under control. "It's just lovely, and so cosy. And it has a garden. Little Amy's over the moon about that. She's already planning on planting nasturtiums and sweet peas in the spring."

"That's nice. Do you miss having them at home?"

"Well, yes, I do. But, of course, Debbie still works in the café with me, and Amy comes after school for her tea."

213

"Ah. It's good that you still get to see so much of her."

Kate felt a tug of sadness. Mike had never had the chance to have a grandchild of his own to bounce on his knee. He'd have made a lovely grandpa.

Music was playing softly, one of the waltzes they had danced to tonight, and she swayed her hands gently in time. "Left foot side, cross behind, side again, cross in front," she recited, going through the movements.

Mike smiled across at her as he drew the car into the kerb outside the café. "You see? You'll get it in no time."

"I'll tell you what, why don't you come in for a cup of tea and we can practise it while it's still fresh in my mind."

As soon as she'd said it she felt a stab of panic. Would he take it the wrong way? Would he think she was being too forward? But he just smiled again.

"That's a good idea."

He turned off the engine and came round to open her door for her — always such a gentleman. She fumbled in her bag for her keys, managing to fit the right one into the lock without shaking too much, and led the way inside.

* * *

Mike followed Kate into the café. As always, it was spotless, the floor and tables were gleaming, the empty glass cabinet on the counter at the back sparkling as she turned on the light.

A door behind the counter led to the stairs up to her flat. He hadn't been up here for several years — not since Sarah died. It hadn't changed much. There were a few more framed photographs — Debbie's wedding, little Amy's first school portrait, with her looking proud as punch in her school uniform.

She was so lucky to have had that. He would have loved to have grandchildren.

"I'll make the tea," Kate suggested. "I . . . don't have anything stronger."

214

"Oh, no. Tea's fine," he assured her quickly. "I'm driving — even though it isn't far."

"Right. Of course."

She disappeared into the kitchen, and he sat down on the sofa, trying to still the thoughts that were spinning in his brain. Nothing could be more inappropriate.

Kate appeared in the doorway again. "Why not put some music on?" she suggested.

"Good idea."

She had a whole shelf of CDs, mostly stuff from the '90s — Elton John, Bryan Adams, George Michael. And Pink Floyd. He smiled as he drew it from the shelf and slid it into the player.

"Hey, do you remember when we went to that Floyd concert. The one at Earl's Court?"

"Of course I remember." Her eyes were bright. "It was amazing."

"It must have been . . . what? '94, '95?"

"October '94."

Oh, how young they'd been then. He and Sarah, and Kate with her Terry, bopping to the music, dazzled by the light show. Now Terry and Sarah were both gone, leaving him and Kate . . .

"Here we are." Kate came back with two cups. "As you like it — milk, no sugar."

"Thank you."

He slid the CD into the player and the music started, the long slow psychedelic introduction. He sat down, sipping his tea. Had it really been so long ago when the four of them had driven up to London, so excited to see their favourite band? So many memories . . .

They listened to several tracks, then as the golden guitar solo on the third track faded away he smiled across at Kate.

"Do you have something we could waltz to?"

"Oh, yes." She jumped up and crossed to the CD player, ejecting the Floyd album. "Amy loves *Sleeping Beauty* — would 'Once Upon a Dream' work?"

"Yes, that's perfect."

It felt so easy, so natural, taking her in his arms and beginning to move to the music. She was concentrating on her steps, and he had to remind himself to do the same. That subtle, feminine perfume was drugging his mind.

He glanced around the room. Sarah had come here often. She would have sat on the sofa where he had just been sitting himself. He could almost see her sitting there, smiling the way she did, nodding her approval.

She was my best friend. What could be better?

Yes, Sarah would want him to be happy again, to find love again. She wouldn't want him to spend the rest of his life alone.

For a long moment, he hesitated. It was a risk . . . "Kate, I . . ." He drew in a steadying breath. "You're my friend and I . . . I don't want to lose that. But . . . do you think there's a chance . . . Could we be more than friends?"

Those soft brown eyes gazed up into his. For a long moment he thought she was going to push him away, tell him not to be ridiculous, but then a slow, sweet smile curved her pretty mouth.

"I . . . I think so. I'd like that."

Warmth flooded through his veins, and he bent his head to brush his lips over hers. He felt a small tremor run through her slim body. Those neat, hardworking hands gripped his shoulders, and her flowery, feminine perfume drifted into his senses.

And a small voice in the back of his head seemed to whisper, *What took you so long?*

CHAPTER TWENTY-NINE

"Hi, Mum."

Kate was swaying and humming along to the lilting melody of 'Fairytale of New York' as she hung gold and silver baubles on the small Christmas tree she had set up in the corner of the café. She turned to greet Debbie with a wide smile.

"Hello there, my luvver. Is it still raining?"

"Pouring." Debbie laughed as she paused in the doorway to shake out her umbrella. "Still, I suppose after the lovely summer we've had we can't really complain."

"Not at all."

"I made some of the cinnamon rolls and some more apple puffs." She lifted the box out of her shopping bag.

"Ah, that's good. Those apple puffs went really well yesterday."

Debbie dropped a quick kiss on her mother's cheek as she passed through to the kitchen. "How's Mike?"

Kate felt the heat rise instantly to her cheeks. "Oh . . . fine."

Debbie's eyes widened. "Mum, you're blushing."

"No, I'm not." She knew she was blushing harder. "I was cooking. It's hot in the kitchen."

217

"Oh? Are you sure you haven't got something to tell me?"

"Of course not. You sound like you're *my* mum."

Debbie laughed. "All right. If you want to keep your secrets . . ."

"There's no secrets. We've just . . . been dancing a few times. And I've enjoyed it."

"Well, that's good."

Except there were secrets — secrets she wasn't ready to tell yet. Not even to her daughter. Secret hopes, secret dreams — secrets of kissing Mike Slade.

She'd always been fond of him, but as a friend, her best friend's husband. And after Sarah died they'd mourned her together. It had never occurred to her to think of him in any other way — until that night when they'd danced at Debbie's wedding.

And it had never occurred to her that he might think of her in any other way. But now she felt as giddy as a girl, wondering if she should dye the grey streaks out of her hair, twisting and turning in front of her bedroom mirror to check on the wrinkles and lumps the years had deposited.

Last night when she went to bed she had picked up the photo of her and Terry she kept on her bedside table. So young, they'd been. Untouched by time, laughing into the camera, all their lives to look forward to.

But time had left him there in the past, while it had swept her on like a leaf floating in a river, passing a single spot on the bank and swirling away downstream, never to go back.

She'd missed him so much for all these years, focussing on bringing up their daughter and running her café. And now . . . She'd always miss him, no one could take his place. But maybe there could be . . . another place . . .

"Anyway, if you're not going to tell me your secret, I'll tell you mine."

"Oh?" Kate turned to stare at her daughter. Her eyes were bright, and there seemed to be a glow about her. A very special glow. "You're . . . ?"

218

"Yes!"

"Oh, my love!" Kate put the box of baubles down on the counter and threw her arms around the girl. "You really are? You're sure?"

"Absolutely sure. I brought the test stick along to show you."

"And Bill?"

"He's over the moon and somewhere out beyond the stars. We were hoping, but we didn't really expect it to happen so quickly."

"Oh . . . Oh . . . I'm crying." Kate brushed her hand across her face as the tears poured down her cheeks. "I'm so happy! Have you told Amy yet?"

"Not yet. Once she knows, the whole town will know!"

Kate laughed, dabbing her eyes. "And you? Are you keeping well?"

"Never better. You know what an easy time I had with Amy. I'm keeping my fingers crossed that this time will be the same."

"Let's hope so." Kate held up her hand with crossed fingers. "Anyway, come and get a cup of coffee and let's sit down for a minute while it's quiet. Oh, maybe not coffee?"

Debbie smiled. "Tea will be fine."

Kate brought two cups of tea and they settled at a table by the window.

"I saw Jess up at the school gates," Debbie remarked. "She'd brought Robyn and Ben." She laughed. "Ben's getting a bit impatient about not being allowed to walk to school on his own yet."

"Well, he's almost eight, and it isn't far. It's quite safe, especially in the winter. I always let you go on your own from when you were seven."

"Yes, but you had the café to run. Anyway, Jess was telling me they've got some interior designers coming down to look at the hotel. I'm dying to see what they come up with."

219

"Yes . . ." Kate really wanted to be as excited about it as everyone else seemed to be, but she couldn't help thinking about Mike. There weren't many jobs for a middle-aged hotel manager within easy reach of Sturcombe.

Which would mean that he'd have to move away. Just when she was starting to feel something special for him.

"Anyway . . ." She managed a bright smile, pushing thoughts of Mike aside for now. "When's the baby due?"

"June. Not very good planning, I'm afraid."

Kate raised one eyebrow in question.

"Right at the start of the summer season. Just when you'll be getting really busy."

"Oh, don't worry about that. I'll manage. You did when I was poorly this summer."

"Well, yes, but . . ."

"But what? If you're going to tell me I can't manage on my own at my age, you can just drink up your tea and go, my girl."

Debbie laughed. "No, of course not. I know you'll manage. And you'll probably be able to get someone in to help over the school holidays — that's the busiest time, and there's always sixth-formers wanting to earn a few quid."

"Yes, that's something to think about. But don't you bother about it. Just look after yourself — and my new granddaughter."

"Or grandson."

"Oh, yes." Kate smiled happily. "A grandson."

CHAPTER THIRTY

"Okay, folks. They're here. All hands on deck. Cue music."

The buzz had been building up for the past couple of weeks, with the decorations going up, the deliveries of heroic quantities of food and drink, the scramble to get all the rooms ready.

"Show time!" Jess pressed the button on the stereo and the jaunty sound of some cheesy Christmas song chimed out.

The first coach load of Turkey-and-Tinsel guests, fifty-two of them, stepped down from the bus and piled up the steps to the reception hall, gazing around in delight at the glittering decorations.

Most of them wouldn't see fifty again, though there were some younger ones who'd come with their parents. And they were clearly intent on having a good time. Santa hats and reindeer antlers were much in evidence, and so were jolly Christmas jumpers with elves and snowmen and Christmas trees.

Whether or not they had known each other before boarding the coach, they were already laughing loudly and joking with each other as they formed a very British queue at the desk to book in and collect their room keys, singing along and jigging to the music as they waited.

Alex had welcomed them all at the door, and was now charming them with his warm Canadian accent. Lisa had come down to help, and she, Jess and Vicky worked in a coordinated relay to get everyone booked in, handing them the key cards for their rooms and inviting them to the Welcome Reception in the ballroom with mince pies and mulled wine.

At last all the guests had been shepherded up to their rooms. "Phew!" Jess breathed a sigh of relief. "So, that's a Turkey-and-Tinsel group!"

She was glad of the distraction. It was a week since she'd seen Paul. Although she was sure she'd done the right thing in telling him she didn't want a relationship with him, she wasn't so sure of her own resolve to stick to that.

Fortunately, he was away. He'd gone to Africa to make a television programme about the development of youth football in some of the poorest areas of Botswana. He'd be gone for another couple of weeks.

"Well done, everyone." Alex came over to the desk, beaming. "Great teamwork. We should have a little while before they start coming down for their mulled wine so I think we have time for a cup of coffee."

* * *

"The radio sah . . . *said* it was going to rain." Shelley shook her head. "Why is that word written 's-a-i-d' when it's pronounced as if it's 's-e-d'?"

Helen Channing smiled. "That's just one of the oddities of the English language, I'm afraid."

"There are so many oddities." Shelley sighed impatiently. "How can anyone ever learn them?"

"By taking it a little bit at a time. Carry on. You're doing great."

Shelley's mouth thinned in frustration. It was too hard. It reminded her of how she had struggled when she was at school. Back then she would shout or throw something, run out of the classroom, burst into tears. But now Helen was waiting patiently, her finger on the line.

"Remember the rule for when there's an 'e' at the end of a word?"

She nodded. "It changes how you say the 'i'. So that's dek . . ."

"No. Think about it in context. What do you think it's likely to be?"

"Dek . . . Deki . . . Oh, this is ridiculous." She flopped back in her chair. It felt as if she was sinking in a wave of misery. "It's no good. I can't do it."

Helen patted her hand. "Okay. Shall we take a break? Let's have a cup of coffee."

"Thanks." Shelley closed her eyes for a moment, then opened them again. "Why won't you let me pay you for lessons?"

Helen laughed. "Because if you pay me, you'll think it's okay to give up when it feels like it's getting too hard. If you're not paying me, you'll feel like you owe me — so you won't give up, will you?"

Shelley laughed. Helen was spot on. "Most people would say it was the other way round."

"You're not most people."

Shelley glanced down at the book in front of her. "Do you really think I can do this?"

"If you decide to."

Decide . . . Ah, *stupid!* "It's decided."

"That's right."

Shelley looked at her sharply. "You did that deliberately, didn't you? To give me a clue."

Helen just laughed.

"But how are you supposed to know if the 'c' sounds like a 'k' or an 's'?"

"Well, mostly if it's before an 'i' or an 'e' it will sound like an 's' — but that isn't a hard-and-fast rule."

"It's a crazy language. It must be really hard for foreign people to learn it. There's so many words that look the same

223

but sound different — like that one we did yesterday, 'cough' and 'though'."

"But you have an advantage. You already have a good vocabulary, so you have a whole store of words that you can guess at when you see them written down. I bet by Christmas you'll be reading a whole book in a week."

"I'll try. And then . . ." She drew in a slow breath. "I'm going to learn to write."

Helen brought the coffee mugs over and set them down on the table. "Good on you. You'll do it. I have every faith in you."

Shelley felt the tears pricking at her eyes again, but this time they weren't of anger or frustration. She could well imagine how much the children Helen had taught at Fowey Road Primary School had loved their deputy headmistress. She already loved her herself.

* * *

One of the guests had left a magazine in their room when they'd checked out. People often did that, and Shelley had always just thrown them away. But in the past few weeks, since she had started working with Helen Channing, she had taken to flicking through them and picking out bits she could read — usually the picture captions and the short reviews on cosmetics and household items.

This one had a double-page spread of tips on how to prepare for the perfect Christmas. She turned the page, and found a question-and-answer interview with an Olympic athlete, and though the paragraphs were longer, she found that she could recognise most of the words.

Sitting down on the edge of the bed, she turned another page to an article about Agatha Christie, the mystery-novel author. To her surprise, she learned that she'd had a house no more than a few miles from Sturcombe. It was so absorbing that she didn't notice the minutes passing — didn't

224

even notice that she'd read three whole pages with barely a hesitation.

It was voices in the corridor outside which brought her quickly to her feet.

"All these light fittings must be replaced, of course. There should be something bronze, baronial." The woman's voice was cool, confident. "Nothing itsy-bitsy."

"Yes. Baronial."

Alex! Swiftly she looked around for a place to hide, but before she could move he appeared in the doorway.

"Oh. Hello, Shelley."

"Hello."

She hadn't seen him since the Remembrance Day parade down in the Memorial Gardens. He'd been there with his grandfather, who'd been proudly wearing a whole row of medals on his chest.

She'd somehow managed to avoid him ever since. Now it was like sticking her finger in the electric socket. She drew in a sharp breath, feeling a sizzle run down her spine, bringing a rush of heat to her cheeks.

"Ah, this is one of your standard guest rooms, I take it?" The woman stepped past him into the room and cast a critical look around. Her eyes swept past Shelley as if she wasn't even there. "It's a good size, and I like the high ceiling and the large window."

She turned to Alex, her lashes fluttering as she laid a possessive hand on his arm. "Thank you so much for inviting me to see this place," she purred. "It's quite amazing. I can really *feel* it, the history, the dignity."

Who was she? His new girlfriend? Of course, she was just the sort he'd go for. Smart, elegant, almost as tall as him — aided by a pair of deadly spiked heels. She was as thin as a whippet, with a bell of dark, glossy hair, dead straight and cut with precision to the exact line of her jaw. Her vivid lime-green talons perfectly matched her flowing lime-green trouser-suit.

225

"I see something bold and vibrant in here." She swept her arms wide. "A sharp Citrus Daze with a brave line of Imperial Purple slashing diagonally across the wall." She gestured wildly with her hand to demonstrate. "A statement."

Shelley blinked. Citrus and *purple*?

To her relief, Alex looked less than impressed. "A statement — yes." He glanced across at Shelley with a smile. "How are you? I haven't seen you for a while."

"Oh, I've been around." She shrugged, attempting an air of casual unconcern. "Busy."

The woman spared Shelley a perfunctory glance then swept past her to the en-suite bathroom. "Now this will all have to be ripped out and replaced. Everything must be black. Very dramatic. With gold fittings."

"Ah, Shelley, this is Georgina. She's an interior designer."

Oh, of course. "Hello." She tried a smile.

All she got in return was a brief, cold look before the woman turned back to Alex. "I see a whole concept. Something medieval — a nod back to the history of the building, but in a way that says twenty-first century."

"It's Victorian."

"Ah, yes. But it can be every period." She trilled with laughter. "I can't wait to begin mood boarding my ideas."

Heaven help us! Behind the woman's back, Shelley rolled her eyes. She didn't intend for Alex to see her, but he did, and the slight crease of his mouth suggested that he was thinking the same thing.

Now the woman had commandeered all his attention again. "I think you should show me some of the other rooms," she purred, tucking her hand into his arm. "Your . . . um . . . assistant can take notes."

Georgina gestured with a flick of her fingers towards the doorway where Lisa was standing. There was nothing to read on her face but a taut smile that didn't reach her eyes.

The interior designer's voice was echoing down the corridor as she drew Alex along with her. "I have to tell you . . ."

226

From the horror in her tone, it was clearly something appalling. "I saw a *dog* in here earlier."

"Yes." His voice was very level. "We're a dog-friendly hotel."

"Oh?" How could you tell from someone's back view that they were wrinkling their nose in distaste? "I really don't think that's a good idea. None of the top-class hotels would ever permit dogs."

"Really? I think there are actually quite a few. The Savoy does, I believe. Besides, I'm getting one myself soon."

Lisa's face cracked as she suppressed her laughter. "Don't worry," she whispered to Shelley. "I don't think it's very likely that she'll be getting the contract."

"Thank goodness for that." Shelley shook her head. "Yellow and purple, in here? I couldn't think of anything more hideous."

"But she's the very latest thing, *dahling*!" Lisa's eyes danced. "She's worked with *so* many celebrities, and they've just *loved* her work."

Shelley giggled. "I'm sure. Aren't you supposed to be taking notes?"

"I'm not bothering — we won't be hiring her. What's that you're reading?"

"Oh . . . um . . ." She quickly tried to hide the magazine behind her back, but realised that there was no point. "Just . . . The guests left it here when they checked out. They didn't want it so I thought there was no harm in me having a look."

"Of course there isn't." Lisa smiled. "What's in it?"

"Just . . . a couple of articles. An interview with that girl who won a gold medal at the Olympics."

"Oh, yes. I remember her. Was it interesting?"

"Yes. And there's a thing on Agatha Christie."

There was a warmth in Lisa's eyes. "Mum said your reading was coming on by leaps and bounds. I knew it would once you got started."

227

"Well, I . . . Your mum's been really lovely, the way she's been teaching me. She's so patient. She hasn't made me feel stupid at all. And I've been practising as much as I can."

"That's good. I think we've got a couple of Agatha Christie paperbacks in the library here, if you'd like to try one. They're not too long. They'd be a good place to start."

"I . . ." She drew in a breath. "Yes, thank you. I'll try."

Lisa nodded. "And how would you feel about trying out the receptionist job? I know you weren't keen before, but now . . . ? There'll be plenty of time for you to train while we're closed for the renovations. What do you say?"

"I . . . um . . ."

"There's going to be a new uniform." Her eyes danced. "Citrus and purple."

Shelley laughed, then drew in a long breath. "Okay, I'll think about it. I'm still a bit slow, though, and some words are just so stupid the way they're spelled. Like, is it even 'spelled' with an 'e-d' at the end, or 'spelt' with a 't'?"

"I think it can be either. You're right, though. English is quite hard. But you're doing great with it. By the time we're ready to reopen after the renovations, you'll be off and running."

"Well, maybe," Shelley conceded doubtfully. "I'll do my best."

"That's all anyone can do."

CHAPTER THIRTY-ONE

"I don't think we need to discuss the Bellingham proposal."

"The lovely Georgina? No, I think not. Of the other two, I tend to favour Verney and Woolfe."

Mike was only listening to the discussion between Paul and Alex with half an ear. He knew he ought to be excited about all the new plans for the Carleton — everyone else was — but somehow it seemed to be passing him by.

The hotel had been his whole life for thirty years, and he had loved it. He still did, but . . . What else was there out there for him? He was fifty-seven years old. Surely not too old to make a fresh start. What was that saying? 'Don't wait until you retire to start living your life.'

Losing Sarah had taught him the truth of that.

He glanced around the small office that had been his retreat for so many years. Why had he never noticed before how dull it was in here? No view, no sunlight. Sarah used to bring in flowers from the garden to put on his desk, to brighten the place up a bit, but since she'd been gone he'd never bothered.

No, he wouldn't miss this room.

Paul and Alex were discussing saunas and gym equipment, studying a page on Paul's laptop. "This company do a good range — good value and good after-sales service. I've used some of their stuff. It's sound."

Alex leaned over to look. "Yeah, seems okay. You're the expert there. I'll leave it to you to draw up a list of what we need and negotiate a price with them."

"Right. Mike, have we got the quotes in for replacing the guest lift?"

"Oh, yes, they're here." With an effort he pulled himself back into the meeting, shuffling through the papers on his desk. "This is the one we've used before."

Alex took the stapled sheets from him. "Hmmm. Would you recommend that we stick with them?"

"Not necessarily." Mike shook his head. "We've had some issues with them in the past regarding repairs. They've let us down a few times."

"Ah. What about the others?"

Mike handed over the tenders, and watched as the two men poured over the details, occasionally grunting or making a comment.

Do what's right for you. It was a big risk, and he'd never really taken a risk in his life. He'd always settled for safe, comfortable. But he felt this was something he had to do.

"Okay, so are we agreed on that?" Paul tossed one of the tenders onto the desk, and held up the other one. "This is the one we'll go with."

"Agreed." Alex nodded. "Right, is there anything else?"

"Er . . . just one thing." Mike opened a drawer in his desk and took out the letter he had written earlier. "This."

Alex frowned as he took it from him. "What is it?"

"My resignation."

"*What?*" Paul stared at him in shock. "Why?"

Mike smiled gently. "Everything's changing, so it seems like it's the right time for me to go. You can make a fresh start with a new manager, along with everything else."

"But . . . Look, we don't want you to go." Alex glanced at Paul, who nodded his confirmation. "You *are* this place. You've been here so long, you know it inside out."

"Exactly." Mike laughed. "I've been here so long I feel as if my backside's permanently rooted to this chair. It's time for me to try something else. I'm planning — I'm hoping — to stay in Sturcombe, and I'd be more than willing to help you through the transition, and to be around at any time if you need me."

Alex sat back in his seat, puffing out a sharp breath. "Well, I . . . We don't want you to go, of course. I hope you don't feel that we're putting you out to grass."

"Of course not. It's entirely my decision." Suddenly he felt a lightness inside him, like a seagull soaring in the high blue sky. "I wish you every success. The old place will be starting a new chapter. And so will I."

"Right . . . Well, okay. We have to agree, of course. Maybe we could meet again later in the week to . . . sort out dates and things. And thank you." Alex held his hand out over the desk. "I have the feeling that if it hadn't been for you, the old place wouldn't have still been here for us to take over."

"Oh, I wouldn't say that."

"No, I know you wouldn't."

* * *

Later that evening Mike was sitting in the kitchen of Kate's café, watching her bake. It was barely a quarter of the size of the hotel's kitchen, but was just as bright and spotless and well-equipped.

She had made two trays of scones and wrapped them in clingfilm, loading them into the large fridge ready to go into the oven in the morning. Now she was kneading a block of pastry.

"Do you do this every night after you've closed the café?" he asked.

She smiled. "Most nights. It depends on what we need in the café. Only for about an hour."

"After you've been on your feet all day?"

231

"It's not a problem. I like cooking."

"You should go on one of those bake-off shows on television."

She laughed, shaking her head firmly. "Oh no. That's not for me."

He liked the way she laughed — free and musical. And the way she worked, neatly and efficiently, no wasted movements. He crept round behind her, swiped a corner of pastry, and popped it into his mouth.

"Mmm, scrummy."

She slapped his hand away playfully. "Hey, hygiene standards. You'll get me shut down."

"There's no one here to see but us." He wrapped his arms around her waist from behind and nuzzled into her neck. "We can do whatever we like."

"Not while I'm cooking," she scolded.

He pulled a disappointed face, making her laugh again.

"Mind you . . ." She gave him a teasing glance, "I've nearly finished. I just need to wrap this and put it in the freezer. And do the washing up."

"The washing up can wait. Why don't we go upstairs and watch television? Or something . . ."

"Or something?"

"Something a little more interesting than watching television, maybe?"

She felt a little fizz run through her veins. Something interesting — at their age? Well, why the hell not? They were only in their fifties, for heaven's sake! She turned her head to kiss the side of his neck. "That sounds like a good idea."

"I thought so."

It took her very little time to wrap the pastry dough in clingfilm and pop it into her big freezer. Then she splashed her hands under the tap to clean off the flour, wiped them quickly on a towel, and with those soft brown eyes gleaming, she took his hand, led him through the small lobby and up the stairs to her flat.

232

CHAPTER THIRTY-TWO

"Phew!" Shelley puffed out a breath that floated like a white cloud in front of her face. "I can't believe these crowds!"

The street was thronged with shoppers too intent on their Christmas lists to pay attention to where they were going. She stepped aside as a harassed mum with a small child and a pushchair steered erratically towards her.

The Christmas lights had been switched on and were twinkling above their heads — snowflakes and angels and Christmas trees — and every shop was festive with tinsel and baubles, Santas and reindeer sleighs. The excitement of the season fizzed in the air like champagne.

Jess laughed. "Only two weeks to go to Christmas. I used to live in Bristol, and it was just as bad — probably worse!"

"I've never been to Bristol," Shelley confessed. "Actually, I've never been to Exeter before either."

"Never?" Jess raised her eyebrows in surprise. "You've lived in Sturcombe for three years."

"I know, but somehow I never got round to it. There was never anything much I needed to buy. But I've really enjoyed today. Thanks for bringing me."

233

"Ah, shopping's always more fun with a friend. Hey, look!" She darted over to a dress-shop window. "Now, that would be perfect for you."

"Oh, I don't know." Shelley frowned at the price tag. "It's a bit expensive."

"But you have to have it. You'll look fabulous in it."

"It is pretty." It was a light turquoise blue, with thin shoulder straps and three floating asymmetric layers of chiffon falling to just above the knees. "But I've never paid that much for a dress before."

"If you don't buy it, I will. Come on."

With a wry smile Shelley followed her into the shop.

This was another first. She'd never even been in a proper dress shop before. But she did want something nice to wear for the hotel's Christmas party.

In previous years she'd always worn the same dress — a pink flowered cotton one she'd bought in a charity shop in London for five pounds. But Jess had already dived into the rack and pulled out this one.

"Here. I think this is your size. Give me your bags and go and try it on."

The changing room was guarded by a dragon . . . Well, okay, just a middle-aged woman in the shop's uniform, who actually smiled at her. "There's an empty cubicle down at the end there."

"Thank you."

Stepping into the cubicle, she pulled the curtain across, hung up her jacket and quickly slipped out of her clothes. Fortunately, the dress had a side zip so it was easy to do up. And then she turned and looked at herself in the long mirror.

Oh . . .

Her eyes looked bluer, and the chiffon layers skimmed over her figure in a way that seemed to enhance her curves and make her legs look longer. And as she moved, it drifted around her like blue smoke.

What would Alex think of it? Her heart fluttered. Alex . . .

234

She'd seen little of him since he'd bought the hotel. Apart from that one time when he'd been showing the interior designer round, he rarely came upstairs, and she had little need to go downstairs. On the few times they had encountered each other, he had been pleasant, friendly, but no more than that.

Maybe she'd just been imagining that he'd wanted something more. She probably had.

Anyway, the dress wasn't just about Alex. She regarded her reflection in the mirror, tilting up her chin. It was a symbol, a statement that she had left her old life behind, that she was making a place for herself in the world. An 'up yours' to all the people who'd called her thick, bad, worthless.

Ten minutes later, with her shopping bags a little heavier and her bank account a little lighter, she and Jess were out in Princesshay again.

"Shall we take a look at the Christmas Market?" Jess suggested. "It's not far."

"Right." They walked down a narrow alley, past the remnants of ancient Roman walls and past the tiny church on the corner that was nearly as old. Turning the corner, they came to the open-air market on the Cathedral Green.

Shelley stared at it in amazement. The place was buzzing. A hundred or more wooden Bavarian huts were clustered around the great medieval Cathedral, its ancient stonework glowing gold against the twilight sky.

Jess took her arm and they plunged in, wandering through the throng between stalls selling pottery, scented candles, jars of honey. Dozens of mingled aromas drifted on the air — spicy mulled wine and roasting chestnuts, crispy potato pancakes with melted cheese, sizzling bratwurst sausages slathered in honey mustard, and more.

"Oh, look at these!" Jess darted to one of the stalls which was selling carved wooden toys. She picked up a small puzzle box. "They'd be perfect for the kids."

"Oh, yes." Shelley bent to examine the display. "I was looking for something for Noah. This would be perfect."

235

They strolled on, pausing from time to time to look at a display of silver jewellery or embroidered blouses. A little further along they came to a stall selling lovely hand-painted silk scarves.

"Oh, I want to get one of those for Helen Channing." Shelley glanced quickly at Jess. "Do you think she'd like one?"

"Of course. They're lovely."

Shelley chose one in subtle shades of green, and handed it to the stallholder. "I'd like this one please."

She wasn't bothered by the cost — this was for Helen. The stallholder wrapped the scarf in tissue paper and handed it over as Shelley tapped her bank card on the terminal.

"Right. I don't know about you, but I could really do with a sit down and a cup of coffee," Jess declared.

"Good thinking. There's a café over there. Let's go and see if we can find a table."

CHAPTER THIRTY-THREE

The sleek dark-green Aston Martin skimmed around the roundabout at the top of Haytor Avenue and continued along the main road, before turning left down Church Road.

After almost a month under the hot African sun, Paul was craving a nice cold English beer. The Smugglers would be just about closing, but he could get a bottle of Doom Bar at the hotel.

And just maybe, Jess might be around. He was a little surprised at how much he had missed her.

It had been a good trip — interesting and worthwhile — but as always, he was glad to be home. He turned into the hotel car park and switched off the engine, unfastened his seatbelt and climbed out.

Neil, the relief night manager, was strolling out of the dining room with a plate of sandwiches as Paul walked in. The sounds of festive fun were spilling out of the ballroom.

"Wow! This lot are certainly getting into the Christmas spirit," he remarked.

Neil laughed. "And this is only their first night. They're nearly all in there. There's a few drinking coffee in the conservatory, and some have gone out for a walk. It's the same every year — each crowd gets wilder than the last one as it gets closer to Christmas. Though I'm amazed they can move after eating all that dinner. I've got a bit of the sirloin in these if you want one, or there's some of Chef's spiced ginger pudding and toffee sauce left."

"Mmm, I can smell it." He sniffed the air appreciatively. "I'm surprised there's any leftovers at all."

He strolled over to the small bar in the lounge, nodded a greeting to the half-dozen guests still lingering in there, and grabbed a bottle of Doom Bar. Snapping off the top, he savoured the spicy aroma of hops and malt as he poured the amber ale into a glass.

"Is this the last lot?" he asked Neil, returning to the reception desk.

"Last but one. These leave on Sunday, then the next lot are here Monday to Thursday of next week. Then that's it."

"And then it's full steam ahead for the renovations. Thanks," he added as he took the proffered sandwich. "How's it going in the annexe?"

"Pretty much nearly done. It'll be ready for Saturday."

"That's good." His sister's wedding. It would have been a shame if they'd had to hold the reception somewhere else, with the hotel full of excitable T'n'T guests.

Then Alex had come up with the excellent idea of getting the large upstairs room in the annexe — which was going to be the hairdressers, spa and gymnasium — finished except for the fitting-out, and using that.

There was another surge of hilarity from the ballroom. "They're supposed to be going down to the Eden Project tomorrow," Neil remarked dryly. "I wonder how many of them will wake up in time?"

"Or wake up with the hangover from hell."

Neil finished his sandwich. "Anyway, I need to do the night audit."

"Can I come and take a look?" Paul asked. "With Mike leaving I'll be getting more involved, so it would be useful to see how it's done, in case I need to step in at any time."

"Sure." Neil picked up the rest of the sandwiches, and they both strolled through into the back office.

* * *

"Wow! It does look fantastic." Jess leaned closer to study the images on Cassie's laptop. "But it's going to be freezing!"

Cassie laughed. "Well, it's on the Arctic Circle, so I expect it will be."

"Robyn's going to love it," Julia remarked.

"So will I. I've been dying to see the Northern Lights."

"It's really nice that you're taking Robyn with you."

"We couldn't have left her out," Cassie responded with a fond smile. "It's important that she doesn't feel that me and Liam getting married changes things between her and her daddy. Anyway, we'll have a proper honeymoon next summer, when she's had a chance to settle. I'm thinking Hawaii." She laughed. "Liam's thinking Kazakhstan to see the Przewalski's horses."

Julia rolled her eyes. "That would be interesting."

"Wouldn't it? Actually, I'm quite keen to see them too, but maybe not on our honeymoon."

The Ellis's family sitting room was warm and cosy, a log fire burning in the grate. Diane was knitting, her feet up on the old cabin trunk that served as a coffee table, Hobo's head resting on her lap. The three men had gone up to Dartmoor to help with the early lambing and were likely to be out all night.

"Anyone for another cup of coffee?" Julia asked as Cassie closed the laptop.

"Not for me, thanks." Jess glanced at her watch. "It's gone eleven — I'd better be getting back. See you soon."

"Goodnight, then." Julia hugged her. "Mind how you go."

Jess laughed. "Like I've got a long walk."

"But the weather's vicious out there. I wouldn't be surprised if we got snow."

"What, down here? I didn't think it ever snowed in South Devon."

"Oh, it does occasionally, and not just on Dartmoor." Diane's needles clicked as she turned a row. "We had a good fall a few years ago, though that was in January."

"It would be great to have a white Christmas." Jess shrugged herself into her coat, wrapped her thick woolly scarf around her neck, and pulled her bobble hat well down over her ears. "Right, I'm ready to face whatever the weather can throw at me."

The weather certainly was vicious. A damp, icy wind was blowing in from the North Atlantic, the sort that seemed to hit you in the face no matter which way you turned.

Fortunately, it was not much more than a hundred yards to the hotel. As she turned into the car park, she smiled at the tall Christmas tree beside the steps, its coloured lights winking red, gold, blue and green.

And then she saw the sleek dark-green car parked in the corner. Dammit, Paul was back. She hadn't realised it would be today. She wasn't ready . . .

But she didn't have to see him yet, she decided. Walking quickly, she crossed to the staff entrance, let herself in, and climbed the stairs to the staff quarters on the top floor.

All was quiet up here. There were only a few live-in staff at the moment, and they would probably have already gone to bed. She wasn't ready for bed yet, though.

In the staffroom she made herself a cup of coffee, then flopped into the least lumpy armchair and flicked on the television. A bit of light comedy would be a distraction.

She'd had plenty to distract her this past month. They'd been hectic, with the Turkey-and-Tinsel groups filling the hotel. There had been endless little wrinkles to sort out — extra pillows requested, a dripping tap which had turned out to simply not have been turned off properly, queries about what time the excursion to Exeter or Dartmoor or the Heligan

240

Gardens was setting off, even though it was all detailed in the programme in their rooms.

But for five years she'd dealt with 'What cc is this bike?' when it was stated right there on the windscreen sticker. 'Do you have this helmet in red?' when they'd had half a dozen colours apart from red on the shelf. And 'Two hundred and fifty quid for a bike lock? That's a bit steep.' *You're riding a Kawasaki Ninja H2 — that's twenty-five grand's worth of bike. You want to put a cheap lock on it and have someone nick it?* And most annoying of all, 'Is there a man I can speak to?' After that, she could cope with a few mildly anxious septuagenarians.

So Paul was back.

She'd hoped that these few weeks without him being around would have given her the chance to regain her equilibrium, that by now she'd be able to keep him safely in the 'friend' zone.

But 'safe' and Paul Channing weren't words you would usually hear in the same sentence.

She forced herself to focus her attention on the television, chuckling with laughter as one of the guys on the comedy show went into one of his famous rants.

His target was people putting their dustbins out and blocking the pavement. "Don't they ever walk down a street themselves? Don't they notice that people have to step out in the road, risking getting knocked down by some lunatic driver who thinks a speed limit is just a suggestion?" His conclusion was that offenders should be hanged.

* * *

"Well, that's it." Neil saved the night audit and closed down the computer. "Okay?"

Paul nodded. "Looks straightforward enough. Hopefully I won't have to do it too often."

"Want any more sandwiches? A coffee?"

241

"No, thanks. It's gone midnight. I think I'll be getting home."

"Right. Goodnight, then."

"Goodnight."

Some of the guests were still carousing in the ballroom. He smiled to himself as he pulled on his overcoat and stepped out into the night. Pausing at the top of the steps, he thrust his hands deep into his pockets.

Neil had switched off the Christmas tree lights and the white floodlights that lit the frontage of the hotel. There was just a security light above the door and a single streetlamp in the lane, so most of the car park was in shadow.

A noise to his left. A fox? A badger? No — someone was curled up on the ground beside the bushes, moaning softly. Someone in a red dress, with long blonde hair — almost certainly one of the Turkey-and-Tinsel crowd.

"Are you . . . ?" There really wasn't much point asking if she was okay — she was lying in a pool of her own vomit. Oh lord, please — not food poisoning! But as he bent over her, the smell of alcohol almost made him throw up himself.

"Come on then, lass. You can't stay here. You'll freeze to death."

She mumbled something incoherent, but let him heave her to her feet. She was young — probably early twenties — and she'd have been quite pretty if she didn't have mascara smudged down her cheeks and her lipstick smeared. There was a long streak of vomit down her dress, and one side of her hair was caked with it. Delightful.

"Let's get you inside and clean you up."

"No, no . . ." She tried to pull away from him as he turned her towards the front doors. She shook her head and stumbled over her own feet. "No' inside. Don' wan' 'em t'see me."

"It doesn't matter."

"Does." She looked panicked. "Had a big row. A great big row." She swung her arm around wildly. "Wiv his ma . . .

She don' like me. Not good enough for 'im." She started to cry, sobbing between hiccups. "Don' wan' 'em t'see me."

Well, he could understand that, given the state she was in. He tried not to breathe in too deeply. "Okay, we can go in the back way." His arm around her waist to hold her up, he coaxed her across the car park to the staff entrance, and up the stairs. "What's your room number?"

"Uh . . . ?"

"Your room number," he repeated patiently. "Do you remember it?"

She blinked up at him, her eyes clearing for a moment. "Um . . . twenty-eight. Uh — two-o-eight."

"Right."

With some difficulty he got her up to the second floor and through the service door to the guest corridor. Keeping his fingers crossed that it was the right room, he opened the door with his pass-key and managed to get her inside. She collapsed on the bed, moaning in misery.

He regarded her with a wry grimace. She needed to get out of that dress and into the shower to get cleaned up. "Look, I need to get someone to come and help you." He didn't know if maybe Jess or someone might be up in the staff quarters.

"No . . ." She shook her head, then moaned again. "Don' wan' anyone t'see me like this. Been sick."

"Yes, you have. So you need to get a shower, clean up your hair."

"No . . ." The young woman had sat up, reaching round awkwardly to try to undo the zip of her dress, but then she gave up and flopped down on the bed again.

"Sheesh!" He shook his head in exasperation. How many times had he put a drunken teammate to bed? And once or twice he'd had been put to bed in the same state himself.

Unfortunately, by now she was completely out of it. Afraid that she might be sick again while he was looking for a female member of staff, he lifted her feet onto the bed and

243

placed her on her side. Then he went to get a towel from the bathroom to put under her head.

"Here, this'll . . ."

Abruptly, the door burst open and a very angry young man erupted into the room.

"What the . . . What's going on in here?" His fists were clenched, his eyes blazing with fury. "That's my wife, you bastard."

"Really? Well, you should have taken better care of her." His voice was cool, patient. "She's had too much to drink, she's thrown her guts up, and now she's passed out."

"And you were going to . . ."

"Come off it, mate." The words were like water off a duck's back. He'd had far cruder insults than that thrown at him on the football field. "I don't know about you, but my taste doesn't run to having sex with unconscious females who smell of alcohol and sick." The girl on the bed moaned and rolled over, mumbled something and snored loudly. "She was upset. She said you'd had a row."

The guy shook his head, frowning. "Nothing serious. Just my mother . . ."

"It was serious to her. So be nice to her, eh? She seems like a good kid."

The guy was staring at him. "You're . . . you're Paul Channing, aren't you?"

"That's right." And before the guy could make up his mind whether to throw a punch or ask for his autograph, he got himself out of the room.

244

CHAPTER THIRTY-FOUR

Jess sat cross-legged on her bed with her laptop, scrolling through the job adverts. Her lip was curled in disgust. Last night . . . She'd heard Paul's voice on the stairs and had peered down to see what was going on — and she'd seen him with that girl.

She'd seen her when the guests had checked in earlier in the day. She was one of the youngest of the group, here with her husband and his family. Jess had wondered at the time whether the girl would get bored among the much older crowd.

Well, apparently she'd decided to relieve the boredom by dumping her husband and going to bed with Paul Channing.

As she'd peeped through a crack in the service door, she'd seen him use his pass-key to open the door of the girl's room, and disappear inside with her.

Well, that hadn't taken him long! He could only have been back for a couple of hours. Dammit, her mum had been right — they were all bastards. Well, most of them.

Thank goodness she hadn't let herself get involved with him. So much for being friends. She wasn't sure she could even bring herself to speak to him.

245

There really wasn't anything worth looking at on the jobs pages. It probably wasn't the best time of year to be searching, with less than two weeks to go to Christmas. Especially for someone with no formal qualifications.

On top of which, she'd have nowhere to live. All the reasons why she hadn't wanted to go to either of her parents when she had first left Glenn were still there, and staying with Jools wasn't an option — she'd still be far too close to Paul Channing.

With a sigh, she closed the laptop, put it aside, and rolled off the bed. At the moment she did have a job, and it would be stupid to just walk out on it, however tempting that might be. She was just going to have to grit her teeth until after Christmas.

The reception desk was busy, as usual. The phone rang intermittently; a steady stream of guests who hadn't gone on the trip to Exeter approached with various enquiries; and there was a delivery of drink for the lounge bar.

This was how she liked it — structured chaos, always keeping her on her toes. Keeping her from dwelling too much on what she'd seen last night.

Hearing voices behind her, her shoulders stiffened: Paul and Mike coming out of the back office. Mike walked over to the dining room, but Paul paused beside the reception desk.

"Good morning. How's it going?"

She spared him the briefest glance and kept her attention focussed on the computer screen.

"Hello?" He moved so that he was in her eyeline. "Anybody in there?"

"Excuse me," she responded tersely. "I'm busy."

He turned his head, letting his gaze wander pointedly around the room. "It seems quiet enough at the moment for you to at least say hello. I haven't seen you for weeks."

She shrugged her shoulders in careless dismissal, as she continued to scroll through the spreadsheet.

246

He hesitated, frowning. "I've obviously done something to upset you."

"What could you possibly do to upset me?" She refused to let herself look at him. "What you choose to do isn't that important to me."

"So I have done something. What? Tell me what it is."

All he got in return was a glare that could crack rocks. She turned an aloof shoulder to him and stalked into the office to get paper for the printer. When she came out, to her relief, he was gone.

CHAPTER THIRTY-FIVE

"It's looking very Christmassy," Jess murmured to her sister.

"Mmm . . . Ben, stop banging your heels."

The organist was playing a Mozart sonata, and heads were turning as a ripple of noise from the back of the church suggested that the bride had arrived.

Julia laughed softly. "They got her here, then. She wanted to skip off to Las Vegas and be married in jeans by an Elvis impersonator."

"That would have been fun! But she looks lovely."

The music changed to Handel's Passacaglia as Cassie and her father began their walk down the aisle. Not in jeans, but in a long white satin dress with a short train, and silk flowers in her hair.

And following them, Liam's little daughter Robyn, in a pretty pink dress, her blonde curls gleaming, her eyes wide and shining.

"Liam looks happy," Jess murmured as the bridegroom turned and held out his hand to take Cassie's, lifting it to his lips to lay a kiss on her fingers.

"He does. He deserves to be. It was such a tragedy, his first wife dying like that."

"I remember her. Robyn looks a lot like her, doesn't she?"

"Mmm. I saw her mum and dad here. They're sitting at the back somewhere."

"Oh, it's nice that they came."

She fell silent as Eva, the vicar, stepped into her place in front of the altar, smiling at the wedding guests in the packed pews. "Dear friends and family, we welcome you today to witness and celebrate the marriage of Cassandra and Liam . . ."

The first hymn was 'Love Divine', the voices rising into the high vaulted roof. As she sang, Jess gazed around the church. It wasn't very big, but it was old. Jools had told her it was built in the thirteenth century, though the Victorians had added the porch and the bell tower.

It had been decked out for Christmas with a large Christmas tree covered in tinsel and shiny baubles on one side of the altar. On the other side was a nativity scene — a wooden stable lined with straw, little plaster figures of Mary and Joseph and the shepherds gathered round the manger, with a couple of sheep, a three-legged cow and a slightly chipped angel perched on the roof.

The end of each pew was trimmed with a sprig of holly, shiny scarlet baubles and a bow of scarlet ribbon. There were garlands of holly and pine around the walls, and the altar itself was decorated with more garlands.

Paul was there, of course, on the other side of the aisle. He was one of the ushers, and he'd escorted his mother to her place in the front pew.

He was looking very smart, in a beautifully tailored morning suit that moulded his wide shoulders to perfection, a white waistcoat and a pale-blue cravat.

But she wasn't going to let her gaze drift in his direction. Anyway, she couldn't really see him properly with all the Ellises and Channings in between.

She hadn't seen him for the past couple of days — he hadn't been down to the hotel. Which suited her just fine. She'd be happy never to see him again. She couldn't wait for Christmas to be over so she could look properly for a new job.

She enjoyed hotel work, so it would be great to find something in that line. Maybe she'd even try something in London. A complete change, a whole new scene.

Cassie and Liam were reciting their vows. *True love, now and forever.* Yeah, well, it seemed to work out for some people. Cassie's mum and dad, and Graham and Diane Ellis, Julia and Lisa. They were the lucky ones.

She could have fallen in love with Paul Channing — there was a lot about him to love. That cock-eyed sense of humour, that easy laugh, his closeness to his family. His consideration for his grandmother and the loyal elderly visitors to the hotel.

And the fact that he didn't play the celebrity, even though he was often on television, commentating on football matches.

But there was that one thing that killed any chance of it stone dead. After her parents' divorce and her experience with Glenn, she was never going to risk getting involved with a man who didn't know the meaning of commitment.

The service ended, and everyone crowded out into the churchyard to pose for photographs, clapping their hands together and hunching their shoulders against the icy cold.

"Heavens, she must be freezing in that dress," Jess murmured to Julia as Cassie laughingly swung little Robyn around while the photographer clicked away.

Julia's eyes danced. "I don't think she's even noticed. I've never seen anyone look so happy."

"Mmm."

From the corner of her eye, Jess noticed Paul strolling towards them, and turned quickly away, crossing to where Kate and Debbie were standing with little Amy. The little girl had a tub of bubble-mix, and was laughing as the bubbles glittered in the winter sunshine.

"Wasn't it a lovely wedding?" Debbie sighed. "I'm so happy for them both."

Kate laughed. "They certainly waited long enough for it. Everyone thought they'd get married ten years ago."

"Oh, but they were far too young then," Debbie protested. "Cassie was only eighteen when she went away. Now she's had all her adventures, and she's home for good."

"Mummy, Mummy, look!" Amy's eyes were alight with excitement. "The horses have come."

Tom Cullen was leading two horses under the lychgate — Missie, Cassie's favourite, a pretty bay with a white blaze down her nose and one slightly crooked ear, and Gitana, Liam's beautiful black mare.

"Wow!" Jess laughed, her eyes wide. "They really are going to ride them down to the hotel?"

"Of course."

The horses' manes and tails were plaited with white ribbon and tiny silk flowers, and they stood posing for the photographer like supermodels.

Liam cupped his hands and lifted Cassie easily into the saddle. She gathered her dress carefully to avoid the stirrups as Liam swung himself up onto Gitana, and his dad handed Robyn up to him to settle on his pommel.

There were more photographs, and then the couple turned the horses and rode out through the lychgate, ducking their heads to avoid the crossbeams, all the guests streaming after them for the short walk down the hill to the hotel.

* * *

"Well, well, will you just look at this!" Arthur gazed round in amazement as he stepped out of the newly installed lift. "Who'd have thought it?"

Alex laughed. "It's certainly looking better than the first time I saw it."

Six weeks ago it had been nothing but a dusty, empty space, with the windows boarded up and only one dim light bulb working. It had been a lot of hard work to get it finished

251

in time, but now the big room above the swimming pool had been transformed from an afterthought into a wonderful new facility.

The boards had all been removed from the long windows around three sides and they'd been thoroughly polished, giving a spectacular view out over the gardens and the wide sweep of the bay. The cool December sunshine flooded in, brightening the whole room.

A light beechwood floor had been laid, the back wall painted a sandy-cream, and the ceiling was dotted with recessed LED lights that could illuminate the space brightly or be dimmed to a subtle glow.

Once it was fitted out, there would be a business suite and conference room up here, as well as the gymnasium, the spa and the hairdressers. But today it was the perfect venue for a wedding reception.

A long buffet table had been set out on one side of the room, flanked at each end by a Christmas tree decorated with baubles and fairy lights.

"Ah, now this looks good." Arthur had made a beeline for it. "How on earth did Chef manage to get all this done, with all them Christmas lot here as well?"

"He had a little help." Alex smiled as Arthur reached out greedily to snatch a fruit kebab. "Kate made the mince pies and tacos, and Vicky did the sushi."

"Sooshee? What's that? Not for me. I'll have one of them sausage rolls, thank you very much."

"You have to wait until the bride and groom get here," Alex reminded him.

"Pah! They'd better hurry themselves up, then."

"They're just having a few more photos taken down on the terrace."

"Haven't they got enough? Must have taken more'n a hundred already."

"They'll want plenty to choose from. Ah, sounds like they're here."

252

The lift doors opened, but it wasn't Liam and Cassie. It was Shelley and the young sous chef from the kitchen, with a catering trolley bearing the wedding cake.

"Oh!" She blinked at him, looked away and looked back again. "I didn't realise anyone was up here yet."

"We came up out of the cold."

"Of course." She smiled warmly at his grandfather. "Hello, Arthur. How are you today?"

"I'm as fit as a flea!"

"That's good. Did you enjoy the wedding?"

"Oh, ah. She's a pretty girl, young Cassie. Young Liam's got himself a good 'un there."

"He has." She flickered a brief smile up at Alex. "Well . . . um . . . We just need to put the cake on the table, and then we'll be gone."

"You're not staying for the reception?"

"Oh no. I nipped up to watch the ceremony, but I'm on duty now."

"Okay." He smiled at her. "I'll see you later then."

"Yes, of course."

Although it was likely that, as usual, she would slip away like one of the piskies from up on the moor.

The cake was placed carefully into the centre of the table. Chef had excelled himself, again. The cake was magnificent — three tiers, covered in intricately piped lace icing, with clusters of silver leaves and white flowers at the base of each tier.

And on the top, instead of the traditional figures of a bride and groom, were little models of Gitana and Missie.

"What's in that punch?" Arthur wanted to know.

"Champagne, ginger ale and vodka."

"Ah . . . I want some of that!"

"In a moment. Here they come now."

Footsteps were heard on the stairs, then the large double doors at the end of the room swung open and Liam and Cassie walked in. A little blonde fairy in a pink dress raced ahead of them.

253

Robyn's eyes were wide with excitement. "Oh, Mummy, Mummy, come and look at the cake!" she squealed.

Cassie smiled. "It's beautiful, isn't it. Hello, Arthur. I hope you didn't get too cold down there?"

"Pah! Everyone fusses, but I was warm as toast. I've got a nice thick overcoat. You young people today never think to wrap up warm, then you complain about the weather."

Cassie laughed. "You're probably right." She smiled at Alex. "You missed the speeches."

"Oh dear, what a pity. Never mind."

"We've videoed them. You can watch them later." She laughed at the expression on his face. "Got you! Only kidding."

"Huh."

* * *

"Hi, there. How was Botswana?"

Paul glanced over at Liam's brother Luke as they climbed the stairs. "Great. The kids are so keen. They all want to play for Manchester United!"

"That's good. Hey, they've done a great job with this place," Luke approved, gazing around as they stepped into the upstairs room. "It was a dump. Do you remember playing cricket in here when it was raining?"

Paul laughed. "Do I! The ball bouncing off the walls like a hand grenade, and stirring up so much dust we'd be choking on it."

He'd taken off his cravat and stuffed it in his pocket, and unfastened the top button of his shirt. He'd been holding back a little, knowing that Jess was ahead of him, and now he was among the last to arrive at the reception.

Most of the other guests were already milling around, chatting and sipping champagne. And there was Jess, with her sister. She'd been wearing a fluffy white fake-fur jacket earlier, but like the other guests she'd left it downstairs in the makeshift cloakroom. Her dress was mauve, in some floaty fabric that almost matched her eyes.

254

She'd seen him, but she instantly looked away, her mouth a thin line. Okay, she was still angry with him. It was frustrating to know that, when he had no idea what he was supposed to have done, but he wasn't going to try to talk to her now. He didn't want to risk a scene at the wedding.

Instead, he wandered over to chat to Diane and Graham Ellis. "Well, it seems to have gone off okay."

"It has."

They all watched as little Robyn dragged a laughing Cassie around by the hand, introducing her to everyone. "This is my mummy!"

"Mummy?" Paul queried quietly.

Diane smiled. "She decided it for herself. She talks about Mummy Natalie, and Mummy Natalie's garden — she loves to go and tend to it up in the churchyard. But I think she decided she wanted Cassie right from the beginning."

Paul nodded. The child couldn't have looked happier, and his sister looked happy too. And as for Liam, he looked like the cat who'd got the cream. Maybe domestic bliss had something going for it after all.

He was conscious that Jess was at the buffet table behind him — he could hear her soft, slightly husky laughter, and her voice as she teased her young nephew Ben for being a greedy little pig.

Dammit, that woman was driving him crazy. He'd thought that several weeks away in Africa would have been an effective cure, but he had found himself repeatedly distracted, remembering that night in his kitchen, the heat of her lips against his, the intensity of her kiss.

It had been a moment of pure connection, and he couldn't shake the feeling that there was still something between them, something worth fighting for.

If her ex hadn't shown up, might it have been different? She'd insisted that it was over, that she wanted nothing to do with him, but the incident had clearly upset her, reminded her of what Lisa had told him — that she was 'off men'.

255

Okay, he'd wait, wait for the right moment. Give her space and time. Try not to let his mind wander back to her every five minutes. And for now, he'd do his best to look happy, join in the conversations around him.

But every now and then, his gaze would flicker over to the buffet table, catching glimpses of Jess's curling red hair, her easy smile, and the way she moved — so graceful, so elegant.

He'd wait. And try not to let his heart crack a little more every time he heard her laughter.

* * *

Though it was barely four o'clock it was already growing dark. Jess stood in the corner between two of the long windows, sipping champagne and gazing out over the inky black waters of the bay.

The small town looked almost like a fairy-land, twinkling lights climbing the slopes above the Esplanade. In the short time she had been here she had fallen in love with the place.

But she couldn't stay. Because she had fallen in love with Paul Channing.

How stupid could you get? The glass of the window was like a mirror against the darkness outside, and she could see him across the room, laughing and chatting with the other guests, flirting with a young cousin of the Ellises.

The DJ was setting up his decks — there would be dancing soon. If she slipped away now, would anyone notice? The last thing she wanted was for Paul to ask her to dance — or worse, not ask her to dance.

Oh dammit, she'd come down here to sort her head out after the way Glenn had behaved, and instead she'd found herself in a far worse mess.

Slipping discreetly along the side of the room she left her champagne glass on a convenient table and faded silently out of the door. No one seemed to have noticed — least of all Paul.

* * *

He had been watching her out of the corner of his eye as she stood there sipping her champagne and gazing out of the window. All the while he was chatting to friends and indulging young Lucy Ellis, his friend's cousin who was almost embarrassingly goggle-eyed at meeting a real live person off the television, he had been constantly aware of her.

And now she was gone — slipping out of the door like a thief in the night.

Should he go after her? At least if he could catch her on her own for just a moment he might be able to talk to her, find out what was wrong. But clearly she didn't want to be caught. He had to let her go.

CHAPTER THIRTY-SIX

"Oh, hello. It's Mr and Mrs Donovan, isn't it?" Shelley smiled warmly at the elderly couple. "Have you enjoyed your stay?"

"We've had a lovely time, dear. I ate so much Christmas pudding at dinner last night that I've had to let my belt out a notch!"

She laughed. "Oh dear. Still, if you can't eat too much at Christmas, it isn't really Christmas."

On the last night of their stay the guests had been served the full Christmas menu of Chef's turkey special, richly basted with butter and his own mix of herbs, with all the trimmings, followed by his amazing Christmas puddings. He always prepared them a year in advance and left them to mature, until just breathing their aroma could put you over the drink-drive limit.

She was enjoying working on reception. She wasn't working here full time — not yet. Only on the days when the Turkey-and-Tinsel groups were arriving and leaving — those days could be very busy, with so many people to be dealt with at once.

But she was learning the ropes, and Lisa was going to teach her how to use the computer while the hotel was closed down for the renovations.

"Phew." Jess sighed deeply. "That's most of them checked out. Well done, Shells. You're doing great."

"I'm loving it. They're all so sweet, and in such a happy mood with Christmas coming."

"Except for that old git in the knitted waistcoat." Jess pulled a face. "You handled him brilliantly."

"Ah well, anyone would be grumpy at having to wear a hideous thing like that. I bet his wife knitted it for him and nags him if he doesn't wear it."

Jess laughed. "You could be right."

Shelley smiled to herself as she checked through the returned key cards. In the past few weeks her life had taken a huge upturn. She was reading avidly. She had found some Agatha Christie paperbacks in the hotel's library stock, and Jess's sister Julia had given her some more, and she was addicted!

Helen Channing had encouraged her to copy out some passages as she learned to write, and she was making progress with that too. The more she practised the skill, the more her confidence grew.

And now here she was on the reception desk, training for a new job. Who'd have thought it?

"Hello."

She turned sharply, her heart thumping. Alex.

"How's it going?"

"Um . . . Very well." She managed a smile. "We're just doing the check-out. Most of the guests have come down. They're sitting around in the lounge having a last drink."

"Everybody happy?"

"No complaints so far." Oh, those eyes. And when he looked at her like that . . .

"That's good. And how are you enjoying your new job?"

"Very much, thank you." She was trying for a casual air, but she wasn't sure that it was working. "Though it isn't actually my job yet. I'm just training."

"Ah, yes."

259

Shelley was vaguely aware that Jess had slipped back through the door to the offices, leaving them alone — just the two of them.

"So, what do you think of the plans for the renovation?" he asked genially.

The staff had all been invited to a meeting where the interior designer had explained her plans and shown a presentation of how it would look. And they had been assured that though the hotel would be closing for two months in the new year, they would all be retained on full wages, and be involved in the preparations for reopening.

"It looks very nice."

"Not too medieval?"

A small bubble of laughter escaped her lips. "I like the colours. And the new light fittings. I think it'll work really well."

"That's good." Oh, she liked his smile. "By the way, I was wondering if you would do me a favour?"

"Oh?" She was instantly wary.

"I'm getting a dog."

Her eyes widened. "Really? You didn't just say that to wind that woman up?"

He laughed. "Well, I did," he confessed. "But then I thought about it and realised that, as I'm staying here, it's the perfect opportunity. We always had dogs when I was growing up, and I miss having one around. So I got in touch with a rescue centre, and met a few of the dogs. They've done a home check, and I've an appointment there tomorrow afternoon to be matched up with one. The thing is, I'm afraid that when I see a pair of sad brown eyes gazing at me, I'll just be a sucker. I need someone to make sure I'm sensible about it, pick the right one."

She laughed outright at that. "You think I'll be sensible?"

"Wouldn't you?"

"Well, I suppose . . ."

"Tomorrow afternoon? I could pick you up at around three?"

260

Three o'clock? She suspected that he had checked her shifts. She really ought to say no, but when he looked at her like that, all trace of reason and common sense flew straight out of the window. "Okay."

"Good. I'll see you then." With a nod and a smile he strolled away.

Shelley let go of her breath in a sigh of exasperation at her own stupidity.

A moment later Jess emerged from the back office, one eyebrow arched in question. "Well?"

"Well what?"

"Are you going with him?"

"How did you know about it?"

Jess's eyes danced. "He asked me this morning what your hours were for the rest of the week."

Shelley laughed, shaking her head. She had been right. He was the sort of man who always had a strategy. "So why don't *you* go with him?" she countered. "You're much more sensible than me."

"Why isn't the moon made of blue cheese? Because it isn't. And you're not sensible if you let a good man like that slip through your fingers."

* * *

A good man . . . Jess sighed, shaking her head. Wouldn't it be nice to meet one of those? All she seemed to get were the arseholes.

Fortunately, the reception desk had been very busy over the past few days, so she was able to use that as an excuse to avoid Paul whenever he was around.

Several times she had seen him chatting to that girl and her husband as though nothing had happened. Clearly he had absolutely no conscience at all. She'd been tempted to tell the husband exactly what she'd seen.

261

And just to add to her bitter mood, everyone was getting into the Christmas spirit, singing along to the Christmas songs playing on an endless loop in reception until she wanted to scream, tear down the garlands and kick the Christmas tree over. The air was filled with the aroma of mulled wine and Chef's splendid Christmas pudding.

At least the group was checking out today.

She was scrolling through the spreadsheet to ensure that all the details had been added correctly and any additional charges totted up when she spotted the girl out of the corner of her eye, with her husband. By the time they reached the desk she had a bland professional smiled fixed in place.

"Excuse me, is Mr Channing around?"

She glanced up, startled to see the girl smiling shyly at her — with her husband standing right there beside her. How barefaced was that?

"No, he isn't." Oops, that wasn't her professional receptionist's voice. "I'm sorry." She forced a formal smile. "I'm not sure where he is at the moment."

"Oh." The husband lifted a tall gift bag onto the counter, the sort that usually held a bottle. It landed with a small clunk. "Would you please give him this, with our thanks."

Jess stared at him blankly. "Thanks?"

The girl leaned forward confidentially. "I got very drunk on our first night here," she explained, glancing quickly around to check there was no one else close enough to hear. "I don't usually drink very much, but . . . well, the wine was so nice. Anyway, I was outside. I'd fallen over and been sick all down my dress. I didn't even realise how cold it was. Mr Channing found me and took me up to our room. He was so kind. I really don't know what would have happened to me if he hadn't been there. I could have frozen to death."

"Oh . . ."

"So we bought him a small gift to say thank you. Does he like whiskey?"

262

"Oh . . . Yes, he does. Very much." Jess blinked, bewildered. She had got it wrong — *very* wrong. Had Glenn curdled her judgement so much that she had been so ready to draw the darkest conclusion?

"Well, would you give this to him with our thanks?"

"Oh . . . Yes, of course." She took the bag and put it on the shelf beneath the reception desk. "Thank you."

"Now we need to settle our bill." The husband produced his wallet. "Name of Barraclough."

"Yes, of course." Somehow she managed to find the right place on the spreadsheet. "Debit or credit card?"

CHAPTER THIRTY-SEVEN

Alex opened the car door for Shelley. "So how do you like the new chariot?"

"It's very nice." She settled into the passenger seat and fastened her seatbelt as he came round to slide behind the wheel. "You decided not to get an Aston Martin then?"

He smiled in dry humour. "I thought Paul might think I was copying him. Besides, having driven the rental Jag for a while, I'd got used to them."

"This one looks as if it would be a lot faster than the one you were renting."

"It is."

"I like the colour better too — this nice metallic grey. More elegant. The red looked a bit flash."

He smiled to himself. These past few weeks he had deliberately backed off, on Lisa's advice: 'She's got some stuff she needs to deal with.' He hadn't pried, but observing her from a distance, happily working on the reception desk — a job she'd repeatedly turned down before, according to Lisa — it seemed that at least some of that stuff had been dealt with.

The wariness hadn't gone completely from her eyes, but she seemed a lot more relaxed, more confident. And she had agreed to come with him today. That was real progress.

264

At the next junction turn left.

"Ah, this is it." The satnav had guided him onto a narrow lane overhung by trees. At the end there was a five-barred gate.

"I'll get it."

Shelley skipped out of the car and ran to open the gate, closing it when Alex had driven through. To their left was the office, a single-storey building, to their right a row of parking spaces. Alex tucked the Jaguar into one and came to join her, and together they walked into the office.

Christmas had arrived here with even more exuberance than the hotel, with a large Christmas tree almost smothered in swathes of tinsel and shiny red, green and gold baubles, and garlands of paperchains around the walls and across the ceiling.

Above the reception desk a shiny gold banner spelled out *Merry Christmas*, along with another that asserted *A DOG IS FOR LIFE NOT JUST FOR CHRISTMAS*.

They were greeted by a middle-aged woman with neat brown hair and a boa of scarlet tinsel wrapped around her neck. The badge on her sweater reminded him that her name was Marion.

"Ah, it's Mr Crocombe, isn't it?"

"Alex."

"So — you've come to pick up a dog. I think they heard you coming." She laughed as she gestured with her hand towards the back of the building, from where a cacophony of frantic barking was echoing. She turned to her computer. "I have your home check here — everything looks fine. You've met with several of our mutts — is there one in particular you're most interested in?"

"I'm thinking . . . Tyson, the Great Dane."

She smiled in delight. "Oh yes — I was really hoping you'd say that. You really seemed to hit it off."

"Why's he here?" Shelley asked.

"People have found him a bit of a challenge. He's just short of ten months old, and he's already been rejected twice."

"Oh . . . ! He's just a puppy."

Marion nodded. "He's a typical Dane — big and bouncy and rather clumsy. But he's very affectionate — he just wants to be loved. And he isn't doing very well in kennels since the last time he was brought back. He's not eating very well, and he's starting to shut down. So — he's your choice?"

"Yes." Shelley spoke before Alex could open his mouth.

He smiled down at her. "I thought you were going to be the sensible one?"

Her eyes danced. "Whatever made you think that?"

Marion rose to her feet. "Come on through and I'll bring him out."

"I didn't think they let people take dogs at Christmas," Shelley murmured, glancing up at the sign above the desk.

"Ah — I exercised my famous Canadian charm and managed to convince her that I'm a responsible person."

A bubble of laughter rose to her lips. "Of course."

They followed Marion into a room behind the office, with a long sofa and a couple of floor cushions, and a box of dog toys.

"This is exciting." Shelley was almost bouncing as she settled on the sofa. "A Great Dane. They're gorgeous dogs."

Alex smiled. It was easy to guess that it was the backstory about the dog being rejected which had hooked her.

"He'll be a challenge," he reminded her.

She quirked an amused eyebrow. "Oh, not like flying a fighter jet at Mach two, or buying a hotel, then?"

The barking from the kennels was going crazy, then the door at the back of the room opened. A large grey head with melancholy dark eyes peered cautiously round, then quickly retreated.

"Come on, boy," Marion urged gently. "There's someone here for you to meet. You remember Alex?"

The dog's head appeared again, drooping and sad. Marion managed to coax him inside, but he tried — not very successfully — to hide behind her. His tail was clamped firmly between his legs, and Alex could see that he was trembling.

266

"Oh, sweetheart!" Shelley slid down onto one of the floor cushions and held out her arms. "You're beautiful." She spoke lightly, as if to a human baby. "Come and have a cuddle."

The huge dog gazed at her for a long moment, uncertain. Then as Marion unclipped his lead, he bounded forward, all giant paws and gangly legs and floppy ears, and scrambled onto Shelley's lap as though he was a tiny puppy. He tucked his head beneath her chin and whimpered softly.

"Oh, you big soppy. You're just a baby, aren't you?" She was laughing, wrapping her arms around him, tears in her eyes as she stroked his long sleek grey body.

Alex laughed. If ever there was a case of love at first sight! "Well, sensible or not, it looks like the decision's been made. Where do I sign?"

* * *

Alex pulled the car into the car park outside the small block of holiday flats.

"Here's your new home, Sweetie," Shelley murmured.

He laughed. "You can't keep calling a dog that size Sweetie."

"Why not? He doesn't look like a Tyson."

He glanced back over his shoulder at the giant pup lying on a blanket on the back seat, watching them both with wary eyes. "No, I suppose not."

Shelley studied the dog for a moment. "How about Tyler?" One floppy ear twitched and the dog lifted his big head. "I think he likes that! Come on then, Tyler. Let's go see where you're going to live."

She unfastened his safety harness and took his lead, but he wasn't at all sure about stepping out of the car — it had taken nearly twenty minutes and half a bag of treats to coax him into it in the first place.

Alex rattled the bag of treats again and it worked like magic. The dog perked up at once and scrambled clumsily out of the car to snaffle the treat. Then he rose effortlessly up on

267

his hind legs to plant his huge front paws on Alex's shoulders and slurped a long pink tongue up his cheek.

"Thank you." Alex laughed and wiped his face with the back of his hand.

Shelley was laughing too. "I think he likes you."

"You reckon?" He scritched the dog behind his ears. "Well, I like you too, you great lummox."

Alex's flat was on the first floor of the block. Fortunately, Tyler didn't have too much trouble with the stairs. Alex opened the door and stood aside for Shelley to go in.

"This is nice." She gazed around the sitting room. The place had the functional look of a holiday apartment, with laminate floors and magnolia walls, black leather furniture and some rather bland prints on the walls.

But it was light and airy, with French windows opening onto a balcony which had a wide view of the bay. And he had a Christmas tree. Not a big one, but nicely decorated with gold baubles and silver stars.

"It's lucky they allow dogs," she remarked.

"I did a deal with the landlord that I'd pay extra rent and cover any damage." Alex smiled dryly. "He was more than happy to be able to find a tenant. Most of the other flats in the block are empty now the season's over."

Tyler was standing in the doorway, a slightly anxious expression on his large, melancholy face. Shelley had brought up the beanbag which Alex had bought from the rescue centre, and set it out on the floor beside one of the two sofas.

"There you are, Sweetie. That's your bed."

"Don't keep calling him Sweetie," Alex reminded her, laughing. "He's already the size of a small horse, and he's going to get bigger."

"He'll always be a Sweetie to me. Come on, Tyler — look. Something for you to lie down on." The dog regarded the beanbag with suspicion. "Look, it's really comfy."

She sat down on it herself, but Tyler was still not convinced. Instead, he sniffed at the sofa, decided he liked it,

268

and clambered up onto it, settling himself with a small huff of breath and laying his big head on his paws.

Shelley laughed. "Well, it looks like he's decided where he's going to sleep."

Alex's mouth quirked into a wry smile. "I get the feeling my life is never going to be the same again. Okay then, boy." He gave the dog a speculative glance. "How about some dinner?"

Tyler was very interested in that. Another purchase from the rescue centre was a large dinner bowl on its own plastic pedestal so he could reach it easily. Alex had barely emptied the tin of meat into it when the dog came bounding into the kitchen and dived into it.

"Wow! He wanted that."

The bowl was empty in moments.

"Right. The next thing is to take him out to do his business," Alex suggested.

"Poo bags." She held a couple out to him.

"Thanks." Another wry smile. "Though I reckon we might need a considerably bigger bag!"

It was only a short walk down to the middle steps. Tyler pranced along beside them, his tongue lolling out, his ears pricked.

"He looks happy," Shelley remarked. "I think he knows he's got a forever home now."

"He walks well on the lead, anyway. They gave him some training at the rescue centre. Let's see what he makes of the steps and the sand."

Not much. It took more coaxing and more treats, but eventually he was persuaded down to the beach. He wasn't too sure about the sand, but reluctantly agreed to try it. The sea, however, was another matter.

Alex let him off the lead and he raced down to the water's edge to sniff at this strange phenomenon. But when a small wave rippled in over his feet, he leaped back as if he had been stung.

Shelley was almost doubled up with laughter. Suddenly a small brown and white terrier streaked past them, barking joyfully, and plunged straight into the water. Tyler stared in astonishment, then with a yap he bounced after him, dancing through the waves as if he hadn't been scared at all.

Tom and Vicky Cullen strolled up to them, laughing, hand in hand. "What on earth have you got there?" Tom's voice lilted with humour.

"Tyler." Alex beamed with pride. "We just got him from the rescue centre."

"Looks like you could have your hands full. He's going to be big — look at the size of those paws."

Alex nodded, untroubled by the prospect. "You could be right."

They all watched the dogs frolicking together, chasing each other and barking with excitement.

"He's a beauty, though," Vicky remarked. "From the rescue centre?"

"That's right. He's had it tough and he's still just a pup — almost ten months."

"Well, he's certainly enjoying himself now. Rufus will show him how."

The two dogs were having the time of their lives. Already firm friends, they splashed through the shallows, raced up the beach and down again, rolling over and over and getting themselves covered in sand.

"He really is happy," Shelley murmured. She felt a warm glow in her heart for the dog — and for the man at her side, who had given the sad, lonely creature a fresh start, a safe home, all the love he deserved.

Alex glanced down at her, smiling. "Could you come back to the flat for a little while? He's taken to you. It might help him settle if you're there."

She hesitated. Was that a good idea? But she did want to help the big dog, and if staying a little while would keep him calm, it would be worth it. "Okay, yes. For an hour or so."

270

"Good. Fish and chips for supper?"

"That would be good."

"Okay. Time to get this mad hound back on the lead." He called the dog's name. Tyler stopped dead in the middle of his game, turning his head, puzzled for a moment. Alex called him again, rattling the bag of treats, and he raced out of the water, hurtling back up the beach.

But in his exuberance he suffered a severe brake failure and crashed into Alex, knocking him over and bouncing on him, licking his face.

"Right . . ." Alex laughed as he sat up. "I think that'll be something to work on."

* * *

The kitchen in the flat was a narrow galley, but well-equipped, with a large fridge-freezer, a ceramic hob and a microwave. "I'm afraid I'm not much of a cook," Shelley confessed. "I've never really had the opportunity to practise."

"Neither am I." Alex laughed. "But I reckon between us we can manage to unwrap a bag of fish and chips."

He took the plates from the cupboard and cutlery from the drawer. "There's salt and vinegar if you want it, and a bottle of wine in the fridge."

She left the wine in the fridge, and filled a jug with water instead and carried it through to the sitting room, setting it out on the table with a couple of glasses.

Tyler had been sniffing around, but he scooted straight over at the sight of her. But instead of knocking her over, as she had half-expected, he plopped his back end neatly on the floor, looking immensely proud of himself.

"Well! What a good boy you are." She bent and kissed the tip of his nose, and in return, got a slurp of a long pink tongue up her cheek.

"Ah, I told you he loves you." Alex's voice was warm. "Thank you for staying."

271

She smiled up at him. The dark glint in his eyes hinted at the truth of what she had suspected — neither of them really believed that she had stayed just for Tyler.

* * *

"Mmm. That was good." Shelley smiled as she laid down her knife and fork.

Alex nodded his agreement. "They do excellent fish and chips down there."

Tyler had been hopefully watching for any titbits from the dining table. Shelley had secretly donated a couple of chips, and she suspected that Alex had too.

"I was a bit scared when you let him off the lead down on the beach. Weren't you worried he might run away?"

He shook his head. "The beach is quite safe for him to run around, and he's not brave enough to run away yet. The trick is to start straight away, while he's still feeling insecure. We're safety to him — and food! Show him that coming when he's called is more exciting than anything else — your tone of voice, a big fuss and a bag full of treats."

"Ah, of course. You're used to having dogs." She rose to her feet and began to clear the table.

"Here, let me," he insisted, taking the plates from her. "I'll put them straight in the dishwasher."

"Oh . . . right."

The table cleared, he smiled at her. "Fancy a movie?"

She hesitated, but temptation got the better of common sense. "What do you have?"

There were half a dozen DVDs on the shelf under the television. They settled on the *Dambusters*.

"You must have seen it before," Shelley objected when he suggested it.

"I have — about a dozen times — but I'll enjoy seeing it again. Those old black-and-white war movies are great." He took the DVD from the shelf and slotted it into the player. "You didn't bring the wine out with the fish and chips."

272

"No . . ."

"Fancy a glass now?"

"Okay."

As they settled on the sofa with their wine, Tyler tried to climb up with them.

"No!" Alex was laughing. "Get down. You're much too big to be a lapdog."

The big dog whined, looking sad. "Ah, you've hurt his feelings," Shelley protested.

"And you'd spoil him rotten."

He managed to persuade the giant pup to climb down. He circled around for a moment, then with a huff laid down — on their feet.

Alex laughed. "Ah well, that'll do." He picked up the remote and flicked it to start the film.

* * *

It felt good to be sitting here like this, his dog sleeping at his feet, Shelley close at his side. She was leaning against his shoulder, the subtle fragrance of her hair drifting on his breath.

Very carefully he eased his arm out from between them and laid it along the back of the sofa. He thought he heard her make a soft sound as she nestled closer, though maybe she was just laughing at the indignant chicken farmer writing his letter of complaint about the low-flying planes over his poultry sheds.

But when he let his arm slip down around her shoulders, the soft sound was definitely one of contentment. He wanted to tell her that he was in love with her, but he had a feeling that she wouldn't trust that word.

Very slowly he let one finger trail into a blonde curl that feathered over her ear. She didn't pull away, so he twirled his finger into the curl again.

Tilting her head back against his shoulder, she looked up at him, those pretty blue eyes uncertain. But when he smiled, she smiled back, that little dimple appearing in her cheek. And he knew that no words were needed — they both knew.

He slid his hand round to cradle her head as he dusted kisses over her trembling eyelids and across her temple, then down to the delicate shell of her ear, finding the tiny sensitive spot behind her lobe that made her sigh with pleasure.

* * *

Shelley felt Alex's breath warm against her cheek. And then at last his mouth met hers, light as a butterfly's wing. His sinuous tongue lapped along her lips, then stole between to swirl into the deep, secret corners within.

The kiss deepened — slow, quiet and achingly tender. A warmth was spreading through her, melting her bones like liquid honey, and she put up her hands to tangle her fingers in his hair, kissing him back.

It could have been moments, it could have been a thousand years before he lifted his head. "Do you think Tyler would mind if we went into the bedroom?" he murmured softly, close to her ear.

Shelley felt her heart flip over. This was the moment that had filled her fantasies for weeks. And now that it was here, she had no doubts.

She glanced down at the big dog, snoozing contentedly at their feet. "I think he's asleep. He must be exhausted from all the excitement of getting a new home."

"We'll try not to disturb him." Alex glanced around the room. "He should be safe enough in here."

Very carefully they eased their feet out from under the big dog. Both suppressing their laughter, they crept hand in hand to the bedroom. Alex closed the door quietly, listening for a moment for heavy paws or an indignant bark. Silence.

"Yes, I think he's asleep." He smiled down at her, his eyes filled with warmth, and glanced towards the bed. "Shall we?"

She could only nod her head — there wasn't enough air in her lungs to speak.

Outside it was dark, the sky mostly covered by clouds, no moon or stars. Alex drew her over to the bed and turned on the low lamp on the table beside it, filling the room with a soft, warm glow.

He drew her into his arms, and his mouth came down to hers again, warm and soft, his sensuous tongue sliding into the corner of her lips, coaxing them apart. He wasn't invading or demanding, as other men she had known had been. And she wasn't surrendering — she was his equal, wanting this as much as he did.

His hands slid up beneath her sweater, smoothing over her back. With a swift movement, she lifted it over her head and tossed it aside — and then did the same with his.

His body was beautiful. In the soft glow of the bedside lamp every muscle was sculpted, his skin was tanned to a pale gold, and a smattering of dark curling hair shadowed his wide chest. Resting her cheek against it she breathed his subtle male scent, letting it drug her senses.

His soft hand stroked down her spine, then round to her midriff and up over the ripe curve of her breast in the dainty lacy cups of her bra, sending little hot shivers running over her skin.

Her head felt light, dizzy, as they tipped together onto the wide, comfortable bed. She gazed up to look deep into his eyes, drowning herself in their mesmerising darkness.

His mouth was hot against her skin and he let his hand trail slowly over her body, caressing her with a warm gentle sensuality that reached right into her heart.

She felt him stroke over the aching swell of her breast, felt the tender bud of her nipple ripen in the tight constraint of her bra. Then with deft fingers he unclipped the lacy scrap and tossed it aside, and his hand brushed over the naked roundness, stirring her responses.

Her own hands were moving down over his wide shoulders and the powerful muscles in his chest, trailing a path

275

through that crisp, black, curling hair that darkened his smooth skin.

He bent his head, dusting a slow path of kisses down over the long column of her throat and along her collar bone, then on to the aching curve of her breasts, circling tantalisingly around first one dainty pink peak, then the other.

She closed her eyes, luxuriating in the strange, sweet rapture of it. Her breathing was shallow, and she heard herself moaning softly as his tongue swirled languorously around one taut, tender nipple. Then he drew it into his mouth, suckling at it with a deep, hungry rhythm, reducing her to a state of quivering helplessness.

He had unfastened the zip of her jeans, and as he tugged them down over her slim thighs, she wriggled herself out of them, then reached out her hands to do the same with his. Her lace-trimmed cotton briefs disappeared along with his jersey boxers.

Propping himself up on his elbow, he let his gaze drift down over her naked body. She closed her eyes, a soft moan escaping her lips as she stretched languorously, savouring his smooth touch stroking up over the soft inner flanks of her thighs.

"Beautiful." His voice was low and husky. "You're so beautiful — every perfect inch of you. Your skin's like silk."

Her breath seemed to be trapped in her lungs as she felt his hand slip into her most intimate core, and with unerring skill, he found the tiny seed-pearl nestling in its secret velvet fold. As his thumb stroked over it, a shock of pleasure sizzled through her.

A low ripple of laughter purred in his throat as he tormented her with the exquisite sensations. She was caught, helpless in the elemental force of her desire until she felt as if she could endure no more of this rapture.

And then she felt the heat of his mouth tracing a languid path of kisses down over her body. With a shimmer of delight, she felt him dip his head between her thighs, and his

276

sensuous, rasping tongue took the place of his thumb, languorously swirling over that acutely sensitive nub, firing her blood with a fever that scalded her brain.

At last he moved to lie above her, pausing briefly to reach over to the bedside table and take something from the drawer. A small foil pack. Teasing him with a mischievous smile, she took it from him and ripped it open, then carefully smoothed the gossamer sheath down over his hard length.

As his mouth closed over hers again, his tongue plundering all the sweet, secret corners within, she twined herself around him, drawing him in. For one long moment they lay still, just absorbing this moment of complete intimacy.

Then they began to move, slowly, in perfect harmony. He was careful to hold his weight from her, but she could sense that he was restraining the driving forces inside him as he built the rhythm, tantalising her with shallow thrusts and circling to stretch her deliciously.

She was long past the point of conscious awareness. Wrapped in her own velvet darkness, she was aware only of the subtle male scent of his body, and the ragged sound of their breathing as the pleasure rose inside her in waves.

Time spun away into an endless eternity, until at last the sheer primitive forces driving them exploded like a million stars, and with a last shuddering climax, they collapsed together on the bed.

277

CHAPTER THIRTY-EIGHT

Shelley lay curled up in the crook of Alex's arm. He was sleeping, his breath lightly stirring her hair. He hadn't turned his back on her, rolled over and ignored her, as other men had. He had snuggled her in, made sure she was comfortable, chatted quietly for a while. It felt so good to be here, warm and protected . . .

But it was dangerous to let yourself feel that way, to let your guard down. *Never rely on anyone — they'll all let you down in the end.* She really ought to leave, now, while he was asleep, before he could persuade her to stay. It would be so easy to let herself hope that this time it could be different.

Yes, she'd leave. In a few minutes, once she was sure he was asleep. It wasn't even midnight yet . . .

A loud crash from the sitting room jerked her upright. Then a second crash, followed by a whine of distress. She scrambled out of bed and snatched open the door.

A large, very distressed puppy was cowering on the floor beside the fallen Christmas tree, the cable for the lights wound round his paw.

"Oh, Sweetie, what's happened?" She knelt beside him and wrapped her arms around his neck. "Did it scare you?"

The dog leaned into her, trembling. She stroked down his long back with a soothing hand, murmuring softly in his ear.

"It's okay, don't be upset. It was just an accident. You're not going to be sent away."

She tipped her head back to look up at Alex, challenging him to confirm the promise. He had pulled on a dressing gown, and handed her the sweater he had been wearing earlier.

"Here — put this on or you'll freeze to death."

"Thanks." As she tugged it on over her head her senses were filled with the subtle male scent of his skin. Maybe he wouldn't notice if she kept it . . .

He had hunkered down beside the big dog, scritching the magic spot behind his ear. "Don't worry, buddy, of course you won't be sent away. It was my fault. I should have realised. It's just a silly old Christmas tree anyway. We'll soon sort it out."

The dog lifted his giant head, liquid brown eyes turning from one to the other. If he didn't understand the words, he seemed to understand the sentiment. Shelley felt the trembling subside as he relaxed, resting against her shoulder.

"There. You're a good boy. Yes, you are."

Alex unwound the light cable and picked up the fallen Christmas tree, putting a couple of the decorations back in place. "There, all done. Now you can go back on your bed, can't you boy?"

"Can't he . . . ?"

"No!" Alex's voice was firm. "I draw the line at letting him sleep on the bed."

"Oh. Well, that's the rule, Tyler. I'm sorry. Daddy's put his foot down." She had to smile as she caught Alex rolling his eyes at being called the dog's 'daddy'. "But you have a lovely comfy bed of your own, don't you? Here, give me a couple of treats and I'll coax him onto it."

Fifteen minutes and a dozen treats later, Tyler finally stopped being suspicious of the large blue beanbag and decided that maybe it was a comfy place to lie after all. As he settled on it with a grunt of contentment, Shelley flopped onto her back, laughing.

"Phew! Now, let's just hope he stays there!"

Alex laughed too, offering her his hand to pull her to her feet. "Let's hope so. I think we deserve a cup of tea after that!"

"I . . . um . . . ought to be getting back to the hotel," she protested.

"Why?"

"Well, I . . . I have to get up for work in the morning."

"That's okay. It's only round the corner. And anyway, I'll have to get up too, to take the mutt out for a w-a-l-k-i-e."

She hesitated, but it was too tempting. "Okay. Do I get breakfast in bed?"

He laughed softly, and dropped a kiss on the tip of her nose. "I think that can be arranged."

* * *

Shelley always appreciated waking up in a warm bed. She appreciated it even more now, with Alex Crocombe's lean, warm body beside her. She breathed in deeply, catching a drift of the unique scent of his skin.

She'd taken a chance, let herself hope. So far it had been all good. It had been three days . . .

Slipping out of bed she reached for her sweater and padded out barefoot to the sitting room. Tyler was asleep on his beanbag, but he woke at once, yawning widely and getting up to stretch his long body. He still had about a year's more growing time — he was going to be enormous!

She paused to ruffle his ears and drop a kiss on his nose, for which she got a long pink tongue lapping up her cheek. Then she strolled over to the window and pulled back the curtains.

"Oh, my goodness!"

"What is it?" Alex, stark naked with his hair adorably ruffled from sleep, appeared in the doorway behind her.

"It's been snowing!"

Wrapping his arms around her from behind, he peered over her shoulder out of the window. "You call that snow? At home we don't even think it's worth mentioning until it's ten feet deep."

"That's because you live practically in the Arctic Circle. But we never get snow here. Well, it snows quite a lot up on Dartmoor, but not down here on the coast." She gazed out of the window at the street below, blanketed in pure white. "It's so beautiful."

He nuzzled into her neck. "Wait till you have to go out and walk in it."

She laughed, turning her head to kiss the stubble along his jaw. "It's a good job the last of the Turkey-and-Tinsel groups left yesterday. They might not have been able to get away if the roads are bad."

"They'll have had the gritter lorries out overnight, and the main roads should be fine."

Shelley glanced down at Tyler. The big dog had come over to lift his paws up onto the windowsill and look out. "What do you make of that, Sweetie?" she asked him.

He turned his head to look up at them as if puzzled to know what was so interesting. Alex scritched the dog's favourite spot behind his ear. "You're going to find out in a bit, buddy. Come on, let's get some breakfast and then we can walk him over to the hotel."

They were in no hurry, though. With the last Turkey-and-Tinsel group gone, there were no more guests in the hotel. It was closing down for Christmas, and after that the renovations would start in earnest.

It was almost eleven o'clock by the time they were ready to set out. They both put on two pairs of socks and bundled themselves up in hats and scarves and gloves against the cold.

The sun was pale and distant in a cloudless blue sky. The bare branches of the trees were outlined in white, the hedges and gardens quiet beneath a blanket of snow that seemed to muffle every sound.

Predictably, Tyler took a fair amount of coaxing to step out into this cold, white, wet stuff. He sniffed at it suspiciously, tapped it with one large paw, and drew back. "Come on, you big coward," Alex urged. "It won't hurt you."

The big dog looked doubtful, but his trust in Alex was enough to convince him to try it. After a few tentative steps he decided that it was safe after all, and pranced along happily beside them, looking inordinately proud of himself.

Alex laughed, dropping his arm around Shelley's shoulders and hugging her close. She smiled up at him, feeling a deep warmth inside her, even though it was so cold that she could see her breath in white puffs.

Three days, and four wonderful nights. Not very long . . . But it felt . . . right. She wasn't going to think about how long it might last. Just take one day at a time.

The snow was actually only about five or six inches deep. Someone had already been out to sweep a path along the pavement, and the gritter lorry had been down Church Road.

But the hotel car park was still a pure, pristine white, smooth as sugar icing and glistening in the pale winter sunshine. That was until Alex let Tyler off his lead.

The dog suddenly decided that this snow stuff was great fun, and began to race around in circles, kicking up showers of white that sparkled in the sunlight as he barked joyously.

"He's having a good time!"

Shelley turned at the sound of laughter. The Ellises were strolling down the lane — Liam and Cassie, Luke and Julia, with Robyn and Ben racing ahead, all bundled up in woolly scarves and bobble hats.

"Especially considering how long it took us to persuade him to come out in it," Alex responded cheerfully. "How are the horses?"

"They're fine — they're not bothered by the snow. We brought them in last night when we got the weather warning, but we turned most of them out to the paddock this morning."

Robyn was bouncing up and down excitedly. "Mummy, can we make a snowman?" she pleaded.

"Another one?" Cassie smiled down at her. "You made two in Suomu."

"Yes, but we had to leave those behind. Now we can make one here."

"Did you have a good time visiting Santa?" Shelley asked her.

"We had an *amazing* time!" The child's eyes were wide. "We went for a ride in a real reindeer sleigh."

"I know. I saw the pictures you sent."

"Daddy said she was a she reindeer, that's why she had antlers. The boy reindeers don't have them at this time of year."

"Is that so?"

"And she was called Bikka. That's nearly the same name as my pony! Isn't that funny!"

Shelley laughed. "It certainly is. When did you get back?" she added to Cassie.

"Last night. We really did have a wonderful time. She was so excited to see Santa."

"It's lovely that she's still at an age to believe in him," Julia remarked. "Ben's beginning to have his doubts."

"Ah, it's a shame that they have to lose that magic."

"Come on, Robyn," Ben called. He had already made a start on piling up snow for the snowman. "Come and help."

The little girl scampered over to join him. The three men were also recruited — not that they were at all reluctant. Soon a magnificent snowman was taking shape, becoming taller than Ben.

The lights on the Christmas tree beside the front steps were winking brightly, casting their jewel colours on the snow. The children's piping voices echoed on the frosty air like birdsong.

Shelley smiled as she watched them. Tyler had stopped chasing himself round the car park and had come over to stand

283

beside her. He leaned against her leg, and she stroked his big head fondly.

Several of the foster homes she had grown up in had had dogs, and she had always loved them — dogs never judged you or let you down.

And there was Alex, laughing as he helped build the snowman, every bit as enthusiastic as the children. He glanced across to her and smiled, and she felt her heart soar.

"Hello!" Vicky and Tom, with Debbie and little Amy, greeted them as they turned in through the entrance. "We came down to get some hot chocolate."

"We did the same," Julia called back. "But we got sidetracked!"

Amy had scampered over to join her friends. Tom had Rufus on his lead, and as soon as he let him off he barked joyfully, trying to run through the snow, though with his little legs he didn't find it as easy as Tyler.

"Come and help with the snowman, Uncle Tom," Ben pleaded. "We're building the biggest one ever!"

Tom laughed. "It certainly looks like it."

"Hey, I saw you building it." Jess come down the steps from the hotel. "I've brought a few things you might need."

"Great. Thank you, Auntie Jess!" Ben ran over and seized the offerings — a carrot for a nose, some Brussels sprouts to make eyes and buttons, and a long red scarf that one of the guests must have left behind.

"How did you get on?" Julia asked Debbie quietly.

"Great! Want to see the scan?"

"Do I!"

The women all huddled round as Debbie took an envelope from her bag and opened it, pulling out the black-and-white printout. Peering over her shoulder, all Shelley could see at first was a pattern of random blobs, but as she looked, they gradually resolved themselves into a recognisable shape.

A baby.

No. Don't even start thinking about that. One day at a time . . .

284

"Does Amy know yet?" Cassie asked.

Debbie shook her head. "Not yet. We want to wait a little longer to tell her. Get the excitement of Christmas out of the way first."

Over at the snowman, progress had been quick with so many helpers. A large ball had been made ready, and with all due ceremony was placed on its shoulders. The eyes and nose were added, and the buttons down his front.

"There!" Ben reached up to wrap the scarf round the snowman's neck. "That's the best snowman *ever!*"

Robyn was bouncing up and down. "He's got to have a name. What's he called?"

"Mr Forsythe!" Jess and Shelley chorused at once.

Everyone laughed. "Mr Forsythe it is."

"Photos!" Julia insisted, pulling out her phone. "Everyone gather round."

They all jumbled together around the snowman, grinning cheesily as she snapped off several photographs. Then Alex took the phone so that she could be in them too.

"Mr Forsythe, we don't like you," Jess declared, scooping up a handful of snow and compacting it tightly in her hands. "You're a very nasty man." Swinging her arm back, she threw the snowball hard and straight, smacking it squarely into the stolid white chest. "There! Serves you right!"

"Serves you right!" Ben echoed. "You're a nasty man." He made a snowball and threw it at the snowman's head.

Robyn squealed with excitement. "Me too! Me too!"

Soon everyone was battering the snowman with snowballs until his nose fell off to loud cheers. Julia's throw missed and hit Liam, who promptly retaliated. Julia laughed. "Hey, sis, let's get him!"

"Whey hey!" Jess was more than willing, and the pair of them ganged up. Luke went to his brother's aid, and Cassie joined in as snowballs flew in all directions.

"Hiya! Is this a private snowball fight or can anyone join in?"

285

It was Lisa and Ollie, with Kyra in her buggy. Noah had already raced over to join his friends.

"Get yourselves some snowballs!" Julia advised. "Women against men!"

"Hey, not fair!" Liam protested. "There's more of you."

"You can have the kids on your side."

With battle-lines drawn, a full-scale snowball fight was launched. The children were racing around shrieking, Tyler and Rufus were bouncing and barking, trying to join in, the grown-ups were laughing and breathless.

Shelley couldn't remember when she'd ever had stupid, crazy fun like this, dodging snowballs and hurling them back, laughing herself silly.

She caught Alex with a good hit on his shoulder, and he chased her round the car park, threatening to stuff snow down her collar. But when he caught her, he snatched her round the waist instead and swung her up in the air.

And when he lowered her to the ground, he kissed her. Right there in front of everyone. And she didn't care who saw them.

"Phew!" At last Lisa puffed out a breath, her hands on her knees. "I'm done. Hot chocolate anyone?"

"Yes, please!" the children all chorused at once.

"Come on, then."

Stamping their feet and brushing the snow from their coats they all piled into the hotel and into the lounge. In moments, big mugs of hot chocolate, topped with swirls of whipped cream and marshmallows, were conjured up. The children's eyes grew wide, and the grown-ups were no less greedy.

"Ha, you've got a moustache!" Ben declared, pointing at Robyn, whose upper lip was streaked with cream.

"So have you!"

Everyone was laughing. It was cosy in the lounge, looking out onto the snow-covered garden. The coloured fairy lights on the Christmas tree were twinkling, the faint scent of pine lingered in the air, and the hot chocolate was sweet and delicious.

Shelley glanced around, feeling a warm glow inside her that wasn't just due to the hot chocolate. Christmas. It had never meant much to her before. In the foster homes where she had grown up she had always felt like an outsider at the family gatherings, had always known that her Christmas presents had been paid for by Social Services.

But this Christmas, for the first time in her life, she felt the kind of warmth and excitement that everyone else seemed to feel. She was with friends.

And Alex.

They were snuggled up on the sofa, his arm around her shoulders, Tyler sprawled across their feet. She wanted to tell him that she loved him, but she didn't quite have the courage yet. Maybe one day — maybe soon.

But for now she was just content to be with him, and take one day at a time.

287

CHAPTER THIRTY-NINE

'Silent night, Holy night
All is calm, all is bright . . .'

Paul loved this old church. He had so many memories — of coming here to Sunday School when he was a kid, and later to Church Parade with the Scouts. And the Christmas carol service — even when he was away with his team he had always tried to get home for it.

All Saints was quite small, but the sound of a hundred voices singing the lovely old Christmas carol rose to fill the high vaulted roof. Built in the thirteenth century from the local hard grey stone, the Victorians had added a square bell tower and a fine stained-glass window over the altar.

There at the front, as every year, was a large Christmas tree on one side of the altar, and on the other beside the pulpit was the nativity scene — the wooden stable, the little plaster figures arranged on the straw, the slightly chipped angel on the roof.

Another memory rose, making him smile. When he and his friends had been about eight or nine years old Alan Cowan had stolen one of the tiny sheep, and tried to cast the blame on

Liam Ellis. Tom Cullen had cornered him in the playground at school the next day and forced him to own up and return it.

'Silent night, Holy night . . .'

Two rows in front of him was the Ellis family. Diane and Graham, Liam with Cassie and little Robyn, newly returned from their honeymoon to Lapland, Luke and Julia with young Ben. And Jess, sitting next to her sister, two heads of rich auburn curls gleaming in the soft light spilling from the sconces along the wall.

He still couldn't figure out what he had done to make her so hostile. That night when she'd come to his house for dinner she'd said they could be friends, even though she didn't want a relationship with him. He'd reluctantly accepted that.

Then the day after he'd got back from Botswana she'd all but bitten his head off.

For the past couple of days he'd avoided coming down to the hotel, wary of antagonising her further. But perhaps this evening the carol concert might put her in a more mellow frame of mind.

The concert continued with a group of children taking it in turns to read extracts from the Christmas story. A prayer, then another favourite carol, someone read a poem, then the congregation sang their hearts out to 'Hark the Herald Angels Sing'.

Finally, Eva brought the service to an end with the traditional blessing, and everyone began to shuffle around, chatting to their neighbours and wishing everyone a Merry Christmas as they filed down the aisle and out into the night.

The snow still lay deep in the churchyard on either side of the swept path, smothering all the graves in white. A single bird had walked across it, leaving its dainty footprints on the pristine surface.

The air was sharp with frost. The sky was smudged with dark grey clouds, obscuring the stars, but the pale moon glimmered though the occasional ragged gap, high, white and stark.

289

His mum and dad had paused to chat with some of their friends. Tom and Vicky Cullen nodded goodnight as they strolled past, hand in hand. Lisa and Ollie stopped to exchange a few words, young Noah skipping around them impatiently.

And there was Jess, at last, with the Ellises. She was wrapped up in a warm parka, a long red scarf wrapped around her throat, a red woollen bobble hat pulled down over her ears.

He caught the moment when she saw him. She glanced towards him then quickly away. Her cheeks were pink, but that could just have been the cold.

The family stopped to shake hands with his parents and wish them Merry Christmas. Jess held back a little — she seemed to have taken a sudden intense interest in the design of the bell tower.

As everyone began to move towards the old wooden lych-gate and out onto Church Road he murmured a brief good-night to his parents and moved over to Jess's side.

"Hi. Did you enjoy the service?"

"Uh, yes." Her shoulders had stiffened, but at least she had replied. "It was very nice. I haven't been to a carol service since I was a kid."

Progress? "What are you doing for Christmas?" he asked, trying a smile.

"I'm staying with Julia."

"Not going to your parents?"

"No." Her head turned towards him, but then away again. "I might go up to see them both in the new year."

He hesitated. It was taking a risk to bring the subject up again, but he needed to clear the air. "Ah . . . We haven't spoken since I got back from Africa."

". . . No."

"Did I do something to upset you?" he asked gently.

"No. It was my fault. I . . . made a mistake." Her voice sounded strained. "I saw you, with a girl — one of the T-and-T people. She was here with her husband."

"Ah . . ." Enlightenment began to dawn.

At last she glanced up at him. "I saw you going into her room, and I assumed . . . I shouldn't have jumped to conclusions like that. I'm sorry."

"It was understandable," he responded gently. "I can imagine how it must have looked."

"I found out when they were checking out. They left that bottle of whiskey for you, and . . . she explained what had happened. I'm sorry, I would have apologised then, but . . ."

"I stayed out of your way." He laughed. "I was afraid you'd chew me up and spit out the bones."

Her smile wavered for a moment. "There'd be a lot to chew."

"There would."

They had reached the Memorial Gardens. The Ellises were some way ahead, past the hotel and already turning into their gate.

The Memorial Gardens lay quiet under a blanket of undisturbed snow, glistening like diamonds in the glow of the single street lamp. The flowerbeds were just undulations, casting weird shadows against the smooth white surface.

Jess paused and Paul watched the white clouds of her breath drifting away on the icy wind. There was no one else around, and the snow seemed to deaden every sound but the wind and the sea.

"Let's go for a walk."

He was a little surprised at her suggestion, but he wasn't going to question the whys and the wherefores.

He reached out tentatively and took her hand, and they strolled down the ramp to the narrow strip of beach left by the incoming tide. The wind was whipping the waves into a fury of white foam far out across the bay, dancing in across the sand then ebbing away to be chased by another.

"I love how the sea is so different all the time," she murmured. "Sometimes so stormy, sometimes as tranquil as a millpond. Every day you never quite know how it will be."

"That's part of the fun of living here. Always the unexpected."

"Where have the beach huts gone?"

"They take them away at the end of October. They're stored in the car park on the top of the hill until April."

"Ah."

They had reached the bottom of the cliff steps and they could go no further as the slope of the beach meant that the sea here ran right up to the cliff wall. Jess climbed the first step, then turned to him. Their heads were level, and she lifted her hands to each side of his face. And kissed him.

He felt as if he'd been tasered. Her mouth was warm and firm on his, her sensuous tongue sliding boldly between his lips, probing its way deep inside.

He'd forgotten to breathe — he'd probably forgotten his own name. His hands slid up into her hair as he kissed her back, their tongues sparring and swirling around each other, their bodies generating enough heat to melt all the snow on Cliff Road.

She drew her head back, her eyes dark as they gazed up at him. "Take me to bed."

He stared at her, stunned. But her eyes told him that she meant it. Fumbling in his pocket for his key, he took her hand, led her up the steps and across the road to his front door.

Dammit. The keyhole. Why couldn't he get the key in? Ah, at last. Jess was laughing, teasing him, as he finally managed to get the door open.

He dragged her inside, slamming the door with his heel and shoving her back against it. Then his mouth was on hers, fiercely possessive, as his hands swept up and down her spine, defining every curve, every valley.

She moved against him, her body restless, her soft moans telling him everything he needed to know.

His hands itched to feel her skin. Hunger roared through him and he deepened their kiss, his tongue sweeping into her mouth, claiming everything she had and demanding more.

292

She gave it to him, surrendering herself to the passion rising between them. Her tongue tangled with his, her breath sighing against his cheek as she met him stroke for stroke. Her hands clutched his shoulders, holding on tightly as she moaned with pleasure.

That soft sound was enough to push him dangerously close to the edge. He tore his mouth from hers, looking down at her through eyes glazed with need. "If we don't move right now, we're not going to make it to the bedroom."

She laughed, a low, throaty sound. "Would you care?"

"The bed's comfortable, but it's up a whole flight of stairs."

Her eyes danced in wicked amusement. "Race you!"

"Right . . ."

She dodged past him, laughing provocatively as he chased her across the hall. They made it halfway up the stairs before he caught her, and they both collapsed, laughing helplessly. His body was hard and aching — he could hardly draw breath without fanning the flames licking at his insides.

"You've got too many clothes on," she protested, fumbling at the buttons of his shirt.

"So have you."

Rolling around on the stairs, they tore at each other's clothes, tossing aside coats and sweaters until they were both down to their underwear. Wriggling out from beneath him, her laughter challenging him, she scrambled a little further up the stairs, but he caught her ankle, clambering over her to claim her mouth again.

Her taste was intoxicating, her kiss sizzling his brain. Everything in him urged him to hurry, to ease the need surging inside him.

But the urge to linger over every second was just as strong. His tongue entwined with hers once more, and he stroked one hand down over her body, relishing the smooth, soft curves beneath his palm.

293

He had dreamed of this moment, painted every detail in his imagination. Somehow, she reached him in a way no other woman had, and although that thought bothered him, it wasn't enough to keep him from taking what she was offering.

* * *

She had dreamed of this moment, but this was no dream. It was far too real. Those hard muscles, those strong, sensitive hands, those sizzling kisses . . . She moaned and writhed beneath him as his hot mouth traced a scalding path down her throat, dragging her to the edge of reason.

His hands laced in her hair as she grasped his shoulders. She wanted him, wanted to feel his smooth muscles move under her hands, wanted to taste every inch of his skin.

With a deft movement, he unhooked her lacy bra and tossed it aside, then his hands were on her breasts, caressing and crushing them beneath his palms, tormenting the ripe peaks with tiny tugs and pinches that sent sparks of electricity zinging through her tautly strung nerve fibres.

Laughing and taunting him some more, she wriggled out from beneath him again and crawled up a few more steps. He caught her, but she twisted free and made it to the landing.

Stumbling over each other's feet, they crashed through the bedroom door and finally managed to tumble onto the bed.

"See? We made it."

She could hardly breathe for laughing, for the urgent desire roiling in the pit of her stomach. She reached for him, dragging him down to her, revelling in the contact of hot, naked flesh, of hard male muscles taut and strong under her hands, of that smattering of rough, curling hair across his wide chest.

"Now, let's see how many points I can earn for this," he growled, bending his head to take one taut pink nipple into his mouth. She gasped and arched against him as he suckled

294

deeply, using his teeth and tongue to torture her with pleasure, making her squirm and gasp for breath.

"A hundred . . . A thousand . . . A million . . ."

She felt the laughter rumble in his chest as she clung to him. Making love had never been like this — fun, playful, crazy. Wild. They rolled on the bed, her hair tangling around them and getting in his mouth; him crushing her beneath his weight to hold her down; her wriggling and twisting to land on top of him.

Somehow her lace knickers had disappeared, and she felt the stroke of his hand up the smooth inner flank of her thighs, his clever fingers exploring the soft velvet folds between, and finding the tiny sensitive seed-pearl that was the focus of all her arousal.

Pressing her lips to his throat, she tasted the dark male flavour of his skin. All her senses were bound up in what his mouth and hands were doing to her. Weak with desire, she could do no more than breathe his name as the ripples of pleasure flooded her veins.

He leaned over to the bedside table and she heard the rip of foil, sensed him smooth the gossamer sheath over his hard length, and she moaned softly as she took him into her, deep and slow, moving together in a dance as old as Eve. Her arms were wrapped around him, clinging to him as the only thing that was real in this wild storm of sensation.

There was no past, no future, only this moment and this man. Higher and higher she rose, spinning dizzily in a vortex of fire, until with a last aching cry, she felt as if she was exploding into a trillion stars, collapsing onto the bed, tangled up in his arms.

* * *

Paul drifted for a long time between sleeping and waking. Jess lay in the crook of his arm, her slow, even breathing warm against his shoulder. She seemed to fit there as if they had both

295

been designed that way. Her glorious autumn hair was spread across the pillow, just as he'd always imagined.

So what now? The whys and wherefores he had refused to consider before came crowding back into his mind. Without being arrogant, he'd known she was attracted to him, but she had seemed set on keeping him at arm's length.

And then, suddenly, she'd changed her mind.

He was at a loss. He'd never been one to ask questions about a relationship before — he'd never needed to. None of them had been important enough.

But this one was. Which was a rather scary thought.

* * *

Jess woke to the pale-grey light of dawn filtering through her window. No, not her window, she realised as she opened her eyes. Memory came back quickly along with the warm ache in her muscles and the sensation of a long hard male body close against hers.

She had slept with Paul Channing.

Turning her head carefully so as not to wake him, she studied his face on the pillow beside her. Those long dark silky lashes lay against his cheeks — a lot of women would kill for lashes like that. A dark morning stubble shadowed his hard jaw, and there was a half-smile on that well-made mouth.

But the niggling voice in the back of her head that she had let herself ignore when he was making love to her was still whispering. Okay, she had been the one to instigate this, and okay he wasn't at all like Glenn.

But he was Paul Channing. The man who changed his girlfriends as often as he changed his socks. Maybe she could last a little longer. After all, she had made him wait longer than he was used to.

But now the clock was ticking. A few weeks, even a month or two, and that would be it. Sayonara.

296

And in the meantime, she would be falling in love with him. In truth, she already had. And if she stayed, she would end up getting her heart shattered beyond repair.

She had to leave — now, before he woke up. Before he could smile at her, before those dark eyes could glint with teasing amusement and blow away every shred of willpower she possessed.

Moving silently, she slipped out of bed and found her clothes, then tiptoed from the room with a last regretful glance back over her shoulder. He was still sleeping, his breathing deep and slow. Her heart creased with pain. Walking away from him now was the hardest thing she'd ever done.

But she had to go.

She crept down the stairs, thankful that none of the treads creaked, and dressed quickly in the hall. Then she eased open the front door and stepped out into the frosty air, closing the door firmly behind her and picking her way carefully though the crisp white snow.

CHAPTER FORTY

"Great party, Mike." Eric, the porter, raised his pint glass in a cheerful toast.

"Yes, it is." Mike raised his gin and tonic in return, smiling as he gazed around the ballroom.

It was two days before Christmas. The last of the Turkey-and-Tinsel groups had gone, and as they did every year before the hotel closed for the holidays the staff and their families, with some friends from the town and other guests, had gathered for a Christmas party.

But this year was different. The hotel wouldn't be reopening in the new year. And when it did reopen, after all the renovations had been completed, he wouldn't be here.

The lights on the Christmas trees and the curtain falls all around the room were twinkling, champagne was flowing and the DJ was playing yet another cheesy Christmas song.

Over on the far side of the dance floor he could see Kate dancing with her new son-in-law, Bill. Very brave of her — hopefully she'd be nimble enough to keep her toes away from his clumsy size twelves.

The song ended and another came on. He watched as Kate made her escape from Bill and wove between the dancers to come back to him. Her smile warmed his heart.

298

He took her hand and bent to kiss her cheek. "You survived?"

"Of course." She laughed. He really liked the way she laughed — soft as a summer breeze. "He's actually getting better. How about you? I bet you were glad to get out of that Santa suit. It must be really hot."

"It is. And the beard tickles."

"But the kids love it."

"They do. Though I think some of them are getting to the age when they don't quite believe it anymore. Especially your Amy. She was giving me some very suspicious looks."

"Ah, she's a bright one. Anyway, come and dance with me."

The song was one they could jive to. Mike felt a small stab of pride in her, that she danced so well. Those pretty brown eyes were laughing as she twirled and spun so lightly on her dainty feet.

When the music changed, he slid his arm around her waist, drawing her closer. Several people cast them curious glances, but he didn't care. He was with Kate, and he wanted everyone to know it.

* * *

Kate let herself relax in Mike's arms. She had been a little shy at first about people knowing that they were together, but why should she mind? She was proud to be with him.

After all the cheesy songs, the DJ was playing a beautiful Christmas ballad — Roy Orbison, one of her favourites. She murmured along to the wistful words — although there wasn't really room to waltz she loved dancing with Mike.

"Debbie's looking well," he remarked, glancing across at Kate's daughter who was dancing with Bill, smiling up into his homely face as if to her he was as handsome as any film star.

Kate smiled too — no need to worry about their happiness.

299

"Have they told Amy about the baby yet?" Mike asked.

"No. They wanted to wait until after the twelve-week scan, and Christmas. She'll be over the moon. Anyway, how about you?" She tipped back her head to look up at him. "How's the job hunting going?"

"Ah, well, yes. That."

"What?"

There was a wry quirk to his mouth. "I haven't really been looking for a new job."

"You've changed your mind about leaving here?"

"No . . . But . . . What you were saying, about needing to employ someone in the café, with Debbie being pregnant?"

Her brow furrowed in confusion. "Yes . . . ?"

"Have you found anyone yet?"

"No." Where was this going? "I thought I'd put up a notice in the window, ask around. There's bound to be a youngster looking for a job."

"Would you consider someone older?"

"Of course."

"Or a man?"

"Well . . . yes, I suppose . . ." She hesitated, the cogs in her brain starting to fall into place. "Did you have anyone in mind?"

He just smiled.

"You?"

"Why not?"

"But . . ." She shook her head — in bewilderment rather than refusal.

"You said I need to do what's right for me," he reminded her.

"Well yes, but . . ."

"Look, if you don't want me, that's okay. I'll understand. It won't make any difference to . . . us."

"Oh, no. I mean, yes, but . . . You'd really want to come and work in the café? After managing the hotel? Wouldn't it be . . ."

"A step down? Yes, but that's exactly what I want. I'm fifty-seven years old. Losing Sarah taught me that time isn't endless. Why waste the time I have doing something that's just a job, something that doesn't make me happy to wake up in the morning? I'd be happy working in the café — with you. What do you say?"

"Oh, Mike. I'd love to have you working with me, if that's really what you want."

"It is."

"Then you've got the job." She laughed, a bubble of happiness growing inside her. She had been so anxious that he would be leaving Sturcombe, just when they were growing close to each other. "When can you start?"

"As soon as you like. And . . . as I'll be moving out of my accommodation here, I was wondering what you'd think about me moving in with you?"

"In my flat?"

"Of course, I can find somewhere else if you'd rather not," he assured her quickly. "If you think it's too soon. I've spoken to Vicky Cullen and she said I can have one of the cottages she's renovating, if I want it."

She smiled up at him, the bubbles of happiness fizzing in her heart. "I don't think it's too soon. Like you said, time isn't endless. Let's make the most of it."

"Let's. I love you, Kate Rowley."

"Oh, Mike. I love you too."

He bent his head, and his mouth brushed over hers, tender and sweet. How lucky was she? In her middle fifties, after twenty-plus years alone since her Terry had died, to have found love again at last.

She hadn't noticed that he had steered her out to the conservatory. As he lifted his head and glanced up, she followed his gaze, and realised that they were under a spray of mistletoe tied to one of the cross struts of the roof.

"You know what?" he murmured. "Let's go three for three."

301

"Three?"

He smiled slowly and tilted his forehead against hers. "Let's get married."

* * *

"Oh, hello." Shelley paused by one of the tables, recognising the two women from the Ladies Golf League. Was it really only a couple of months since they'd been here before? It felt like half a lifetime — so much had changed. Now she could smile with a confidence she hadn't known then. "How do you do?"

"Ah, it's Shelley, isn't it? How nice to see you again." The older of the two extended her hand. "It's a very lively party, isn't it?"

"Yes, it is." Shelley laughed, glancing round at the ballroom. Everyone was enjoying themselves, dancing and singing along to the cheesy Christmas songs the DJ was playing. With the lights lowered, the room was transformed into a smart disco or nightclub.

"It was kind of Mr Crocombe to invite us," the other woman — Mrs Lavis? — said. "We've been discussing our plans for next season."

"Oh?"

"You'll be pleased to know that we intend to bring several of our regional ladies' tournaments here. And we're negotiating to host a round of the national tournament, too."

Shelley smiled in delight. "Ah, that's good." They had been hoping for that. The contract would secure bookings for quite a few weeks over the whole year. "We'll be pleased to have you."

"I'm not saying that it was entirely because of what you did to help us in dealing with Mr Gibbons," Mrs Booth confided, smiling, "but it was certainly a factor in our consideration."

Mrs Lavis nodded. "We felt that your courage in coming forward deserved some reward."

302

"Oh." She wasn't sure what to say to that. "Well . . . thank you."

"We've been looking at the display board about the plans for the hotel. It's going to look fabulous. Really elegant."

"Yes, it is." And not yellow and purple, thank goodness!

"I love those new waterfall chandeliers you're putting in here. And the wall lights in the corridors upstairs give a much nicer light than ceiling lights."

"I'm looking forward to trying out the spa. We were talking to Mike earlier. He said they've already started on that."

"Oh, yes. It's in the annexe, so they were able to make a start even while there were guests here."

"Such a charming man." She glanced eagerly around the ballroom. "Is he still here?"

"Yes, I . . . um . . . think he's just popped outside for a minute." She smiled to herself. The staff often teased Mike gently about how many of the older women guests took such an interest in him.

"He told us he's leaving."

"He's taking early retirement. We'll all be sad to see him go. But he plans to stay in Sturcombe, and he'll still be coming in to help Alex get the hang of running the place."

"That's good. Well, Merry Christmas, my dear."

"Merry Christmas."

Shelley wandered around the side of the room, watching the dancing. Everyone was thoroughly enjoying themselves. Santa hats and reindeer antlers and sparkling garlands of tinsel were the dress code, and the champagne was free.

"Ah, there you are. Come and dance with me, eh?"

Shelley glanced round as Alex came up behind her, her heart skipping. She knew it was crazy to let herself fall in love with him, but she couldn't help herself. If it all ended tomorrow . . . Well, she'd survive.

He drew her out onto the dance floor and slipped his arms around her, drawing her close and moving with her to the music, and she let herself stop thinking about tomorrow, next week, next month.

She was with him for now, and that was enough.

"Where have you been?" he asked, smiling down at her.

"Chatting to the ladies from the golf league. They said they'd been looking at the display boards in the lounge."

"What did they think of it?"

"They loved it. They told me they're bringing more tournaments here."

He nodded. "We agreed terms this afternoon."

"That's good."

He was a good dancer, easy on the rhythm. And it felt so good being in his arms. If people were staring, shocked to see her with him, why should she care?

He was the most attractive man in the room, so far as she was concerned. Some might pick Lisa's brother Paul, or maybe Tom Cullen or Liam Ellis, but for her there was no contest.

"Anyway, where have you been?" she asked.

"I took Tyler for a walk, and popped in to see Grandpa."

"Ah. How is he?"

"Fine. He was just getting off to bed. Grumbling about Marcus being away, though Carol seems nice enough."

"Marcus'll be back in a few days. He deserves to have Christmas off."

Alex laughed dryly. "Try telling that to my grandfather! Anyway, then we walked on up the hill."

"Oh?"

"I noticed a for-sale sign when I drove past yesterday, so I thought I'd go up and take a look."

Her brow furrowed in thought. "You mean the old Ellicot place?"

"Is that what it is? Big old house, set well back from the road. I couldn't get inside, obviously, but I managed to look in through a couple of windows. The rooms look pretty big, and the garden at the back is huge. Tyler would love it."

304

She glanced up at him in surprise. "You're going to buy it?"

"I think I might. I'll speak to the estate agent in the new year to arrange a viewing." He smiled down at her again. "Will you come up with me to have a look?"

She laughed a little unsteadily. "You want me to give you sensible advice, after I landed you with Tyler?"

His eyes glinted with warm amusement. "Well, that turned out pretty well."

"It did." She had to smile at the thought. "Where is he now?"

"In Mike's office. He's okay in there. I can pop in from time to time to check on him."

"With a bit of sausage roll?"

"Of course."

"He's not bothered by the noise of the party?" she asked.

"He's better there than on his own in the flat. He doesn't like being alone."

She laughed softly. "Big baby."

* * *

Another cheesy Christmas song began, and Alex laughed, shaking his head. "Oh no, not this one. This is really doing my head in. Let's go outside."

"It's freezing out there," she objected.

"The conservatory then."

He kept his arm around her waist as they threaded their way through the dancers. She looked absolutely gorgeous tonight, her pixie blonde hair curling around her head, her blue eyes sparkling.

Her dress was a light greeny-blue, some kind of floaty fabric that swirled around her as she moved and flirted to just above her knees.

"I like your dress," he murmured.

"Oh . . . !" Her eyes lit up. "Thank you. Jess picked it for me. We went into Exeter last week to go shopping."

It struck him to the heart how much that simple compliment seemed to mean to her. He guessed that she had never owned a pretty dress like that before, much less received any compliments.

The small jewellery box he had picked up yesterday was burning a hole in his pocket. Was he moving too fast? But moving fast was what he did. And Jess had told him that she had almost run away a few weeks ago — Lisa had persuaded her to stay. He didn't want to risk that happening again.

* * *

"Phew!"

Shelley huffed out a breath. It was cooler in the conservatory after the heat of the ballroom, where everyone was jumping around and singing along raucously to the music. She'd noticed that even the two golf ladies were on their feet, joining in.

Alex drew her round into the shelter of a flourishing Areca palm, sliding his arms around her and drawing her close.

"About the house . . ."

She glanced up at him, a question in her eyes.

"The thing is, Tyler said that he won't move in there unless you come too."

She laughed at his nonsense. "He did?"

He nodded, pretending to be solemn. "He was most insistent about it. In fact, he said it would be most improper of me to just ask you to move in with us. He can be really quite prudish at times."

"Oh . . . ?"

He glanced up, and she followed his gaze. Above their heads was a spray of mistletoe.

"So . . . I got you an early Christmas present." He took something out of his pocket and put it into her hand. "Well, it's not really a Christmas present."

She hesitated. It was a jewellery box. A small one. The sort that often held earrings, or dainty little pendants on gold chains.

"Open it," he urged softly.

Gulping down the constriction in her throat, she lifted the lid. A ring. A sapphire, surrounded by diamonds. It caught the light from the ballroom and flashed like fire.

"I love you, Shelley." There was a warmth, a whole world of meaning in his voice. "Will you marry me?"

She had to close her eyes for a few seconds. When she opened them, he was still there, still smiling at her, and that beautiful ring was still in her hand.

Happiness bubbled up into laughter. "Did Tyler tell you to ask me that?"

"Of course he did. What shall I tell him?"

"Uh . . ." She drew in a long, slow breath. "You'd better tell him I said yes."

His smile could have melted the winter frost out in the garden as he slipped the ring onto her finger. It was a perfect fit. His mouth came down to hers in a long, deep, tender kiss — a kiss under the mistletoe, for a lifetime of love.

***

Jess stood on the terrace, leaning on the cold stone balustrade as she watched the wind-whipped waves roll in and crash in fountains of spray against the rocks below.

The stars were glittering pinpricks of light, high and stark and cold in the ink-dark sky, and the moon gleamed like silver on the snow that still blanketed the garden.

It was freezing out here. Her breath was puffing out in clouds of white, and there were goosebumps all down her bare arms. But she didn't care — the icy cold just suited her mood.

Christmas, and everyone was merry. Behind her the ballroom was full of happy people dancing to a seemingly endless string of jolly Christmas songs as the fairy lights on the tall Christmas tree winked silver and gold.

Maybe it was the Christmas spirit, or maybe there was something in the air, but everyone seemed to be falling in love. There had been two weddings in the summer, then Cassie and Liam's wedding just last week.

Now Alex and Shelley were in the conservatory, under the mistletoe, locked together as if they'd been covered in superglue. Even Mike and Kate were canoodling like a pair of teenagers. She had to admit that it was lovely to see them finding happiness together at last, though.

But for herself, the ice had crept into her heart. Oh, it was her own stupid fault. She should never have let herself fall in love with Paul Channing.

Hadn't she learned her lesson with Glenn? Some men just weren't cut out for commitment, and if you expected it from them then you were doomed to disappointment.

A soft footfall came from behind her. She stiffened — she didn't need to turn her head to know who it was.

"It's cold out here."

She shrugged her slim shoulders in a gesture of casual dismissal. "I don't mind."

"Cold doesn't bother you anyway?"

"You've been watching *Frozen* too many times," she retorted on a note of sardonic humour.

His laugh was low, husky, and she felt him gently put his jacket around her shoulders. "Here."

He was standing so close that it was a struggle to breathe. She felt as if her lungs were clamped in a vice. The memory of last night was so vivid it felt as if he was touching her.

And now . . . Oh, she ached for that touch. Ached to feel the slow, sensuous stroke of his hand over her skin, to feel his breath warm against her cheek, his hot mouth on hers.

"Why did you leave like that?" He spoke quietly but insistently. "I woke up this morning and you were gone."

She forced a note of casual mockery into her voice. "I bet that was a first for you."

"Just tell me why." Now there was a thread of tension creeping in. "Don't I deserve that, at least?"

"I just . . . It just seemed like the best thing to do."

"Why? Did you regret sleeping with me?"

"Yes . . . No . . . I don't know." She turned her head away. "Don't ask difficult questions."

He laughed without humour. "It doesn't seem that difficult to me. A simple yes or no would do."

"*Simple?*"

"Okay." She heard him drag in a heavy breath. "Just tell me one thing. Was it because of Glenn?"

She spun back to him, startled. "Glenn? Why would it have anything to do with him?"

"I don't know. I couldn't think of any other reason. It couldn't have been about that girl the other night because you know what happened there." He shook his head. "Please, just tell me why."

"Why should there be a why? It was just . . ." She could feel herself crumbling. "Oh dammit, I just wanted to be with you, to make love with you — even if it was only for one night. I've wanted that from the beginning, from the first time we met. I'm leaving after Christmas . . ."

He frowned sharply. "Why?"

"Because . . . It would be too easy to stay. But I won't be just another in your long string of girlfriends."

He shook his head, lifting his hands to rest lightly on her shoulders. "You wouldn't be. I don't want anyone else but you. Ever. Just you."

She stared up at him, not sure if she could believe him.

He laughed softly. "Cassie told me weeks ago that I'd met my match."

"She did?"

"Lisa was a little more forthright about it. She said I'd be an idiot to let you go. She can be an interfering little madam, my sister, but she's mostly right. When she told me where to find you, she gave me this."

309

He plucked something out of the buttonhole of his jacket — she hadn't noticed it when he had put it round her shoulders. A sprig of mistletoe.

"They say that if you kiss under the mistletoe on Christmas Eve, you'll have a lifetime of love."

"It isn't Christmas Eve."

He glanced at his watch. "It is now."

* * *

"I thought you said your sister was off men?"

"I thought you said your brother changes his girlfriends as often as he changes his socks?"

"I don't think he'll be changing this one."

"You could be right."

Lisa frowned at her empty champagne glass. "I think we need a refill."

Julia tipped her own glass upside down — there wasn't a drop left. "You could be right."

"Come on, then."

The two of them linked arms and wove their slightly tipsy way back through the dancers, picking up fresh flutes of champagne from one of the waiters as they passed.

PLANYOURTRIP.COM

CARLETON HOTEL
Sturcombe, South Devon

The Carleton Hotel is an idyllic forty-two-bedroom, four-star Spa Hotel, set in 2.3 acres of lush sub-tropical gardens. Situated in an elevated position, it provides stunning views over the golden sandy beach of Sturcombe Bay. Built in 1862, it has recently been taken into private ownership and has undergone an extensive renovation to an exceptionally high standard.

Among the many amenities is a fine-dining restaurant which has been awarded a coveted Three AA Rosette Award. There is also a large ballroom/function room, a business suite with conference room, a conservatory, lounge and large terrace. The annexe houses a 25-metre heated indoor swimming pool which overlooks the gardens and the bay, a state-of-the-art gymnasium, and a luxurious aromatherapy spa. The hotel also offers an all-inclusive wedding service.

Located next to the eighteen-hole Sturcombe Golf Course, the hotel hosts local and national tournaments as well as Stay'n'Play vacations. It is close to Dartmoor and offers horse-riding and trekking and a range of corporate team-building activities. Both the hotel and the beach are dog-friendly.

Guest reviews

★ ★ ★ ★ ★ **Just Perfect**
Thank you to all the staff at the Carleton for making our wedding perfect. The setting was stunning, the hotel was beautiful, and all the staff were so helpful. Jess, the wedding co-ordinator, had her own wedding there in May — what could be a better recommendation?

★ ★ ★ ★ ★ **History repeating**
My grandparents spent their honeymoon at the Carleton nearly sixty years ago and have been back for their anniversary every year since. The staff always make it extra special for them. So where else was I going to have my wedding? We thought about going to the Caribbean, but having it in Devon meant my grandparents could come too. I'm so glad we did, and like Nanna and Gramps, we plan to come back for every anniversary.

★ ★ ★ ★ ★ *Gastronome*
We had to choose our wedding location carefully as my husband's family is French and own a chain of restaurants in Paris, so I didn't want them to be disappointed with the food. I needn't have worried — my father-in-law was so impressed he tried to poach the chef!

★ ★ ★ ★ ★ **Had a great time**
We're just back from a three-day team-building event laid on by our company, and boy did we have a great time! Not only are the hotel and location stunning, but we were able to play a couple of rounds of golf, use the well-equipped gym, and relax in the fabulous spa. The highlight? Paintballing on Dartmoor, led by ex-player and football pundit Paul Channing! Highly recommended.

★ ★ ★ ★ ★ **Merry Golf Widows**
We don't play golf, so when our husbands go for golf trips we either stay home or get to twiddle our thumbs in some dull hotel while they're out on the course. Not this time! With a fabulous swimming pool, spa and hairdresser, as well as a wonderful garden to explore, the hotel was everything we could have wanted. And with luxury minibus excursions to Exeter, the Eden Centre or Heligan Gardens we didn't have enough time and have insisted on coming back very soon.

★ ★ ★ ★ ★ **Scribblers Spree**
Hi, fans! We're on a writers' retreat in beautiful South Devon. The Carleton has the most amazing history — cue inspiration for a dozen new stories. Yesterday we were taken on a trip to Dartmoor, with a talk by an expert on local folklore. And on top of that, the setting is the most beautiful little bay, with a pretty town behind it. I've already filled half a notebook!

★ ★ ★ ★ ★ **Woof Woof**
It isn't easy to find somewhere to enjoy a holiday when you have two Great Danes. We've given up on taking them abroad, but so many English hotels

are sniffy about having dogs. Not so the Carleton. Dogs are allowed everywhere except the restaurant. Smaller dogs can stay in the main hotel, but with our giants we chose one of the two self-catering apartments in the gardens. It was really comfortable and just as luxurious as the hotel itself. And to our delight, the owner and his wife have a Dane too!

THE END

THE CHOC LIT STORY

Established in 2009, Choc Lit is an independent, award-winning publisher dedicated to creating a delicious selection of quality women's fiction.

We have won 18 awards, including Publisher of the Year and the Romantic Novel of the Year, and have been shortlisted for countless others. In 2023, we were shortlisted for Publisher of the Year by the Romantic Novelists' Association.

All our novels are selected by genuine readers. We are proud to publish talented first-time authors, as well as established writers whose books we love introducing to a new generation of readers.

In 2023, we became a Joffe Books company. Best known for publishing a wide range of commercial fiction, Joffe Books has its roots in women's fiction. Today it is one of the largest independent publishers in the UK.

We love to hear from you, so please email us about absolutely anything bookish at choc-lit@joffebooks.com.

If you want to receive free books every Friday and hear about all our new releases, join our mailing list here: www.joffebooks.com/freebooks.